THE
PROTECTOR

MARLISS
MELTON

ISBN: 1460951816
ISBN-13: 9781460951811
Library of Congress Control Number: 2011903206

This story is dedicated to all the guardians of this world. Thank you for your steadfast protection. Not only do you shelter the weak, but you keep idealists like me believing in a better tomorrow.

PROLOGUE

Eryn McClellan, the only English-as-a-second-language teacher at Edmund Burke School, made a point of loudly latching shut her briefcase. At the sharp *snap, snap*, the Afghani senior who'd enrolled midway through the year glanced up from the sentences he was writing.

"Are you leaving?" Itzak Dharker looked overwrought at the thought of her departure.

"I'm sorry, honey, but I need to get home and walk my dog," she said. "Besides, I'm sure your parents are wondering where you are." She hoped that was the case, at least.

Her words met with a ducked chin and a deep scowl. Or maybe his parents didn't care, she considered, feeling sorry for him.

Gripping his pencil tighter, Itzak glared down at a worksheet on subject-verb agreement. Seconds ticked by and, still, he hadn't moved.

Eryn gnawed on the inside of her cheek. Something in Itzak's personal life clearly kept him from wanting to go home. She debated asking him what it was, whether to involve herself; after all, the boy was eighteen, practically an adult now.

To her relief, he popped open his binder and carefully inserted the pages he'd been working on. Urging him on, Eryn scooped up her purse and briefcase and crossed to the door to wait. At last, Itzak unfurled his lanky body from the desk, slung his backpack over one shoulder, and plodded out the door, avoiding eye contact.

Clearly he didn't want to discuss what was bothering him, which was certainly his prerogative. Shutting and locking the door, she turned and drew back, startled to find him just inches away.

"Miss McClellan..."

His tortured expression filled her with dismay. "Yes, Itzak?"

"Can you open the library for me? I left my math book there. We will go out the back door, yes?"

She searched his desperate gaze. What was he up to, thinking he could lure her into a private alley filled with nothing but garbage dumpsters? "I'm sorry, honey, but I don't have a key to the library," she told him steadily.

Her words prompted a grimace. A tickle of foreboding feathered Eryn's spine. She needed to handle this kid with velvet gloves, not forgetting the male-dominant culture from which he came.

He took a sudden step closer, making her pulse race. "I will keep you safe," he growled with sudden urgency.

Okay... Her father had explained to her when she was young that the crawling sensation making her tingle all over was her *spidy-sense,* and she had better the hell listen to it. "It's getting late, Itzak," she retorted, channeling her father's voice.

Breaking toward the stairs while pretending their conversation hadn't happened, she dug in her purse for her cell phone and nearly plowed into Itzak as he darted ahead of her, pulling open the door to the stairwell.

The dim and deserted stairwell.

She should never have stayed after school so late with a male student. Flourishing her cell phone, she stepped reluctantly through the door.

"Who are you calling?" he asked, chasing her down the stairs as she hurried for the ground floor. The door thudded shut above them.

"A friend." She thumbed the number as fast as she could.

In the cool stairwell, she could feel Itzak's body heat, he followed her so closely. With the phone to her ear, she heard nothing but silence. A harried glance at the display confirmed she had no reception.

"Who is this friend?" Itzak's voice echoed off the cinderblock walls.

"Just someone," she replied, turning at the landing.

If he suddenly grabbed her, she had two options: run or fight. In the skirt and heels she'd selected that morning, she'd be more likely to break her neck than get away.

"You have a boyfriend?"

God, if she'd known he had a crush on her, she would never have stayed alone with him. "No," she said, practically running down the last few steps.

She was nearly free. Lunging for the exit, Eryn pushed it open, bursting onto a bustling street corner in downtown Washington, D.C. A brisk

March chill dispelled her fears, but not entirely. Her *spidy-sense* was still creeping, and her muscles flexed with the instinct to distance herself.

"Good bye, Itzak," she called, turning right toward the Van Ness Metro stop. She expected him to head the other way since he lived further down Connecticut Avenue, not far from the zoo.

Without a backward glance, she walked briskly down the sidewalk, redialing her department chair's number and getting through this time. "Cindy, call me back," she said, having to leave a voicemail. "I need to talk to you about a situation. It's urgent."

Putting her phone away, she detected footsteps immediately behind her. A quick glance back confirmed that Itzak was dogging her heels, walking just to her left, and casting fearful looks behind him.

Oh, help. Eryn tried making eye contact with the pedestrians thronging around her, but they were too caught up in their evening commute to even notice her plight. It was up to her to put an end to this monkey business.

She abruptly halted. "Listen, Itzak—" To her astonishment, he seized her wrist in a grip that cut her lecture short.

"This way," he hissed. Even with so many eyes on them, he managed to pull her toward a row of shops.

Her heels slid on the sidewalk as she resisted him. "Itzak, you can't do this!" she warned, but he wasn't even looking at her. He was staring fixedly at the black taxicab turning onto Connecticut out of the nearest intersection. He muttered what sounded like a prayer in Dari.

Eryn, too, stared at the taxi. An ominous feeling rose up inside her as it drew alongside the curb. She realized, as Itzak's grip tightened, that he could pull her into that taxi without a soul stopping them.

Frantic, she struggled to secure her freedom. Her briefcase tumbled to the sidewalk, but Itzak didn't notice. His attention was riveted to the passenger window sliding open. In the taxi's dark interior, Eryn could just make out a man of Middle Eastern origin wearing glasses. He summoned Itzak over on a note of authority.

"No!" Eryn protested, horrified to have her thoughts confirmed.

To her surprise, Itzak jerked her behind him, shouting back what was clearly a refusal. Suddenly his words to her earlier made sense: *I will keep you safe.*

Safe from whom?

Eryn stole another peek at the driver. All she could see of him now was the finger that he shook at Itzak in dire warning. In the next instant, rubber squealed on asphalt, and the taxi drove away.

Itzak's grasp went slack.

Eryn pulled him roughly around. "Itzak," she reprimanded, "what are you involved in?"

He didn't answer, just stood there, staring after the taxi, his breath coming in shallow gasps.

"Listen, you can't just go around abducting women here," she added, trying to catch his eye. "It isn't done!"

His frightened gaze swiveled abruptly toward her. "You must run away," he whispered. "My beautiful teacher, you must run. He will not stop until he takes your head!" he added, gripping her suddenly and giving her a little shake.

She heard the words but refused to dwell on them. "Okay, calm down, Itzak. That kind of thing doesn't happen in America. We'll go to the police, and we'll tell them everything you know. They'll find that man and arrest him—"

"No!" He cut her off, blanching. "I am sorry," he added, his voice cracking. And then he fled from her, moving against the tide of pedestrians as he ran in the direction of his home.

Eryn watched his backpack bob up and down until it disappeared. Jerking a fearful gaze at the heavy traffic, she sought any sign of black taxi. There were two, one coming from either direction. She quickly moved behind the crowd, and they roared past, neither one even slowing.

Everything appeared as it always did. People rushed toward the entrance to the metro station, bumping into her as she went to salvage her briefcase, which was being trampled on. Maybe she'd just imagined that she'd nearly been kidnapped.

But Itzak's warning played over and over in her head, keeping her pulse unsteady. *My beautiful teacher, you must run. He will not stop until he takes your head.*

The warning carried distinctly jihadist overtones. People didn't go just around "taking" other people's heads in America, but she was the daughter of the top U.S. Commander in Afghanistan. A couple of Afghanis with ties to the insurgency might have a real motive for abducting her.

They'd probably intended on grabbing her in the alley behind the school's rear exit. Or had Itzak wanted to take that route to avoid being seen by the taxi driver?

Dear God, if that man knew where she worked, how could she be sure he didn't know where she lived?

Envisioning the taxi cab lying in wait, she shuddered.

She didn't dare go home, not without getting help first. A call to Kabul, Afghanistan during peak calling hours was going to cost an arm and a leg, but her father would know exactly what to do. General McClellan would do everything in his power to protect his only daughter.

CHAPTER ONE

Isaac Thackeray Calhoun imbedded the head of the ax into the log he was splitting and went to silence his beeping watch. The watch, linked to the security system that monitored his sixty-three acres, alerted him that someone was now trespassing on his property.

Ike pricked his ears and tested the atmosphere. Over the cry of a red-tail hawk and the sloughing of a spring breeze, he could hear a vehicle fighting its way up his mountain. *Who the hell?* He wasn't expecting visitors.

Abandoning the log pile, he strode to the towering oak tree and ascended twelve slat rungs to a platform that offered a bird's-eye view of Overlook Mountain and Jollet's Hollow.

The spume of dust rising over the budding treetops confirmed the intruder was coming up fast, in what sounded like an eight-cylinder pick-up conquering the steep, gravel drive with ease.

Four years in Afghanistan had conditioned Ike to expect the worst. Sliding down the thick rope he used for conditioning, he hit the ground running. His old, clapboard cabin, twenty yards away, housed an arsenal of weapons, all of which he kept locked and loaded.

Retrieving his Python .357 Magnum, he returned outside and stepped gingerly through the bed of winter squash at the side of his cabin. He lowered the brim of his baseball cap, leaned his 6'-2" frame into the shadows, and waited.

Within seconds, a black Ford pick-up with Pennsylvania plates swerved to a stop in Ike's front yard. Shining like a new penny under a coating of road dust, the well-cared for truck spoke volumes about the man who drove it.

Ike could just make out broad shoulders and dark sunglasses through the tinted windows. The intruder looked like any one of the first responders who took Ike's survival and security course. Except the spring session had just ended, and he wasn't due for more trainees till July.

If it wasn't business, and it sure as hell wasn't pleasure, that left nothing but trouble.

The engine died, and Ike tensed as the driver's door opened. A pair of cowboy boots emerged, followed by jeans, a plaid shirt, and aviator sunglasses. The intruder was lean and blond with hair buzzed high and tight. Closing the truck door, he cut across the grassy yard while scanning his surroundings with eyes that never stopped moving.

There was something familiar about the way the man moved, a confidence in his stride that prompted Ike to steal a closer peek at his face. The intruder spotted him, reaching for the small of his back.

"Leave it," Ike barked and the man froze. Aiming high over the porch rail, Ike stalked him.

Two hands shot into the air. "Goddamn it, LT, don't fuckin' shoot me! It's me, Cougar Johnson."

Ike hesitated at the exasperated announcement. The intruder didn't look much like the twenty-year-old teammate he had left behind last year. But Afghanistan had a way of aging a man.

"How'd you find me?" he demanded. He'd been living off the grid, doing everything in his power to leave the past behind.

"How 'bout you put the gun down, then we talk?" Cougar kept his eyes on the Python.

"How 'bout you jump back in your truck and haul ass off my mountain?" Ike countered, only he knew Cougar wouldn't do it. The boy never did have any stopping-sense.

Proving him right, Cougar whipped off his sunglasses. "I had a hell of a time finding you," he accused.

If Ike had wanted to be found he'd have listed himself in the goddamn phone book.

Getting no response, Cougar cast a wider look around. "So this is where you retired, huh? Not bad." To Ike's irritation, he dragged a porch chair closer and perched his ass right on it. "I wondered where you'd holed up after you left."

Guilt bubbled up, burning and raw after all these months.

Undeterred by his silence, the boy continued a one-sided conversation. "So, I guess you heard Spellman stepped on a mine?" he said, a hard glint in his brown eyes.

Ike had not heard. He did everything in his power to avoid getting news from the outside.

"They managed to save him," Cougar added, his voice roughening. "But he lost his left arm and both legs. Fuckin' shame, ya know?"

Spellman had been Ike's spotter, the most careful guy he had ever known, not the type to put his foot down carelessly.

Johnson's face contorted with the scorn Ike knew was coming. "He never did get over what happened, I reckon," the kid added, reckless enough to bring up the past. "After you left, he couldn't stop thinking everything was his fault. Figured he should've done something different." Cougar glowered down at him, awaiting a reaction.

Ike didn't give him one. He had learned to *be* nothing, *need* nothing, *feel* nothing. It was the only way he could live with himself, day after grueling day. "Why're you here?" His tone would have sent any other man running for dear life.

But not Cougar. The kid looked like he wanted to jump off the porch and whoop his ass. Ike considered letting him try when Cougar's words, quietly measured, stopped his breath.

"McClellan needs you."

Ike choked on his own spit. With three simple words, Cougar had shattered his self-imposed isolation.

The Commander of ISAF, the International Security Assistance Force, had been more of a father to him than his own daddy ever was. He might have been the leader of every coalition soldier in Afghanistan, but to Ike, he was a confidant who understood what it was like to be an executioner, commended for taking human lives.

Stanley, as he'd insisted Ike call him when it was just the two of them, had been a sniper, too, with the Marines two decades earlier. Many a night, they'd lingered at the Watering Hole in Kabul baring their sins, granting clemency, from one killer to another. Stanley had trusted Ike to keep his teammates alive. Ike would never forget the look on his face when he'd returned from the mission with four body bags.

"McClellan told me to tell you, 'You owe him,'" Cougar added.

Three more words guaranteed to bring Isaac Calhoun down off his precious mountain. He couldn't bring himself to disappoint Stanley ever again.

Lowering the nose of the Python, Ike rumbled a growl of defeat. Whatever the Commander asked of him, he would do. Yeah, he'd do it. But then he'd come right back here and shoot the next fucker who tried to drag him off his mountain.

* * *

"I'll be back for lunch."

FBI Special Agent Jackson Maddox's voice reminded Eryn of a Jamaican steel drum. "You know the drill, ma'am," he added. "Stay away from the windows. Keep the doors locked. You'll be fine." White teeth flashed against his mocha-colored skin as he sent her an encouraging smile.

Fine? She wanted to scream at the agent for using such a vague, insubstantial word. *Fine?* Her student Itzak had been found with his throat slit the very night he'd changed his mind about abducting her. She'd been removed from everything that was safe and familiar and brought to this sterile environment, where communication with the outside world was strictly forbidden. And she hadn't been allowed any communication with her father since the day of the incident. How in hell did that make her fine?

Fifteen days! She'd been at this safe house for over two weeks and all the FBI had learned was that Itzak had ties to the Brotherhood of Islam, a local Muslim group with an extremist element. They hadn't arrested anybody.

Somewhere out there lurking in the shadows, sat a killer, mocking the Bureau's attempts to identify him, while Eryn wasted away behind locked doors and cameras, waiting for the other shoe to drop.

Oh, no. She was far from fine, but if she opened her mouth to admit it, she was certain she would burst into tears.

"You okay, ma'am?" Jackson's blue-green eyes, so startling against his dusky complexion, reflected sympathy.

Given the lump in her throat, all she could do was nod at him.

"Dial one if you need me," he reminded her.

Hugging herself against the tremors that had started up again, she trailed him toward the door, wishing desperately that she could just walk out into the world like he did each morning. She missed her freedom almost as much as she missed talking to her father. It made so little sense that they refused her that harmless concession.

"Try to sleep," Jackson added, stepping outside. Fresh, spring air taunted her as it wafted in.

Thanks to the prescription the FBI's psychologist had given her, sleeping was about all she had been doing. It left her feeling more isolated, more cut off than ever. What she would rather do was to slip quietly away from here, just disappear, to someplace where neither Itzak's killer nor the FBI could find her, ever again.

Jackson shut the door between them, waiting for Eryn to bolt all three locks behind him, just as she'd done from day one. Moving toward the window, which she'd been told never to approach, she tabbed the blinds to watch jealously as Jackson slipped into a dark green car and pulled away.

The sudden stillness in the townhouse plucked at her tautly strung nerves. The downy hair on her forearms prickled.

Why was it that whenever he left, she felt suddenly like prey?

A wet nose bumped her hand, and she looked down to see her Golden Shepherd gazing mournfully up at her.

"I know, Winston." She stroked the dark ears inherited from his German Shepherd sire. His mother, a Golden Retriever, had contributed to Winston's blond undercoat, as well as to his docile personality. Turning to the nondescript kitchen, she went to feed her loyal dog.

* * *

"Why the hell is UPS at our door?" demanded Jackson's boss, Supervisory Special Agent Brad Caine.

The two men sat three feet apart, watching live video feed of the safe house on split-screen monitors that occupied most of the back wall of their Mobile Command Center. The giant silver RV stood at the far end of a shopping center one mile from the safe house.

Jackson barely heard his supervisor's muttered question. He was busy studying the feed from cameras three and four at the back of the safe house. Camera three showed an empty, fenced-in yard, where nothing of interest was happening. Camera four showed the yards of the condos backing up to theirs. In one such yard sat a man Jackson had tentatively identified as National Guardsman Hal Houston, only he wore no markings on his military-issue jacket to confirm it. More curious still, he was sporting gloves on a fine, spring day with temperatures already in the fifties.

"Maddox," Caine called again, and Jackson dragged his attention to his supervisor's monitor, where the split screen showed two different angles of a man in a UPS uniform standing at the front door of the safe house.

Jackson sprang from his seat for a closer look. "Is that a terrorist?" he exclaimed. The man looked more Indian than Afghani, though it was hard to tell for certain.

"Nah, it's the UPS guy. I've seen him before. But why's he bringing us a package?"

"How do you know it's not a bomb?" Jackson asked. After so many tours in Iraq, every mysterious object tended to look like a bomb.

Caine snatched up the phone to contact the agent watching the safe house from across the street. "Ringo, what's up with UPS?" he said.

"Don't know." Jackson could hear Ringo's tinny voice through the speaker. "I've seen him around before. Did we ask for a package?"

"Hell, no."

"So, what do we do?"

"Go tell him no one's home and you'll hold the package for them," Caine suggested.

"What if it's a bomb?" Jackson repeated.

Caine sent him a scowl. "We're not in Iraq, Rookie."

Jackson glanced back at his own monitor. Nothing had changed. The back yard still stood empty. The neighbor was still sitting in his own yard, wearing gloves. Something didn't feel right. "One of us should stay with Eryn," he asserted, and not for the first time.

As usual, Brad Caine just ignored him.

CHAPTER TWO

Eryn snatched her head up, startled. Winston pushed to all fours, his ears twitching. *Who on earth would be ringing the doorbell?* she wondered as the chime faded.

Her imagination supplied an immediate answer. *The taxi driver!* He had tracked her down, and now he would finish what he'd started.

That can't be. How would he know where to find me?

There was only one way to know for sure, and that was to go to the door and take a look.

Rising on jittery knees, Eryn traversed the short hallway from the kitchen. Her breath rasped in the silence as she tiptoed toward the solid panel door and put an eye to the peep hole.

She drew back uncertainly. The familiar-looking uniform was reassuring, but the man wearing it was as foreign as all of her students. And why would UPS bring a package to a safe house? It had to be a trick, a way to get her to open the door.

Retreating to the kitchen, she snatched up the phone and pushed one for Jackson. "There's a man at the door with a box," she whispered when he answered.

"It's just UPS." While his words were encouraging, the thread of tension underlying them was not. "Don't answer, Eryn. Stay right where you are."

How did Jackson know who was at the door? "What's in the box?" she asked, even as her mind supplied an answer: a pipe bomb, of course. Wasn't that what terrorists always put in boxes?

Suddenly, the caller gave a forceful knock. Panic flooded Eryn's arteries. He had overheard her whispering! He knew she was in here!

"I have to go!"

"Eryn, wait! Stay on the phone with me—"

She hung up on him abruptly. Her father had promised her that the FBI would keep her safe. But she didn't feel safe here, not at all.

Snatching her purse from off the kitchen counter, she whirled toward the basement stairs. "Winston, come!"

He shot past her on the narrow steps, knocking her off her feet so that she skidded down the last six treads on her bottom. Leaping up, she raced him to the door. "Quiet!" she hissed when he barked with excitement.

The rear exit was as heavily bolted as the front. No doubt there were cameras guarding it, as well. Ignoring the frantic voice that whispered that it wasn't safe to leave, Eryn twisted the locks and yanked the stubborn door open.

It wasn't safe to stay, either. Another day of this uncertainty and she'd lose her mind. Besides, she'd been assured she was a guest here, not a prisoner. She could call it quits whenever she felt like it.

And today she desperately wanted to call it quits.

Winston bounded past her as she stepped into the fenced yard and drew up short.

Now what? There was no gate or exit out of the enclosure, only a section of the fence that looked like it was propped in place.

Crossing over to it, she gave a push and, to her astonishment, a six-foot partition keeled right over. Grabbing her dog's collar, she waded cautiously into the grassy alley that divided the rows of condominiums.

She sensed the stranger before she actually saw him; he blended with the shrubbery so well that she would have looked right through him if his green stare hadn't drawn her gaze.

He stood up slowly, never breaking eye contact. *Too tall. Too broad.* Eryn stepped back, her heart jumping.

She wheeled and ran the other way. The muscles in her legs, weak from inactivity, strained to carry her as fast and as far away as possible. She should have listened to her *spidy-sense* days ago.

Well, I'll be damned, thought Ike. He'd been studying the back of the safe-house waiting for Cougar to show up when the part of the fence he'd compromised keeled over and out stepped the woman he was supposed to recover, all blue eyes and wild hair.

Up till then he'd had no idea how Cougar had planned to retrieve her without the FBI agents' knowledge. He stood up, relieved. She'd saved them a hell of a lot of trouble.

Or not.

To his incredulity, she took one look at him, clutched her handbag to her chest, and sprinted the other way, up the grassy alley with the dog at her side, heading in the *opposite* direction from his getaway vehicle.

Sonofabitch.

The other camera, tucked under the rear eaves was filming her exodus. It would film him, too, if he went after her, but the odds of snagging her were better now than they'd ever be, especially if the FBI caught her first.

So Ike took off after her.

The girl was surprisingly fleet-footed. She had almost made it to the tree line before he curled a gloved hand around her elbow and swung her around. Lunging for the dog's collar at the same time, he pulled them both to a jarring halt. "Wrong way," he grated.

"Let go of me!" Her voice came out high and thin. "I'm not going back." She struggled against his grasp, proving more difficult than the dog, who eyed him warily.

The odds of a successful nab and grab depended significantly on the amount of time it took to seize the recovery target and disappear. Ike had two minutes, tops, to make them disappear.

Ignoring Eryn's shriek, he banded an arm around her waist and plucked her off her feet. "Come," he said, relying on the dog to follow his mistress. He carried the squirming woman into a fenceless back yard where he hid them all behind a utility shed.

She was a wriggling bundle of resistance. "Let me go!"

He had to pin her to the shed's wall. "Quiet," he ordered, covering her mouth with a gloved hand. Her face went waxen; her pupils dilated. Christ, she was terrified of him, and he had mere seconds in which to reassure her.

"Look, I'm not with the FBI and I'm not a terrorist," he said, peering around the corner of the shed for any sign of pursuit. "Your father sent me."

She sucked a startled breath through her nose.

That's right, princess. "The safe word is *Lancaster.* He said you'd understand that." Not that he did.

Looking back into her eyes, he was relieved to see her fear fade. Suddenly, she looked more like the teenager in the photo on Stanley's desk at HQ, all freckles and periwinkle eyes. Except the lithe body crushed under his most definitely belonged to a woman.

Easing his hand off her mouth, he saw that her jaw now bore the imprint of his glove.

"Lancaster," she whispered, touching the tip of her tongue to her full upper lip.

She was too beautiful. Aware that his right thigh was wedged between hers, Ike eased his weight off of her. They needed to get moving. "I'm here to take you somewhere safe," he added, measuring the distance to his car as she took stock of him.

"Do I know you?" she asked.

"Isaac Calhoun." He glanced at his watch. No more time to chat.

But then she gave a cry of relief and threw her arms around him, hugging him tightly. "Thank you!" she cried, leaving an impression of soft breasts and fragrant hair.

Ike disguised his sudden befuddlement by tying a short rope to the dog's collar in a makeshift leash. "We need to go. Can you run?"

"Of course." She seemed more than eager, looping the strap of her purse over her head.

He swept the area one more time. "Now." Seizing her hand, he tugged her back into the grassy alley toward the condo he'd been using.

Sliding open the rear entrance, he pulled her and the dog inside and locked it behind them. In seconds, they were stepping out the front door. The man who owned the place happened to be in the service, making him compliant to the Commander's strange request for a house key.

Everything was legal, right down to the parking space, one lot south of the one fronting the safe house.

"Look casual," he said, ushering Eryn to an older-model Mercedes.

They passed a young mother buckling her baby into the back of a van. The rest of the parking lot stood deserted, with most residents away at work.

Ike opened the door. No alarm sounded yet. He might just pull this off.

Ten seconds left. He trundled Eryn into the front seat. "Head down," he said, pressing her head to her knees.

He opened the back door for the dog. "In, boy," he said, but the dog balked.

"Winston, come!" Eryn called, popping up in order to coax her dog into the back.

It all came down to time. He could leave the dog if he had to, but then he'd have a hysterical woman on his hands.

With the last precious seconds ticking off the clock, Ike muscled the dog into the back, slammed the door shut, and rounded the vehicle to slip behind the wheel.

Two minutes and five seconds had passed since he'd grabbed her. The odds were against them already.

Pulling briskly out of the parking space, he took the route out of the area suggested by the GPS device stuck to his dash. He had programmed it to guide him through a maze of back roads, avoiding Randolph Road and Viers Mill, where the FBI had parked their RV.

A sudden explosion shattered the morning quiet, so loud that the windows of the car reverberated. Eryn screamed and ducked. Ike, startled by the sound, swerved and recovered. *What the hell was that?* He increased his speed.

"It was a bomb!" Eryn cried. "I knew it was a bomb!"

He glanced at her sharply. "What was? Where?"

"The UPS man was knocking on the front door. He had a package in his hand. I knew it was a bomb!"

No way. Terrorists had just tried killing her again? "Did you see him? Did you recognize him?"

"Yes. No. I don't know. There was a man at the door with a box. He might have been the one who killed Itzak. I couldn't tell."

The surface of Ike's skin abruptly cooled. He increased his speed, not at all surprised to hear sirens wailing in the distance.

Eryn, who looked like she was going to throw up, peered fearfully through the back window.

"Head down," he reminded her. At least the bomb, if that's what it was, would make it harder for the FBI to pursue them. But would they deem him responsible when they replayed the surveillance tapes?

Cued by the GPS, he swerved right, cutting through a middle-class subdivision, past a busy elementary school with kids pouring out of yellow busses.

Out the corner of his eye, he watched Eryn drop her face into her hands and rock herself. The shock had finally gotten to her. He braced himself for the sight of her vomiting or, worse yet, sobbing hysterically. But, with a sharp sniff, she dashed the moisture off her cheeks and turned her lowered head to look at him.

"You s-saved me, Ike," she said in a shaky voice.

Startled to hear his nickname, he looked back at her. "Why'd you call me that?"

"Ike? That's what my f-father calls you, right? I recognize you f-from pictures in his e-m-mails." Dragging her purse closer, she started fumbling through it.

"That wasn't me," he said, amazed that she could talk without biting her tongue. Not that he blamed her for being shaken. Christ, if terrorists had just bombed the safe house, then that had been one hell of a close call. If she hadn't run out to greet him, she might well have been killed.

He swallowed convulsively as he imagined telling Stanley that he'd been too late.

"Sure it w-was you," she insisted. "You had a b-beard back then, and your hair was reddish gold." She fished a prescription bottle out of her purse and wrestled with the safety lid.

The comment proved she knew exactly who he was. Before the cluster-fuck that had left most of his squad dead, he'd had the coloration of a young man. Grief and guilt had turned his hair silver, practically overnight.

"But your eyes are the same," she chattered on, shaking a pill into her palm. "I never forget a face. It's a gift, I guess."

He glanced at her, surprised she found his face memorable at all. He had no exceptional features, no disfiguring scars. Pretending to scan the road signs even though the GPS would tell him the way, he focused on the mission.

"Do you have any water?" she asked.

"No." He glanced curiously at the pill.

She swallowed it anyway, making a face that told him it was lodged in her throat.

The GPS prompted him to turn right in fifty yards. As he swung onto a boulevard jammed with service stations and auto parts stores, the sound of sirens grew louder. Flashing blue lights bore directly down on them.

Ah, shit! But the black and white cruiser screamed past without even slowing. Probably heading to the scene of the explosion, he figured. Something sure as hell had happened.

"That was close," Eryn commented, clutching her purse with white-knuckled fingers.

He slowed, searching for the narrow entrance to the garage where his Durango was parked.

There. He braked abruptly, grabbing Eryn's shoulder to keep her head from plowing into the dashboard. As he swerved into the alleyway between two buildings to a lot in the rear, she glanced up. "Why are we here?" she asked.

The yard behind the mechanic's shop was crammed with dilapidated European cars. "Changing vehicles," he said.

Cougar could tell her the whole story once he finally checked in. What the hell was keeping him, anyway? As Ike saw it, he had done his part. Cougar could do the rest. He never wanted to see Eryn McClellan again.

She made him think about the past. She brought urgency and agitation to the present. He would rather just exist in limbo, wanting nothing for himself.

* * *

Farshad of Helmand province chuckled. The eruption of brick and mortar, human limbs and glass, had sent the agent who'd burst out of the opposite building flying backward through the air and crashing into a parked car. He had filmed it all on his digital camera to share with his students later.

Inhaling the stimulating stench of black powder, Farshad filmed the injured agent as he slowly recovered. Like a startled owl, he blinked, then crawled toward the dismembered body of the UPS employee, whose death he had unwittingly instigated. Farshad hadn't intended to kill him but with the agent interfering, he'd been forced to detonate the bomb. Ah, well. Americans called such casualties "collateral damage."

Through the lens of his digital camera, he savored the heat of the blast, the roar and crackle of destruction. Peace filled his heart. It was finally over. After three long years, his son, Osman, had been avenged. Oh, marvelous day, for Allah had prevailed over the Great Satan!

Of course, Farshad would have preferred cutting off his target's head. But there was justice in blowing her up, he comforted himself. After all, Osman had died similarly, having been crushed under rubble in the air-strike ordered by his victim's father.

Of course, if Itzak had not been corrupted by the West, Farshad's revenge would have happened the way he'd envisioned it. Itzak's cowardice had resulted in the target being moved to this complex in Silver Spring, Maryland. Farshad had found her by following the agent who came to her house to collect her dog. Stupid Americans. They had underestimated his ability to blend in, to watch and to wait, assessing the enemy while searching for vulnerabilities. But the safe house had made it next to impossible to execute her as he had planned.

That was when the patience he preached to his students back in Helmand paid off. He had come up with another plan, and it had born fruit.

Hearing a car approach, Farshad lowered his camera in time to see two agents leap out of their green sedan. These were the two who left every morning to observe the safe house from a mobile unit parked nearby. Farshad had followed them to it, one day, using his cousin's taxi. As they rushed pell-mell into the smoking hole left by the blast, his pulse quickened. Any moment now, they would emerge bearing his victim's maimed body, lamenting her death.

Hidden within the shadows on the north side of the complex, he readied his camera.

But they did not appear again for many minutes. And when they did, they were covered in soot and empty-handed.

A cold sweat breached Farshad's pores. His hands grew slippery.

"Where is she?" the blond agent raged at one still outside.

The agent with the glasses looked stricken. He got up and joined the other two.

Inept Americans. Did they not know how to search the rubble?

All three went back into the building. Farshad loosed the collar about his neck. His heart thumped; sweat coursed down his face. They ought to have found her by now.

An ambulance barreled into the complex, followed by fire trucks and police cars. It was dangerous to remain, but Farshad stayed in his hiding place, rooted by disbelief.

When minutes turned to hours and there was still no body, he was forced to consider the impossible: His victim had escaped. But how?

Allah's will?

Never. He knew what Allah wanted. If the Commander's daughter had survived the blast, then there was only one reason: His enemy had taken action, as usual, to conspire against him.

I will find her, Farshad swore, dropping his camera into his suit pocket. He slipped from his hiding place as agents dispersed to search the area. *I will find her, and I will have my vengeance, yet.*

CHAPTER THREE

Eryn let Ike Calhoun whisk her from the Mercedes and into the back seat of a burgundy Dodge Durango. Shutting Winston into the cargo area, he jumped behind the wheel and sped them away from Silver Spring with efficiency that had her groping for her seatbelt. Within minutes, they were leaving the city's limits, headed toward the rolling hills of the Maryland countryside.

Seated behind tinted glass, Eryn took comfort from the fact that she couldn't be seen by anyone else on the road. Only Ike and maybe her father knew where she was right now. The knowledge helped to soothe her frayed nerves. With relief, she felt her medication taking effect. Her trembling had subsided. Her muscles relaxed and her breathing deepened.

I'm not going to die today. The realization slowed her heart to an acceptable tempo.

Studying her savior from the back seat, she wondered if she should thank him now or later. He sat rigidly at the wheel, his jaw still jumping. Every now and then, his vigilant gaze trekked toward the rearview mirror to skewer her, making her pulse leap.

Ike Calhoun. Up to about a year ago, her father used to speak of the Navy SEAL by that name regularly and with affection. He'd even emailed her digital photos of a smiling, bearded warrior with commentaries like "The son I never had" or "You'd like this one, Eryn."

She had liked the looks of him. But the clean-shaven, grimfaced man at the wheel scarcely resembled the Ike Calhoun her father knew. If not for the green-as-grass eyes or the familiar angles of his nose and cheekbones, she'd have thought him a different man.

A memory worked its way loose. Something had happened to disappoint her father. There'd been a wartime tragedy, a toll of casualties. Her father had been vague on the details since they revolved around Special

Ops, but one thing had come across very clearly: He had opposed Ike's decision to quit the military.

As Eryn watched, Ike tugged off his gloves and set them aside, revealing hands that had been exposed to the elements. Long, powerful-looking fingers lightly and expertly gripped the steering wheel.

Why had her father sent him, of all people? And where was he taking her? The questions vied for articulation, but her tongue felt suddenly immobile. Her thoughts were growing foggier by the moment. Maybe she shouldn't have taken that pill.

She assured herself that wherever they were headed, it was bound to be safer than the FBI's so-called safe house. She was in good hands now. Her father, who'd probably been fed-up with the FBI's insistence on no communication, had intervened again on her behalf.

Tipping her head against the headrest, Eryn let her weighty eyelids close. Her body relaxed into the cloth seat as she heaved a great sigh of relief. Winston's hot breath fanned her cheek. *I could be dead read right now, but I'm not.* She could feel her heart beating slowly and steadily in her chest, proof that she was still alive.

* * *

"Who the hell are we looking at?" SSA Caine demanded, as he, Jackson, and Ringo hovered over a screenshot of the man who'd taken their client.

Unable to find their client's body in the rubble, they had hastened to the Mobile Command Center to review their surveillance tapes. It was then that they realized camera three by the back door had been sabotaged, having failed to capture Eryn's panicked departure, which camera four had picked up—only they hadn't seen that, having been riveted to cameras two and three showing the UPS man on their front stoop.

No one had been more dismayed than Jackson to see the suspicious neighbor drawing Eryn into his condominium.

Of course, she was no longer there. No one was. A quick search of the building and several well-placed phone calls revealed that Sergeant Hal Houston was drilling with the National Guard that weekend, which made the identity of the man occupying his condo a complete unknown.

All the agents could make out under the bill of the man's cap was a straight nose, tightly-held lips, and a firm jaw. He was thirtyish, Caucasian, physically fit, and he'd left no fingerprints.

Hence the gloves, Jackson thought, berating himself even more severely than his supervisor had.

"He doesn't look like a terrorist," Ringo mused. One of the lenses of the agent's glasses was cracked. He had a nasty contusion on his right shoulder. But he'd refused to let the ambulance take him to the hospital.

"Because he's not," Jackson murmured, and both his colleagues frowned at him.

"Are you guessing again, Maddox?" Caine needled.

"With all due respect, sir, I can tell you who he is," Jackson insisted. "I've seen his kind before."

Caine folded his arms over his chest. "Okay, Rookie," he said with measured patience. "Tell us. Who is he?"

"A professional soldier, sir, sent by McClellan to get his daughter back." He was sure of it.

Caine's upper lip curled, but he didn't look as incredulous as Jackson thought he'd be. "What about the explosion? Was that McClellan's doing, too?"

"No, sir. That was the work of the terrorist."

"And this guy just happened to be waiting out back when the bomb went off."

Jackson had to admit the timing was remarkable, but McClellan had been badgering their field office about his daughter for days. He'd overheard Director Bloomberg telling Caine that McClellan was becoming a real pain in the ass. The Commander had wanted his daughter released to his personal representatives, while Bloomberg maintained that Eryn wanted to remain with the FBI. The bottom line was that McClellan now had what he wanted. At least Jackson hoped that was the case.

"Hold onto that theory, Rookie," Caine advised, causing Ringo to divide a puzzled glance between them. "Right now, we still have to eliminate the UPS man as the suspect. Either he martyred himself for Allah, or he was at the wrong place at the wrong time. Ringo, I'm volunteering you to get in touch with UPS. Find out everything you can about the driver. We'll want the original packing slip for the box and a copy of their surveillance tape."

"Yes, sir." Ringo darted out of the sound room.

As the biometric lock on the door to the MCC clicked shut, Caine applied himself to transferring their image of the soldier over to their facial recognition program. The software took measurements and compared them to tens of thousands of archived images. Caine sent Jackson an indecipherable glance as the computer went to work. It finally chimed, reporting 668 possible matches for the image.

"Shit," Caine muttered.

Jackson hid a private smile. He wondered if Caine had any clue what kind of special operator McClellan would have picked for the job. Not only had the man arrived in the nick of time, but he'd sabotaged camera three without any of them realizing till it was too late.

"Sir," he said, recalling his incredulity when the bomb had detonated. "How did the terrorists find the safe house? You must have been followed when you went to collect our client's dog."

"Don't be stupid, Jackson. Nobody followed me. We leaked the address of the safe house to the Brotherhood."

For ten seconds, Jackson couldn't speak. "But...why?" he finally managed.

Caine shot him an impatient glance. "Oh, come on, Rookie. You know how the game goes: No bait, no fish. Don't look so horrified," he added. "You, of all people, should appreciate what'll happen if we don't make an example out of these bastards. This is the New Face of Terror that the CIA's been warning us about: Strike at the U.S. military by targeting their families back in the States. We're the FBI, Maddox. It's our job to see the bigger picture."

"But, sir," Jackson sputtered, "she could have been killed!"

"She isn't dead, is she?"

Jackson sat back, stunned and disillusioned.

"Look at it this way," his supervisor added more quietly. "We needed evidence. Now we have a body, the remnants of a bomb, and soon a packing slip. We are going to find these bastards, Maddox. And we are going to make such an example out of them that this new trend in terror will be snuffed out forever. Now, are you with me? Or don't you have the balls for it?"

"I'm with you." Jackson had squelched the devastation wrought by extremists in Iraq.

Odd, but what had happened today at a location that was supposed to be a closely guarded secret had the same smell and feel as that hot, unpredictable warzone.

* * *

Ike pushed out of the SUV into the smell of country air and horse manure. He'd tried calling Cougar while driving; only the winding road that took them far from the D.C. Beltway made cellular reception intermittent. Plus, the throw-away phone he'd bought for the mission was a cheap piece of crap that only worked when he tilted his head thirty degrees to the south.

Ike had made up his mind. Cougar, who'd been AWOL from the get-go, could damn well take over from here.

Glancing back at the Durango, he assured himself that Stanley's daughter still slept. That pill she'd gulped down earlier had knocked her out, saving him the stress of listening to her nervous prattle. If the fates were kind, he could hand her off to Cougar without having to dredge up another word.

Nothing personal, but she was just the kind of woman who made *feeling* nothing, *being* nothing difficult. The less time he spent with her, the better.

"Come on," he muttered, willing Cougar to answer. He had gotten Ike into this mess, and now he was nowhere to be found.

After ten persistent minutes, Ike finally made contact.

"Where the hell are you?" he growled with relief. "I've got the package. Tell me where to rendezvous and I'll hand it off."

"Change of plans, LT."

Ike scowled at the cryptic message. "What do you mean?"

"I can't leave Carrie right now."

Cougar's older wife—and the source for his nickname—had health issues. She'd been diagnosed with breast cancer when Cougar joined Ike's team.

"Can't leave her," Ike repeated. What did that mean?

"I've got hospice people all over the place. I can't keep the package here."

Hospice people. Oh, Christ, then Cougar's wife was...dying. "Damn." Ike felt like the ground had just shifted. "I'm sorry, man."

"Yeah, me too."

At a loss for what more to say, he listened to Cougar's labored breathing. The kid was holding it together, one breath at a time.

"What do you want me to do?" he finally asked. They still had a mutual problem to deal with.

"Pops said you can keep the package."

"No." Ike's refusal was immediate and visceral.

"Once the excitement dies down, he'll give you a call."

He felt a distinctive throbbing in his temples. "Negative. My place isn't right for her. There has to be another way," he insisted, abandoning their code-speak.

"Well, there isn't any other way!" Cougar exploded without warning into rage. "Carrie's gonna die and there's nothing anyone can fucking do about it!"

"I wasn't saying—"

"I know what you were saying. Why don't you think about someone other than your fucking self, you selfish bastard?"

Pain whipped through Ike. Cougar wasn't just talking about their current situation. He was making reference to the incident at Yaqubai. He closed his eyes and brought up a hand to squeeze the back of his neck. "I can't take her to my place," he reiterated.

"Fuck you, LT. You wanna quit? Then you call the Commander yourself and tell him."

"Don't hang up—"

The click in Ike's ear sounded like a gun shot. Flinching, he hurled the cheap phone across the length of the barn into a bayberry bush.

Sonofabitch!

Scraping his fingers through the silver spikes of his hair, he glared at his Durango and grimaced. Now what? He couldn't just leave Eryn on the side of a country road. But taking her to his refuge was unthinkable.

The place was a dump, which was fine for him. He'd wanted seclusion, not some ritzy resort up in the mountains. After three years in Afghanistan, his cabin was a big step up. Blue eyes, on the other hand, had probably never roughed it in her life.

Damn it, the last thing he needed was some beautiful, untouchable female underfoot. Keep her? What the hell was Stanley thinking?

Roused by a wet nose, Eryn awoke with a start. The events of the morning came rushing back to her. Her leaping heart subsided as she realized she was still safe in the Durango, only it had been parked by an old barn, set some distance from a country road. The breeze wafting through the cracked window smelled of hay. Winston whined, asking to be let out.

Where was Ike Calhoun?

Twisting in her seat, she searched the area frantically. There he was, standing in the shadow of the barn, raking a hand through his hair. Relief morphed into uncertainty as she beheld his rigid stance. Every line of his densely muscled body screamed frustration.

Why had they stopped here, and why did he look so irate? They'd made it safely out of Silver Spring. They hadn't been followed as far as she could tell, yet anger seemed to roll off him as he stalked toward the Durango with a menacing scowl.

Eryn held her breath. He didn't look much like her savior now. Shrinking against the door, she clutched her dog's collar as Ike raised the cargo hatch. Seeing her awake, he wiped all expression off his face. "Dog needs a walk," he said shortly, scooping up the rope still attached to Winston's collar and giving it a tug.

"What about me?" Eryn asked, wishing she didn't sound so scared.

"You stay put," he said, slamming the hatch shut behind him.

Stay put? The dog was being afforded a walk, so why not her?

Shivering with uncertainty, she waited anxious minutes for them to return. At last, Ike shut Winston into the back again and slid behind the wheel. As he donned his seatbelt, she scrounged up the courage to ask him what was next.

He gunned the engine, shooting back onto the country road, driving like the hounds of hell had given chase. "Um, where are you taking me?" she called.

His grip tightened on the steering wheel, but he didn't answer.

His silence turned her mouth desert-dry. "You haven't explained why my father sent you," she persisted, her breath coming in gasps.

"Not now," he growled.

Talk to me! Her imagination, quick to help out, offered possibilities. Maybe he wasn't working for her father. Maybe he'd just overheard the story about Lancaster, using it to gain her cooperation, and he was actually in league with the terrorists!

He could have been the one to mail the bomb to the safe house, forcing her to flee out the back. It made sense, didn't it? And now he was driving her to some remote spot to cut her head off!

Oh my God! Eryn peered out the window, noting their speed and measuring her chances for survival if she jumped out.

"Relax." Her rescuer/abductor spoke up suddenly. "You're headed somewhere safe. That's all you need to know."

Oh, really? She glared at the back of his head, relived but furious. Who was he to tell her what she did or didn't need to know?

He tipped the rearview mirror. As their gazes clashed, Eryn's stomach flip-flopped. The memory of how solid, how male he had felt pinning her to the shed sent a shiver of awareness through her. In any kind of physical struggle, she would be helpless against him.

Edging toward the far side of her seat, away from the trajectory of his gaze, she clutched Winston's collar and hung on tight. She felt like she'd gone from one scary situation straight to another. What was her father thinking?

* * *

SSA Caine ended his phone call with a satisfied smirk. *"The Washington Post* says the Brotherhood of Islam just took credit for the bombing."

"Just like we expected," Ringo replied. He had returned from the UPS store with a packing slip, cash in a Ziploc baggie, and a copy of their surveillance tape. Somewhere along the way, he'd produced a new pair of glasses.

To Jackson, the news still came as a surprise. Targeting McClellan's daughter was an ambitious step up from detonating C-4 explosives in a trashcan by the Washington Monument, which the Brotherhood had done last year, injuring no one.

"Why didn't our asset warn us?" Jackson demanded. Since the C-4 incident, the FBI had kept close tabs on the Brotherhood, recruiting an active member to be their eyes and ears.

"Mustafa says the bombing was never discussed online," Caine retorted.

"If it was never discussed, then how was it coordinated?"

"If I knew that, Jackson, I'd be arresting someone," his supervisor answered irritably. Caine looked back at the monitors in front of them. "Damn it, we have to be missing something!"

Whoever had mailed the bomb had to have stood within 300 meters of the safe house to detonate it. The perp had probably gotten even closer than that in order to assess the building's security. At some point, his image might have been picked up by their cameras, providing they could tell him apart from neighbors or passersby.

But nothing from the last forty-eight hours had helped to narrow their search. "Keep going back," Caine ordered.

They reviewed seventy two hours of footage. Still, there seemed to be nothing out of the ordinary, just neighbors going through day-to-day motions; the same stuff they'd been watching live for two weeks. In fact, the only person besides themselves and the UPS man to come within five yards of the safe house was Pedro, the groundskeeper for the condominium complex.

Jackson remembered watching him live as he spread mulch around each of the buildings. The same question popped into his head now. "Why the baseball cap?"

Caine lunged toward Jackson's monitor. He toggled the keys, zooming in on Pedro's face just as the gardener glanced discreetly at the camera. The hat concealed his eyes, but they could tell right away he wasn't Pedro.

"Got you, you sonofabitch!" Caine exclaimed, freezing the man's image. "Jackson, go see if you can find Pedro in his shed. Bring him here for questioning."

"Yes, sir." Jackson rolled out of his seat, heading swiftly for the exit. He had a pretty good hunch Pedro was history.

* * *

Turning between the pillars that flanked the head of his driveway, Ike went to silence his watch as it signaled their intrusion. A glance over his shoulder revealed that Eryn McClellan had finally succumbed to exhaustion. She lay in an ungainly sprawl across the seat behind him. Her seatbelt looked like it was strangling her.

Over the last half hour he'd watched her fight the effects of the drug she'd taken. She had obviously wanted to stay awake, just in case he had abducted her himself. While he admired her tenacity, the fact that she'd popped that pill in the first place really worried him.

It'd be just his luck for Stanley's daughter to have turned into a prescription pill abuser. Given his zero-tolerance for drugs, this was going to make her stay at his cabin a living nightmare. He shuddered at the thought of her going through DT's. Hell if he would carry her into his house, either. A girl who popped pills wouldn't think twice before accusing him of something he hadn't done.

And who would Stanley believe then?

Christ, how'd he get into this mess, anyway? He'd holed up on Overlook Mountain for a reason: to keep the rest of the goddamn world away. They would have all been better off just leaving him the hell alone.

With an impatient tap on the brakes, he switched the old transmission out of two-wheel into four-wheel drive. "Wake up," he called.

A backward glance revealed that she was still out cold, her head lolling in a way that guaranteed a crick in the neck. "Hey." He reached over the seat and lightly shook her knee, keeping a wary eye on the dog, who looked to be part German Shepherd. "Wake up," he repeated, smoothing the roughness out of his voice.

She came awake with a frightened gasp followed by a moan as she grabbed her neck. He started forward with a lurch, ignoring a stab of pity for her. "We're here," he said, tackling the steep gravel track to his cabin.

Her pallor and her wide-eyed silence assured him she'd realized by now he wasn't the knight-in-shining armor she'd first taken him for. He knew he ought to explain what had happened to his original plan with Cougar, except that he didn't want to discuss it. Didn't want to contemplate what sharing his space with her would entail.

He had never agreed to be a babysitter. Hell, he would never have answered Stanley's call for a favor if he'd known he would have to bring the woman back with him.

The guys on his team would laugh their asses off.

His decision to quit the war and abandon his teammates had obviously come full circle. Right now, karma had him by the balls and it wasn't letting go.

Eryn looked wildly around them. Having fallen back asleep, she had had no idea where they were, other than the fact that they were obviously in the Blue Ridge Mountains. She'd seen signs to Skyline Drive and to a ski resort earlier, but she couldn't pin her location on a map to save her life.

She prayed to God she wouldn't have to.

Ike was driving her up a forested mountain on a road that only a four-wheel-drive vehicle could handle. Through the light foliage on her left, she could just make out a clear creek tumbling over a rocky streambed. To her right, a precipitous drop gave way to a vivid green valley dotted with tiny farmsteads and circumscribed by blue-tinged mountains. A view she would certainly have enjoyed under any other circumstances struck her as threatening for its unfamiliarity.

She had to flex her jaw to clear the pressure building in her ears. Her mouth felt like it had been swabbed with cotton. She needed a bathroom and a glass of water, in that order, but would Ike Calhoun provide her with either?

Negotiating a hairpin turn that threatened to send them careening over the precipice, he sped them onto a bit of level land, where they came to a stop.

There in front of them stood a rustic cabin under the shade of a mammoth oak tree. A log pile and a rusty tin bucket littered the yard. Blooming forsythia and cherry blossoms added color to the otherwise depressing setting. *This is it?*

As he killed the engine and went to let the dog out, she pushed out of the rear seat and discovered that her legs refused to hold her. Clinging to the door, she waited for the unexpected weakness to pass.

Winston bounded into the yard, found a patch of buttercups and started rolling in it. As far as he was concerned, they'd arrived in heaven.

"You coming?" Ike called, heading for the house.

Eryn hiked her purse higher. Shutting the truck door, she willed her legs to carry her toward the listing front porch. *Please, God, let this place have indoor plumbing.*

Ike stood at the open screen door, watching her progress through narrowed eyes. Unlocking the inner door, he shoved it open. "I never expected company," he admitted.

She clutched the porch rail for support. "Then why am I here?" Not to knock her father's choice for a champion, but Ike was about as welcoming as a hangman, and this place was just a bit remote for her taste.

"Been asking myself the same question," he gritted, telling her nothing. With a jerk of his head, he gestured for her to enter.

Eryn called her dog for protection before venturing into the shadowy interior.

The dwelling was woefully primitive, without a hint of the rustic charm for which it had the potential. Its furnishings belonged to a past era. A brown sofa set, crude coffee table, and a woodstove took up most of the large room. A field-table stood adjacent to the front window, flanked by ladder-back chairs. Drab cabinets and ancient appliances lined the far wall, creating what was meant to be a kitchen.

Welcome to the mountains.

On the other hand, the place couldn't be cleaner, she had to admit. Every surface was free of clutter, not a speck of dust in sight. Even the worn hardwood floor shone with a dull luster. She felt secure enough to release her dog.

"You'll sleep upstairs," Ike said, inferring that the tightly shut door behind him led to his bedroom. "Bathroom's under the stairs over there."

Glimpsing white-washed paneling behind a half-closed door, Eryn started toward it. *Thank you!*

"There's no TV," he continued, stalling her progress. "No radio, nothing but books. So if you're expecting entertainment, you came to the wrong place," he added, unnecessarily.

Going rigid, she glared back at him. *Wow. Two whole sentences this time.* "I didn't come here," she reminded him. "You brought me, remember?"

With a hard look, he headed up the flight of stairs in front of them, taking two steps at a time. She guessed she was supposed to follow. *Darn it!*

Putting off her bladder, Eryn chased him to the low door at the height of the stairs and stepped into a child-sized room with a slanted ceiling and a dormered window. The flaking paint was vaguely yellow in hue. The mattress on the antique frame looked like it had been in use for decades. The single dresser was missing two drawers.

"It's pretty basic." The chagrin in Ike's voice made him seem less heartless.

"It's fine," she assured him. She'd seen worse while living overseas.

"I'll help you make the bed," he offered, pulling open the remaining dresser drawers to produce sheets and a blanket.

They worked in silence to dress the bed together. Ike made quick work of the job, tugging and tucking with the same ruthless efficiency he'd demonstrated while snatching her from the FBI.

Eryn sheathed her pillow and set it at the head of the bed. "I, uh, I need to use the restroom," she added, hurrying for the stairs.

The absence of a railing made her wary. So did the weakness in her legs. She'd made it halfway down the steps when her knees abruptly folded, causing her to ride the remainder of the treads on her bottom, just like at the safe house—only Ike's wooden steps were more slippery. And harder.

By the time she caught herself near the last step, her purse had fallen off her shoulder, spilling its contents all along the steps, including her pill bottle, which rolled clear to the door.

With a whimper of humility, Eryn checked to see if her tailbone was broken. Miraculously, she hadn't peed in her pants. She was conscious of Ike stepping gingerly around her. He dropped into a crouch at her feet and caught her chin between his thumb and forefinger.

"You hurt?" he demanded, angling her head so he could see her face.

His touch made her nerves jangle. "No." She jerked her chin from his warm grasp. Ignoring his outstretched hand, she rose under her own steam and swept all her stuff back into her purse, including a tampon with a worn wrapper. Pushing wordlessly past her host, she fled, red-faced, to the bathroom.

CHAPTER FOUR

Eryn had to flip the light switch to confirm what her fingers were telling her. No, the door did not have a lock. With a strangled moan, she turned to eye the bare facilities.

The sink and tub were stained by mineral deposits that told her the water came from a well. The room was as stark as the rest of the house, with the exception of the claw-footed bathtub, adding a hint of vintage charm. But as basic as the amenities were, at least they worked.

She went to wash her hands at the sink and realized there was just one spigot. *Cold* water. The only towel was government-issued, with the name CALHOUN printed on it. Heck if she would touch that. Maybe there were more towels in the closet?

Only it wasn't a closet, she realized, shutting the door abruptly. A glimpse of Spartan furnishings and a whiff of her host's woodsy scent told her there were two ways to access his bedroom.

Turning back to use the towel, she caught sight of her reflection in the speckled mirror. *Gads.* The morning had taken its toll on her. Setting her purse on the sink, she grubbed inside it for her bronzing powder.

A knock at the door nearly startled her into dropping it. "Yes?"

"I'm coming in," came the gruff warning, and the door swung inward.

Baffled, Eryn stepped back. Ike Calhoun's disapproving gaze went straight to the compact in her hands. "What are you taking?" he demanded.

She showed it to him. "Nothing. I'm putting on make-up."

"I meant earlier. What's in the pill bottle?"

"What's it to you?" The rude rejoinder appalled her but, really, was it any of his business?

His eyes narrowed and he put out a hand. "Give it over." He looked like he'd wait till Christmas or next Easter, but, by God, she'd give up the goods.

With an exclamation of disgust, Eryn took the bottle from her purse and thrust it at him. "Fine, have a look. The FBI's psychologist prescribed it to me for anxiety."

Angling the bottle toward the light, he read the label. Then, with an inscrutable glance, he twisted off the cap, stepped over to the toilet, and upended the little blue pills into the bowl.

"No!" Eryn cried in horror. "What did you just do?" She couldn't believe what her eyes were telling her.

"You don't need those," he insisted, sliding the empty container into his pants pocket.

Blood rushed to Eryn's head, pushed by a heart that had started galloping. "Are you crazy?" The thought of being without her pills terrified her. Images of Itzak with his neck slit open made her prickle all over. "How am I supposed to sleep?" she demanded.

"You'll be fine," he insisted.

"Fine?" Her fears manifested into fury. That was the same damn word Jackson had used within hours of the safe house blowing up. "You call hiding in this hovel out in the middle of nowhere fine?" She was aghast at her own rudeness but unable to help herself.

Ike folded massive arms across his chest. "I don't give a damn what you think of this place," he retorted in a voice that could freeze water. "My job is to protect you—from yourself, if necessary. Right now, you're so strung out, you can barely stand up."

"Strung out?" Her mouth popped open. "You think I'm a drug addict?" She could barely spit the words out.

He shrugged impassively. "You tell me."

"I already told you!" *You asshole!* "Those pills were for anxiety. I need them to sleep. You have no idea what I've been through!"

"I don't care about what you've been through. I'm not your therapist."

She gasped. His callousness was a slap in the face. She tried again. "You don't know what it's like—"

"To know someone died because of you? To think you could have stopped it? To want your goddamn life back?" Each word brought him an inch closer. A ruddy stain crept out of his collar and up his neck to stand on his cheekbones.

She stared at him, speechless, not altogether certain if he was talking about her or something that had happened to *him*. This wasn't the time to ask, either, not when he loomed over her, his breath rasping in the volatile silence.

He visibly reigned himself in. "You'll thank me later," he muttered, turning away.

The pompous statement brought her anger roaring back. "The hell I will!" With no control over her impulses, Eryn shoved him toward the door.

He turned back with a look of incredulity.

She wanted him *gone*—all six-foot-something, 200-some-odd pounds of him. "Get out!" She knew she was seconds away from a meltdown. She could feel it gaining momentum inside of her. In desperation, she shoved him a second time.

All her shove accomplished was to make him widen his stance and drop his arms. The extent of her absolute helplessness broke over her. Mortified, Eryn whirled around and pressed her hands to her burning eyes, fighting down the geyser rising up her throat.

Awkward silence filled the small space.

A tortured sob escaped her. Her lungs convulsed. She couldn't contain it. Ike's hostility coming on top of the fear she'd lived with these past weeks—the thought of Itzak's last horrifying moments, her near run-in with a bomb this morning—coalesced into a storm breaking over her with fury.

It sounded like someone else sobbing as she succumbed to the deluge. And Ike had thrown away her only comfort, dooming her to nightmares in which she envisioned her own violent death at the hands of a faceless terrorist. How could he have done that to her, the heartless bastard?

Over her gut-wrenching sobs, she discerned a longsuffering sigh.

In the next instant, firm hands settled on her shoulders, drawing her around. Begrudgingly, she let him pull her to the rigid but warm wall of his body. A thick arm banded her shoulders, holding her securely.

"It's okay," he muttered, sounding subdued. "You'll feel better once it's out of your system."

He meant the medicine, she realized, with a surge of resentment. How could he even think for a moment that she was a drug user! With a moan of outrage, she gripped his jacket to shake sense into him, only to cling to him, instead.

Trying to draw comfort from such a hardened man was lesson in futility. Then again, nothing about the past two weeks made any sense. At the very most, he was an anchor holding her fast, as muddied waters threatened to sweep her away.

Moment by moment, her sobs subsided and her self-control returned.

Gathering what little remained of her dignity, Eryn dashed the wetness from her face, sniffed, and stepped back. "I'm sorry," she apologized, staring at the cracks in the tiled floor, aware of his emotionless scrutiny.

"You'll feel better in a day or two," he finally predicted. With a glance at the toilet bowl and the dissolving pills, he left her standing there, bitterly humiliated, feeling like a junkie in rehab.

Screw you, she thought, glaring after him.

The spoiled princess was sulking over her lost meds, Ike decided, as he carried two bowls of stew from the stove to the field table that served as a dinette.

Eryn sat stiffly in a ladder-back chair, clutching a glass of ice water. The sinking sun spotlighted her puffy, red-rimmed eyes and spiked eyelashes. How she managed to look beautiful, even regal, on the heels of her emotional outburst was a mystery to him. But thanks to her meltdown, her softness and her scent were now imprinted on his senses, giving rise to a nagging sexual awareness.

"Back up," he snapped at Winston, who stepped into his path while sniffing the air appreciatively. At his sharp tone, the Shepherd mix lay down, put his head between his paws, and gazed up pitifully.

"He's hungry," Eryn growled in defense of her dog.

Ike felt like an ogre. Placing Eryn's dinner in front of her, he braced himself for a negative response. Being the daughter of a four-star general, he imagined she was used to eating at fancy restaurants and officers' clubs. He doubted she'd ever seen grub like this before.

When she studied the unappetizing mush without comment, he dropped into the seat opposite hers and dug in wordlessly, watching her reaction out the corner of his eye.

She lifted her spoon, took a small bite, chewed and swallowed. "Do you always eat MRE's?" she asked him.

That got his attention. "How do you know this is an MRE?" She'd been upstairs when he'd dumped the stew out of the Meal-Ready-to-Eat Pouch.

"'Cause that's all we ate after my mother died," she said, stirring her stew. "That's when I learned to cook."

Now he really felt like an ogre. The memory of Stanley's moist gaze as he talked about his wife at the Watering Hole returned to Ike with clarity. He wondered if Cougar would grieve for Carrie as long as Stanley had grieved for Irene—over a decade now. "You don't have to eat it," he heard himself offer. "I'll find you something else." Except the only thing growing in his garden was winter squash.

"You know, I could cook while I'm here," she suggested unexpectedly. "I make a really mean lasagna."

Ike's mouth watered. When was the last time he'd tasted home-cooked lasagna?

"We'll buy groceries," he decided. "Tomorrow."

"How long am I going to be here?"

The question agitated him all over again. "Depends on whether the FBI can find the bomber and whether they can prove he murdered your student."

She put her spoon down, looking suddenly ill. "You heard about Itzak?"

"Yes." Stanley had relayed the story to Cougar, who'd told it to Ike. Her Afghani student had plotted with another man to abduct her on her evening commute, only the kid had changed his mind at the last instant and ended up paying for his loyalty with his life.

"He had ties to the Brotherhood of Islam. That's a faith-based group in D.C."

"I know what it is." Bunch of homegrown terrorists, he thought.

"The FBI says they want to avenge my father's actions in Afghanistan by...by attacking me." She lifted a dainty hand to her neck as if protecting it.

Disturbed by the look on her face, Ike heard himself say, "No one's going to find you here."

She nodded, blinking rapidly to staunch the tears that made her eyes luminous.

"Eat your food," he ordered. It annoyed him that he could feel himself getting sucked into her predicament. It had nothing to do with him—not anymore.

She poked at her stew but didn't eat. "Listen, I don't mean to be a nuisance," she said with hesitancy, "but I don't have any clothes." Her gravity conveyed that the world would stop turning. "Plus, I need a toothbrush."

Her perfect, white smile had probably cost a fortune in orthodontics. "I have an extra. Never been used," he added when her eyes just widened. "You going to eat that or not?"

She took a genteel bite to appease him. Ike acknowledged that she'd probably never called anyone crazy in her entire life, nor told anyone his house was a hovel. He had managed to bring out the worst in her, which had amounted to a storm of weeping and mild epithets, making her more appealing than ever, damn it.

Truth was, she'd been through hell lately—like nothing she'd ever experienced before. He could at least try to be nice, whether she abused drugs or not.

"Did you get a look at the man in the taxi?" They might as well hash it out now while they were on the subject.

She fought to swallow the bite she'd taken. "Not really. It was dusk. I couldn't make out his face, just the fact that he wore glasses."

"Didn't anyone get the plates?"

She shook her head again. "No one even noticed. They would have gotten away with it if Itzak hadn't changed his mind." She bit her trembling lower lip. "He saved my life."

Poor kid was probably half in love with her.

"Did he say anything that could help identify the driver?"

All color slipped from her face as she gave a nod. "He told me to run, that the driver of the taxi would find me, and...he would take my head."

The stew in Ike's gut threatened a return. He stared at Eryn, aghast. Beheading the enemy was a fun little game that fundamentalists liked to play overseas. To date, it wasn't a pastime of homegrown terrorists. That meant they were probably acting at the behest of the Taliban or al Qaeda. Had the FBI considered that?

Feeling thoroughly worked up, he thrust his chair back and crossed to the woodstove where he busied himself stoking the flames, adding enough firewood to last till midnight.

"Why did my father send you, Ike?"

The soft question, spoken just over his shoulder, startled him. He hadn't heard Eryn leave the table.

Shutting the iron door, he brushed dirt off his hands and rose to face her. His first impulse was to shelter her from the truth, but then he decided it was best that she knew. "He figured the FBI was using you as bait."

Air whooshed from her lungs but she didn't look too surprised. "That's what it felt like," she admitted, proving herself more astute than he'd given her credit for. As he watched, she hugged herself in an effort to quell the tremors shook her entire body. He started to reach for her, then thought better of it.

"I'm scared," she whispered. The pleading look in her violet-blue eyes begged for his comfort.

Ike's heart trotted. All this touchy-feely stuff awakened emotions in him he'd spent the last twelve months—a lifetime maybe—trying to deny. She made him *want* what he could never have.

"Give your dinner to the dog," he said, fleeing for the door. What he needed right now was fresh air and a clearer perspective.

"Where are you going?" she asked, whirling with a panicked look.

"Not far." He couldn't get out fast enough.

"Ike?"

With one foot out the door, he glanced back.

"I'm sorry," she said, unsettling him further.

"For what?"

"For intruding on your space."

He didn't want her feeling bad for him, not after the way he'd treated her today. Not when he looked at her and thought about sex.

Not going to happen. Without a word, he kept right on going, pushing into sharply cooler air, shutting the door behind him.

The sun was starting to set behind the adjacent landmasses, Green Mountain and Lairds Knob. Stalking up the trail he'd extended for his survival course, Ike hiked through the sparse, shadowed woods to the man-sized boulder that marked the first tenth of a mile. Climbing onto its lichen-covered surface, he dangled his feet off the edge and admired the burnished horizon.

Eryn's struggle was a manifestation of the war he wanted no more part of. Recruiting Ike had been Stanley's way of getting him back into the game, the sonofabitch.

It wasn't like Ike had a choice, either. He'd do anything to make up for the mistake that had cost four teammates their lives. Stanley knew that. He knew Ike wouldn't fuck up again. He knew he'd keep Eryn safe from any threat that might come up his mountain.

Keeping her safe from himself? Now that was going to be the real test.

CHAPTER FIVE

"Okay, so the UPS man didn't martyr himself," Ringo stated, bringing them up-to-date on his findings. "Ashwin Patel has been a U.S. citizen from the age of two, plus he practiced Hindu."

"That could have been a cover," Caine insisted.

"The manager said some little shit came in and mailed the package, paying for it in cash." Ringo set aside the baggie with the cash in it for the Emergency Response Team to take back to Quantico for fingerprinting. "It's all on the tape, which has been rewound for us."

Caine inserted the old cassette tape into a compatible player, and they all watched with baited breath.

"That's the kid," said Ringo.

"Christ," Caine exclaimed. "What is he, like fifteen years old?"

The little shit, Jackson determined. The boy was probably too young even to be in their system.

Despite the cool thermostat setting in the sound room, Caine had sweat stains under his arm pits. "How the hell are we going to find a kid that young?"

"Learner's permit if we're lucky," Jackson drawled. He thought to himself that the mastermind behind the attack was pretty damn clever.

As Caine queried their facial recognition software, Jackson studied the boy's every nuance. Unlike the man pretending to be Pedro, he made no attempt to disguise his face. He smiled at the cashier, paid seven fifty in cash, and left. He's not the bomber, Jackson realized. In deference to Caine's worsening mood, he said, instead, "The kid has no idea what's in the box."

"Yeah, I think someone paid him to send it," Ringo agreed.

Ignoring both of his subordinates, Caine snatched up the report coming in from NCIC. "Patel comes up clean," he relayed, stating what they'd already guessed.

The UPS driver was not a suspect. The kid who mailed the box knew nothing, was nobody, as their facial recognition system attested when it flashed NO MATCH.

SSA Caine wiped his sleeve across his forehead. "We've got nothing," he admitted, looking stunned. "They bombed our fucking safe house, and we don't have a fucking lead!"

"ERT might come up with something," Ringo offered.

The Emergency Response Team was analyzing what was left of the bomb.

"Why don't we ask our asset if he recognizes any of our suspects," Jackson suggested.

Caine glared at him. "Of course we're going to ask him." He started printing off the picture of the unidentified youth. "You two make yourselves useful," he said, thrusting the photo at Ringo. "Go canvas the neighborhood and be quick about it. Then we'll go after our client."

On his way to the exit, Jackson stopped and backtracked. "Did you say our client, sir?"

"That's what I said, Rookie." Caine sounded smug.

"How are we supposed to find her?" Jackson had assumed—and been glad about it—that Eryn McClellan was as good as gone.

Caine sent him a small, superior smile. "I'm tracking her," he admitted.

Ringo had also circled back. "How?" he demanded.

"Bought the dog a special collar last week. Looks just like the old one but it has a SIM card which gives us the dog's global positioning. You can buy them at any pet store." Turning to his open laptop, Caine tapped a key and displayed a map with a neon dot blinking at its center. "They're 125 miles southwest of here, outside of a town called Elkton."

Jackson looked from the neon dot to Caine's satisfied smirk and arrived at a startling conclusion. "You knew her father would come for her."

"Suspected," Caine corrected. "What I *knew* was if he came for his daughter, he'd also take the dog."

"Yes, but why would we want to take her back?" It didn't make sense to Jackson.

Caine flushed with anger. "We're the Counterterrorism Division, Maddox," he said through clenched teeth. "If we're going to find the terrorists, we need to find the girl."

Not necessarily, but he wasn't going to argue with his boss. "We can't force her to return to us, sir," he pointed out.

"Who says we're going to force her?" Caine glanced at the flashing light, his face pinched with disapproval. "I just want to know who this soldier is. If he looks legit, maybe I'll forget that he destroyed federally owned property."

"He didn't bomb the safe house," Jackson insisted, thoroughly disillusioned. He had assumed when applying to the FBI that they operated with the integrity as the Marine Corp. Evidently not.

"Prove it," Caine shot back.

Jackson sighed. McClellan's elite soldier wouldn't like the FBI hounding him. Nor would he appreciate being framed for something he hadn't done. Having insight into the man's lethal skills, Jackson liked even less the idea of pissing him off.

* * *

Eryn couldn't sleep. She lay on a lumpy mattress, staring at grotesque shadows creeping across the attic's sloped ceilings while replaying the day's events in disbelief.

If she hadn't heeded her instincts and fled the safe house, she could be dead right now. *They used me as bait!* The realization filled her with fury. Had Jackson known? How could he have been so thoughtful and considerate and still have left her there to fend for herself?

She wondered if her entire life would be like this, running from place to place in fear.

Whenever she closed her eyes, all she could envisioned was the terror Itzak must have felt when the taxi driver caught up to him. Recalling his parting words to her, he must have known the man would come after him with a knife. And now, because of her, her student was dead, buried in a Muslim cemetery in the heart of the city. She'd wanted desperately to attend his funeral, but, of course, the FBI agents had convinced her it wasn't safe.

Eryn kicked off the covers. Heat from the woodstove was rising through the cracks in the floorboards, turning the attic into an oven. Damn Isaac Calhoun for dumping her pills into the toilet! She'd be sleeping like a baby if he hadn't.

Straining her ears, she listened for him, but all she could hear was Winston snoring next to her bed and firewood crackling in the woodstove downstairs. A creaking sound outside her window had her sitting up abruptly.

What was that? Wind howled and the panes of the window rattled. The creaking came again. Her overwrought imagination spawned visions of terrorists skulking around the cabin, dousing it in lighter fluid. All it would take to end her life would be the strike of a match.

Frightened by the direction of her thoughts, she leapt from the bed and squirmed into her jeans. Another gust of wind sent her flying down the stairs in fight or flight mode. As much as she resented Ike for taking away her only comfort, he *was* her protector.

But he wasn't there. A knock at his bedroom door resulted in silence. Her clammy skin sprouted goose bumps in the cooler air. "Ike?" When he didn't answer, she slowly turned the doorknob. His bed, illumined by moonlight, lay empty and still neatly made.

She whirled to face the empty cabin. Fear skated up her bare arms. Where was he? Crossing to the window, she went to peek outside. In that same instant, a silhouette loomed against the glass, snuffing out the moon glow.

With a muffled scream, Eryn jumped back.

The boards on the porch creaked. Then the door groaned open, admitting a breath of cold air. Eryn ducked behind the recliner, not altogether certain who she was hiding from. Winston came barreling down the stairs to defend her, and Ike's "Easy boy," had her melting into a boneless puddle on the floor. It was just Ike.

The light came on. A pair of running shoes walked into her line of sight. She craned her neck to find him frowning down at her.

"What's wrong?"

"N-nothing," she said, coming unsteadily to her feet. "I didn't know that was you outside."

His gaze skimmed over her camisole, reminding her that she'd discarded her bra so she could sleep more comfortably.

"What do you need?"

"I can't sleep," she said, folding her arms against his all-seeing gaze. "You shouldn't have thrown away my pills."

He shrugged. "Nothing I can do now."

Heartless man. You could reassure me. "What time is it?" she asked.

He glanced at his watch. "Zero hundred hours."

Midnight. "And you haven't even gone to bed yet?"

He pushed his hands into his pockets. "Don't sleep much," he admitted.

"Then you can't sleep either." Maybe they could play a board game or something.

But the way his eyes touched on her bare arms told her he was thinking of something else. Her body prickled with sudden awareness and not a little caution.

"Does anyone know I'm here besides my father?" she asked, bringing up the Commander intentionally. Ike's allegiance to her father would keep him from doing anything inappropriate.

"Just Cougar."

"Who's he?"

"Former teammate. You were supposed to go with him," Ike added, with resentment that cast light on what had put him in such a foul mood earlier. "But he never showed up. His wife is sick. She's dying."

"Cancer?" she guessed, with a twinge of compassion for the faceless Cougar.

"Yeah," he said.

She thought she detected some compassion in the single syllable. "But, I'm safe here, too, right?" she added, still craving reassurance.

His gaze dropped to the strip of bare flesh above her low-rise jeans. "Go back to bed," he said, in lieu of an affirmative.

The inference that her virtue might be at risk made her pulse quicken. Did he honestly find her alluring? He sure had an odd way of showing it.

"You mentioned books I could read?" she said, taking her chances.

He swiveled wordlessly toward his bedroom. Returning with a handful of books, he dumped them on the coffee table.

Her stomach rumbled. "And I don't suppose there's something I could eat?"

His gaze jumped at her so predatorily that Eryn caught her breath. Perhaps it was reckless of her to push him, but she was more intrigued than frightened by his body language.

Turning toward the kitchen, he grubbed inside a cupboard, coming away with a foil-wrapped nutrition bar which he thrust at her en route to the door. "Go back to bed," he repeated, exiting swiftly.

A puff of cold air left her shivering and alone. *Just as I thought*, she considered with a rueful smile. *He wouldn't dare lay a hand on General McClellan's daughter.*

Bending over the pile of books, she refused to admit to a tiny pang of disappointment.

A vision of Eryn's ripe breasts, so clearly outlined beneath her strappy little top burned the backs of Ike's eyeballs. Their generous shape, the shadow of her hardened nipples, abraded his nerves like the rasp of a cat's tongue.

Christ, it wasn't like she needed to be any easier on the eyes.

Stalking to where his driveway began its descent, Ike gnawed on the hankering inside of him, then pushed it ruthlessly aside. Wanting more than what he already had was dangerous. It upset the delicate balance he had struck for himself, here in the Blue Ridge Mountains.

Up here on Overlook, nothing ever happened to disturb the peace. Nothing but his dreams forced him to recall the past. In the present time, his only preoccupation was survival, which he excelled at, which was why he taught that skill to others. In his solitude, he could almost convince himself that the enemy no longer existed. After all, Osama Bin Laden was dead. A significant dent had been put into The War on Terror.

Only, Eryn's circumstances indicated otherwise, reawakening the disturbing feeling that the enemy was still out there, multiplying.

Tonight he needed the tranquility of the Blue Ridge to settle his perturbation. Drawing a deep breath, he centered his awareness then expanded it outward into the chilly night, seeking unexpected disturbances.

The gurgle of Naked Creek, the whisper of the wind, the scent of granite and mountain laurel soothed his disquiet, as they always did. But the faint rumbling of a large gas engine, idling near the base of his mountain, roused it again.

Ike stiffened, concentrating all his energy on identifying the potential threat.

* * *

"He's got her up there," Brad Caine determined, glancing from his tracking program to the mountain looming over them.

In the reversed cones of the RV's headlights, brick pillars bookended a gravel driveway which snaked precipitously though the dark trees. Amidst a web of semi-naked branches, a distant light twinkled near the pinnacle of the mountain. Resentment vied with curiosity as Brad pondered who General McClellan felt was better suited than the FBI to protect his daughter.

Hearing Maddox's phone call come to a close, he craned his neck to look back at him. "Well?" he prompted.

"Sheriff's Office says they have no idea who lives up there." The rookie's light-colored eyes cut through the darkness, seeming to mock him.

More like they're just too fucking lazy to look it up, Brad thought.

"They said their records aren't digital. But if we show up at Town Hall tomorrow, they'll search their files. Office opens at o'eight hundred."

Brad sat back more heavily in the captain's chair beside the driver's seat. Luring the terrorists to the safe house had produced neither the quantity nor the quality of the leads he'd expected. Didn't it just figure he'd run into more dead ends while chasing down their client?

"I don't even think our car could get up that hill," Ringo chimed in. Their green sedan was trailered to the RV to make local driving more convenient. "Are we sure Eryn's safe with this guy?"

"She's safe," said the rookie with confidence that set Brad's teeth on edge. "The soldier works for her father; he's not going to hurt her."

"Shut up, Maddox." Brad couldn't take anymore wisdom from a man who'd been a special agent for all of three months. He thought he had it all figured out, but he knew nothing about the internal politics of the FBI: what it took to get promoted, to be named a special agent in charge. Brad had been fighting for a SAC slot for eleven long years.

"Yes, sir," the rookie said, his words respectful, his tone insubordinate.

Ringo flicked a nervous glance between them. "Where to from here?" he asked.

The Mobile Command Center had cushions to sleep on but the mattresses were as hard as rocks, and Brad had lower back issues. "Let's go to that motel we passed on 33," he said.

"Elkton Motel," the rookie supplied, his memory annoyingly accurate. It was bright, young men like him who made it hard for the older guys to get the positions of authority that they deserved.

Ringo backed carefully onto Naked Creek Road and pointed their RV back toward civilization. Hah, Brad thought. Civilized wasn't the word to describe a county whose records were still kept in file cabinets.

* * *

Four minutes and ten seconds was exactly how long the unidentified vehicle idled at the base of his mountain.

It was possibly a delivery truck, Ike told himself, the kind that brought fresh ingredients to breakfast joints opening at the crack of dawn. Only how could anyone get that lost heading into Elkton?

As the gears grated and the accelerating engine faded, he eyed his watch, waiting. His advanced security system combined Doppler technology with a passive infrared sensor that did a fair job of distinguishing between human and natural intrusion. If anyone had dismounted from the vehicle to hoof it up his mountain, he would be alerted. Digital images would be forwarded wirelessly from strategically positioned cameras to his laptop. But there was no intrusion; no reason for his heart to beat so unevenly.

Damn Stanley for reminding him of the war he'd walked away from! The Blue Ridge Mountains were as different as the ragged peaks of South Eastern Afghanistan as day was from night, and that was how Ike preferred it. He'd deliberately kept the radio off, refused to buy a television, and avoided surfing the Internet for news. But whenever he went to town, the headlines jumped off the magazines and papers, letting him know that the war raged on without him. Plus it had taken on a new expression of home-grown terrorism.

The golden sense of security Americans enjoyed within their borders would be shattered if these new terrorists weren't stopped.

But that wasn't his problem. Some other sniper could thin the ranks of Taliban and al Qaeda and do a better job of it. Homeland Security and the FBI could deal with the homegrown threat. They didn't need him to win this war.

Oh, really? Then why is Eryn running for her life?

He pushed his cold hands into his pockets, determined not to think about it.

* * *

"Our asset doesn't recognize the kid from the UPS store," Brad announced, his voice disembodied in the dark motel room.

A minute ago, his cell phone had awakened him and Ringo—but not Jackson, who'd just returned from a morning run. Fourteen years in the Marine Corps had conditioned the jarhead to roll out of bed before dawn and run five miles.

That's because the kid's not a terrorist, Jackson wanted to say, only why get on Caine's bad side first thing in the morning?

"What about the guy pretending to be Pedro?" Ringo asked, stifling a yawn. "Did the asset recognize him?"

"Couldn't see enough of his face," said Caine, who'd begun to sound perpetually pissed off.

"Pedro hasn't shown up yet?" Jackson already knew the answer; he just wanted to make a point in a roundabout way.

"Not yet." Caine swung his feet out of the bed he'd claimed for himself, forcing his subordinates to share. He reached for his laptop to consult the tracking program. "Our client's still on the mountain."

"What time is it?" Ringo asked.

"Seven thirty," said Caine. "If Town Hall opens at eight we'd better get moving."

For whatever good it would do them. Jackson didn't comprehend Caine's need to identify McClellan's soldier. If the man was as highly skilled as Jackson suspected, they weren't ever going to get her back. She was as good as lost to them. And he hated to say it, but that was probably the best thing for her.

* * *

"There's no hot water."

Hearing a quaver in Eryn's voice, Ike turned from the window to realize she wasn't showering before their trip to town, after all. Her hair fell in a riotous, unruly mass that had defied her attempt to tame it with the comb in her purse. Her bloodshot eyes were rimmed by dark circles, and her eyes were watering.

Stressing or detoxing? he wondered. She looked like she was barely holding it together. Empathy, unwanted and inexplicable, caught him off-guard.

"Let's just go," she said. "Maybe the water will be warmer in the afternoon. I'll shower then."

He wanted to shrug off his pity for her, but it wouldn't leave him. Princesses didn't do cold showers, obviously. They shouldn't have to.

God damn it. "Wait here," he said.

Going outside he found the big tin cauldron he used for his trainees to dunk their canteens in. Carrying it inside, he set it on the woodstove, went outside for the hose, cranked it on, and dragged it through the house to fill the cauldron, kinking the line so water wouldn't dribble across the hardwood floor.

The tremulous smile Eryn sent him eased his irritation.

But thirty minutes later, as she dawdled in the bathtub, he regretted warming her bathwater because now he was sitting on the couch getting hot and bothered as he pictured her lolling in his tub. The scent of his soap stole out from under the closed door. The haunting tune she hummed reminded him of a mermaid's enchantment, luring sailors foolish enough to listen to their deaths.

Shaking off his trance, Ike ordered himself to get up and walk the dog.

Half way to the door, he heard Eryn pull the plug. The mental image of her rising from the water, her nymph-like body wet and gleaming, assailed him. She'd be reaching for the extra towel he'd located, nipples hardening in the colder air, goose bumps playing tag across her thighs and ass.

"Winston, come," he called. She'd awakened his dormant desires the minute he'd laid eyes on her. So what? There were lots of things Ike craved that he did fine without—aged whiskey, a hot tub, a big old horse to ride. Eryn would be just one more thing that he denied himself.

* * *

Jackson balanced the file he was perusing on his left arm so he could reach for his buzzing phone with his right. "Maddox," he answered, recognizing his supervisor's number.

"She's moving," said Caine, who got to enjoy breakfast at a local bakery while Jackson and Ringo searched the records at Town Hall. "Finish up over there and come get me."

"Yes, sir." Jackson put his phone away and closed the file. "Ringo," he said, jerking his head toward the door. "Ma'am, we'll need to borrow these." Tucking the files under his arms he started walking briskly past the secretary.

"Oh, no you don't." She jumped up and wrestled the files from him. "These originals don't go anywhere," she exclaimed. "If you'll just sit tight, I'll make you some copies."

With a rueful smile, Jackson nodded and motioned Ringo to wait. Even in the civilian sector, there were hoops to jump through.

* * *

"Thank you," Eryn said, as Ike reversed direction and pointed the Durango down the mountain. Winston strained against the back seat, content and quiet whereas, moments before, he'd set up such a ruckus that she had begged Ike to bring him along. Ike might be armed with a pistol under his denim jacket and a rifle on the floor behind his seat, but the dog was *her* security blanket.

"Welcome," he muttered, negotiating the sharp turn that put them on the steeply descending driveway.

The lofty view, even more impressive when viewed from the front seat, made up for his less-than-friendly tone. The valley below boasted tiny toy houses, barns, and pastel-colored fruit trees. Nothing bad could possibly happen out there, she told herself.

Ike's set profile told her otherwise.

Her gaze slid to his competent grip on the steering wheel, and her stomach flip-flopped as she imagined how it would feel to have those large, dexterous-looking hands touching her. Were hands that ruthless-looking capable of giving pleasure? Something told her yes, absolutely. He'd warmed her bathwater for her, hadn't he? Obviously, he knew how to show consideration.

"Are you originally from here?" she asked, letting her curiosity show.

"No," he said. "Ohio."

"What made you settle in Virginia?"

He shrugged, kept his eyes straight ahead, said nothing.

As the silence thickened, she heaved an inner sigh. She was going to have to stay here with him for how long? The man's communication skills were one step above Winston's.

Just as she'd reconciled herself to silence, he asked her, "Who is Lancaster?"

"A bear." She shot him a smile.

His expression turned quizzical.

"My favorite stuffed animal," she clarified. "I got him when I was a kid, back when we toured England, while we were living in Germany. Of course, only Dad would know that, which was why he chose it as the safe word. Now you do, too," she pointed out.

Ike nodded and went back into his shell. He maneuvered around a pothole, slowed where rainwater had eroded away the gravel. "You're dad's a good man," he said as they bounced across the chasm.

Eryn's eyes flooded with tears, making her realize how much she'd missed talking to her father. "Can I call him?" she begged. "We always talk on Sundays."

"No." Ike shook his head. "NSA is monitoring his phone calls. He doesn't want anyone knowing where you are. Sorry," he added, glancing her way and seeing her pained expression.

She turned her head to hide her disappointment. The creek raced alongside them, colorful quartzite glimmering under the rush of clear water. Once she'd collected herself, she looked back at Ike and was struck by the isolation that seemed to encase him. "Do you have family?" she asked him. "In Ohio, maybe?"

"Far as I know."

She found the statement odd. "As far as you know?"

He lifted a hand and punched on the radio, cutting their conversation short.

Her mouth hung open. How rude! Obviously, he didn't want her knowing anything about him. Fine. She didn't want to get personal with him, anyway. He was nothing more to her than her protector.

Then why are your feelings hurt? she asked herself.

Averting her face, she refused to look at him, refused to even think about it.

CHAPTER SIX

Eryn McClellan was giving him the silent treatment, Ike realized, mildly amused. She had managed to go twenty minutes without speaking a word—probably a record for her. In the process, she'd bitten her lower lip so many times it looked liked she'd been thoroughly kissed. Damn it, now he was thinking of kissing her.

Don't even look at her, he ordered himself.

But he couldn't keep his eyes off her. Without a speck of make-up, with her freshly washed hair tied into a damp knot, wearing yesterday's clothing and a haunted look on her face, Eryn was like no other woman in Elkton, population 2,000.

She was too damn graceful. Her complexion was too clear, and when she spoke—which she was bound to do soon—she used proper, grammatical English that sounded nothing like the mountain twang from *this here part of Virginia.*

And shopping for clothing at Dollar General was clearly an unaccustomed chore for her. "There's hardly anything my size," she groused, breaking her silence after sifting unsuccessfully through the racks. At last, she held up a yellow sweater, laid it over her chest to see if it would fit, then lobbed it wordlessly toward the shopping cart.

And missed.

Ike's ribs tickled. Unsettled by the giddy sensation, he moved toward the display window, resigned to wait.

With one eye on the parking lot and the other on Eryn, he watched her fill her cart with another sweater, a pair of jeans, and a pink, velour sweat suit. He wondered if there was a plan to her selection-choices or if it was all hit or miss. As she moved toward a rack of pastel-colored panties and bras, his pulse quickened. He made himself look the other way, but not before he pictured her wearing what she picked out.

For Christ's sake, think of something else.

As she turned toward the rear of the store for toiletries, he stayed where he was, affording her privacy. Finally, with a look of resignation, she headed for the register.

He joined her just as she unzipped one of the pockets in her purse. "I'll pay," he said, pulling out his wallet.

Incredulity shone in her eyes as she raised her head to look at him. "I've got it," she told him.

"Cash," he said, reminding her that credit cards could be traced.

She caught her lip between her teeth and adjusted her hair. "Oh." She started to retreat with her cart.

Amused, Ike caught it back and handed the cashier three twenty dollar bills.

"I'll repay you," Eryn muttered, looking flustered and humiliated.

He walked away without a word. As he approached the exit, he caught sight of a man in overalls petting Winston's head through the Durango's rear window.

Bringing the dog was a big mistake. Luckily, the man wandered off.

"Is my Dad paying you to keep me?" Eryn's sharp question drew Ike's attention to where she stood behind him with her purchases.

"What? No." There'd never been any discussion of money. Loyalty wasn't something a leader had to pay for.

Grabbing half the bags to lighten her load, Ike herded her out the door, moving toward the grocery store on the opposite end of the strip mall. As he loped along the covered walkway, he suffered the sudden suspicion that they were being watched.

Who? He searched the broad parking lot for the culprit. His nape prickled. *Where?*

Seizing Eryn's elbow, he drew her between himself and the building and lengthened his stride. Dropping her purchases in a grocery cart, he pushed it briskly through the automatic doors. To his exasperation, Eryn slowed to a stop, just inside the breezeway.

Ike drew up short, backed up. "What are you doing?" he demanded, when she closed her eyes.

She hushed him. "Visualizing what we need."

He cast an uneasy glance out the windows but still saw no reason for his concern.

She started forward as suddenly as she had stopped, and he chased after her, fighting to keep his gaze from sliding downward—which it did, anyway.

Now why did Stanley's daughter have to have the sweetest, heart-shaped ass imaginable? Fucking karma, he thought.

For the next half hour, Eryn browsed while Ike's blood pressure steadily increased. He watched her compare the contents of two boxes of bread crumbs, while he listened to the ticking of his watch, the voices in the store, different kinds of footsteps. The woman could not be rushed, apparently.

Finally, she placed one box in the shopping cart and put the other back. "Why that one?" He just had to know why so much effort had gone into her decision.

"Less preservatives. I have to be careful what I eat."

"Watching your weight?"

She cut him an odd look. "Cancer runs in my family," she said.

He felt like he'd been slapped awake. This wasn't the first time his assumptions had been off the mark. Like assuming she'd been addicted to those pills. If she steered clear of preservatives, she probably avoided drugs—duh. Remembering his harshness with her, he cringed inwardly, his face growing hot.

But then he wondered if the FBI had prescribed the pills to keep her docile, and that kept his mind off his idiocy.

He was still pondering the FBI's underhanded tactics when they cashed out minutes later. Adding their groceries and Winston's dog food to Eryn's earlier purchases, Ike pushed the cart outside. The instant they stepped into the cool sunshine, he was ambushed by the feeling that someone was watching them again.

Damn it! Who was it, and where the fuck were they?

"Wait," he said, catching Eryn's arm as she made to rush ahead and greet her dog.

Aware of the soft delicacy of her wrist, he raked the rooftop behind them for signs of a sniper. Nothing. He was conscious of her wide-eyed scrutiny as she finally took note of his vigilance.

"What's wrong?" she asked.

"Nothing. Keep walking." One by one, he assessed every car in the parking lot, yet he still saw nothing to explain his unease. "I'll get the bags. You get in." He unlocked the doors with his remote key. "Sit here," he said, forcing her into the middle in lieu of the front.

"Why?" Her voice had climbed an octave.

"Just do it," he said, tossing in the groceries after her. At that precise moment, his roaming gaze fell on an all-silver motor coach parked by the bank on the far side of the parking lot, behind a row of blooming Bradford pears. The FBI had monitored their safe house from a motor coach just like it. He hadn't seen it for himself, but it fit Cougar's description.

As he squinted across the distance, sunlight glanced off a reflective surface just inside a tinted window.

Ike's adrenaline spiked. He ducked out of sight. Binoculars made that kind of glare. So did an older model rifle scope. Neither was a welcome possibility. Pressure descended like a vise on his chest.

No fucking way. The FBI had found them? How? He'd been so careful to leave no trace.

Breaking out in a cold sweat, he slipped into the driver's seat and reviewed his options. His Dodge Durango had four-wheel drive. The RV, on the other hand, was a big, lumbering mass of metal he could easily outstrip on the open road. He'd outrun them, then. He'd take Eryn back to his cabin and hunker in.

Stanley didn't want his daughter in FBI custody and hell if Ike was going to quietly hand her over. It wasn't Uncle Sam he owed his allegiance to, not anymore.

* * *

"He just saw you," Jackson announced, turning from the tinted window in disgust. He knew they should have brought the Taurus, which was far less obtrusive than the 40-foot Mobile Command Center.

"Don't be ridiculous." Caine lowered the binoculars, while flicking him a dismissive look.

"We'll follow him," Ringo offered, springing from the second seat at the computer console.

"Wait." Caine watched the Durango barrel toward the exit. "Let him go. He'll outrun us. Plus he'll know we're here."

Too late, Jackson thought.

"Man!" Ringo's eyes were huge behind the lenses of his back-up glasses. "Who is this guy?"

"We know who he is," Caine said, checking the report just faxed over from the Virginia Department of Motor Vehicles. "And the license plate confirms it: Isaac Thackery Calhoun. Ringo, run NCIC on him right now. Check with the Sheriff's Office. Maybe they have a rap sheet on him."

Jackson gestured to the disappearing vehicle. "Sir, he already saw us. The man has the instincts of a wild animal. No terrorist's going to get close to her. Aren't we happy with that?"

Caine's expression turned mulish. "He's only one man, Maddox," he retorted. "And if I don't think he's the right man, then, by God, we'll get her back."

It was all Jackson could do not to roll his eyes. SSA Caine was going to have to learn this lesson the hard way. Men like Isaac Calhoun were ghosts. In a war, you never heard or saw them coming, but when the sun came up, you sure as hell knew they'd been there.

* * *

Ike exited the parking lot and accelerated swiftly. Don't fucking follow me, he prayed, one eye glued to the rearview mirror.

He drove a hundred yards. The RV didn't move.

Half a mile. His heart rate slowed. The RV remained in the parking lot, motionless.

A full mile. Nothing.

Expelling a long breath, Ike reviewed what he'd seen and felt. Maybe it wasn't the Feds. Maybe it was just a regular old motor coach, belonging to retirees from New Jersey.

With the sweat on his palms drying, he veered off the four-lane highway, cutting through the downtown area before turning right on Red Brush Road, where there was nothing but farms and churches and domestic livestock, all back-dropped by looming mountains. Not a single car passed them on the winding, hilly roadway, and that was just the way Ike liked it.

But what if isolation had wreaked havoc with his instincts? Being alone day after day, month after month, it could have over-sensitized him. There wasn't a snowball's chance in hell the FBI could have tracked him down that quickly. Hell, it had taken Cougar twelve days!

"Ike?"

The query drew his gaze to the rearview mirror. The size of Eryn's blue eyes struck him with remorse. He'd scared the crap out of her with his erratic behavior. "We're good," he said.

"What did you see?" she asked shakily.

The freckles on the bridge of her nose were more apparent when her face was chalk-white. "Thought I saw something. It was nothing," he assured her.

"You said no one followed us," she reminded him.

"They didn't. We're good. I'm just a little out of touch." He hated to admit he had a problem, but that had to be it. Too much time alone had left him paranoid.

She seemed to accept his explanation, lapsing into thoughtful quiet.

Or had someone who knew the Commander's plans leaked them to the FBI? That might have been the case if Stanley didn't play his cards so close. A more likely scenario was that the FBI had put a tracking device on Eryn, the fuckers. It was probably in that gargantuan purse of hers.

Eryn wasn't going to like it, but when they got back to the cabin, he'd have to do a strip search.

Right. A vision of him yanking her clothes off and feeling her up flashed through his thoughts like a jag of lightning. If she was his, he'd do that every day, several times a day till he could keep his hands off her. Made him envy the bastard who eventually claimed the privilege.

Imagine being the love of her life.

He sucked in a sharp breath. One thing was certain: It wouldn't be him.

Eryn trailed Ike into the cabin. Conscious of his brooding silence, she went straight upstairs to put away her purchases then came back down to help him with the groceries.

"I've got this," he said, his head buried in the refrigerator. "Go get your purse," he added unexpectedly. "I need to search it."

She drew up short and stared at him. "Why?" Surely he didn't think she was carrying more drugs around.

"I want to know if the FBI's tracking you."

What? She groped for the chair, needing something solid to hang onto. "But you said—"

He turned and looked at her. "I know what I said. Indulge me." He jerked his head, gesturing for her to fetch her purse.

With rising foreboding, Eryn trudged back upstairs to retrieve her purse. She didn't know what was worse: Ike being out of touch with reality or the FBI tracking them.

By the time she brought it down, Ike had put most of the food away.

"On the table," he instructed, closing the cupboards and stacking the paper bags.

Eryn's purse had been a gift from her father who'd found it at an Afghan bazaar. It had more pockets and pouches than the Hindu Kush had caves. Unsnapping and unzipping every compartment, she stepped back and let Ike look.

And, boy, did he look. There wasn't a pocket or pouch or metal catch that didn't suffer his scrutiny. He sifted through wrappers and pens, an address book, a fingernail file, paper clips and credit cards, the tampon with the worn wrapper. Eryn fidgeted. Okay, maybe it was time to toss out extraneous stuff, only you never knew what you might need if you got kidnapped.

She swallowed an inappropriate giggle.

Ike found a business card from Special Agent Jackson Maddox. He studied it dispassionately before putting it back.

"What are you looking for, exactly?" she asked him.

"Transceiver or a GPS device. Metal or plastic-coated. Might be circular or rectangular, about an inch in diameter." Several minutes later, he gave up. "I don't see anything suspicious," he admitted. Frowning thoughtfully, he handed her purse back.

"Then they're not following me," she concluded.

He cut a glance at her attire. "I need you to take your clothes off. I mean, change your clothes," he added, a ruddy stain rising up his neck. "Bring me what you're wearing."

"You think they hid something in my clothes?" she asked too horrified to analyze his blush.

"In your clothes, in your skin. Do you have any new cuts?"

Her jaw dropped. He had to be kidding. She shook her head wordlessly.

She thought she detected a hint of a smile at the corners of his mouth. "Bring me your clothes," he said again.

Shocked and wondering if the FBI could have stooped to sticking implants under her skin, Eryn replaced the contents of her purse and dashed back upstairs.

Stripping her clothes off, she examined her body as well as she could without a mirror. Nothing suspicious caught her eye—no strange incisions, just lots of bruises from falling down the stairs. Twice. With a shrug, she dressed in the new underwear Ike had paid for, while reminding herself to pay him back. Trying on the new jeans and the violet sweater, she looked critically down at herself.

The sweater was snug in the chest; the jeans too baggy. But what did you expect when you shopped at Dollar General? With a mutter of disgust, she gathered up her dirty clothes and carried them downstairs.

Ike was examining the dog's collar, paying special attention to Winston's ID tag. He straightened to inspect her offering as she laid it on the table.

Squirming self-consciously, Eryn watched him examine the seams and pockets of her jeans. After a while, he set them aside, sifted through her underwear and camisole, then picked up her black bra. Watching him run his thumb along the underwire flustered her. In his rough hands, the satin garment looked especially delicate, sexy. She darted a furtive glance at his profile and noticed his neck was ruddy again.

"Don't see anything," he muttered, dropping the bra like a hot grenade.

She strove for normalcy. "So I can wear this stuff again once it's washed?"

"Sure."

She looked around, a little worried. "Um, how do you wash your clothes here?"

"By hand," he said, with that same suggestion of a smile at the edges of his mouth.

He had to be teasing her again. "You mean, down by the creek on the rocks?" She could only hope she was being facetious.

"You have a problem with that?" he asked, his green eyes glinting.

Nope," she said, affecting false confidence and a mountain twang. "Once the laundry's done, I'll just hoe the garden and bottle some moonshine," she told him, angling her face to his.

The smile lurking at the edges of his mouth deepened, putting a bubbly feeling in her chest. "You do that," he said with a slow nod. "But not before you cook some vittles, woman."

Eryn laughed aloud at his impersonation of a mountain man. "Wow. It's scary how well you do that," she remarked.

"Yeah, well…" All traces of his smile disappeared, puncturing her bubble of contentment. "I've been here a while."

She didn't know what to say to that.

He tipped his head at the refrigerator. "Go ahead and start." And then he turned toward a kitchen drawer, pulling out what looked like a bag of beef jerky. Calling for the dog to follow, he left the cabin without a word of explanation.

Curious, Eryn crossed to the window to observe him. He strode to the middle of the yard where he turned and faced the dog. The sun cast comical shadows onto the virgin grass. "Sit," she heard Ike command, and the dog immediately sat.

Eryn snorted. Ike was going to try to put Winston through obedience training? "Good luck with that," she murmured, watching a little longer before recalling she had a meal to cook.

Maybe Ike would resent her less once he tasted her cooking, she considered.

* * *

"So, gentlemen, let's tell Sheriff Olsen, here, who lives on Overlook Mountain, since he doesn't seem to have a clue." Brad Caine's mocking tone filled the cramped meeting room in the basement of Town Hall, where the Rockingham County Sheriff's Office was located.

Embarrassed by his supervisor's rudeness, Jackson glanced at the bushy-browed sheriff and realized the man wasn't the least bit intimidated.

"Maddox, you start," Caine said.

Jackson glanced at the notes in his hand, information supplied by their analysts an hour earlier—none of which had come as a surprise to him. "The landowner's name is Isaac T. Calhoun. Prior to March of last year, he worked for the U.S. Navy as a SEAL sniper. He served in Africa, Iraq, and Afghanistan and is credited with eighteen kills. Last March, he resigned his commission and purchased sixty-three acres on Overlook Mountain."

"You know, Sheriff," Caine interrupted. "It might pay to get to know the constituents who voted you into office."

Sheriff Olsen slid him a hard look but, again, said nothing. Caine gestured for Ringo to take over.

"Right, ah, according to the Rockingham Treasurer's Office, Mr. Calhoun owns and operates a business here called ITC Survival and Security Training. He teaches tactical defense and survival strategies to private citizens, corporations, and *law enforcement officials*," Ringo added, giving special emphasis to the latter. "Calhoun is paid up on his taxes and has no outstanding debts."

"Sounds like a sterling citizen," Caine mocked. "Have you ever taken his course, Sheriff?"

"No."

"But some of your subordinates have."

The Sheriff shrugged. "What do you want with him?"

"Sorry, but that's a matter of national security. We'd like to talk to someone in your office who's taken ITC Survival and Security Training," Caine requested.

"My deputies are all on patrol. I'm understaffed out here."

"Right," Caine sneered. "I can see that it's a busy place."

The small room fell quiet. The Sheriff scratched his bristled chin. "You might try talking to my nephew," he suggested, finally. "Works for security over at the ski resort." He jerked his chin in the direction of Massanutten Mountain, a well-known vacation spot for yuppies living near the capital.

"What's his name?"

"Dwayne Barnes."

Caine gestured for Ringo to take down the name. "You wouldn't happen to have a record of the firearms in Mr. Calhoun's possession, would you, Sheriff?" he asked off the cuff.

Olsen belted out a short, startled laugh. "This ain't the city, gentlemen," he countered. "Out here, it's a man's constitutional right to bear arms." He abruptly pushed his chair back. "Now, if you'll excuse me, I got a job to do."

"Does Calhoun teach ordinance?" Caine persisted.

"Don't rightly know," said the lawman, heading for the exit. "You'll have to ask Dwayne that question."

"What's the best way to get a hold of him?"

Olsen looked over his shoulder. "You're the FBI," he said. "Reckon you can figure that out." Without another word, he marched from the meeting room, leaving the door ajar behind him.

"Well, I can see that the LE won't be any help," Caine murmured, referring to the local law enforcement. "What's the saying?" he smirked. "There's honor among thieves?"

"So what's next?" Ringo asked him.

"We interview the nephew," Caine decided, glancing at the name Ringo had jotted down. "But I want you to find some dirt on him first. We'll get more out of him that way."

Jackson rubbed his aching eyeballs. Caine wouldn't recognize honor if it jumped up and socked him in the nose.

* * *

No tracking device could only mean one thing, Ike assured himself. The FBI was *not* tracking Eryn; that *hadn't* been their RV at the shopping center. He was just overly precautious given that it was Stanley's daughter he was protecting.

Still, his gut insisted that he needed to keep vigilant. He couldn't afford to underestimate the FBI, who had gobs of information and spy satellites at their disposal. He couldn't, for a moment, let his guard down. And the only way to stay sharp was to train.

Given the paucity of trainees, Ike had turned his attention to Winston. The dog looked to be half German Shepherd. Surely he could be trained to stave off attackers, the way the military trained their K-9 units. Ike had seen how it was done. Moreover, training the dog would help to keep his thoughts off Eryn, whose spunky personality was undermining his resolve to keep her at arm's distance. He'd almost busted a gut when she'd talked with that mountain twang. Made him want to keep her up here all to himself, pregnant and barefooted.

Don't go there, he warned himself. But all he could think about was how strange and stimulating it felt to have her around. He couldn't dwell on the past, not while every cell in his body was aware of her in the here and now. His mind, meanwhile, seemed incapable of tactical thought.

Fortunately, Winston remained focused throughout their first training session. Within an hour's time, he could reliably sit, lie down, stay, fetch, and drop. But as the aroma of sausage and garlic wafted from the cabin, even the dog lost focus.

How much longer? Ike wondered, his stomach rumbling.

As he tossed the stick a final time, Winston watched it sail through the air, falling just short of the blackberry bushes. "Stay," Ike said.

The dog whimpered.

"Quiet." Ike glanced at his watch. Forty five seconds seemed interminable, even to him. "Okay," he said, releasing the dog to shoot across the yard and claim his prize.

Trotting back with the stick, Winston indulged in a game of keep-away, exacerbating Ike's desire to go back inside the cabin. Giving up on the hopeless canine, he chased his shadow to the cabin, eager to see what Eryn had concocted.

The stillness inside prompted him to make a stealthy entrance. Spotting Eryn asleep on the couch, he edged around for an unguarded look.

She had obviously just meant to rest for a moment and succumbed to exhaustion. She lay in an ungainly sprawl, with one arm out-flung, a smudge of tomato sauce on her cheek, her legs splayed. Amber hair cascaded over the sofa's arm, glinting with copper, bronze, and golden highlights where they caught the sunlight.

Looking at her made Ike's chest feel tight and his groin feel heavy. The urge to bend over and trail a hand through her silky hair had him curling his fingers toward his palm. He stood entranced for several minutes, content to watch her breasts rise and fall under the tight yellow sweater.

But then his gaze trekked helplessly lower, over her trim waist to the gap between her parted thighs. He could just imagine how warm and soft she felt there. Inhaling deeply, he imagined he could smell her woman's scent, a musky perfume that exacerbated his arousal. What color was her pubic hair? he wondered, growing harder, still.

You'll never know, asshole. Women like Eryn didn't bother with guys like him. It might have sounded like she was flirting with him last night, but she wasn't. She had more sense than that, choosing lovers who were intelligent but tender, capable of offering her the stability she was used to.

Ike had never questioned his intelligence. But when it came to his mental state, he'd been as stable as a mine field this past year. And he'd always been about as tender as a drill sergeant.

Dampened by his self-assessment, he tore himself away from drooling over her and stalked to the bathroom, shutting the door intentionally loudly. He heard Eryn lurch from the couch and run for the stove.

"Shoot, shoot, shoot!" she cried, sounding distraught. The oven door groaned open. "Oh, yes!" she added, releasing a delicious aroma.

Ike met his gaze, dark with desire, in the speckled mirror. *Get it under control, man.*

Her appeal was eroding his resolve, and he couldn't let it. If he wanted Stanley's respect back, he needed to return his daughter to him, unscathed and untainted. That meant keeping his distance, no matter how badly she got to him.

CHAPTER SEVEN

Farshad studied the leader of the Brotherhood of Islam with contempt that he kept hidden behind a pious smile.

"Why does the media say we take credit for the bombing?" Imam Abdullah Nasser railed. He stood in the robes of a cleric before the kneeled gathering of devoted followers. "Did I order the persecution of General McClellan's daughter?" His indignant voice echoed under the mosque's domed roof.

The congregants, the majority of them moderate Muslims, murmured that he had not. Farshad tried to guess which young man in attendance was the one he was cultivating to replace Itzak.

In the online chat room where the extremists gathered every other night, his name was Vengeance. Farshad had coaxed him into a more private arena to feel out his loyalties. Eventually, he had passed him the user name and password to a fictitious, email account where they shared emails with one another, saving them in the draft folder without ever having to hit SEND.

Over the course of a week, Farshad learned that his new recruit was Shahbaz Wahidi, a twenty-three-year-old auto mechanic and a lover of violent video games. Shahbaz had been born in America, but his parents, illiterate and uneducated immigrants, had found themselves no better off in D.C. than in Pakistan. Isolated from their relatives, disillusioned and embittered, they had taught their son to hate everything American.

From where he sat, Farshad couldn't see anyone with grease under his fingernails. Nor could he have picked out any of the other extremists who met online. Not even the informant, who'd mentioned the address of the safe house *after* Farshad had found it himself, was known to him.

Imam Nasser's voice cut into his thoughts as it rolled out over the congregants. "Mustafa Masoud, are you here?"

"Here, your eminence," said one of the worshipers.

"Stand."

A slender Afghani-American rose to tower over his kneeling companions.

"Why does this rumor exist?" Imam Nasser asked.

Why would Nasser ask the man such a question? Farshad wondered. Was it possible that he was the informant, the man whose sister was married to an FBI clerk?

"Imam, *The Washington Post* received a phone call from someone in the Brotherhood claiming responsibility," Mustafa explained. "They, in turn, called the FBI."

Farshad's hopes rose as his suspicions doubled. Knowing who the informant was meant he wouldn't have to enter the online chat in order to question him about the whereabouts of his target.

Farshad would send Shahbaz to ask the man in person. Yes, it was time to put his new recruit to work, at no risk to himself. Shahbaz could not identify him anymore than he could identify the Shahbaz.

"This is a lie!" Imam Nasser railed, thrusting a finger in the air. "We are a peaceful organization seeking the creation of a global Islamist state! Our *Ummah* is governed by Mohammed's law. *Sharia* forbids the murder of innocent people."

Farshad hid a sneer. *Your interpretation of the law is weak.*

"Let all thoughts of persecution cease," the cleric demanded with a stern gaze all around. "*Sharia* means unity through love, never through hatred. Now let us pray all together."

Farshad had no need to pray. Allah had already spoken to him.

* * *

The look on Ike's face as he savored his lasagna had Eryn biting her lower lip to keep her pleasure from showing. She willed the flush of satisfaction from her cheeks. It was obvious by the reverent way he chewed each bite that he loved it, though he hadn't said a single word.

Words weren't always necessary, she assured herself. She ought to know that from teaching English to speakers of other languages. Body language conveyed thoughts just as effectively, if not more so. But she wasn't comfortable sitting at a table across from someone and saying *nothing*. Seeking some way to fill the silence, she attempted to continue the conversation he had aborted earlier. "So, you grew up in Ohio. Which part?"

He shot her a dry look. "Small town outside of Columbus," he admitted shortly.

"Anywhere else?"

"No."

She couldn't imagine growing up in just one place. "I've lived in Northern Virginia, South Korea, Japan, Germany, and Jordan," she offered, ticking off each locale on her fingers. She looked over at him, awaiting a response.

It took him several seconds to respond. "Which was your favorite?"

"Germany." She didn't have to think about it. "Oh, my gosh, every kid should have such an experience! On weekends we'd take the train into bordering countries, even across the channel to England to sightsee. That's where I got Lancaster, remember? You've been to Europe, haven't you?"

"Turkey," he said, getting up for a second helping.

"Oh, I've been there, too. I went on this fantastic archaeological dig with my mother when I was eleven. She was crazy about ceramics. Everywhere we went, she collected pieces. And on this dig in particular we got to uncover a mosaic that dated back to the Byzantine era."

Ike sat across from her again, his gaze lingering on her face, which she knew was lit up with nostalgia. "So where have you done your tours?" she asked, trying to put the focus back on him.

He stabbed at his dinner. "The usual tourist traps," he said, his mouth quirking with cynicism. "You know, Iraq, Darfur...Afghanistan."

She could only imagine what his adult years must have been like, trading one hellhole for another. "I didn't care much for the Middle East," she admitted, "though don't tell my students that. There's just not enough foliage. I need color. I need *green*." *Like the color of your eyes,* she almost added.

"Jordan's not bad," he said, forking up a bite.

"I guess not. Dad got orders to go to Iraq the same week my mother was told her cancer was spreading. She wanted to be close to him, and Jordan was the only stable country with decent hospitals."

Ike lowered his fork. It chinked against his plate. "Stanley talked a lot about your mother."

His confession put a weight on Eryn's chest. "They were crazy about each other," she agreed. "If Mom hadn't been sick, I'd probably have a dozen siblings."

A log in the woodstove popped and sprayed sparks. Ike cut the edge of his lasagna with the side of his fork, but he didn't eat it.

"Are you an only child?" she asked, crossing her fingers that he would give her an answer this time.

"Have an older brother," he said shortly.

"Were you close?"

"He beat me up to keep me in my place."

His words told her more than he knew. "I guess having a sibling doesn't guarantee you'll get along," she said, subdued.

He grunted in agreement, stuck his food into his mouth and chewed.

Eryn's goal had been to get *him* to talk, but maybe if she set the bar, he'd follow her example. "I was thirteen when my mother died. We brought her body home and buried her in Arlington so that she and Dad could be together again one day." She hadn't meant to get emotional about it, but tears rushed unbidden to her eyes and spilled over. Embarrassed, she dabbed her wet cheeks with her napkin.

"I'm sorry," Ike murmured, looking uncomfortable. He put his fork down, pushed his plate away, and brooded.

Here it comes, she thought, sensing the words building in him. He was going to tell her something of himself now.

"I was wondering..."

"Yes?" She realized she was holding her breath in anticipation of his disclosure. She was that keen to get to know him better.

"Did Stanley ever teach you how to shoot?"

The question was so unexpected that her mind went blank for a moment. All she could do was stare at him, disappointed. "No," she finally managed, expelling her held breath. "He-he tried teaching me Hapkido when I was a teenager, but I figured I had him to keep me safe. Why do you ask?" She was curious despite herself.

"I want to teach you to shoot."

"I thought I had you for that," she said stiffly.

"You do." He blinked as though just realizing that she was annoyed with him. "We'll can talk about it later," he suggested.

"No. That's fine. Obviously this is something you've been thinking about."

His expression was a mix of wariness and determination. "Look, eventually you'll have to go back to your own life," he said, distancing himself with his words rather than drawing nearer. "You should learn to defend yourself. What would it hurt?"

She had to concede that learning to shoot couldn't hurt anything. The thought of returning to D.C. as vulnerable as when she'd left it terrified her. "Fine," she agreed. "You can teach me how to shoot." She envisioned what that would look like—lots of one-on-one time with Ike. Maybe it just took time to get to know him. "When do we start?" she asked, her optimism returning.

"Tomorrow." He excused himself from the table.

Eryn watched him wash his plate in the sink. "Did you like your dinner?" She knew he had, she just wanted to *hear* it.

He glanced up, obviously surprised. "Dinner was excellent," he assured her, making her glow inwardly. Drying his hands, he felt over the top of the kitchen cabinet and came away with a gun. "This is a Glock," he said, carrying it toward her and extending it out for her to take. It fit snugly in the palm of his hand.

Eryn refused to take it from him. She'd never talked weapons over dinner before. Her gaze flickered to the rifle he kept hidden under the sofa. "How many more weapons do you have tucked away?" she asked him tartly.

"Plenty," he admitted, avoiding her searching look.

His answer underscored how very different their worlds were. She had grown up with a silver spoon in her mouth. He'd grown up as his older brother's punching bag. Their differences put a gulf between them where Eryn craved some commonality. Did she and Ike have anything in common, aside from their mutual affection for her father?

"I'll clean up supper," she offered, slipping from the table and turning her back on him.

Or did she just crave a friend right now to stave off her loneliness and fear?

* * *

Returning to his parents' home, Shahbaz Wahidi logged into the fictitious online email account, eager for the Teacher's feedback about Imam Nasser's sermon.

Just as he expected, the Teacher had scripted a lengthy and caustic retort about the imam's weak interpretation of the *Qu'ran*. Following his rant, the Teacher gave Shahbaz his first assignment: to approach Mustafa Masoud in person and ask him if he could please discover where the Commander's daughter had disappeared to.

Shahbaz's heart trotted with excitement. As it turned out, he knew where Mustafa worked: at the Wardman Park Marriot Hotel behind the concierge desk.

Shahbaz rubbed his hands in anticipation. All his life, he had dreamed of punishing America for advertising itself as the land of the free, home of the brave. *Hah!* His life had been nothing but a cesspool of unfairness and discrimination. Finding himself under the guidance of the mysterious Teacher was providence. To be chosen for such a task was a privilege.

Hastily, Shahbaz typed a succinct reply, saving it as a draft for the Teacher to read the next time he logged on: *I will do it tonight.*

Mustafa Masoud finished with a hotel guest before giving his attention to the broad-faced youth lurking nearby. He had recognized the boy as a member of the Brotherhood, possibly one of the extremists who betrayed their political leaning by their aversion to authority.

"Do you want something?" Mustafa asked, mentally comparing him to the photos of the suspects involved in the safe-house bombing. He was too old to be the youngster filmed at the UPS store; his eyes too widely spaced to be the suspect posing as the gardener.

With a furtive glance around, the boy sidled closer and announced in an undertone, "I am Vengeance from the online chat."

Mustafa pretended to neaten the stack of maps of the D.C. metro system. He was not surprised; but he was startled to be approached so overtly.

"What do you need from me?" Thank Allah the hotel lobby was virtually empty.

The burly youngster leaned closer, scarcely moving his lips as he made his request. "We wish to know where the girl was taken."

Confirmation of his suspicions sent a chill up Mustafa's spine. Pretending to adjust his tie pin, he snapped off a photo of the youth with the tiny camera the FBI had loaned to him. "Who is we?" he asked, in the hopes of learning more.

"I cannot tell you that." The boy glanced toward the door as if having second thoughts. "Can you help us find the girl or not?"

Mustafa feigned disinterest. "I can try," he said with a shrug.

"Good. When you know something, call this number." The boy slid a scrap of paper with a number on it across the concierge desk. Without another word, he turned and darted through the turnstile.

Mustafa called a colleague from behind the check-in counter. "Cover me for a minute, will you? I have to use the bathroom."

In the employee lounge, he took off his tie pin, stuck the end of it into the tiny port on his Blackberry and forwarded the photograph of Vengeance to the FBI, along with a text quoting the youth's exact words and including the phone number given to him.

Perhaps this was the break the FBI had been waiting for. If they were lucky, the number would lead them straight to the terrorists threatening the Commander's daughter. Then he, Mustafa Masoud, a follower of true Islam and an American patriot, would be a hero.

* * *

"Rise and shine."

Eryn awoke from a nightmare in which she was struggling to assemble the components of a handgun while Itzak's killer threw his shoulder against her locked door.

She cringed to see a silhouette looming over her. But then she made out just enough of Ike's face in the starlight to recognize him. "Oh, it's you." She fell limply back against the pillow.

"Time to start your training."

Relief turned into denial. "I just fell asleep," she protested, snuggling deeper into her bedding.

He tugged down the sheet and blanket without warning, exposing her to the now-cold air in the attic.

Eryn shrieked. She had stripped down to nearly nothing when the attic had felt like a furnace several hours ago.

Ike sprang back. "Get dressed," he ordered, his tone telling her he'd seen plenty of pale skin, despite the dark. "Sweats, T-shirt, and running shoes." He backed toward the stairs.

"All I have is my Skechers," she called, rubbing her sticky eyelids. "And why are we shooting in the dark?"

"First we train, then we shoot," he said over his shoulder.

"Train for what?" She hadn't signed up for this.

"For the worst," she thought she heard him say as he melted out of sight. "Keep the lights off."

Clutching the blanket to her body, she considered what *the worst* meant. To her, it meant her dream, still so fresh in her memory, becoming real.

God forbid she would ever come face to face with Itzak's killer, who wanted to decapitate her. But better to be armed than defenseless. Rolling out of the bed, she felt in the dark for her new, pink velour sweat suit.

Five minutes later, she joined Ike downstairs, finding him at the kitchen table wearing what looked, in the dark, to be an Army-green hoodie.

"Why no light?" she whispered.

"Light betrays you to the enemy."

She had never actually thought of that. To Ike it was probably second nature.

"Eat and let's go," he said, handing her a power bar like the one he'd given her the night before.

With no appetite to speak of, she choked it down.

Ike stood up abruptly. "Ready?"

"I guess." It was hard to whip up her enthusiasm.

Cold air enveloped her as she followed him through the door and off the porch. Shuddering, she drew hood of her jacket over her ears and knotted the pulls.

A hint of buttery sunlight edged the adjacent mountaintops, but the sky was still an indigo sea sparkling with stars. Down in the dark valley, a rooster crowed. Only farmers and newspaper delivery boys had any business being up at this hour.

And soldiers training for the worst, she amended with a shudder.

"Warm up." Ike turned beneath the tree and started doing jumping jacks.

Eryn followed his example, her breath forming a cloudy vapor before her. They did fifty jumping jacks then something Ike called burpees, which entailed dropping to the damp ground and jumping up again, keeping her feet together. Then they stretched their quads and hamstrings.

"All set?" He straightened abruptly.

"All set for what?" she asked, mentally counting back to her last workout at the gym.

"Running."

She didn't care for the word running. Jogging was more her style.

"Follow me," he said, taking off.

Crap! Eryn hurried after him. His dark form blended instantly with the vegetation growing up behind the cabin. She found herself on a path that formed a dim tunnel through the woods.

Whatever you do, don't twist an ankle, she cautioned herself, promptly stubbing her toe on a rock.

They were running uphill on a rugged, rain-eroded trail. Her calves and ankles immediately protested. Her lungs strained. But she refused to be a victim, running scared. If she wanted her life back, she would need to learn a lot from Ike.

With renewed vigor, she pushed herself to catch up with him. Her breath sawed in the backwoods stillness. The scent of sap and minerals filled her nostrils. Her fingers, ears and nose stung from the cold, but she managed to close the gap between them.

At last the path leveled off, and she fell into a rhythm she felt she could sustain. As they wound through the hickory and chestnut trees, the sun began to rise, shooting golden beams through the forest, illumining the tree trunks yellowed with lichen. A woodpecker hammered out a hollow-sounding percussion, while warblers and goldfinches darted through the undergrowth in search of grubs. If her body didn't hurt so darn much, she might actually enjoy this quality time with Mother Nature.

She saw Ike glance back and increased her speed to impress him. She realized she could scarcely hear him over the sound of rushing water, which grew louder with every step. Ike slowed down, and she joined him, gasping for breath, at the lip of a ravine, where, over the centuries, melting snows had carved a deep, rocky gorge. Water gushed through it, crashing and swilling in its haste to get down the mountain.

"Naked Creek," he announced, looking and sounding rested.

"Pretty." Dabbing her runny nose with a sleeve, she squeezed the stitch in her side, praying they would rest awhile before turning back.

"We're going to cross," he said.

Eryn's eyes flew wide. The climb down to the water looked deadly. "How?" she squeaked.

"Zip line." He stepped over to a tree.

As he reached up to crank a pulley, she spied a thick wire strung from one side of the gorge to the next, camouflaged by the silvery sky.

Making its way toward them was a device that looked like a set of handlebars with a bungee cord dangling from the center and a belt attached to the bungee cord. "Oh, no. I'm not going on that." She edged away from him. "Let's just run back."

"Sure, you are," he said, grabbing the handles and pulling them closer. "Over here." He gestured with his head.

She held her ground. "What's any of this got to do with learning how to shoot?" she demanded.

"Everything." He reached out and caught her elbow, pulling her closer. Holding her gaze with a burning look he added, "You think shooting is about pulling a trigger and hitting a target?" His warm breath fanned her cheek. "It's not. It's about learning to separate yourself from something that scares you shitless. You want to shoot? First you have to learn to think through your fear."

She'd never heard him say so much at once, in a voice that was rough and cynical and made her prickle all over. "Okay," she conceded with her heart pounding, "but only if you come with me."

His eyes narrowed. He inclined his head in agreement. "Okay."

"Hold me tight," she added, as he guided her into position under the bars. Ike would never let her plunge into deadly rapids, she assured herself.

"Hands here and here." He placed her hands where he wanted them. The bar felt cold beneath her aching fingers; his body blessedly warm, as he took up position directly behind her. She had to resist the urge to lean against him, to draw reassurance from his strength.

As she measured the distance to the other side of the ravine, her knees began to knock, her arms to tingle. She felt him loop the broad leather belt around her waist, and her heart began to hammer.

"Once you're airborne, lift your feet out in front of you. That'll keep you moving," he instructed, backing them up.

She could hardly breathe.

"When you reach the other side, you'll hit a stop. Let go and jump to the ground. Take the belt off."

"I thought you were coming with me!" she cried with sudden panic.

"Right behind you," he amended. "Ready? Run!" He didn't give her the chance to decipher whether she was in this alone or not before he pushed the handlebars into a running glide.

The next thing Eryn knew, the land under her feet was gone, and she was gliding through thin air, all alone.

A squeal of terror erupted from her throat. She glanced down at the deadly rush of water and sharp rocks. Fear sucked the strength from her grip. Her momentum slowed; her fingers started to slip on the handlebars. She would never make it to the other side.

"Feet up!" Ike shouted, his voice echoing in the gorge.

"I hate you!" she yelled back, lifting her feet and regaining her speed. Trees and rocks rushed toward her. Then, suddenly, she was sailing over solid ground. She hit a stop, and remembering his instructions, let go of the bar. Landing on shaky knees, she unfurled her cramped fingers and glared over her shoulder at him.

Ike stood on the opposite side with his arms crossed, wearing a crooked smile. "You did good," he called.

"Well," she muttered, correcting his grammar. With her entire body quaking, she fumbled to release the belt around her middle and realized it would have kept her from falling, even if she had let go.

As Ike drew the bar back to his side, her emotions seesawed between euphoria and outrage. She had done it! But he had lied to her! How was she supposed to trust a man who didn't keep his word?

As she watched Ike glide effortlessly toward her, her anger heated to a boil. He dropped to the ground while the bar was still moving, released the belt and approached her warily. "You want to hit me, go ahead," he offered.

Eryn's chin went up. "I don't believe in violence," she retorted.

"Yeah, you do."

He was right, damn him. She wouldn't be subjecting herself to this kind of training if she didn't believe in fighting back. Without a hint of forewarning, she drew back her foot and kicked him in the shin.

"Ow!" With an incredulous laugh, he bent over to rub his injured leg.

"You lied to me!" she raged, annoyed by his amusement, though his rusty laugh was music to her ears.

"Not technically."

She made to kick him again, only this time he caught her heel, causing her to lose her balance. As she toppled over, he seized her arm and pulled her upright. She felt like a doll in his hands, a feeling that both thrilled and annoyed her.

He kept hold of her. "Look," he said, his touch disturbingly warm, even through the sleeve of her sweatshirt, "you did something you didn't think you could do, right?"

"I suppose."

"That's the first step to overcoming fear." His gaze slid intently toward her mouth.

"So the end justifies the means." Her voice sounded huskier than usual. Her blood warmed with the expectation that he would try to kiss her.

"Exactly," he said, releasing her, instead.

Disappointed, she just stared. Did she want him to kiss her?

"You want to survive, you conquer your fear," he added tersely. "Stop and feel, and you'll end up dead."

Not again. Here she was trying to establish a rapport with him, and he was picturing her dead. When would she learn?

"Let's move." He gestured downhill. "One more mile back to the cabin. Then we'll eat breakfast."

Taking off at an easy lope, he left her scrounging for the strength to hurry after him. At least gravity was on their side now.

As she chased his shadow, his chilling words echoed in her head. *Stop and feel, and you'll end up dead.*

Was that what had happened to Ike? Had he learned to shut off his emotions to survive? That would explain why he rarely smiled; why he behaved like he was more machine than man.

Yet there was wisdom in his advice. God forbid she should come face to face with terrorists again, but if she did, thinking through her fear might be the only thing that saved her.

On the other hand, what was the point of living, if you could no longer *feel*?

CHAPTER EIGHT

Maybe training Eryn wasn't such a good idea, Ike considered.

He was used to training men. There were no women on the SEAL Teams. He hadn't had a woman enroll in his survival and security course yet, either. If he didn't know better, he'd have guessed that the double X-chromosome interfered with accuracy. Eryn had fired twenty-five rounds at the plywood silhouette standing fifty feet away, and she still hadn't hit it.

How could she be Stanley's daughter and be such a miserable shot? Jesus, at this rate, she'd need to cart around a cannon and be close enough to shake the enemy's hand in order to shoot him!

Maybe if they'd gotten an earlier start today. But their four-course brunch, followed by a nap for Eryn, had taken up most of the morning. If she could shoot like she cooked they'd be in business, but obviously she couldn't. The sky was starting to mellow, and the trees were casting long shadows, and she was still off by a country mile. "We'll try again tomorrow," he suggested.

"Are you thinking I can't do this?" Eryn whirled to face him. As he ducked and broke right, she sheepishly pointed the Glock at the ground. "Sorry." Her mouth drooped with defeat.

Determined to end things on a positive note, Ike heaved a sigh. Damn it, he was going to have to put his arms around her.

Easy, he ordered his libido as he drew her back around.

Her target was one of a dozen plywood silhouettes studding a clearing of wildflowers—an area known to his trainees as The Range. "Loosen up," he said, feeling tension in her shoulders. "Let me see your grip."

No wonder she kept missing. "That's not what I showed you. Slide your right hand higher. Your forefinger needs to rest along the frame—like that, thumbs crossed. Now think of pushing with the right hand, pulling with the left. Got it?"

"I think so."

"Go ahead and aim." She smelled like peaches, with sunshine and woman thrown in to distract him. He tried holding his breath.

"Like this?"

What the hell was she aiming at? "Are you using the sights on the pistol?"

"I'm pointing at the target!"

Bracing himself for contact, he edged closer. "Remember your two sights. Keep your target in both of them, but your focus is on the V-post."

"Oh." Her tone made it clear she'd forgotten that part.

The nose of the gun wavered. Up. Down. Left. Right. Suddenly, she froze. "I've got it!"

"Hold it there." He didn't want her to miss. Gritting his teeth against the feel of her soft ass against his thighs, he moved closer till her back was molded to his front. Then he put his arms around her, cupping her hands to steady them. They were touching from shoulder to toe, and it felt like heaven.

"Breathe," he said, as much to himself as to her, and she exhaled. "Now squeeze."

Crack! The bullet ripped into the target. At the same time, the recoil pushed her up against him. It was all he could do to disguise his burgeoning erection.

"That's a kill," he said, backing away swiftly, but even five feet away, he could still feel her, smell her.

To his puzzlement, she just stared at the target with her shoulders slumped.

Ike edged around her to peek at her reaction, and her eyes, identical in color to the violets in the grass, shifted in his direction. "That made me think of Itzak," she admitted sadly.

He was startled to find his hand in her hair, smoothing it where it bumped up over the ear muffs. "Think of the one who killed him next time," he suggested, snatching his hand back. "Try again, by yourself this time."

Giving her room, he watched her reconsider her target. As her face hardened and her eyes narrowed, he decided maybe she had some of Stanley in her, after all. Respect mingled with pity and roiled inside of him, heating to a furious boil. If it were up to him, the fuckers plotting her death would meet a premature and grisly end.

His gaze dropped to where the snug velour sweat suit clung to her amazing curves. Protecting her hadn't proven all that rough. She hadn't complained about the lack of creature comforts. She cooked; she kept the house neat. For the most part, she left him alone when she wasn't trying to crawl into his head. He was starting to enjoy her company.

And that in itself was dangerous. He needed to minimize her effect on him, somehow. Maybe a trip to Elkton was in order. He could look for the RV he'd seen yesterday—ascertain that it wasn't the FBI's RV. He could stop in at the local pub and ask TJ if he'd seen any strangers in suits. Hook up with TJ's sister for a quick coupling. That might just take the edge off his lust.

Only who would protect Eryn while he did all that? There wasn't anyone he trusted to look after her. Bottom line, her safety mattered more than this hankering inside him.

Crack! Thunk! The sound of her bullet hitting its mark brought him sharply to the present.

"I did it!" She remembered to engage the safety before rushing at him with her arms out flung.

There was no avoiding her effusive embrace. "All by myself!" she cried, throwing her arms around him. Her soft breasts were crushed against his chest, her warm breath sighed against his neck. Her beautiful face seemed lit from the inside out, like a lantern.

He forced himself to study the target. "Nice job." Fighting to keep his hands from palming her ass, he gently disengaged himself. "Do it two more times, and we'll call it a day."

* * *

The FBI interview with the Sheriff's nephew took place at 9 **P.M.**, just outside of the security office at Massanutten Resort. Children scrambled on the playground equipment lit up by halogen lamps. Fruit bats darted in the darkening sky. Dwayne Barnes, heavily bearded and built like a lumberjack, jumped out of his skin as the three agents surrounded him the minute he stepped from his place of work. The look of dread on his face told Jackson he'd been expecting this moment.

"Dwayne Barnes?" Caine flashed his badge. "Brad Caine, FBI. Special Agents Maddox and Ringo," he added introducing his companions. "We'd like a word with you." Caine gestured to the solitary RV parked on the far end of the lot, and Dwayne gave a reluctant nod.

Inside the Mobile Command Center, they handed him a Diet Coke, a Ho-Ho pastry, and kicked off the interview with the usual questions tailored to put the mountain man at ease, but he was so enamored with the amenities that came with the RV that he couldn't stop staring at them.

"Ya'll have two refrigerators," he marveled.

"That's a beverage bar," Caine said shortly. "What can you tell us about Isaac Calhoun?"

Dwayne lowered his half-eaten snack cake. "Who? Oh, you mean, LT."

Caine's upper lip curled. "Still calls himself Lieutenant, does he?"

"Well, no. But folks call him that 'cause of his military bearing." Dwayne shrugged. "What do you want to know?"

"How do you know him?"

"Took ITC Survival and Security Training last fall."

"What was that like?"

Dwayne shrugged. "Tough. Learned a lot. Got recertified."

A sheaf of papers hit the table in front of him, making him jump.

"What's this?" Dwayne frowned down at the first page. "Why's my name on this?"

"This is the Class 1 misdemeanor you were charged with several years back, Mr. Barnes," said Caine. "The one your uncle kept secret from your employer? I wonder how they'd react to learning that you lied to them all this time. You think they'd let you keep your job here?"

Dwayne Barnes visibly swallowed.

"You wouldn't want them knowing you grew and sold your own marijuana, would you?"

A long moment passed before the man finally buckled. "No, sir."

"That's the spirit," Caine continued. "Now, why don't you start by telling us everything you know about LT?"

Two hours later, they sent the mountain man on his way. While Caine disappeared into the sound room to update their supervisor at the Washington Field Office, Jackson mulled over the information Dwayne had shared with them. None of it made Ike Calhoun look like a man you wanted to tangle with. When Caine finally emerged, Jackson took one look at the smirk on his face and his stomach fell.

"The SAC says we need to take her back," the supervisor announced, cheerily. "He doesn't think our client is safe with this former sniper, and neither do I."

"Sir," Jackson protested, "there's nothing in Calhoun's record to suggest he's a menace."

"You're wrong, Rookie. There's a reason his men wound up dead on that mountain in Afghanistan. The circumstances are all hush, hush, but the rumor is he got them all killed."

"Since when do we base our decisions on rumor?" Jackson asked, his temperature rising.

"Look at the facts, Maddox." Caine's syllables grew clipped. "The man is a trained killer. He's offed eighteen terrorists and, according to Dwayne Barnes, he has enough weapons on his property to start World War Three. That, in my opinion, makes him dangerous."

Jackson threw up his hands. "That's exactly why McClellan chose him to protect his daughter. Why can't we just respect his wishes and get back to the business of catching terrorists?"

"Why can't you just shut the fuck up and do as you're told?"

Ringo stared at the Coke in his hand like he'd never seen one like it.

"There's no call for profanity, sir," Jackson countered, holding Caine's gaze without flinching. "We should be able to discuss this like professionals."

"There's nothing to discuss," Caine insisted, his fair complexion mottling with rage. "I give the orders. You do as I say. Get used to it, Rookie."

"This isn't about me, sir." It was all Jackson could do to keep his voice level. "This is about a former Navy SEAL. SEALs are trained to fulfill a mission at any risk. He got his order straight from General McClellan. He is *not* going to hand Eryn back to us without a fight."

"I expect he won't," Caine agreed, snatching up the document with which he'd blackmailed Barnes. "But last time I checked, we were law in this land, not some renegade vigilante."

Ringo spoke up quietly. "What about Calhoun's security system?"

"We're going to use it against him," Caine decided, smacking his open palm with the sheaf of papers. "Tomorrow morning, Rookie, *you* are going to hit up Town Hall for the plats of his property."

Jackson expelled a long, shuddering breath.

"Give me a hard time about it, Maddox," Caine added, thrusting a threatening finger at him, "and I'll personally escort you to the Bureau's back door. Ringo," he barked, pivoting toward the sound room, "get us out of here."

* * *

"Who lives here?" Eryn asked, holding on tight as Ike drove them through the broad, shallow creek at the base of the mountain and out the other side. He slowed to a stop before a modest mobile home basking in afternoon sunlight and backing up to a sharply rising forest.

"An acquaintance," Ike said. "Name's Dwayne."

"I thought we were going to do laundry."

"My machines are here."

"Oh." She reconsidered the dismal looking trailer. "Is Dwayne even home?"

"Not yet." Ike killed the engine and fetched the laundry bag from the back seat, slinging it over his shoulder. As he rounded the vehicle, his gaze did that unnerving, scanning thing that stirred her apprehension.

"Hop out," he said, opening her door.

"What about Winston?"

"I cracked the windows. He can wait."

Calling reassurance to her dog, Eryn trailed Ike to the front door. "Do you have a key?" she asked, as they mounted the rickety steps.

He turned the doorknob. "No one locks up out here."

You do, she thought, remembering how he'd secured the cabin when they left.

She found herself in the smallest living room imaginable. Shag carpeting complimented the camouflage pattern of the sofa and the deer's head mounted to the wall. *Oh my.*

"In here." Ike led the way to a slightly larger kitchen. The cabinetry was as functional as it was in Ike's cabin, making the brand new, heavy-duty washer and dryer set look out of place against the far wall.

"Have a seat." He dumped their bundle on the dryer.

Eryn sat tentatively at the breakfast table. "Need help?"

"I've got it."

Brushing a crumb from the table's sticky surface, Eyrn propped her chin on her hand and watched. Ike was dumping all the clothes into the washer at once. "Umm…" She cringed.

He sent her a questioning look.

"You're not going to wash those all together are you?"

"That's what I usually do."

"Well, you might want to wash the whites separately. Otherwise, my sweat suit's going to turn your underwear pink."

With lightning-quick reflexes, he snatched back the colored clothing, clearly unnerved by the thought of owning pink underwear. Eryn hid a smile behind her hand.

"Oh, hot water," she instructed as he went to start the white load. "Gosh, I would have thought the Navy taught you some laundry basics," she commented. "They taught you how to make a bed, right?"

Closing the machine, he denied it. "Taught myself."

"What about your mother?"

He looked away. "What about her?"

"You had a mother, right?" For all she knew, he'd been raised by wolves.

"Affirmative."

"Didn't she teach you how to do laundry?"

"Don't remember." He pushed wordlessly off the appliance and stalked into the other room. Eryn jumped up to follow.

She found him easing into the only armchair available. He pulled down the brim of his baseball cap and folded his arms across his chest. "What are we doing?" she asked him.

"Waiting."

She cast her eyes toward the ceiling. "Okay. Are you sure Dwayne won't mind?"

"Positive."

Eryn looked around for somewhere to sit. The camouflaged sofa with the deer head looming over it was out of the question. "What about your family?" she heard herself demand.

"What about them?" His tone was as remote as Timbuktu.

"You don't even know if they're still in Ohio. Why don't you keep in touch?" The puzzle of his past was starting to frustrate her.

But not him, obviously. He looked like he was already half asleep. "Don't know," he said.

"Don't you ever call?" If her mother were still alive, she would call her every day.

He tugged the brim of his cap even lower and tucked his chin to his chest.

He couldn't make it any more obvious that he was done talking. Eryn propped her hands on her hips. She glared at his unresponsive figure. "I'll be in the kitchen," she announced, retracing her footsteps.

Thumping down at the table, she fumed over Ike's refusal to make general conversation. With a shrug and a defeated sigh, she gingerly crossed her arms on the sticky table, laid her aching head on her arms and shut her

eyes. Another poor night's sleep followed by a second day of intensive training had taken its toll. Her limbs grew slack and weighted. She tumbled
into oblivion without meaning to.

* * *

Elkton Motel was an all-brick relic from the 1950's. From its tin roof
to the used campers set up on the perimeter to provide overflow during
peak tourist season, it looked like a haven for biker groups touring the Blue
Ridge. The FBI's Mobile Command Center, large, sleek and silver, looked
as out of place amidst the campers as a Ferrari in a lot full of Volkswagen
Beetles.

Scooping up the plats of Calhoun's property from the seat beside him,
Jackson got out of the Taurus and approached the RV with leaden feet. He
was really starting to dislike his boss.

As he stepped up and in, Ringo put a finger to his lips and gestured
toward the sound room. Their supervisor was talking on his cell phone, a
finger stuck in one ear.

Jackson could tell by his "Whatever you say, sir" that he was kissing up
to Bloomberg, again. He turned to the beverage bar for an iced tea, needing
to cool his simmering resentment.

He hadn't taken more than a swallow when Caine called them back.
"We've got a new suspect," he announced, dropping in front of a moni-
tor. "Our asset was approached by a young man desiring to know where
McClellan's daughter was taken."

Pleased that *someone* in D.C. was still working the investigation, Jackson watched as Caine opened an attachment displaying a grainy photo of a
vacant-eyed youth.

Jackson frowned. *Not another one.*

"Another kid," Ringo exclaimed. "How many more are there?"

"Eight extremists meet online, Ringo, so you do the math," Caine
retorted. "But this is the first time Mustafa's been approached in person.
This one's not too bright. Left our asset with a cell number registered to
a twenty-three-year-old Pakistani named Shahbaz Wahidi. He's an auto-
mechanic, still lives with his parents."

Jackson frowned at the photo in puzzlement. "Why did this kid
expose himself? He could have made the same request of our asset
online."

"Maybe they suspect that we've stumbled on their chat room," Caine suggested.

Ringo pushed his glasses higher. "So what are we going to tell this Shahbaz Wahidi?"

"We'll tell him Eryn McClellan is staying with a friend of her father's," Caine answered. "We'll make it a city address, somewhere convenient for the terrorists, since we're tight on time."

Jackson pinched the ridge of his nose and shook his head. Why hadn't they offered up a false address in the first place, instead of putting Eryn at risk?

"Oh, one more thing." Caine opened a second attachment showing the image of a badly decomposing body with a ravaged neck. "Pedro was found in his shed under fifty-pound bags of Weed and Feed. As you can see, his throat was slit like Itzak's."

Goosebumps sprouted on Jackson's forearms. "Same weapon?"

"Forensics says it was the same six-inch blade. Severed his vocal chords before he could scream."

Déjà vu mushroomed in Jackson's brain. Suddenly, he was back in Iraq, hearing the news that several of his missing Marines had been found with their throats slit. He swallowed hard. "Sir, this isn't the work of a rebellious teenager," he whispered.

Caine didn't even look at him. "You got another theory for us, hotshot?"

One neatly slit throat was a fluke. Two of them meant someone out there had learned a lethal skill. "Ever tried slitting someone's throat, sir?" Jackson asked.

"Of course not."

"Well, I have." He let himself remember the sneak attack on Mosul. "It takes hours of training to finesse. For that matter, so does building a pipe bomb."

Caine leaned back in his seat. "What are you saying, Maddox?"

Jackson deliberated risking Caine's wrath by going out on a limb. "I think we're dealing with a non-native threat, sir," he ventured.

Caine gave a bark of laughter. "The problem with you, Rookie, is that you're still jumpy from your last tour. The Brotherhood has claimed responsibility. We don't need to start inventing suspects."

Jackson looked back at the grisly picture. Fine. All he could do was make suggestions. But he couldn't shake his conviction that Eryn's would-be killer had come across the ocean to avenge her father's actions.

"Ho, sir!" Ringo exclaimed, pointing at Jackson's laptop which stood open on the console. "Our client's not on the mountain anymore."

* * *

Ike was amused to note that Stanley's princess drooled. As he folded his briefs and T-shirts into neat little squares, he watched saliva trickle from the corner of her slightly parted lips toward the wet spot on the table. The dryer hummed with the second load, but Eryn slept on, oblivious.

Maybe I'm pushing her too hard, he considered with a twinge of guilt. It wasn't like she'd signed up to take his course. Leaving her as vulnerable as a baby, on the other hand, would be a huge disservice to her. Teaching her to shoot, to think through her fear, made perfect sense.

If he could just do it without wanting something more, without getting sucked back into the War on Terror. Extremists weren't his problem anymore; they were hers. The most he could do was to teach her to defend herself. His job would be a hell of a lot easier, though, if she'd stop insisting that they get better acquainted.

It was none of her business what kind of family he came from, whether he called his mother or not. He didn't need to hear her dismay, which only made him feel ashamed and then cheated. Hell, not everyone had parents who adored them.

The only people who'd ever treated Ike like family were Stanley and his brothers in Team Five. They'd lived through glory and hell together, day in and day out for years. They knew each others' secrets, weaknesses, and strengths. Hell, they could practically read each others' minds.

A sudden pain lanced Ike's chest. Damn it, he still missed them— the ones who were gone forever and those he hoped still lived. He leaned against the dryer, racked by grief.

Where was Spellman recuperating, he wondered, after stepping on that mine?

It came as a relief to hear Winston barking out front. Counting on the dryer noise to keep Eryn unaware of what was going on, Ike hurried from the kitchen to intercept Dwayne Barnes in his front yard.

He found the thickset mountain man sitting in his F150 just looking at Ike's Durango. Seeing Ike step out of his trailer, Dwayne pushed slowly out of his truck and approached him with a less-than-enthusiastic step. "Hey, LT." He stopped about three yards away and gave his bushy beard a scratch. "What's new with you?"

Usually Dwayne was all boisterous handshakes and claps on the back. Ike searched his guarded expression. "Not much. You?"

"Oh, same ol', same ol'." Dwayne rocked for an awkward moment on his feet. "I see you got yourself a dog," he observed, jerking his thumb at Winston.

Ike acknowledged the comment with a nod. "You just come from work?" he asked.

"Naw, I'm takin' the day off."

"You go into town?"

"Yep. Had to buy lumber for my new deck."

Ike glanced toward the planks filling the back of Dwayne's Ford. "Happen to see a large silver RV anywhere?"

The man stared down at the grass. "Can't say I did," he answered unconvincingly.

Ike's sixth sense told him Dwayne was lying. The mountain man shuffled his feet. He cleared his throat. Beads of perspiration dotted his forehead. "You got something to tell me, Dwayne?" Ike invited, softly.

"No," said Dwayne, just a little too quickly.

"That right? Maybe you need me to jog your memory." The threat was accompanied by a widening of his stance.

"All right!" Dwayne threw up his hands. "I'll tell you what I know." He sent Ike a tortured look. "There's some FBI guys in town, LT, and they're askin' all about you."

The confession wasn't altogether unexpected, but it struck Ike squarely in the solar plexus. He took a step closer, pitched his voice low. "What are they asking?"

"They wanted to know what you were like, if you were right in the head, and all. They wanted me to list the weapons you have."

Dwayne's words made Ike's blood boil. "You told them," he guessed.

"I had to!" Dwayne took a precautionary step back. "They knew something about me. Something that would've cost me my job."

"You sold me out," Ike accused, incredulous.

"Aw, hell, you got nothin' to hide!" Dwayne protested. "You're a freakin' war hero, LT."

"I want to know *exactly* what you told them," Ike hissed.

"That you had a security system," Dwayne admitted. "That you'd know they was comin', and there wasn't a snowball's chance in hell they'd catch you, if you didn't want to be caught."

"Just like your favorite movie, *Rambo*," Ike elaborated.

"Exactly," Dwayne agreed.

Shit!

Ike thought of Eryn still sleeping in Dwayne's kitchen. If the man got a look at her, there was no telling what kinds of rumors would start to fly. No one needed to know who she was, let alone where she was located.

Planting a hand on Dwayne's massive chest, Ike propelled him toward his vehicle. "I think you'd better take a drive, Dwayne, before I break your fucking nose."

"I'm sorry, LT! I'll make it up to you, I swear it."

"Go," Ike ordered.

With a resigned look, Dwayne slumped back to his truck. He stepped in, revved the engine, and took off with a spray of gravel.

Good riddance, thought Ike, but then he felt his nape prickle. Turning, he found Eryn standing on Dwayne's front stoop, staring in astonishment at the retreating Ford. "Was that Dwayne?" she asked.

"No," he lied, stalking back to the trailer.

As he hustled her inside, she shot him a reproachful look. "Why on earth did you chase him off?" she demanded.

"Time to leave," he said, ignoring the question and continuing into the kitchen. There, he scraped the colored clothes out of the dryer and stuffed them into the laundry bag on top of the whites.

Eryn didn't move an inch as he passed her again en route to the door. "Now," he urged.

"I don't think so." Her chin was angled upward, her hands planted on her hips. "You need to explain what I just saw."

It was obvious to Ike she wasn't going to move an inch unless she got some answers. His temples throbbed. He peered through the cracked front door, half expecting to see the FBI barreling through Naked Creek. "Dwayne took my course last fall," he admitted shortly. "I teach survival and security."

Her brow furrowed as she processed his statement. "So, that's what the trails are for," she guessed aloud. "And the shooting range."

"Right."

"Dwayne took your course, and that's why he agreed to house your machines here."

"Exactly."

"Then why'd you chase him off his land?"

"I didn't. He forgot something."

"You're lying."

Ike had had enough of the fifth degree. "You gonna come on your own, or do I need to carry you?" he threatened.

Eryn's back stiffened. After a measuring look, she apparently decided she wouldn't put it past him to throw her over his shoulder. She marched mutinously out of the door, sending him a look that should have left him in cinders. Amused despite the urgent situation, Ike trundled her into his SUV, tossed the laundry bag onto the back seat, and took off.

With haste that bounced them in their seats, he sped them away from Dwayne's trailer, spraying water twenty feet into the air as he sluiced through Naked Creek and out the other side.

No Feds or the local cops in sight.

As he rushed them toward his mountain, leaving a trail of dust hanging in the air behind them, he was sharply aware of Eryn's silence. She sat stiffly in the opposite seat clutching the safety handle, her mouth drawn into a firm pink line.

Her irritation with him unsettled him. Just like everything else about her, it went straight under his skin to affect his nervous system. And, damn it, before she'd come into his life, he hadn't been aware that he'd even *had* a nervous system.

"Why don't you tell me anything?" she demanded as he flew toward his property.

"Like what?"

"Like the fact that you teach survival training? Like why you chased that poor man off his property."

"Trust me, you don't need to pity him." His temper flared again at the thought of Dwayne's betrayal.

"Okay, then, give me one good reason for your hostility."

"I can give you several."

"Go ahead."

But he couldn't because he'd assured her just the other day that the FBI hadn't followed them, and he didn't want her losing faith in him. Worse than that, if the FBI was in town, then the fucking terrorists probably weren't all that far behind. She sure as hell didn't need to know that.

Swinging between the pillars, he silenced his watch, shifted fluidly into four-wheel drive, then took off again, using the need for concentration to avoid her expectant gaze. What she didn't know couldn't hurt her, he assured himself.

* * *

"Damn it, we missed him!" Caine looked from his laptop to the long stretch of country road blocked at the far end by a lumpy mountain. "It's too late. They're back on his property."

Ringo, who was driving the Taurus, let up abruptly on the gas, and the seatbelt strapping Jackson into the rear seat jerked tight at the abrupt change in speed. He had to take it off in order to put it back on.

It was just another sign of how totally ineffective their approach was. He couldn't even say if they were on the side of the law anymore.

As a Marine, Jackson had been one of the good guys. Sure, he'd done some dirty deeds in the line of duty, but he'd never shot at women, children, or upright men. And, as far as he was concerned, Isaac Calhoun was an upright man. Any special ops warrior was a hero in his eyes, whether the men under his command got killed or not.

"Turn around." Caine gave an angry gesture, and Ringo swung into a tractor road to pull a U-turn, pointing them back toward town.

"Don't worry," Caine added after a minute of tense silence. "We'll get her back tomorrow night."

Jackson's pulse accelerated. "Sir, I'd just as soon not run into a SEAL in the dead of night," he announced. Their plan to lure Calhoun away from the cabin wasn't going to work the way Caine figured it would.

"I don't want to hear excuses, Maddox. He's not a SEAL anymore."

"How am I supposed to convince Eryn to come with me?" Jackson asked.

"You don't give her any a choice, Rookie. Or does it turn your stomach to manhandle a woman?"

Jackson met Ringo's quick glance into the mirror. Did Caine really just say that?

"Besides, she won't give you any trouble," Caine predicted, "not if she's still taking her pills."

Jackson had to let the statement run through his head twice. "Are you telling me we drugged her, sir?" His voice came out an octave too high.

Caine made a sound of disgust. "Of course not. She was overwrought by her students' death. She had gone without sleep for days, remember that?"

Turning in his seat, Caine whipped off his amber-lensed Oakley sunglasses and pinned him with a hard stare. "You're not a Marine with an

M-16 and a Beretta, anymore, Maddox. You're a special agent. Start looking at the bigger picture."

It was Caine who couldn't see the bigger picture, Jackson realized. His
perceptions were too clouded by ambition. Protecting Eryn wasn't his pri-
ority. He wanted to make a name for himself, in whatever way he could—
either by catching the terrorists or by creating a situation in which Calhoun
looked like a terrorist.

It really made no difference to Caine who the bad guys were.

CHAPTER NINE

As their altitude climbed, so did the tension in the cab of Ike's Durango. The only sound cutting through the thickly charged silence was that of gravel hitting the undercarriage.

Ike made the last sharp turn with relief, barreling into his front yard to brake beside the log pile. He cut the engine and was diving out the door when Eryn grabbed him and refused to let go, her nails digging into his biceps.

"Oh, no you don't." Her tone would have made a room full of adolescents sit up and take notice. "I don't know who taught you to keep everything bottled inside of you, Isaac Calhoun. Maybe that's how you were raised, but it's bad for your health, and it's driving me effing crazy!"

Effing? He found himself smiling. How cute was it that she couldn't bring herself to curse even when she was furious?

"Now tell me what Dwayne said that's making you act so strange, or I'll..." A riotous pink suffused her face and her chest heaved.

"You'll what?" He was tempted to push her over the edge just to see what she would do.

"I will hurt you!" she vowed, balling a hand into a fist.

He just had to laugh. Even in the sticky situation he was in, the chuckle felt good, rolling up from his gut with a rush of warmth.

She glared at his mouth in astonishment. "Are you mocking me?"

"'Course not."

"Then stop smirking, and tell me what the heck is going on!"

He wasn't about to tell her the truth and send her back into the panicky state she'd arrived in. What he could do, however, was to derail this little tirade with a kiss. One, it was the only way he knew to shut her up. Two, he'd been dying to taste her sweet mouth for days now.

Flashing out a hand, he palmed the side of her head, lowered his head, and crushed his lips to hers.

There, nothing to be heard but silence.

She froze against him, her eyes flashing with outrage, and she wasn't kissing him back.

Ike's pride wavered. He had to get a response, to prove he was firmly in control of the situation. She could just let go, trusting him to look out for her.

Ignoring the voice in his head that cautioned him against it, Ike shifted gears. Coercion wasn't the way. He needed to coax her the way he tamed wild animals, with patience and tenderness. With that new objective, he gentled the contact and nibbled on her unresponsive lips until they warmed and softened like handled butter.

That's it, honey. Trust me. I got it all under control.

The sound of her breath hitching was music to his ears. Her eyes sank shut, and the same lips that had resisted him seconds earlier parted willingly when he laid his thumb lightly against her chin. Anticipation whipped through him as he stroked his tongue into her mouth, meeting hers in a warm, delicious glide. *Oh, yeah.*

Suddenly she was as welcoming as the petals of a flower spreading in the sun. She kissed him back with enthusiasm that made his heart trot. Her kiss was as sweet and sultry as a wet dream. It gained force inside him like an afternoon thunderstorm.

On some unconscious level, Ike realized his awareness had shrunk to the proportions of the vehicle. All he was aware of was Eryn's taste, her smell, her texture. Nothing else existed. Alarm bells sounded in his head. He broke contact with a groan, hauled himself back into his seat, and forced his senses back into the world around him.

The FBI could have had the place surrounded, and he wouldn't have noticed.

"You're dangerous," he stated, aware that their kiss had rendered her speechless.

As for himself, he'd just learned a sobering lesson. Where Eryn was concerned, he *wasn't* in control. She could *not* trust him to keep her safe. Stanley had made a huge mistake in choosing him to be her protector. He had to get the hell away from her and stay there.

Groping for the latch, he stumbled out of the truck before he got another genius idea.

"Whoa, daddy," Eryn breathed, falling weakly against her seat. Who'd have guessed that Ike Calhoun could kiss like that?

Actually, the kiss had started out exactly as she'd expected. It had been nothing more than a strategy to shut her up. But then he had gentled it into something compelling, unexpected, with sensuality that had sparked an immediate response in her.

Too stunned to move, she watched him carry their laundry into the cabin. The tense look on his face, paired with that comment about her being dangerous told her he wasn't going to kiss her again, not if he could help it.

Drat.

She may not have gotten answers to her questions, but she'd learned more about Ike from that one kiss than from anything he'd ever told her!

Pleasure shimmered in her as she relived his unexpected tenderness, his restrained passion. It was as if the kiss had created a window in the wall he kept between them. Through it, she had glimpsed the real Ike. He wasn't just the terse, resentful soldier who had brought her so begrudgingly to his cabin. He was a complex human being, vulnerable, lonely, wracked by guilt.

My God, there was so much more to him than she'd realized!

And if she was eager to get to know him before, now she was consumed with curiosity. Who was Ike Calhoun, really? What did he want out of life? Could she help him overcome the tragedy that had sent him into self-punishing isolation?

Ike couldn't get that kiss out of his head. It was supposed to have been a simple thing, an indulgence he'd allowed himself because—hey, he was human. Only, he'd seriously miscalculated his own weakness. The moment Eryn started kissing him back, his self-control had vanished. All he could think about was getting more.

Which is never going to happen, he sternly warned himself.

Plus, his timing sucked. The FBI was circling like the Union Army closing in on the Confederates. He needed to focus. He figured he had twenty-four hours, tops, to work up a plan so that Eryn didn't fall back into their clutches. He shouldn't even be *thinking* about what might have happened if he hadn't reined himself in.

Retreating into his room, he shut the door and put away his clean clothes. He waited till he heard Eryn slip into the bathroom before he placed her clothing on the stairs. Then he eased outside with the dog right behind him, desperate to avoid running into her while his body was still primed like an engine pumped full of high octane fuel.

With Winston on his heels, he hiked up the trail toward the boulder where he did his clearest thinking. How had the FBI done it? They had to have access to technology or information he was unaware of.

He wished to hell he could call up Stanley for advice, only Cougar had warned him that any direct communication would be intercepted.

Arriving at the top of the rise, Ike clambered onto the sun-warmed boulder and threw himself down on it. A stiff breeze ruffled the soft material of his T-shirt. Storm clouds lined the horizon, tracking a path in his direction.

The wind carried the memory of the kiss back to him. He pushed it away, resolutely.

He figured he had two choices. One, he could hole up on his mountain and defend it by force. With rabbit and fowl in abundance this time of year, survival was not an issue. But if the FBI launched a forcible attack, he'd have to fight to protect Eryn, who might wind up getting hurt. Option one didn't look so good.

Option two was to leave the area undetected and head off somewhere equally remote. But until he knew how the Feds had found them in the first place, leaving wouldn't guarantee that they wouldn't be followed again.

So, until he thought of something better, they had to stay put. *Damn it.* The memory of Eryn's responsiveness made his gut clench. He should have known her kiss would taste like something he could never get enough of.

How the hell was he going to live in the same space as her and not want more?

Eryn stood on the front porch, listening to the birds twitter. Ike and the dog were gone. Her heart pattered. Surely he hadn't abandoned her.

No, he wouldn't do that. Besides, the Durango was still parked under the tree. He had to be walking the dog, giving himself time to ponder whatever it was that Dwayne had told him. Hopefully he would realize he could tell her what it was. It wouldn't kill him to share his concerns. Nor would they send her into a mindless panic, not so long as she still had his protection.

To distract herself, she decided she would concoct another of her specialty recipes. Sharing another hearty meal at the table might induce Ike to talk. If that didn't work, another kiss might do the trick. Only, she would have to make the first move. Given his remark about her being dangerous, she was sure he would keep himself firmly in check.

His kiss was like a drug she desperately needed more of, a crystal ball that offered insight into who he really was. If he refused to kiss her again out of, what—fear?—then she would have to make the first move. Sexual excitement kept her blood at a low simmer.

With her arms elbow-deep in pastry dough, she finally heard Ike's voice out front, speaking to Winston. Sighing her relief, Eryn rolled out the dough by hand. She cut it into strips and laid it atop the contents of the shepherd's pie. Then she slipped the dish into the pre-warmed oven, scrubbed her hands clean, and ventured outside to watch.

An unpredictable breeze played havoc with her hair as she pushed the door open. Dark clouds surged across the valley toward them, bearing the scent of rain. Hovering on the top porch step, Eryn watched Winston heed Ike's every command with no more reward than a pat on the head. "Wow," she murmured, impressed by Ike's accomplishment.

But then he offered Winston a stick from the log pile, and she frowned. *What's this?*

"Sic," he said, urging the dog to bite it. "Good boy," he added when the dog growled.

Eryn's puzzlement deepened. It wasn't till Ike tossed aside the stick and started wrapping a towel around his forearm that she realized his intent. *Oh, no.*

"Sic," he said again, offering the dog his arm.

"He's not going to bite you," she called out, betraying her presence.

Ike visibly stiffened, but he kept his back to her, not acknowledging her comment.

Who did he think he was, teaching her docile Shepherd mix to bite?

"Winston, sic," he repeated, thrusting his arm in the dog's face.

Winston barked. His blond coat shimmered in the uncertain light as he backed away.

"Stop it!" Eryn demanded.

"Sic."

The dog barked again. He turned in a circle, chasing his tail, but he wouldn't attack Ike's arm.

"You're upsetting him," she cried, leaping off the porch to intervene.

Ike's head swiveled. His green gaze singed her as he took in her approach. The memory of their kiss seemed to thicken the air around them—or maybe it was ozone from the approaching storm.

"Come stand right here," he said, crooking a finger at her.

She approached him warily. "Why?"

"You're going help me. When I grab your wrist, I want you to scream and struggle." He squared off against her.

"Uh…" She wanted no part in training Winston to be aggressive, but the prospect of Ike touching her caused her to waver.

"Play on his protective urges," he added, mistaking her hesitation for agreement. "Then maybe his Shepherd instincts will kick in."

"It still won't work," she insisted. In his heart of hearts, Winston was all Retriever.

Fast as a trap, Ike caught her wrist, his grip like a shackle.

"Okay, that actually hurts," she admitted, somewhat surprised. The clouds surged ever nearer, emitting ominous rolls of thunder.

"Struggle," he said, loosening his grip at once.

It was still unbreakable. This wasn't nearly as pleasant as the kiss they'd shared. Eryn tried peeling back his fingers with her free hand, but it was useless. "Okay, please let go; you're wasting your time."

Ike held her fast. "Tell him to sic." She could tell by the look on his face he wasn't going to release her till she did it.

Stubborn man. "It's not going to work!"

"Do it."

"Winston, sic!" she raged, clenching her fists.

The dog just looked at her, obviously confused.

With a stifled curse, Ike dropped her arm and stalked away, dragging a hand through the spikes of his hair.

"What did you expect? I told you he wouldn't attack," she scolded.

He threw his hands up. "Why didn't Stanley teach you to defend yourself?" he railed. "I can't believe you're so goddamn helpless."

The accusation stung. "I am not helpless. Don't discount me like that!"

He folded his arms and considered her as he might an unsolvable problem.

"Here, I'll prove it," she added, hunting for a weapon. Spying the stick Ike had used earlier, she snatched it up and wielded it like a bat. "Try grabbing me now," she invited.

"Put it down." Ike's voice came out low and flat.

"I don't think so. Earlier in the truck you called me dangerous. Now you say I'm helpless. Which is it, Isaac? You can't have both."

He had her angry now, and it wasn't because he was training her dog to be aggressive—not really. It was because she could sense the distance he kept putting between them. He couldn't make it any clearer that he considered that kiss a mistake, but it wasn't. At least when he kissed, he communicated *something!*

"You'll end up with a splinter. That's not the way to hold it," he bit out.

"Then teach me how to fight," she demanded.

"No."

"Why not? You taught me to shoot."

He narrowed his eyes, saying nothing.

"You know what I think? I think you're afraid of me, Isaac." She tossed out the accusation with unaccustomed recklessness. But she needed to rattle his cage a little, to goad him into letting his guard down so she could kiss him this time. "You're afraid you'll kiss me, and you won't be able to stop," she added, with sudden insight.

His answer was a short, bitter laugh, but he didn't deny it, she noticed with a private thrill. "You teach defense in your survival course, don't you?" She pressed what she sensed was her advantage.

"To men," he retorted.

"What's the difference?"

His gaze flicked to her breasts and lower. "There are a couple differences."

The bold inference flustered her. She knew she was playing with fire but she couldn't seem to help herself. "And why would those prevent me from learning to defend myself?"

A muscle in the side of his jaw jumped. "You going to use that stick?" he asked her softly, "or just stand there running your mouth?"

Bingo. With a smirk of triumph, she rushed at him while swinging the stick at his butt. *That'll teach him.*

Except the stick never made contact with his backside. In a move too quick to see, he grabbed her weapon, whipped her around, and pulled her back to front against his larger frame.

"This isn't a game, Eryn," he grated in her ear. She could feel his heart pounding against her back. The stick, placed like a bar against her shoulders, kept her pinned against him. "If you know what's good for you, you'll keep your distance, understand?" The hard ridge under his zipper was as much a threat as his words.

If he was trying to intimidate her, he was succeeding. She didn't know if her knees trembled from fear, chagrin at being told off for pushing too far, or because she felt the substantive proof that he could ravish her right here, right now, with or without her participation. "I—I understand," she said.

He released her wordlessly and stepped back, hurling the stick toward the woodpile, apparently furious with himself.

Eryn fled for the porch. A backward glance saw him striding across the darkening yard to the long rope dangling from the oak tree. Pausing again at the door, she saw him pull himself, hand over hand, up the length of the rope, his feet dangling. He disappeared into what looked like a tree house.

Rain began to pelt the yard. Winston streaked past her, up the steps, toward shelter. Eryn followed him inside, leaving Ike outside to weather the storm.

She went straight to the bathroom, flicked on the light and studied her flushed face in the mirror.

What are you doing, Eryn?

Her reflection provided no answers. It wasn't her style to taunt a man into losing control, especially not one as dangerous and battle-hardened as Ike, but some small voice insisted that he needed her to force him out of his protective shell. The hunger revealed in his kiss today—the volatility he'd just warned her about—sparked an unexpected yearning to soothe him.

She was crazy to consider it. The man had been a sniper; he was a recluse with a murky, tortured past.

And yet her father trusted him with her keeping. That said something, didn't it?

Forget about him, she advised herself. *Eat your dinner, read a book, and go to bed.*

As long as Ike kept to himself, then he deserved to wallow in his isolation. Who was she to force him to deal with his issues?

Cutting herself a portion of shepherd's pie, she ate it standing up, fighting all the while to keep her gaze from sliding to the window, where the sky had darkened to black. Occasionally, jags of lightning lit up the yard as bright as day, revealing snapshots of Ike, stripped to his jeans, punishing himself with push-ups and pull-ups and those drills called burpees.

He'd rather be struck by lightning than spend time alone with me.

Feeling like a cat with its fur rubbed wrong, Eryn dumped her plate in the sink without washing it. She'd agreed to cook for him, but he could damn well do the dishes.

Snatching up her book, she stormed upstairs to bed.

Ike took an ice-cold shower. It did as little to abate his craving for Eryn as exercise had. He'd driven his body to the brink of exhaustion, to no avail.

Eating his supper all alone, he moaned aloud as the buttery crust, creamy vegetables, and seasoned beef melted in his mouth. He would have gone for a second helping, only the silence overhead, coupled with his concerns about the FBI, had whittled away his appetite.

He caught himself listening for her upstairs. Was she sleeping? Reading? Christ, he hoped she wasn't crying. He cringed to recall how harshly he'd dealt with her.

It wasn't her fault he'd lost his mind and kissed her today. He had no excuse, only that he'd wanted to lock lips with her from the moment she touched her tongue to her upper lip the day he'd grabbed her at the safe house. She had to know by now that she had that effect on men.

You're afraid you'll kiss me, and you won't be able to stop. Damn right, he was. But why wasn't she?

He could only suppose her desperate circumstances had skewed with her judgment. He supposed it was only natural for a girl in her predicament to be drawn to the one man who could defend her. With him, she could forget she was being hunted by terrorists.

But if there *were* no terrorists, the story would be different, wouldn't it?

If she weren't running scared, he'd be the last man she would want comforting her. He was a rough and ready soldier, a man who'd abandoned his teammates when they needed him most; a man who hadn't called his mother in a decade. He had no business even looking at her.

She was vulnerable right now. If he took advantage of that, what would that make him? Plus one time would never be enough. He would want her for as long as she could stand him—which wouldn't be for very long, he acknowledged with bitterness. Sooner or later, he would come up short, unable to give her the stability she was used to.

His life had gone to shit the day he'd watched his teammates die, knowing all the while that he could have prevented it.

Dropping his face into his hands, Ike rubbed his gritty eyes. Aw, hell, he needed to explain this to Eryn so she didn't keep pushing the issue.

He put it off as long as possible, tidying the kitchen until it gleamed. She had left a mess intentionally, he realized, amused by her subtle punishment. When there was no more putting it off, he turned toward the stairs, hoping to find her fast asleep.

Her scent ambushed him halfway up the steps, undermining his noble intentions. Over the groaning of the risers, he heard the sound of a page being turned. She was reading, he realized, peeking through the half-open doorway.

He drew back with a start. Eryn lay on her stomach across the bed, wearing nothing but that strappy top she'd worn the other night and white lace panties. *Oh, fuck.*

At his quick retreat, the floorboards squeaked, and she shrieked, fumbling to cover herself. He hovered in the hallway, torn between the common-sense urge to run like hell and his determination to set the record straight once and for all.

"Okay, it's safe," she called, her voice wobbling.

Safe, right. He peered around the door frame, staying right where he was. She had wrapped the sheet around her like a toga, but the tops of her shoulders and most of her legs were still bare.

"It gets hot up here," she said with a proud lift to her chin.

No kidding. "You could open the window," he suggested.

"I've tried. It's stuck."

Her answer left him no choice but to wade into the room to un-stick the window. Chill, moist air wafted in as he jimmied it open, cooling his scalding mental image of Eryn laying across her bed practically naked.

By the time he turned around, she had pulled the sheet over her shoulders. *Smart girl.* "Came to apologize," he said, edging toward the exit.

"For what?"

Why did women do this? "I was out of line today," he added. *Obviously.*

"Which part?"

Damn it. "Eryn, you're not…" He cut himself off, afraid that he would either offend her somehow or make himself sound depraved.

For a change, she kept absolutely mute as he struggled to articulate his thoughts. "Look, I'm not going to betray your father's trust," he finally ground out, deciding that was the safest excuse handy. "He trusts me to watch over you, not—" *fuck your brains out.*

"Take advantage of me?" she delicately supplied.

"Exactly." He jammed his fingers into his pockets to disguise his erection.

A crooked little smile seized her lips, making his pulse quicken. "I get it," she told him, blushing prettily. "You don't have to beat yourself up, Ike. If it's any consolation, I'm not opposed to being…taken advantage of." Her voice trailed to a husky whisper as her lashes swept downward concealing her gaze.

Not helping.

Swear to God, all she had to do right now was to drop the sheet, and he'd be across the room burying his face between her thighs.

Calling on his last ounce of restraint, Ike turned briskly toward the stairs. "Shut the window if it rains again," he called, fleeing from the temptation she embodied.

"Sleep tight," she sang out.

He pushed into his room and firmly shut the door. *Sleep tight?* Right. She had to know she had him too worked up to sleep. Besides, he couldn't afford to sleep, not when he had some serious planning to do.

Turning his lock against the desire to return to her, he spread an oil-stained towel over his dresser top. He then set out the lubricant and cloth needed to clean his sniper rifle. For the next hour, he'd lose himself in mindless routine.

If the Feds made a move tonight, at least he wouldn't be caught with his pants down. Some comfort that was.

Eryn collapsed onto the mattress, half euphoric, half chagrined. What on earth had compelled her to say those words, *I'm not opposed to being taken advantage of?*

She covered her hot face with her hands. Had she known what she was saying? It wasn't like her to be so forward.

But how else was she going to get to know Ike when he refused to talk to her? And she just *had* to get to know him better. His kiss had shot roots of curiosity deep into the soils of her mind.

The real Ike was lonely and despairing. He needed her.

Yet there was no way to comfort him if he didn't let her in. And letting her in clearly terrified him. That line about not betraying her father's trust—hogwash. It was fear that held him back. She could see it so clearly now. He was afraid of her; afraid of intimacy, period.

That was why he lived in this crumbling cottage, in deep seclusion!

Poor man. A picture of what he used to look like flashed before her eyes. What had happened to the confident warrior her father had so loved?

It could only be the incident her father had mentioned, the one she couldn't remember, except the part about lives being lost. Friends of Ike's most likely. He blamed himself. He'd quit the military because he felt he'd let them down. For a man who took his duties seriously, their deaths would have been a crushing blow. That had to have been what happened.

And until he discussed the past with someone else, the guilt would fester in him, like a tumor.

But who was she to force him to talk? And what made her think she could play counselor when she'd never experienced that depth of guilt and grief herself?

It's better I don't try, she told herself, with a sigh of disappointment.

She and Ike were two very different people; it wasn't like their futures were likely to bring them together again. Having tried the impractical route back in college, she'd long ago decided not to waste her time on bachelors without promise. She was holding out for Mr. Right.

And Ike was so not that guy.

Seeing rain splatter the window sill, she rolled out of bed, dragging the sheet behind her to close the draft and shut off the light.

As she sprawled back across the lumpy mattress in the dark, the memory of Ike's hard body had her touching herself. Pleasure gripped her as she envisioned his rough hands on her breasts, relived the thrill of his tongue tangling with hers. *Oh, Ike.* She moaned, arching toward her fingers in an effort to appease the ache pulsing inside her.

But her decision to leave Ike alone made her sudden climax an unfulfilling one.

She wanted more. She wanted all of him, every mysterious, tortured part of him. But that desire was impractical, if not impossible. The man would barely even talk to her, let alone share his life with her. Practicality won the day, whether she wanted it to, or not.

CHAPTER TEN

"I have information for you," Mustafa said, calling the number on the narrow scrap of paper. To his disappointment, he recognized the voice on the other end as belonging to the same young man who'd approached him at the hotel.

And to his further disappointment, it was Vengeance who entered the McDonald's on Connecticut Avenue half an hour later, where they had arranged to meet. Two FBI agents sat in a dark blue Buick parked across the street, listening to the conversation via Mustafa's Blackberry.

The McDonald's, which stood across from the National Zoo, stayed open until midnight, one hour from now. Aside from the two employees tidying up in back, Mustafa and Vengeance had the dining area to themselves.

Once small talk was out of the way, Mustafa slid an envelope across the table. The boy picked it up, opened it, and read the address written inside.

"She is here?" he asked incredulously, "in D.C.?"

"Yes. The house belongs to a friend of her father's, an old Marine colonel," Mustafa explained, relating what he'd been told to say.

The boy's brow furrowed. "Why isn't she better protected? Doesn't the FBI take us seriously?" His grip tightened on the square of paper.

Who is us? Mustafa wondered. Was it the Taliban? Al Qaeda? "She's no longer under the protection of the FBI," he lied. "Her father dismissed them. He thinks he knows better how to keep her safe."

"He thinks he is indestructible," Vengeance concluded with a sneer. "We will bring him to his knees."

"Yes," Mustafa agreed. "But...who else is involved? Can they be trusted?" he asked, feigning concern.

The boy became guarded. "It is not safe for you to know," he said, putting the note back inside the envelope and pocketing it. He came abruptly to his feet and inclined his head. "Thank you." Without a backward glance, he headed for the exit.

Mustafa remained in his seat. No sooner had the door closed behind Vengeance than he heard an engine turn over. He wondered if the agents would detain and question the youth. Probably not, for that would undermine the trap they were trying to set.

Let it work, Mustafa prayed, swallowing his last sip of coffee.

* * *

Ike's eyes abruptly opened. He had stretched out on his neatly made bed with the intent of catching just enough shut-eye to keep his reflexes sharp. He must have slept longer than he'd intended, for the driving rain that had lulled him to sleep had abated. Moonlight now shone through the cracks of his lowered blind.

Checking his watch to see what time it was, he found it flashing, and he jerked upright. Images had been forwarded from the cameras guarding his property to his laptop, meaning someone was near his invisible fence.

Oh, hell, not the FBI!

Slipping out of bed and into the chair at his desk, he opened his Mac-Book Pro and logged on. A total of twelve image files awaited his perusal.

A cold sweat formed on the small of his back as he studied each image. For the past couple of hours, three men in dark pants and windbreakers had followed his property line along the northwest boundary, but never crossing onto his land. They were reconnoitering. A steep cliff finally forced them to retrace their footsteps and leave.

Didn't they know he could see them? Hadn't Dwayne told them all about his high tech security system? And what were they looking for—a vulnerability? They wouldn't find one.

Ike leaned back in his chair. What to do? he wondered.

The creaking of treads jerked his attention to his door. By the sound of it, Eryn was also up and moving down the stairs. With a stab of his finger he put his laptop into hibernation and closed it, plunging his room into moonlit darkness.

Memories of how she'd looked tonight, stretched across her bed in her undergarments, sent tongues of desire licking over him. He remained glued to his seat, wondering what the hell she was up to. If she knew what was good for her, she'd go right back upstairs.

A light knock at the door dashed that fragile hope. His heart began to pound, his jeans to grow suddenly snug. He didn't trust himself to speak.

The doorknob slowly turned. His mouth turned dry as she poked her burnished head into the room. "Ike?" She was looking toward his empty bed.

"Here."

As she eased inside, he was relieved to see she'd put on some clothes, having pulled on her pink sweat pants. "I had a bad dream," she announced with a hitch in her voice.

Concern edged his lustful thoughts aside. "It was just a dream," he said, meaning to reassure her.

"But it seemed so real." She hugged herself. "The taxi driver that killed Itzak brought me to this cabin, only it was different, creepy and dark with chains on the walls. He locked me up. And he—he hurt me," she finished, her voice trailing to a whisper.

Ike's stomach clenched at the violent image she'd so delicately depicted. "He won't find you here," he promised, fighting the impulse to cross the room and haul her into the reassuring embrace he knew she needed. He gripped the chair he was sitting in until his knuckles ached.

"I know, but..." She weaved on her feet a moment. "Can I please sleep in your bed?" She gnawed her lower lip as she waited for his answer, a sight that nearly did him in. "This isn't—I mean, I just want—"

"—to sleep," he finished, understanding perfectly. He knew about nightmares. But putting her in his bed was as rash an idea as kissing her to shut her up. "Go ahead," he heard himself say. *Idiot!*

With a whisper of thanks, she pulled back the blankets and wriggled under them. As he watched her curl into a ball to warm herself, he felt himself being torn right down the middle.

"Don't you ever sleep?" she asked, stifling a huge yawn. She fluffed his pillow, cozied into it.

Don't think I'd sleep much over there. "Later."

"Mmmm." At last, she ceased her shivering and went quiet.

In the next instant, he was certain he heard her soft snore.

He shook his head, incredulous. Seductive and sweet and not opposed to being taken advantage of. *Jesus.* And he was no better than the terrorist in her dream for wanting to keep her here all to himself. Only it was pleasure, not pain, that he wanted to inflict on her. Pleasure like she'd never experienced.

To think that someone wanted to *destroy* her in the most horrific and violent way imaginable. It turned his stomach. In his line of work he'd been forced to watch several taped executions. The victim remained conscious for several seconds *after* the head was severed from the body.

Ike's ardor evaporated. What if the terrorist was never caught? What if there was a whole network of the fuckers, each determined to finish her off? Then Eryn was doomed to nightmares and looking over her shoulder for the rest of her goddamn life.

The realization shook the bars of something caged deep inside of him. He had to do something.

I already am, he told himself. I'm toughening her mentally, teaching her to shoot.

Not good enough.

Then he'd teach her to defend herself, damn it. He'd bite the bullet and do it for her sake.

And let Eryn fight the terrorists? What kind of man does that make you?

Reprimanded by his conscience, Ike threw himself out of the chair, and went into the living room to feed another log into the woodstove. He then sat on the couch and dropped his face into his hands. Winston got up, padded over, and nudged him.

Ike petted him absently. Eryn's fate wasn't his problem. The War on Terror was not his problem. There were others who could hold the line. Safeguard the innocent.

Then why did he feel so damn responsible?

* * *

Using Google Maps, Farshad studied the street view of the address given to Shahbaz by the informant. *Her father thinks she is safer here with his friend, the Colonel,* Shahbaz had written in their shared online account.

Safer how? Farshad mentally scoffed. The dwelling was situated in a neighborhood within walking distance of the brownstone where he lived with his second cousins. The lot was deep, with plenty of trees and shrubs for a killer to hide behind. The windows were extensive and uncovered.

So near, so easy, Farshad thought. The Commander had to be mocking him. Had his daughter not nearly lost her life twice already? What was to stop him from planting a bomb like the last one at this location, to wait until he knew she was close, and then detonate it? There would be little satisfaction in that.

It smelled like a trap, even more so than the other safe house. Might the FBI, now suspicious of an intelligence leak, have purposefully disseminated false information?

I will soon find out, Farshad determined.

* * *

Eryn awoke to sunlight and birdsong. She looked around, surprised to find herself in Ike's bed, but then she remembered the nightmare and how she'd crept downstairs looking for consolation. He had offered her the sanctuary of his bed, which had kept the dream from recurring.

Not that she would ask to sleep here again. It would leave her pride in tatters to be ordered back upstairs, like some kind of tramp.

She stretched, enjoying for a moment the play of light across the ceiling and the worn softness of his sheets. But then she heard Ike's voice in the yard, and she threw back the covers.

Clear skies greeted her as she pushed outside. Last night's storm left the mountain with a freshly-washed look and smell. At the sound of the screen door falling shut, Ike broke away from training the dog. "Morning," he said, coming closer.

"Hi, no running today?" she asked, crossing her fingers.

"Not today. I've decided to teach you self-defense." He looked away when he said it.

It took Eryn a second to recognize her victory. Goose bumps sprouted on her arms. "What made you change your mind?"

"Decided it couldn't hurt," he said, glancing at her quickly. "Go put some clothes on," he added, on a surlier note. "And find something to eat. You'll need the energy."

Eryn dashed inside, eager to get started. So, Ike had decided he could teach her how to fight while not betraying her father's trust. Practicality fled in the face of her sudden anticipation.

We'll just see about that, she thought.

* * *

The ringtone on Brad Caine's cell phone startled all three agents awake. Jackson was halfway out of the motel bed before realizing the sound was not an alarm summoning the Marines to the site of a car bombing. He wasn't even in Iraq. He sat back down on his side of the bed, letting his adrenaline subside, and listened to Caine's end of the conversation.

"Did they bring him in for questioning?" He sounded excited.

Jackson's scalp prickled. It sounded like a terrorist may have fallen for the trap.

"What do you mean, he's not the guy. How do you know that?" Silence followed as Caine listened intently. "Like hell, it was a mistake. Sir, the kid was Afghani, right? Trust me, he's one of them. They're all kids."

On the other end of the line the Supervisor in Charge must have spelled out why the boy in question had been released.

Caine dropped his face into his hand. He stayed on the phone a few minutes longer, then put it away.

Jackson waited for him to collect himself before asking, "What happened?"

"Some pizza boy showed up at the mock safe house," Caine muttered with disgust. "The boxes made the agents nervous and they jumped him. Only the kid has no apparent ties to the terrorists. The request for pizza came from a disposable cell phone that was used just once to call in the order."

"Nothing links him to the Brotherhood?"

"Nothing. Our asset says he knows the kid and that his parents are third-generation moderates. You can bet an extremist called in the order, though. Bet he was watching the whole goddamn time. Now they know the place is crawling with agents!"

Jackson swallowed his disappointment.

Ringo, who'd been pretending to sleep levered himself on one elbow. "It's worse than that," he declared.

Caine and Jackson turned to look at him.

"Our asset may have just lost his credibility. Why would the terrorists trust another word he says?"

Caine snatched up his cell phone and placed a brief call. "Tell Mustafa to watch his back," he warned.

* * *

If Ike found it as difficult to train a female as he alleged it would be yesterday, he didn't show it.

Disgruntled, Eryn blew away the tendril of hair sticking to her cheek. Every time he repositioned her to correct her form, her pulse accelerated and her nerves jangled. Ike's set expression told her he suffered no such reaction. The man was all business.

"You kick like a girl, Eryn," he commented as the sun edged higher, making her perspire in her pink sweat suit.

"I am a girl," she muttered. Today he didn't seem to notice. Instead, he gave her detailed instructions on how to wallop the thick pad he had secured to the base of the oak tree. "Pack some punch behind it. Envision the taxi driver."

She didn't want to even think about that man. She wanted Ike to look at her the way he had last night, like he was holding himself back by a thread. He might not be Mr. Right, but for some reason, that didn't seem to matter at this time in her life. He could be Mr. Right Here, Right Now if he took the initiative, only he didn't. He was too intent on molding her into a martial artist.

Plucking the sticky tank top from her damp chest, she panted with frustration.

"Eryn." Ike's short tone had her drawing up guiltily.

"What?"

"Are you listening or daydreaming?"

"Um..." She licked the sweat off her upper lip.

"I said to practice the sweep."

"Oh." She thought for a moment, but all the moves he'd taught her had blurred into one indistinct waste of energy. "How do you do that again?"

He sent her an incredulous look shook his head in disgust. "This isn't working," he declared.

"Yes, it is! I'm sorry. I'll pay closer attention."

The look in his eyes as he suddenly started to stalk her had her backing up hastily.

But it was too late. Moving with inhuman speed, he grabbed her, spun her, and locked an arm around her neck. "Let's try it this way," he said in her ear.

Eryn struggled ineffectually. He wasn't thinking of kissing her again, that was certain. The pressure in her head started to build.

"That won't get you anywhere," he said with no emotion. "Think, Eryn. What do you do?"

She wheezed in a breath. "I don't know!" She hoped he'd let her go, but no such luck. Stars floated across her eyes.

"You change the dynamics."

"How?" She would pay attention now.

"Shrug your shoulders and jab your chin into my arm."

She did so and was rewarded with a sweet breath of oxygen. It gave her a burst of clarity, helping her to recall the sweep she'd drawn a blank on earlier. Aha! That would do the trick.

Bending abruptly at the waist, Eryn swung her right leg around Ike's, hooking his ankle with her foot. Then she twisted in the same direction, wrenched the opposite way, and wrested free.

"Yes, Eryn!" Ike's eyes blazed with approval as she staggered away from him.

Only, it wasn't enough to just to breathe again. Adrenaline urged her to retaliate. She leveled him with a roundhouse kick that packed all the power she could put into it.

"Now tell me I kick like a girl!" she demanded. The resulting thud had him stumbling sideways, clasping his ribs. Eryn felt slightly sick. Ike's growing smile sent her deeper into confusion.

She wheeled away and staggered toward the porch, where she threw herself down on the middle step and willed the pressure building in her eyes to subside.

In her peripheral vision she saw Ike venture closer. He had wiped the smile off his face but was still clutching the ribs she'd kicked.

Eryn flushed. "Sorry if I hurt you," she mumbled.

"Don't apologize," he shot back. "I deserved it."

She flicked him a reproachful look. "You are not supposed to *hurt* me."

He stiffened. "Are you hurt?"

"No." But her feelings were.

Ike sighed. "Look, there's no nice way to teach someone how to fight for their life. I can't sugar-coat it for you, Eryn. Your father has enemies who want you dead!"

Her skin seemed to shrink at the blunt reminder.

He lowered himself onto the step beside her. For a long time, they sat in silence, at a stalemate. "I will protect you for as long as you need me," he finally swore on a low, fervent note. "But I can't be with you forever."

Turning her head, Eryn searched his shadowed gaze and wondered at her sudden sense of loss.

"Even if the terrorists are caught, the world is full of predators. I want you to be strong, Eryn. It...it bothers me to think of how helpless you are," he added through his teeth.

She felt her jaw unhinge. Did Ike Calhoun just confess to his feelings? Maybe there was hope for him yet in the communication department.

Suddenly she wasn't mad at him, anymore. Instead, she was terrified of the grim picture he'd just painted. Ike was right. She was pathetically helpless. Without him around to protect her, she was a walking target for her father's enemies. *Dear Lord.*

Hearing Ike's muttered curse, she realized her eyes were welling with tears.

He grimaced and started reaching for her.

"Don't." She put out a hand, denying herself the comfort she craved more than anything. She wasn't here to be comforted. She was here to learn from Ike, to pick up anything and everything she could, to fight for her future. That was why her father had picked him, of all people, to be her protector.

She pushed to her feet. "Teach me something else," she demanded, gesturing for him to rise.

Ike searched her face with uncertainty. "I think you broke my ribs," he stalled.

"You're full of it." It would take more than a kick from a girl to slow him down. "Come on, Ike. It's like you said: people want me dead. Let's not make it easy for them. Are you going to teach me or not?"

The crooked smile that stripped years off his craggy face made her heart flutter.

"Now you sound like your father," he remarked, rolling to his feet.

Hmmm. She would rather Ike saw her as a woman than a former-Marine mentor, but there would be time for that later. Right now she was going to try to learn everything he could teach her.

* * *

Mustafa slipped into the side entrance of his father's two-story colonial with an uneasy knot in the pit of his stomach. The kitchen was deserted. The house, which was always stirring with tenants coming and going, seemed vaguely threatening. Given the events over on Brandywine Street, it wasn't any wonder Mustafa felt perturbed.

Advised by agents about the mix-up with the pizza boy, he had immediately called Vengeance to warn him that the address he'd provided was, in fact, a trap. Allah willing, the extremists would still consider him an ally. Trust was a fragile thing among murderers and thieves.

As he climbed the rear stairwell to his room, he called to his father, surprised when no one answered. Even the two tenants renting rooms appeared to be out. The silence made his footfalls sound louder, made his scalp tighten.

Unlocking his bedroom door, he pushed it cautiously open. It groaned inward into a darkened room.

Hadn't he parted the drapes that morning?

He flicked the light switch, but the lamp across the room did not come on. With a steadying breath, Mustafa plunged into the darkness. The door slammed abruptly shut behind him. He whirled to see the shadow of a stranger locking the door.

A flashlight flared, catching his startled face in its glare. "Who are you?" he demanded, flinching from the bright invasion, his heart racing.

"You know who I am," said a gentle voice, in strange-sounding English.

He recognized the voice as belonging to the Afghani teacher who'd addressed the Brotherhood several months ago, at Imam Nasser's invitation. "What do you want?"

"Your traitorous head on a stake," came the ominous reply.

Mustafa, whose heart stopped on a down-stroke, rushed to appease him. "You don't understand. I only share what my sister can glean from her husband. I have nothing to hide." Slipping his hand into his pocket, he blindly punched in the password to unlock his Blackberry, then speed-dialed the number the FBI had given him in case of emergencies.

The light wavered as the stranger stepped nearer, causing Mustafa to snatch his hand from his pocket. It would take the agents several minutes to arrive. In the meantime, if he could get to his pistol...

He headed for the bedside table where he kept it.

"You work for the FBI," the man accused, pursuing him.

"No." Mustafa denied it, bumping into a bookcase in the dark and becoming disoriented. Had his room been rearranged? "My sister's husband is a clerk on the counterterrorist squad," he insisted.

His words prompted a disbelieving laugh. "You are an abomination to Islam. I have read your notes with the transcriptions of the online chat."

Mustafa bumped into the couch where his bed was supposed to be. *Allah have mercy.* Where was his pistol?

"Looking for this?" Something metallic glinted in the Teacher's hand.

Mustafa bolted in a sudden panic toward the door, only to crash into a table and spill onto the Kurdish carpet with a yelp of fear.

The stranger straddled him to keep him pinned. He seized Mustafa's thick hair and yanked his head back. The sound of a switchblade ringing free froze Mustafa's blood, as did the feel of its razor edge against his Adam's apple.

"Tell me where to find the Commander's daughter," the Teacher demanded.

Mustafa considered fabricating an answer. Would it save his life? Probably not. "I really don't know," he admitted, his heart sinking. At least he would die defending true Islam.

In the next instant Mustafa felt a sharp intrusion, heard the cartilage in his throat split. He screamed, only to feel a geyser of blood spray his chin, its coppery odor overpowering. Light shimmered briefly in the darkness. And then...nothing.

Farshad wiped his blade clean on the back of the dead man's shoulders and stood up. Over the burble of blood seeping from his victim came the sound of tires squealing on pavement.

Snapping the switch blade shut, he crossed to the window in time to see a dark-colored Buick jerk to a stop in Mustafa's driveway. It expelled two men, who raced toward separate entrances.

Surprised, Farshad glanced back at the dead man. Had he summoned help, somehow? He could hear the new arrivals throwing their shoulders against locked doors downstairs. It wouldn't take them long to gain entry.

Quelling his panic, Farshad wrenched open the window, stuck one leg outside, then the other, and sat for a moment on the sill, looking down. It was a straight drop to the hedge.

Behind and below came the sound of doors crashing open, feet thundering up the stairs.

Praying his middle-aged body would survive the fall, Farshad jumped.

He hit a mature holly bush, feet first, palms down. It slowed his descent, even as dozens of stiff, thorny leaves pierced his clothing and broke his skin. Over his grunt of pain, he heard a shout of alarm above him.

Wrenching free, Farshad staggered across the dimly lit lawn into the shadows. As he glanced back, the drapes at Mustafa's window parted, and a man stuck his head through the opening.

Farshad fled into the night.

Had he been reckless in confronting the informant? Perhaps he should have sent Shahbaz to do the deed. But Shahbaz was neither stealthy nor bright enough to have wheedled his way inside. He could not have silenced an old man and a tenant with lethal efficiency, nor discovered Mustafa's transcriptions of the extremists' rhetoric in the online chat.

Only he, Farshad, could have accomplished such feats, proof that Allah protected him, still.

As for the whereabouts of the Commander's daughter, Allah would have to reveal that secret as well, and soon, for the FBI was casting their nets everywhere trying to identify him.

In the meantime, he would leave Shahbaz a letter, warning him that the FBI special agents were bound to pick him up for questioning. He was to tell them nothing about the way they communicated.

Fortunately, Shahbaz still could not identify Farshad if his life depended on it.

CHAPTER ELEVEN

The fog that blanketed the cabin cast an ethereal light on Eryn's sleeping face, making her look like an angel. No one would look at her and know that she packed a wallop when she kicked. He had bruises all over his body to prove it.

When she finally retired to her room last night, it had taken all of Ike's willpower not to offer her his bed. To his relief, she'd marched up the stairs without asking. He'd heard the springs on her mattress creak briefly, then all went still and silent. For a change, she had slept like the dead.

Given how hard she'd worked that day, he regretted having to rouse her now, just hours into a full night's sleep. But he couldn't risk leaving her sleeping and alone.

"Eryn." He gave her shoulder a gentle shake.

She lurched awake, grabbing him hard with both hands, her eyes wide open.

"It's just me," he said, impressed with her reflexes.

"Ike." She fell limply against her pillow and blinked up at him. "Are you wearing a cap?"

"Yes." It was a ski mask, actually, but he'd rolled it up so that it looked like a cap. "I need you to wake up."

"We're training now?" she moaned, casting a glance at the fog-shrouded window. "What time is it?"

"Zero-one-hundred hours. We're not training." He didn't want to tell her what they were doing yet. "Just get dressed and come downstairs." He stood up, ignoring her shocked silence. "Keep the lights off and dress warm," he added. Marshalling the willpower to avoid looking back, he trotted down the stairs.

Eryn wriggled into a pair of jeans, donned one of the sweaters she'd bought at Dollar General, but she couldn't find a second sock in the dark. Giving up, she pushed her bare feet into her Skechers and crept downstairs. She spied Ike standing by the armchair.

A thick fog at the window illumined his all-black attire: black sweater, black jeans. With the cap covering his silver hair, he looked younger and more dangerous than ever.

Foreboding twisted her insides. "What's going on?"

"Intruders," he said calmly. "I need to see who they are."

I, not we. She locked her knees as fear threaded through her body. "You're going to leave me here?"

"I'm going to put you somewhere safe. Winston will keep you company."

Mystified, she allowed him to lead her to the bathroom, where he shut the door, pulled the blind, and snapped on a pen light.

This is safe? She watched in confusion as he rounded the bathtub, shone the light on the whitewashed paneling behind it, and ran his fingers over the grooves.

With a *snick*, the paneling pulled away, and cold air spilled into the room. A dark, musty-smelling maw now stood where the wall used to be.

"The cellar," he explained, pointing a shaft of blue light down the stairwell. "You'll be safe down here."

Eryn eyed the sharply descending steps in astonishment. She had bathed and showered in this tub and never once suspected there were stairs behind it.

"I don't like dark spaces," she informed him.

"You'll be fine." He pulled her, resisting, toward the opening. "I won't be gone long. There's a cot and a blanket. You can sleep."

"Who could sleep down there?"

Ignoring her protests, he herded her down the steps with Winston right behind them.

Eryn's foreboding rose as she touched down on an earthen floor. "Please." She clung to his arm. "I can help you, Ike. I'm not helpless anymore."

He pried her hand loose. "Here, I'll leave you a light." Striking a match, he held it to a lantern that was hanging from the ceiling.

The brightening wick drove back the shadows, revealing a cellar packed with military paraphernalia. Eryn looked around in astonishment. Ghillie suits hung like shag carpets on the far wall. Firearms of every shape and size had been mounted on the other three. Half-opened boxes showed stores of artillery, ammunition, and battle dress uniforms underfoot. Winston sniffed at them cautiously.

"If you hear anyone upstairs, douse this flame," Ike instructed, recapturing her attention. "The light bleeds through the floorboards. If Winston makes a sound, tell him 'Quiet.' You can also make him 'Sic,' but that's not going to happen."

"Who would I sic him on?" Ike's precautions, like all these weapons, seemed excessive. The last two times he'd suspected interference, nothing had happened.

"That's what I'm going to find out," he said, telling her nothing.

She felt his hand on her head one minute; the next, he was up the stairs, shutting her in.

The panel closed with a *click*. Floorboards creaked overhead, then all was silent save for the sound of Winston padding about, sniffing boxes.

Eryn shivered. Eying the uncomfortable looking cot, she crossed the room to sit on the coarse blanket and to think.

Ike was grim and tense again. Oh, God, was it possible he suffered from Post Traumatic Stress Disorder? He'd certainly seen enough of combat to have picked it up.

Her gaze touched wonderingly on the fearsome collection in front of her. Poor man, did he need all these weapons just to make him feel safe?

But then she noticed four boxes labeled by size. Those were for his survival and security course. Maybe all of these weapons were for his course.

In that case, Ike wasn't paranoid. That was the good part. The bad part was there probably *were* intruders on his property! Who could it be? The FBI? Terrorists?

Disturbed, Eryn called her dog over. As he sidled up to the cot, she threw her arms around him, petting him distractedly.

Winston rumbled his pleasure. He liked for her to remove his collar now and then and give his neck a good scratching. With nothing else to do, Eryn obliged him, fumbling with the catch on his collar. Puzzled, she leaned closer.

Wait, this wasn't Winston's collar. It was the same color, same material, but the buckle plate was different.

Figuring out how to release it, she took off the collar and studied it in the flickering light. When and where had Winston gotten a new collar?

The answer hit her with a corresponding outbreak of goose bumps: *At the safe house when she'd been too drugged to notice the difference.* But there'd been nothing wrong with the old collar. Why would Winston need a new one?

And then it hit her.

With a gasp, she dropped the collar on the cot and jumped to her feet, backing away from it.

Metal or plastic-coated, Ike had said when he'd searched for the transceiver. My God, then the FBI had been stalking them, using the collar, all along!

Maybe Ike already knew that. Maybe that was the secret he'd been keeping from her.

She gave a half-hysterical laugh. Hey, at least he wasn't crazy.

Concealed by a stunted cypress and the ghostly fog, Ike watched two federal agents through the eye holes in his ski mask, as they wended their way along his southern-most boundary. Unlike last night, they'd crossed his property line at one point—intentionally or by mistake?

He hadn't been content to study the images on his laptop. He'd wanted to know what the hell they were up to, and that entailed getting close enough to listen to their conversation.

But by the time he reached their location, up where his property abutted the Shenandoah National Forest, there were only two men, not three. The wet mist muted the beams of their flashlights as they picked their way along the rocks.

Straining to hear their conversation, Ike searched for the third agent's heat signature through his rifle's scope. He'd feel a whole lot better knowing where that man was. Perhaps he'd returned to their vehicle, which they would have parked on Skyline Drive, the only road within miles of Ike's southern boundary.

"You sure this will work?" the curly-haired agent asked his partner.

"I'm not sure of anything," retorted the other man. "Just keep quiet and keep your eyes peeled."

Peeled for what? Ike wondered, thoroughly unsettled. An answer occurred to him at once. For him, of course. They had activated his alarm tonight in order to draw him out while...oh, fuck, while the third man went to the cabin to look for Eryn.

Aw, hell, he'd heard something in the forest earlier, which he'd convinced himself was a bear or a deer. After all, the agents hadn't done anything last night but reconnoiter. But that was just to lull him into a false sense of security. Tonight they were going for recovery.

Scuttling from his hiding place, Ike accidentally kicked a pebble loose. As it clattered down the slope, the agents pivoted, swinging their lights in his direction.

"Freeze! FBI! Get down on your knees and put your hands behind your head."

Like hell, thought Ike, who was fairly sure they couldn't see him. He continued his descent, moving on all fours to keep his balance.

A bullet whizzed over his ski mask, fired from a 9mm pistol that shattered the quiet. Now that was a lucky shot. Ike's temper flared. He considered returning fire to teach the agents a lesson: No one but an idiot fired at a Navy SEAL sniper. But they were no doubt hoping to goad him, so they'd have something to charge him if they ever managed to catch him.

Bounding down the precipice into the tree line, he had to grab at tree branches to slow his descent. It wouldn't do Eryn any good if he broke his neck; on the other hand, he couldn't get to her fast enough.

The sound of his pounding heart became indistinct from the thudding of his boots as he crashed downhill toward the trail that would carry him back to her. Stanley would be so pissed if he let the FBI take her back.

Was that a gun shot?

Eryn froze at the sound, her heart palpitating. Then the FBI was already here, and Ike was out there trying to chase them off his land. *Oh, my God!*

No sooner had she arrived at that awful realization than the cabin's front door groaned open. Recalling Ike's warning about the lantern, she snuffed the flame, plunging the cellar into total darkness.

Please, let it be Ike, she prayed, straining to hear over the blood rushing past her eardrums.

The intruder closed the door quietly behind him. Footfalls, heavier than Ike's, moved stealthily across the floorboards above her. Winston growled low in his throat, and Eryn crouched beside him, hushing him and clutching him for reassurance.

It could only be the FBI. She glanced back at the collar, hidden in the dark on the cot but still broadcasting her location. *What do I do?*

Think through your fear, Ike's voice whispered in her head. The cellar was hidden. Maybe if she stayed put, whoever was looking for her would give up. Or Ike would come back and chase them off.

Fractured light sliced through the floorboards as the intruder switched on a flashlight.

Eryn considered arming herself. She was surrounded by weapons, none of which she knew how to use.

Upstairs, the bathroom door swung open. Winston growled again, and she squeezed him tighter, her heart pounding.

"Eryn," called a familiar voice. "It's Jackson. I know you're under the house. Are you okay?" He sounded genuinely worried.

Jackson. She'd always trusted Jackson, only she didn't want to go back with him. She felt safer with Ike.

But then Winston, recognizing Jackson's voice, tossed up his head and barked in greeting.

"Eryn?" Jackson's voice sounded closer, like he was standing right at the height of the stairs. "How do I get to you?" He opened and closed Ike's second bedroom door.

"Go away," she called. "I don't want to leave with you. I'm safer here."

"Come on, Eryn. He's got you down in the basement. That's kind of creepy, don't you think?"

"It's not like that. He's protecting me."

"We can protect you, too." He started tapping on the wall, searching for the stairs.

"Right, like you did at the safe house?"

"You're right. That was a trap that backfired. I had no idea my boss had leaked the location of the safe house. I swear I'll protect you better next time. You trust me, right?"

"Go away! I like it here."

He sighed. "It's not that simple, Eryn. Either you can tell me where you are, or I'll just break this wall down. Ah." With a *snick*, the darkness suddenly lifted. Bright light shone down the stairwell. Jackson had found the way in.

Eryn pushed to her feet as he descended the steps. "Stay," she ordered, gripping Winston's scruff as he attempted to rush at the agent. Jackson pinned them in the beam of his flashlight, and she blinked at him defiantly.

"Are you okay?" He looked her over thoroughly.

"I already told you. I'm fine."

The light slid away from her to pan the four walls. "Holy Christ," he whispered, as surprised as she had been by the quantity of weapons assembled in one place.

Now. "Sic, Winston!" Eryn released her dog.

With a mock-ferocious growl, the Shepherd mix lunged at Jackson, toppling him. Eryn dashed past them up the wooden stairs. She sped out of the bathroom, through the living room and out the front door. Vaulting off the porch, she headed straight for Ike's lookout up the huge oak tree.

* * *

A rash of barking confirmed Ike's worst fears. He berated himself for not anticipating the FBI's strategy. As a former Spec Ops commando, he was trained to think outside the box. In that regard, he had failed the Commander tonight.

Sprinting down the last treacherous path, he approached the cabin at a speed he knew was reckless. But how would he ever redeem himself in Stanley's eyes if he let Eryn be taken?

At the verge of bursting into the clearing, he threw himself against a tree, caught his breath, and queried his senses.

The wavering light of a flashlight silvered the tiny leaves in the woods around him. A man's voice, cajoling but tinged with desperation, was calling Eryn's name.

She's mine, thought Ike, raising his sniper rifle. Peering through the crosshairs, he caught site of his target in the yard. It was the third agent, sure enough, the light-skinned black man, young and physically fit. As he searched the fog-shrouded shrubs, Winston loped happily alongside him, his tail wagging a mile a minute.

If the dog was out of the cellar, then where the hell was Eryn?

Setting his rifle to fire a single round, Ike aimed it well above the agent's head and pulled the trigger.

Crack! The agent sank into a crouch, dropping his light, which sputtered and died. But in the next instant, he fired back, his bullet hitting the ground within a yard of Ike's position.

Luck had nothing to do with this man's accuracy. Ike broke cover, darting to a new location.

"Don't shoot, Calhoun," the man called suddenly, with a healthy dose of respect in his voice. "That's not going to help your cause any."

"Get off my property," Ike growled back.

"I'm going," the other man assured him. "But this isn't over, not by a long shot. I came here to warn you, Calhoun. My boss wants Miss McClellan back in FBI custody, and he'll stop at nothing to get her. If you don't surrender her willingly, you're going to find yourself in a heap of trouble."

"Go before I change my mind and shoot your ass," said Ike, unimpressed.

The agent bolted from cover. Ike listened to him sprint into the woods, confident of his direction, even in the dark. He had to have had prior military service. It was possible the man would even double back, but Ike didn't think so. The agent had inferred that the FBI would seek some legal means of detaining him.

Out of nowhere, Winston barreled into him, planting his front paws on his chest. Ike went to pull him down and found his collar missing.

"Eryn?" he called, his worry rushing back. He sought her heat signature. Nothing. Aside from a raccoon, cowering under a bush, the yard was deserted. Christ, if she'd run off into the fog, she could have stepped over an unseen cliff and plunged to her death.

"Where is she, boy?" he asked the dog. "Find Eryn."

Loping to the oak tree, the Shepherd mix lifted his leg, and Ike groaned.

"I'm up here." The sound of her voice, coming from way up in the branches, snatched his head up.

Well, I'll be damned.

She'd found a good hiding spot, albeit a cold one. He climbed the slat rungs swiftly, concerned about her state of mind. When his head crested the crow's nest, he found her huddled on the floor, her face as pale as the moon.

"You're in trouble, Ike," she stated, wringing her hands. "You're in trouble because of me."

"It doesn't matter," he insisted, moving closer. Thank God she was safe.

"They followed us here." Words tumbled out of her mouth barely making sense. "It was Winston's collar. I didn't realize it, but they'd swapped out his old one for a new one. The tracking devise is in the buckle plate, I think."

Stunned, he just looked at her. "But...couldn't you tell it was a different collar?"

She shook her head. "I never noticed. I guess with those pills I was taking..."

"It's not your fault." Her self-reproach had him rushing to reassure her. "I missed it, too. If the collar has a tracking device, I should have noticed."

She gave him a sudden, unexpected shove. "Why didn't you tell me that the FBI followed us?" she demanded, suddenly irate. "You knew all along, didn't you? You saw them when we went shopping. And then Dwayne confirmed it, didn't he?"

"Yeah," he admitted, bracing himself for the return of her panic.

"Why didn't you tell me?" She smacked him in the shoulder with a balled fist.

Because protecting her was his *job*. Catching her hand, he found it ice-cold.

"Oh, Ike." Her fierce demeanor softened as he warmed her fingers between his palms, saying nothing. "Why do you keep so quiet?" she whispered with a searching look.

Her hands were so delicate, so smooth.

"Don't you know it's unhealthy to bottle everything inside you?" she added, stroking the side of his face.

He felt his insides melt. "I'm all right," he assured her, his voice turning raspy.

"Are you?" She didn't seem convinced.

"So what happened?" he asked, unused to the spotlight. "How'd you get away from the agent?"

"Jackson," she said, giving him a name. She sat up taller, her proud little smile lighting up the darkness. "I thought through my fear," she told him on a proud note. "I sic'ed Winston on him, just like you said I could, and I got away."

Visualizing it, he just had to grin. "You did great," he acknowledged. "Just, uh...do me a favor and don't tell your dad about tonight. I should never have left you by yourself."

"Yeah, I was starting to think you had PTSD."

"What?" He didn't follow her.

"I thought you were imagining intruders," she added with a rueful smile. "That's what happens when you don't talk to me. My imagination takes flight."

"You thought I was crazy?" What the hell kind of opinion did she have of him, anyway?

"PTSD isn't crazy. It's a completely natural reaction to unprecedented levels of stress." She gave a sudden shudder. Her lower lip trembled. "In fact, I think I have a touch of it myself," she added, tears glimmering in the dark.

Ike's indignation evaporated. Her efforts to be brave and resourceful made her irresistible. He pulled her roughly into his lap and wrapped his arms around her to quell her tremors. With a sigh of relief, Eryn leaned into him and snuggled closer.

The lingering adrenaline inside him heightened his awareness of her to painful levels, turning him instantly hard. Maybe this wasn't such a good idea.

Eryn's head shifted on his shoulder as she tilted her face toward his. In the next instant, her lips landed warmly on his chin.

What the hell. Ike couldn't ignore the unspoken invitation. With a groan, he crushed his lips to hers. The lure of her darting tongue immediately beguiled him. By the time he thought he should scrounge up some self-restraint, he came up empty-handed. The well was all dried up.

And he honestly didn't give a shit.

If Stanley hadn't wanted Ike to touch his precious daughter, then he should've found a more reputable man to protect her. Eryn was too beautiful, too sweet, too delectable to resist. And, despite the training that made Ike one of the best warriors in the world, he was still flesh and blood, with basic, male needs. And one need in particular had a powerful grip on him.

Eryn's heart trotted at the message in Ike's kiss. It was a kiss of desperation, of surrender. She felt as if she'd pried open a door, and his true essence was pouring out like rays of sunshine bearing his heat and energy. She'd been waiting for this moment, for him to emerge from his private prison since the day they'd met.

Somewhere between the glide and retreat of his clever tongue, she managed a suggestion: "Let's go inside."

He went still at her whispered words, and she kicked herself for talking at all, when body language had sufficed just fine.

"I have to check my laptop," he divulged. "See what the agents are doing."

His words were an unpleasant reminder of what she had already managed to put out of her mind. "You think they'll be back tonight?" *Oh, please, no.* She wanted to weep at the FBI's awful timing. Here Ike was finally letting down his guard, and the agents wouldn't leave them alone long enough for her to get to know him better.

"Probably tomorrow," he replied, giving her hope. His lips hovered over hers, caressing them lightly, regretfully. "But we should leave."

"What? Tonight?" Her hopes plummeted.

"That way we'll be gone when they return."

"No." She curled her fingers into the dense muscles of his back. "I don't want to leave, not tonight. Make love to me first, Ike," she added, startled by her directness, but not at all ashamed. "Please." So what if he wasn't Mr. Right? Her life had taken a drastic detour in the past month. What guarantee did she have that she would even live long enough to find *the one*?

Ike was the only man in her life who mattered, a man fully capable of satisfying her needs. She could trust him. She wanted him. Why deny herself the experience when there might never be another?

At her words, he drew a deep breath. His eyes glittered with unmistakable desire.

"You said they'll be back in the morning. We still have time," she assured him.

"We might," he agreed. "I'll know more once I check my laptop."

His words implied that his laptop was linked to the same high tech security system that was also linked to his watch. She felt safer knowing that, though it was Ike himself who made her feel secure. "Let's go check it, then," she urged, squirming out of his arms.

"Not that way." He caught her back, rolling smoothly to his feet. "Best way to get down is to use the rope." She watched in wonder as he reached into the branches, caught the top of the dangling rope, and held out his hand to her. "Come on, princess. We'll go down together."

The endearment made her heart flutter; still, she clung to the far side of the crow's nest, uncommitted. "That's what you said the last time," she reminded him.

"Boy Scout's honor this time." His teeth flashed in the dark.

"You were a Boy Scout?" Skeptical, she nonetheless took his proffered hand and let him pull her to the opening on the other side of the crow's nest.

"Eagle Scout," he said without conceit. "Now, reach for this and hug it tight. Once you're on I'll swing around you."

Glancing into the void below, she balked. But the only way to get back into the cabin was to reach the ground again, and reaching the ground was high on her list of priorities tonight.

With a squeal of fear, she clasped the rope with both hands and stepped off the crow's nest. Clamping her thighs around the rope, she managed not to plummeting thirty feet.

In the next instant, Ike was behind her, his hands above hers, his feet below. "Loosen your grip," he said.

Together they glided slowly and gracefully down the smooth length of the rope. By the time her feet touched the ground, Eryn felt that, with Ike, she could do anything. Anything at all.

On spongy knees she tottered toward the porch, her hand firmly held in his, her heart leaping with the anticipation of getting to know him, intimately.

When Eryn slipped into the bathroom with a breathless excuse, Ike went straight to his laptop, accessing the images there and studying them intently.

There were four new images waiting for him. The first showed the agents regrouping near the spot where he'd left them. The one in charge appeared to be irate, chewing out the one who'd gone in for the recovery— Jackson, Eryn had called him, with respect in her voice.

The next three images showed all the agents retreating up to Skyline Drive. Ike expelled a sigh of relief and guessed that they'd go back to wherever they were staying. Come morning, they'd procure a warrant for his arrest, citing some lame charge. By midmorning, they'd be back.

Only he and Eryn wouldn't be here. At least they didn't need to leave right away. His blood warmed at the prospect of fulfilling Eryn's request. *Make love to me first, Ike.*

Unless she'd changed her mind....

Glancing at the bathroom door, he steeled himself to accept that distinct possibility. He could never accurately guess her next move. Would she emerge fully dressed and announce that she had spoken impulsively? Hell, he wouldn't blame her if she did. All he really had to offer her were a few hours of reprieve from the nightmare that had become her life. She could get that from any man. He happened to be the one on hand.

But then the door swung open revealing Eryn's hourglass figure, cast into silhouette by the light behind her, and there was no mistaking her nudity, with the exception of the barely-there, black panties on her hips. Ike's heart suspended its beat.

Thank you, Jesus. She hadn't changed her mind. If anything, her state of undress sent a very clear message: She wanted all of him.

Ike set aside his laptop, keeping it open just in case. Thoughts of packing up and shipping out flew from his mind. He was in no hurry to go anywhere. Not with Eryn standing in front of him like a virgin sacrifice, offering him more than any mortal man deserved.

He rolled slowly to his feet, his body strangely weighted. "You don't have to do this, Eryn," he felt it only fair to warn her. What if he hurt her? What if her father found out? How would he ever look Stanley in the eye again?

Her answer was to float toward him and slip her arms around him. The feel of her naked breasts through the material of his sweater made him groan.

"I know I don't have to." Her eyes were translucent in the shadows as she tipped her face toward his. "But I want to, Ike, more than I've ever wanted anything."

Christ, she knew exactly what to say, not only to reassure him but to arouse him. She wanted to make love to him. It was nothing short of wondrous. Gathering her soft curves in his rough hands, he felt like he'd been given a rare and amazing gift. Afraid that she might evaporate into thin air or disintegrate like a dream, he lowered his head and kissed her cautiously.

Deep inside, he could feel himself trembling. He knew what he was, what he had to offer—which was nothing. But he could no more push her away than he could stop his own heart from beating. Besides, there was one thing that he could give her—more pleasure than she had ever known or would ever know again.

Sweeping back the long locks of hair that covered her torso, he beheld her naked breasts for the first time. They were everything he'd imagined— full and high and tipped with berry-like nipples that made his mouth water. Drawn to them at once, he ducked his head and ravished the velvety nubbins with as much restraint as he could manage.

For a night that had promised to end badly, this one was turning out to be the best goddamn night of his life.

CHAPTER TWELVE

"Jesus Christ." The shock in Caine's voice brought Jackson fully awake. He'd been nodding off in the back of the Taurus on the return ride from Skyline Drive to Elkton Motel.

"What wrong?" Ringo asked, tearing his gaze from the steep, winding highway illumined by their headlights.

Caine lowered his cell phone to share the news. "Our asset was murdered," he told them, grimly. "His throat was slit, just like Pedro's."

Holy shit, thought Jackson, swiping a hand over his stinging eyes.

"The perp was still on the scene when our agents answered Mustafa's summons, but he jumped out the window and escaped. Lucky for us, he left his blood all over the holly bushes. They're running his DNA right now."

"Was it Shahbaz Wahidi?" Ringo asked.

"No. They brought Wahidi in for questioning, hoping he'd spill something, but he has an air-tight alibi. We've intercepted all his emails, monitored his phone calls, and nothing. He doesn't seem to be in contact with anyone."

The news drove the fog from Jackson's head, leaving his thoughts sharper. He was becoming more and more convinced that Shahbaz—and Itzak before him—were red herrings, employed by the real terrorist to divert suspicion from himself onto the Brotherhood.

As he mulled over ways to prove it, he overheard Caine update their supervisor on the failed attempt to wrest Eryn from Calhoun's cabin. He made a point of mentioning how the ex-SEAL's cellar was packed with ammunition and that he'd fired his rifle at Jackson, driving him away.

"That's right, sir. Yes, sir." Caine's tone grew smug. "My thoughts exactly. We'll need at least fifty HRT members to surround his property, plus a helicopter. The sooner they get here, the better."

Jackson couldn't believe what he was hearing. They were planning to utilize the FBI's Hostage Rescue Team. "You can't be serious," he exclaimed the instant Caine pulled his phone from his ear.

"I'm as serious as a heart attack, Rookie."

"Come on, sir. We haven't even established dialogue with the man," Jackson argued.

"You want to reason with him?" Caine's eyes glinted as he twisted in his seat to glare back at him. "He fucking tried to shoot you."

"He aimed well above my head," Jackson insisted, though at the time, the bullet had felt pretty damn close.

"He has a smear on his military record, not to mention enough weaponry in his basement to start a revolution. You saw it for yourself."

The so-called smear on Calhoun's record was nothing more than a case of extremely bad luck. "The man needs the weapons for the business he operates. Look, can't we at least give him a chance to do the right thing?"

"You said it yourself, Maddox. He's not going to just hand her over."

"Maybe if he knows the consequences."

"Fine," Caine gave in unexpectedly. "You want to talk to Calhoun, go right ahead. As soon as it's daylight, take the Taurus and go. I'll give you till noon to bring him in."

Was he serious?

Ringo drove them off the highway into Elkton Motel's parking lot where he double-parked by the RV and killed the motor. The motel's neon sign buzzed in the sudden silence. Jackson queried the wisdom of setting off Calhoun's alarm and barreling up his steep gravel driveway unannounced.

"What's the matter, Maddox?" Caine taunted. "Change your mind?" He pushed his door open, stepping out. Ringo did likewise.

"I'll go," Jackson decided.

Ringo poked his head back in the car. "I'll go with you," he volunteered.

"No, you won't," said Caine, slamming his door shut. "I'll need your help coordinating with HRT and the National Guard."

Ringo sent Jackson an apologetic grimace before following Caine to their room.

Jackson stayed in the car for a moment. He hoped to hell Calhoun's integrity was as rock-solid as he intuited to be. In about six hours, he'd find out.

* * *

Cradling Ike's head in her hands, Eryn transferred his lips to her other aching breast and gasped her pleasure. The way he lapped and suckled on the sensitive peaks sent darts of pleasure zinging to her womb. If he kept this up much longer, her legs were going to buckle.

She tried concentrating on his callused hands which were now touching her the way she'd fantasized, raising a trail of goose bumps as he swept them from her shoulders to her hips, molding, caressing, shaping. He slid them over the fullness of her backside, squeezed and lifted. Eryn moaned. In the next instant, he swept her off her feet and spilled her gently onto the bedspread.

He pulled away to take his clothes off. Eryn's heart rate doubled as she watched him undress. He scrabbled at his laces, shucking his boots in record time. He hauled his sweater and T-shirt off simultaneously, revealing mounds of sculpted muscle and a thatch of auburn hair that glinted in the muted light. Every square inch of his torso was honed to perfection.

"Oh, Ike, you're beautiful," she exclaimed, coming to her elbows to see him better. He sent her an incredulous look.

Her gaze locked eagerly on the hands now unfastening his pants. She touched her tongue to her upper lip.

With a jerk and a tug, he dropped his jeans and stripped off his boxers. Eryn managed to glimpse just an eyeful before he pushed her back against the mattress. Seizing the elastic of her panties, he yanked them off in one impatient movement that startled a laugh out of her.

"*You're* beautiful," he corrected, taking a moment to gaze down at her.

His hungry gaze made her face heat self-consciously. Stroking her hands up the muscled length of his arms, she pulled his head down for a kiss. *Talk to me without words. Tell me all about you...*

He sank gently over her, melting her with the purposeful forays of his lips, teeth and tongue. Loving the weight of his body on hers, Eryn gave her hands free rein. From his broad shoulders, to the dense contours of his pectorals, to the resilient steel of his buttocks, she reveled in his undiluted masculinity.

When he moved his lips to her neck, her collarbones, her breasts, her entire body went taut with anticipation. He lathed her nipples into stiffness, and she arched helplessly toward the pleasurable torment, all too conscious of his arousal brushing her thigh, warm and velvety and distinctly present. Heavens, would she be able to accommodate all of that?

But then he was moving lower, giving her something altogether different to dwell on. His lips followed the curve of her ribs to traverse the plane of her belly. As his tongue swirled in and around her naval, her blood came to a flash boil. His lips brushed the curls at the apex of her thighs and her hips came off the bed. *Oh, yes. Oh, please.*

"Copper," he breathed, his breath warm against her skin.

She whispered aloud the plea in her head.

There was no mistaking the flash of white in the darkness for anything but a smile. "What'd you say?"

Unable to repeat herself, she spread her thighs wordlessly.

He chuckled. "That's what I thought I heard." And then he ducked his head, obliging her.

Dear God. In her mind's eye, Eryn saw herself as if from a distance, on the pinnacle of a mountain that had been shaped in ancient days by great land masses colliding, causing an up-thrust of granite thousands of feet high. When Ike touched her there, it felt like the mountains were being shaped all over again, his world and hers colliding.

Heat flowed along her ravines and passageways as Ike took his time moving toward the epicenter of her pleasure. He circled it, compressed and agitated it, instigating tremors of delight that rippled through her, each one more powerful than the last. She turned molten, unstable, volatile. The result of their worlds colliding was going to be tumultuous.

"Yes," she cried, as he slipped a finger into her chasm. He added a second digit, stroked and stretched. The incursion was all that was needed to push her over the edge. She felt herself folding and faulting, becoming a changed woman. The sensations were so raw, so organic that she screamed his name out loud. Aftershocks shook her endlessly before giving way to a stunned calm.

When she opened her eyes again, she found him studying her in wonder.

"Sorry," she apologized, grateful that he couldn't see the images in her head.

"What the hell for?" He lunged across her body reaching for the bed-side table. As his erection came within inches of her hand, she caught it deliberately, enraptured by its velvety texture, awed by its size. *Speaking of upheaval.* She wanted to put her mouth on it, to rock his world the way he'd just rocked hers.

He pulled deliberately away. "It's been a while," he apologized. Watching him tear open a condom wrapper with his teeth, it hit her that she hadn't given a thought to birth control. *Oh, smart, Eryn.* Thank God Ike had more common sense than she!

Covering himself with the same efficiency that he did all things, he settled back over her. The intent expression on his face made her toes curl.

"You good?" he asked thickly.

"I hope so."

He tensed. "What does that mean?"

"It means I hope we fit," she said breathlessly.

He huffed out a laugh of relief. She could feel his heart trotting against her crushed breasts. "We'll fit," he promised, and then he kissed her thoroughly, reawakening her senses.

It occurred to Eryn that the true collision of their worlds was yet to come. She braced herself. Yet the smooth head of his engorgement met no resistance as he probed her entrance. Moist heat flooded her, easing his way.

He took possession of her so slowly, so thoroughly that each gentle incursion stripped the air from her lungs, even as it filled her with a delicious desperation for more.

"Still okay?" he gritted. She realized every muscle in his body was rigid from holding himself back. A light layer of sweat sheened his bare skin. His heart was pounding.

"Oh, yes," she gasped, awed by her affect on him, her response *to* him. Together they made a new creation.

One more thrust and their hips came solidly together. Eryn gave a cry of rapture. Every inch of him was buried deep inside her, and—guess what?—they fit, just right.

With his forehead pressed to hers, he gasped for breath.

Her hips undulated with the need to satisfy a deep itch. "Please don't stop," she begged.

"You're going to make me come," he warned.

The thought of him teetering on that brink made her inner muscles clench, drawing up a rush of pleasure so intense that it mushroomed into another climax. He caught her cry of surrender in a searing kiss.

The arc of her ecstasy was just beginning to fall when Ike tore his mouth from hers, buried his face in the crook of her neck, and shuddered in stoic silence. As her rapture faded into warm contentment, Eryn smiled.

Even in the throes of sexual release, her protector was the strong, silent type.

Holy fuck, Ike thought, clawing his way back to consciousness.

Eryn lay beneath him, her dreamy smile lit by the suggestion of dawn that framed the closed blind. Outside, a couple of song birds twittered optimistically. Down in Jollet's Hollow, the rooster crowed. All was peaceful and calm. He could only hope the agents who had tried to outsmart him last night were fast asleep.

Shutting them out of his thoughts, he focused on the woman embracing him so tenderly, now putting her lips to his chin, in what was fast becoming a habit. A chuckle rasped in his throat at he recalled her lack of inhibition.

"You should laugh more often," she remarked, tipping her head back to look at him. Her eyes looked iridescent in the shadows. "I like the sound of it."

As long as she continued to surprise him, he'd continue to laugh. Who knew Stanley's daughter would as amazing in bed as everywhere else? Christ, if there was one more endearing thing about her, he was going to fall head over heels in love with her.

Panic followed swiftly on the heels of that thought. Using the condom as an excuse, he started scooting off the bed, but Eryn caught him back, snuggling against him. His traitorous body, all too glad to feel her nakedness against him, gathered her closer. As she laid her head on his chest, he stared down at her in wonderment, at an utter loss for words.

She began to comb her fingers through his golden chest hairs. "Tell me why your hair turned silver, Ike," she requested sleepily. "What happened? What made you leave the military?"

He had no intention of telling her anything. It wasn't something he ever talked about, ever even let himself think about. But the same spirit of intimacy that kept him in the bed brought the memory, haltingly, out of his mouth. He heard himself tell her how his reconnaissance squad had stumbled onto a pair of boys herding their goats in the Hindu Kush.

"There wasn't anything in the handbook to tell us how to deal with them," he recounted, recalling his queasy dread. "We knew they'd run and tell the elders they'd seen soldiers on the pass. But we couldn't just kill them in cold blood. Christ, they were only kids."

"Oh, Ike." She tightened her grip on him.

He found himself reliving the moment, right down to the feel of grit between his teeth and the lightheadedness that resulted from an arduous climb at ridiculous altitudes. "I was the OIC. I let the guys cast a vote, but the final decision was mine." A familiar pain, one he thought he'd pushed away for good, wracked him. "Even as I let the kids walk, I knew I was sealing our death sentences."

Eryn's fervent embrace took the edge off his agony. "What happened?"

"We tried to retreat, but we were too far up the mountain to get back down. There was nowhere to hide that they wouldn't find us. About fifty Taliban came after us, shelling out more firepower than we could match. One by one, I watched my men get shot, killed."

"Oh, sweetheart." She kissed his throat, her tenderness melting him. The endearment had him spilling out the rest.

"Spellman and I found a hollow log. We hid in it as they rained RPGs down on us. Finally, the air support we'd called in came down and drove the Taliban away. But, by then, it was too late. Four of my men were dead. My decision got 'em all killed."

Eryn went rigid. She shot to her elbow. "What? How can you say that?" she demanded.

He couldn't believe he was discussing this with her, though it had been easier to talk about than he'd thought it would be. "I was the OIC," he said dully.

"So? Ike, you told me you let your men cast a vote. What was their decision?"

He rubbed his eyes. "One of them said we should just shoot them quietly. The other four wanted to let them go."

"So it wasn't your decision that got them killed," she said in vehement defense of him.

"All right, Eryn," he agreed, with intent to dismiss the conversation. He soothed her back against the pillows. "I'll be right back," he added, rolling out of bed to address the condom situation.

As he eased into the bathroom, he shivered at the cool air wafting out of the still-open cellar door. He cleaned himself up quickly then went back into the bedroom, fully anticipating another round of mind-blowing sex.

He found Eryn huddled under the covers, freshly asleep. Her hair, gilded by the light that framed the blind, lay like a shimmering scarf over her shoulder.

My woman, he thought, rocked by a sudden possessiveness. At least, she was his for now. He wanted to wake her up, to make love to her again like they had all the time in the world. But they didn't. They needed to leave Overlook Mountain before the Feds came back.

It was better this way. He knew the more he got used to her, the more he would want to keep her. Christ, he couldn't believe he'd told her about the incident. He hadn't even *thought* about it for months, but the current circumstances had made it come rushing to the foreground, as if it had happened only yesterday.

At least she'd defended him. That came as a huge relief. If only her father felt the same way.

Resisting the urge to join her, he turned and hunted for the clothes he'd discarded earlier. As much as he wanted to bridge reality with his dreamy relationship projections, he had a job to do.

Dressing with haste, he jogged down into the cellar with Winston on his heels. As he lit the gas lamp, he spotted the dog's collar on the cot and went to pick it up.

He could see, now, how the buckle plate might serve a dual function. Scrounging up a screwdriver, he pried it apart where the two molded halves came together. Sure enough, as they separated, a SIM card, a tiny antenna and a battery, all wired together, fell into his hand. *Sonofabitch.* He laid them carefully aside. Then he squeezed the two halves back together and buckled the collar onto the dog.

It was time to plan for their exodus. But as he considered what they would need to take with them, memories of the past hour kept interfering with his thoughts.

There weren't any more rules of engagement for eluding the FBI than there'd been for dealing with innocent shepherd boys. All he had were Stanley's directives to keep Eryn away from them and, of course, from the terrorists.

Stanley hadn't made a clear distinction between the two, but there sure as hell was a big one. Ike had no problem offing terrorists. Firing at a federal agent, on the other hand, could get him convicted—hell, he was probably in trouble already for shooting at Jackson.

He couldn't blaze his way out of the situation. He would have to be clever and resourceful. And he couldn't let Eryn—or any burgeoning feelings he might have for her—distract him from his primary mission.

Stripping off his black sweater, he donned a military issue T-shirt, fresh out of the package. He found a box labeled XL and pulled out a starched set of BDU's, trading his black attire for woodland patterned camouflage.

Donning battle dress made him feel like he still had options; he was still in control.

In a previously unopened box, he found a small set for Eryn to wear. He headed upstairs to wake her up.

But when he got there, he couldn't immediately do it.

He stood over her, riding the ebb and flow of each breath; reminding himself that this thing between them—the perfect chemistry, his deep-down fulfillment—meant nothing. He'd never be more to Eryn than a source of comfort and distraction. She was Stanley's daughter. She deserved the sun and moon, so much more than he could give her right now.

With common sense urging haste, he stroked his finger over her cheek. "Eryn, wake up."

The corners of her mouth pulled down in a pout.

The look made his heart contract. *Sorry, princess.* Time was running out.

Eryn pried her heavy eyelids open. As she met Ike's gaze, memories of their lovemaking caused a wave of pleasure to roll through her and made every extremity tingle.

"Time to get up," he said, banishing her contentment. "We have to leave," he added.

She lifted her head off the pillow, noticing his change in attire, the alert manner in which he held himself. "Already?" she asked, dismayed.

"Already," he confirmed.

"But..." Her heart sank. She'd hoped they wouldn't have to leave, after all, that Ike would have thought of an alternative course of action. "Where will we go?"

"Somewhere safe." He turned from the bed, lifted a folded set of BDUs off his dresser, and tossed them down next to her. "Put these on. We have ten minutes."

She was about to ask a zillion questions when he picked up his laptop and disappeared into the bathroom. She could hear him moving swiftly down the wooden steps into the cellar.

Numb with exhaustion, Eryn scooted to the edge of the bed to search the floor for her underwear. Recalling how he'd hauled them off her made her blush. She had no regrets about what had followed—none at all. Ike had finally shared the awful tragedy that had changed his life. He'd opened up to her, at last!

Damn the FBI for not just leaving them alone. She'd have been perfectly happy to stay here with Ike for as long as it took them to catch the terrorists.

Shivering in the cool air, she dressed quickly in the BDU's he'd given her. The stiff, starchy canvas abraded her sensitized skin. There was only one reason he could have told her to put them on, she realized with an unpleasant start. They were going to have to blend with the forest, to hide from the FBI.

Realizing she still had no socks to wear, she dashed upstairs to fetch a pair. She ran into Winston on her way back down. "You put Winston's collar back on?" she called out, perplexed.

"Took out the tracking device." Ike's voice came from the cellar steps. "You were right."

"So where is it now?" she asked.

Stepping in her line of sight, he patted a pocket on his thigh.

"Don't you want to burn it or something?"

"I have a better plan." His gaze slid to the dog who sat expectantly at the bedroom door, and all expression vanished from his face.

Eryn's gut tightened. She had learned to recognize that look. "What's wrong?" she demanded.

He met her gaze reluctantly. "We need to leave the dog here," he announced.

"No." She glanced at Winston with heightened alarm. "Why?"

"We can't take him with us, Eryn. The agents will find him when they search the cabin. They'll take good care of him."

"How do you know that? What if they don't come? We can't just leave him!" Tears scalded her eyes. "Please, Ike."

"Don't ask me," he retorted, looking away. "It's not what I want. We have to cross the zip line. We have to rappel down a cliff. He can't do all that."

"Why can't we go a different way? You won't even tell me where we're going!" She stamped her foot on the floor, using it as an excuse to get her heel in her shoe.

"I told you, somewhere safe."

"Details, Isaac!" she demanded.

A hint of humor lit his shadowed gaze. "Okay. I have a friend who owns a vineyard twelve miles west of here. We're walking there. Hopefully, he'll give us a car so we can drive to Pennsylvania."

"Pennsylvania?" Her heart sank. "What's in Pennsylvania?"

"Cougar. He was supposed to take you in the first place."

"So you're just going to pass me off to Cougar?" *After what we shared?*

He swung a packed rucksack on his back. "Come on, it's not like that," he muttered, avoiding her gaze.

"Then what's it like?" She needed to hear something, *anything* to indicate that last night had meant as much to him as it had to her.

"I have to get you away from here, that's all," he insisted. Setting his jaw, he went into the living room and reached under the sofa.

Eryn sank weakly onto the edge of the bed, where she met Winston's questioning gaze. A lump clogged her throat at the thought of leaving him. Attuned to her emotional state, he padded over.

"Come on, boy," Ike called from the door. "Let's walk."

Winston looked back and forth between them, obviously torn, but the call of nature claimed victory, and he followed Ike outside.

"Coward!" Eryn shouted, as Ike shut the door soundlessly behind him. Walking the dog was an excuse to avoid communicating.

Blotting her tears with a starched sleeve, she looked around. She wondered if she would ever see the cabin again. She'd just started to like it here, especially when Ike went out of his way to heat her bathwater. The peaceful view had lulled her into a sense of security. She'd even forgotten from time to time that someone wanted her dead.

With a sharp sniff, she pushed to her feet. Winston would hate being left behind, but she knew the agents, especially Jackson, would look after him. And Ike would have an easier time getting her out of the area undetected.

For her father's sake, she owed it to Ike to cooperate. And when the time came to part ways, she wouldn't cling like a vine, either. She'd known from the start they had no future together.

Ignoring the ache in her chest, she plodded to the bathroom to use the facilities. A glance in the mirror showed a pale-faced woman with uncertainty in her eyes, not at all how she'd looked hours earlier, anticipating making love with Ike.

CHAPTER THIRTEEN

"Time to run, princess." Ike swept the clearing with that all-seeing look that made Eryn's stomach knot. Every tree, every leaf, every blade of grass was scrutinized and dismissed in under a millisecond. Finally, his eyes came to rest on Eryn as she hiked her purse onto her shoulder.

She nodded. At least she wasn't toting a rucksack that looked like it weighed sixty pounds.

"Here, why don't you give me that?" He slid his pack off his shoulders. "You're going to need your arms free."

With a sigh and feeling guilty for adding to Ike's burden, she watched him drop her purse on top of the assorted gear he'd collected for their exodus. "Sorry," she mumbled.

"Don't be," he said, swinging the pack back onto his shoulders. "I've carried more."

Winston's frantic barks, merging with the scratching of his claws at the door, drew her attention back at the cabin behind them.

Ike deliberately caught her eye. "He'll be alright. Promise," he added, lifting a hand to stroke her cheek. "Come on, babe," he urged. "You set the pace."

As with their previous runs, she tackled the steep incline with all she had. But her legs felt like rubber as she stumbled over the moist, uneven earth. A near-sleepless night gave her very little energy to call upon. She tried telling herself this was just another training run; that they'd be back to the cabin for a leisurely breakfast. Only, she knew it wasn't, and they wouldn't. They were running headlong into reality.

She arrived at the tree line out of breath, more than glad to stop when Ike called, "Wait," and veered suddenly off the path. He mounted a man-sized boulder.

Watching him, she listened to the wind rustle the tender leaves on the trees. Ike pulled binoculars from his pack and peered out over the valley. He went suddenly still, his back stiffening.

"What do you see?" she asked.

He put the binoculars away and leapt lightly down beside her. "We might have company coming," he admitted, avoiding her gaze. As if on cue, his watch began to beep. He silenced it with a push of his thumb.

"The FBI?"

He gave a nod. "You trust me?"

"Yes."

"We need to move fast. No talking, no slowing down. No questioning my orders. Clear enough?"

She swallowed hard. "Crystal."

He sent her a tiny crooked smile that alleviated her fear. Chucking her under the chin, he spun her around and gave her a push. "Now run!" he said.

* * *

The Taurus barely made it up the gravel driveway. Slipping sideways on a hairpin turn, Jackson was relieved to arrive at the cabin, at last. It looked far less sinister in the daylight than it had in the dark. He parked beside Calhoun's Dodge Durango and killed the overheated engine.

Calhoun was likely still here since his truck was here, Jackson reasoned, leaving his gun in the glove compartment. He wore a Kevlar vest under his dress shirt, just in case. But the ex-SEAL wouldn't shoot an unarmed man; Jackson was counting on that.

As he opened the car door, he was hit by a torrent of barking. He approached the cabin cautiously, his hands by his sides where Calhoun could see them. Aside from the dog, the only sound was that of birds twittering, the wind blowing. The area struck him as deserted, unthreatening. He hoped he hadn't come too late.

The planks on the porch groaned as he crossed them. He rapped firmly on the screen door. Winston scratched the inner door and whined.

"Isaac Calhoun! This is Special Agent Maddox. I'd like to talk to you." Jackson's booming voice sounded ridiculous in the peaceful quiet.

Getting no reply, he cracked the screen door and found the inner door unlocked. As he pushed it inward, Winston tried barreling past him, only

Jackson caught him by his collar and muscled him back inside. He shut the door and looked around, noting details that had changed since the night before. A kitchen cabinet stood open. The smell of toast still hung in the air.

Despairing that he'd come too late, he pushed into the bathroom, where he opened the cellar door and peered into the darkness, making sure that Eryn wasn't down there. Of course, she wasn't. Nor was there any evidence suggesting she'd been forced to stay there for any length of time.

He went back upstairs, poked his head into the master bedroom. The unmade bed caught his eye. Twisted sheets and dented pillows suggested they had shared the bed, been intimate. Having pegged Eryn as the prim and proper type, it made him wonder if she'd known Calhoun prior to this week. That sure would have made it easier for the former SEAL to coax her from the safe house, would have given him an edge.

Winston clawed at the exit, recapturing his attention. The dog's desperation to get out made Jackson wonder if he knew where Ike and Eryn had gone. He hunted briefly for a leash. Finding nothing suitable, he gave up, deciding he would take his chances. "You know where they went, boy?" he asked, pulling the door open. "Show me."

Winston bolted out of the screen door with Jackson right behind him. The dog disappeared around the cabin. It was all Jackson could do to keep him in sight as the Shepherd mix hightailed it up the well-worn path that led to Calhoun's southern boundary and Skyline Drive. It was exactly the route the FBI had expected him to take, if and when he fled. An HRT squad lay in wait on Skyline Drive.

Torn between his commitment to duty and his lack of respect for his supervisor, Jackson considered whether to call his supervisor or blow him off. The Marine in him had him pulling out his phone as he ran.

"Well, Rookie?" Caine prompted when he picked up.

"Sir," Jackson gasped for breath. "They'd already left the cabin by foot by the time I got here. I think they're hiking up to Skyline Drive. I'm right behind them."

"I know where they are, Maddox. I've been tracking their movements for the last half hour."

What? Jackson's gaze went to the dog's red collar. Half hour? But he and Winston had only been running for ten minutes, unless...unless the GPS device wasn't even *on* the dog. Calhoun must have discovered it, in which case, he would use it as a decoy. Jackson felt a surge of relief.

"You can fall back, Rookie. Obviously your plan didn't pan out. We'll leave it to HRT to get our client back." Caine severed the call abruptly, sparing Jackson from having to tell him the truth.

He dropped his phone back into his jacket pocket and kept right on running. One, he couldn't leave Winston running off into the forest by himself. Two, he wanted to warn Calhoun about the HRT, convince him to surrender peacefully or face the consequences.

The path ahead of him forked abruptly. A steep climb to the left led to Calhoun's southern boundary and an ambush. The path to the right led to an impassable gorge. With Eryn tagging along, Calhoun probably hadn't gone that way. But Winston's bushy tail said otherwise as it disappeared ahead of him. Jackson picked up his pace.

Here and there, the imprint of a sole corroborated the dog's tracking ability. Plumbing the light brush ahead, Jackson sensed that he was closing in. The sound of rushing water swelled with every step.

He arrived abruptly at the gorge, which was far more impressive in real life than when viewed via satellite.

Winston eyed the sheer drop to the streambed and barked his frustration. A metallic humming sound snatched Jackson's gaze to a sturdy steel wire that spanned the ravine. *So that's how they got across.* Reaching up to touch it, he detected a subtle vibration. It hadn't been long since they'd used it, either. But the bar, if there was one, had been taken down.

He could maybe use his belt to slide across, if he could get enough momentum, but then he'd have to leave the dog behind. "Calhoun!" he shouted, fairly certain the man was within range to overhear him. "You should surrender or face charges. We have your property surrounded."

The warning echoed back at him, mocking his good intentions. He applied himself to calming Winston's agitation. "It's okay, boy. We'll get her back."

His ringing cell phone had him groping in his pocket. "Maddox."

It was Caine. "Get your ass down here, Rookie. Calhoun is moving down the north side of the mountain. We'll intercept him at the bottom."

Jackson consulted the compass on his watch. "The north side, sir? I've got him headed west." North was where all the tumbling water was headed.

"Negative. I've got him on GPS, remember?"

Ah, decoy time. Calhoun must have dropped the SIM card into the rapids while crossing to the other side. In an airtight container, it would flow downhill for hours, sending the FBI on a wild goose chase. Jackson found himself grinning.

"We'll be looking for him from the air," Caine added, shouting over the whopping of a helicopter's rotors.

Oh, Jesus. The air support team was getting underway.

Jackson took one last look at the other side of the ravine. Maybe Calhoun didn't need his help. His odds were looking pretty good right now, and Jackson didn't respect his supervisor enough to correct his assumptions.

Finding a granola bar tucked inside his jacket, he waved it under Winston's nose and turned him around. "I got you, buddy," he said, leading him by the collar.

* * *

Eryn felt like her insides had been knotted together and then stapled, but she gritted her teeth and forced one foot in front of the other. After crossing the gorge, they had veered off the path and waded through a deep forest traveling down the shadowed side of the mountain.

It seemed a sacrilege to disturb the quiet. She tried moving on the soles of her feet like Ike, who scarcely made a sound as he stepped through last year's fallen leaves. Beams of sunlight, slanting through the tree trunks, imbued the cool air with warmth as the sun rose steadily higher. She was soon perspiring in her BDUs.

Despite the warning shouted across the ravine half an hour earlier in a voice belonging to Jackson Maddox, they did not come across any more FBI agents. Eryn's worries subsided, especially when Ike took her hand and kept her anchored next to him. The strength of his grip and the calm, self-assured way he moved through the forest eased her worries that they would be caught. He knew what he was doing.

Then, unexpectedly, he dropped to a crouch, startling her as he hauled her down beside him. With a warning, "Shhh," he put his forefinger to his lips and searched the shadowy forest, listening intently.

Eryn did the same. Over the creaking of branches, she heard a muted conversation and a stifled cough floating up from the area below. Ike hefted his rifle, and she gasped, but he only used it to peer through the scope. Lowering it again, he sent her a thought-filled look that stirred her uneasiness. He shook off his rucksack, opening the flap to take out his sturdy laptop.

Curious, Eryn watched him rouse it from hibernation and access a program. One by one, he opened image files. They all showed pictures of men in uniform, toting rifles, their faces concealed by helmets and camo paint, moving stealthily uphill.

It dawned on Eryn that those were the same men she could hear below them. Startled, she looked up at Ike, who appeared tense but not the least bit harried. "What do we do?" she whispered.

He shut the laptop, slipping it back into his rucksack. "I'm going to distract them. Need to leave you here for just a minute. When you hear an explosion, drop down and cover your head. Stay that way till I get back."

Eryn's mouth fell open. *Explosion?* She watched him withdraw a weapon from his rucksack, something she didn't have a name for, but it looked lethal. "How long will you be?" she whispered as he tucked it under one arm and hefted his rifle.

"Ten minutes, tops." He planted a swift kiss on her forehead. "Keep your head down and wait for me." Leaves rustled at his departure. In an instant, he had disappeared from sight, and all was quiet.

Eryn swallowed hard. Her heart beat so loudly she couldn't hear the soldiers anymore. Who'd have thought the FBI would send soldiers after them! She and Ike were evidently in big trouble now. Would they be shot at if they were spotted?

A sudden *boom!* shattered the quiet and shook the ground. With a squeak of fear, Eryn dove onto her stomach and landed on a rock. *Ooooph.* The percussion faded almost at once. Shouting took its place. She could sense movement below her. With her face buried in dry leaves, she prayed no one would stumble upon her.

Suddenly, Ike was back, hauling her to her feet and swinging his pack over his shoulder. "Run," he said.

She didn't need much encouragement. Breaking into a mad dash, she clung to Ike's hand as he pulled her downhill to the right, away from the melee.

In her peripheral vision, she caught flashes of movement. Men raced uphill to their left, shouting orders and warnings. Ike caught her back suddenly, crowding her against a tree trunk, where he held perfectly still, his stare enjoining her to do the same. And then they were running again, slipping and sliding down the steep grade.

Eryn's lungs ached. Her legs wind-milled beneath her. The shouts behind them grew more distant.

We did it! she marveled. We made it past the soldiers. Suddenly, Ike yanked her to a halt, preventing her just in time from plunging off a cliff.

"Oh, my God!" She scrambled away from the rocky edge, watching in horror as the rocks she'd kicked loose plummeted out of sight. "How do we get down?" she asked, looking for a way around the sheer drop.

"We rappel." In the next instant, he pulled a rope and harness from his pack.

* * *

"Land her on the road," Caine called to the pilot. Being certified to fly himself, he occupied the co-pilot's seat which offered a bird's eye view through the rounded windscreen. He hadn't caught sight of the suspect or their client yet, but according to his tracking program, they were right below him, moving along the streambed. He shouted over his shoulder at the squad leader in the back. "Prepare your men, Sergeant!"

Sergeant Malloy gave a thumbs-up and issued orders to his men who sat on benches soldered to the exterior walls of the chopper on either side of the open doors, their legs dangling in the air. At his order, they lowering their visors and adjusted their Heckler and Koch submachine guns.

"Right here," said Caine, and the MH-6 Little Bird wobbled briefly in the air before dropping lightly onto the dirt road, within a hundred meters of the suspect's location.

Sergeant Malloy shouted, "Go!" and six men, outfitted in bulletproof vests and helmets, jumped off the perches on either side and fanned toward the brush that lined Naked Creek.

Confident Isaac Calhoun would be arrested shortly, Caine sat back in his seat and waited. No sense putting himself in danger if the former sniper started popping off shots.

As he watched, the air support team melted cautiously into the vegetation. His cell phone started ringing. Ringo, who was in direct contact with the HRT unit coordinator, was calling him. "Caine here."

"Sir," Ringo exclaimed, "the team on Calhoun's west boundary reports that he just detonated a claymore mine. They suspect it was a decoy and that he may have gone right past them."

What? "I told you, Ringo, he's following the creek on the northeast side. We're about to arrest him now."

"You sure about that?" Ringo didn't sound convinced. "Jackson said he saw the suspect heading west. Isn't that the side the cliff is on?"

The damn cliff. They'd run into it the first night, forcing them to turn back. No way in hell could Eryn McClellan climb down something like that. "Stand by," Caine commanded, as Sergeant Malloy jogged out of the tree line, back toward the chopper.

Caine cracked his door to talk to him. "Where is he?" he shouted over the spooling rotors.

"Not here, sir."

Caine glanced down at his tracking program, comparing its report to the sergeant's, and nearly had a heart attack. "He's practically on top of us!"

"I don't think so, sir," Malloy said. "But we did find this." He extended what looked like a fat pill bottle in his gloved hand.

Caine took it, thinking it was nothing. But then he read Eryn McClellan's name on the bottle. Several small components rattled inside. With a sinking sensation in his stomach and a good idea of what he was going to find, he twisted off the safety lid. A SIM card, antenna, and a battery, all still connected and functional, fell into his hand.

Fuck! "Summon your men," Caine said to the sergeant, aware that his face was hot with chagrin. "We're heading to the mountain's west side."

* * *

Half an hour later, Eryn was numb with fear and pouring rivers of sweat. "Just relax," Ike said in her ear. "Don't use up all your strength holding onto me."

Relax? How could anyone relax while dangling in thin air a hundred yards from the ground, while counting on a slim nylon rope, an anchor, and a pulley to lower them down? She reminded herself that she could always count on Ike, who would never let her come to harm.

But then she made the mistake of gauging their progress. *Oh, God.* There was nothing but jagged, gray rock below them. If the rope snapped they'd crack open like eggs and die.

Their only harness was strapped around Ike's hips and between his legs. Eryn sat on his thighs, facing him, her arms and legs hooked tightly around him, competing with the pack on his back and the rifle on his shoulder. In order to work the pulley, he had to leave both hands free, meaning it was completely up to her to remain in his lap and not slip off.

"How do you know the anchor's going to hold?" she asked for the umpteenth time.

"It'll hold." Suddenly, he went perfectly still.

Glancing up, Eryn saw him searching the blue sky. "What?" she breathed. In the next instant, she had her answer. He was listening to the distant clatter of a helicopter.

"Is that for us?" Her voice sounded unnaturally high.

"Probably. We need to move faster. Hold tight." He swung them out. *Zip!* Down the rope they slid, coming to a jarring halt that nearly unseated her. Eryn swallowed a scream. Ike repeated the motion three more times. The helicopter thundered closer.

"Rope's not quite long enough."

His announcement froze the blood in her veins. "What?"

Out of nowhere, he produced a knife. "We're going to jump. It's not far. I'll protect you."

He didn't give her a chance to argue. In the next instant, he pushed them away from the wall of granite while cutting one of the two lines of rope simultaneously. For a terrible second, they just hung there. Suddenly, they plummeted.

Eryn screamed and squeezed her eyes shut. They hit the ground hard, Ike on his back, Eryn on her hands and knees. As she fell against him, his breath came out with a *whoosh*.

"Ike!" She levered herself off him. "Oh, my God are you hurt?" She would never forgive herself if he'd broken his back.

Ike gritted his teeth, shook his head, and sucked in a painful breath. Grateful to his pack for breaking his fall, he ignored the contusions along his spine and forced himself to sit up. In just seconds, the helicopter would be right on top of them.

He gave the rope in his hand a yank, pulling the rest of it down to snake around them. Shrugging off his pack, he tore into it. "Quick, put this on," he said, lobbing a Ghillie suit at Eryn while putting away the rope and tunneling into a suit of his own. There was very little tree coverage on this side, just shrubs and bushes.

"Keep your head down and hold still," he instructed, helping her disappear into her own grassy suit. Then he pushed her head to the ground. Just then, the helo broke over the ridge above them.

Ike froze. Peering through the netted hood of the suit that camouflaged him, he watched the incoming bird. He could see three men on either perch, guns pointed at the ground. If this were a war, Ike would put his rifle to his shoulder, fix the crosshairs on the fuel tank, and turn the helo into a ball of fire. But this wasn't a war. Those men were like him, defenders of the peace.

"We should surrender," Eryn suggested in a muffled, frightened voice.

"No," he said. "They won't see us." Not without thermal imaging goggles, which he could tell the soldiers weren't wearing.

The helo circled round them, flying so low that the rotor wash flattened the wild wheat in the field behind them. Then it banked sharply to the north, increased its elevation and thundered out of sight. Eryn sat up slowly, pulling back her hood. Perspiration dotted her forehead. Her hair looked wildly disheveled. "How much farther?" she asked on an exhausted note.

He wished he could wave a magic wand and transport them. Or better yet, call on teammates to pick them up.

"Not far," he lied. "We cross this field. At the foot of that mountain, there's an old road that isn't used any more. We follow that, and then we're almost there. Come on. You can make it," he added, pulling her to her feet.

She swayed for a moment, prompting him to grub in his pack for his canteen. "Here, drink some water."

As she drank her fill, he eyed the sky nervously. Just because the helo hadn't seen them, it didn't mean they were out of the woods yet. He looked back at Eryn and his heart hurt. "I need you to run for me," he said, reluctantly. "Just one more time."

She screwed the lid on the canteen and handed it back. "Okay," she said.

He'd never realized how much of her father she had in her. He felt his eyes sting. "I'm sorry, princess."

She managed a weak smile at the endearment. "Don't be. It's not your fault." Dragging his pack off the ground, she thrust it at him and started to run.

"Whoa." He grabbed her back, pointed her in the right direction, then released her. Together, they cut through the knee-high grass, heading for the deer-stand and the old mountain road Dwayne Barnes had shown him last year.

On the other side of the field, Jollet's Hollow yielded to Green Mountain. Ike spotted the deer-stand in the forked trunk of a birch tree overlooking the hollow. "Road's just over this rise," he assured her, pointing into the forest.

Eryn nodded. Ike had to push her up the leaf-slick incline, one palm on her rounded bottom. She crawled the last few feet on her hands and knees, panting for breath, but she didn't complain.

Just as he gained the rise behind her, his sixth sense whispered words of danger.

Too late. He should have made certain the road was clear first. A police cruiser stood directly in their path, parked on a road obscured by the passing of decades. The Sheriff of Rockingham County leaned against it, gripping his holstered side arm.

"Drop your weapons, Calhoun," he drawled on a note of authority.

Berating himself viciously, Ike eased his sniper rifle off his shoulder and placed it slowly at his feet. He flicked a pale-faced Eryn a reassuring look. He still had his Python, his Gerber blade, and the Glock in his pack.

"Take it easy, Calhoun. We're not here to arrest you," the Sheriff drawled.

We?

The passenger door opened suddenly, and Dwayne Barnes emerged from behind the tinted windows to send Ike a conciliatory grin. "I figured you'd come this way," he said.

"You need our help, LT," added his uncle. "Between the FBI's Hostage Rescue Team and the State Police, there are over two hundred men in uniform out there looking for you. Every road in and out of the county is blocked."

"Oh, my God," Eryn whispered.

"We'll take you anywhere you want to go," said Dwayne, with a level look.

Was he serious? Ike looked back at the Sheriff, who nodded his agreement.

"The government boys have got it all wrong," insisted Olsen. "You've been good to us, LT. You're a patriot, not an outlaw. We'd like to help you out."

Humbled by the locals' sense of loyalty, Ike glanced down at Eryn, who squirmed out of the Ghillie suit as she came to her feet. Dwayne and his uncle both fell silent as she emerged like a butterfly from a cocoon. "Hello, I'm Eryn," she said, stepping forward to shake the Sheriff's hand, then Dwayne's as he rounded the car to greet her.

A warm tide of respect washed over Ike as he watched her. The woman had been to hell and back. She'd been scared out of her wits and pushed to her limits, but there she was, all manners and grace, shaking hands with the Sheriff like she'd arrived to share a pot of tea. He fucking loved her.

Rocked by the realization, he let the others bask in her presence while he pulled himself together and mulled over their offer. He, for one, didn't need their help. He could slip past any hastily assembled barricade, especially under the cover of darkness. But Eryn could use a break. "Can you take us to Naked Creek Vineyards?" he said, cutting through the pleasantries.

"Not a problem," said Sheriff Olsen. "There's just one thing. You'll have to travel in the trunk." Rounding the car, he lifted the hatch and sent Eryn an apologetic grimace. "They're searching all the cars that come through."

Ike had decided the men were trustworthy. Scooping up his rifle, he guided Eryn toward the trunk and stuffed his pack and both Ghillie suits inside. Then he helped her in.

"This is a first," she admitted, climbing awkwardly into the enclosed space. She laid her head on his pack.

Dividing a final look between Barnes and Olsen, Ike eased in next to her and twisted onto his back, holding his rifle in readiness across his chest.

The Sheriff sidled around, took one last look at them, and wordlessly shut the trunk, snuffing out the sunlight.

CHAPTER FOURTEEN

In the cramped trunk of the police car, Eryn shifted closer. "Ike," she called, as the tires rumbled over debris. He could feel tension in the fingers gripping his arm. "Are you sure this is a good idea?" The cruiser started backing down the road.

He'd just been wondering if a reward hadn't been posted for their capture. "They let me keep my rifle," he reassured them both. "They never would have done that if they weren't going to let us go."

With a weapon in his possession, he simply could not be apprehended. "If something happens, I'm going to take offensive action. You stay behind me, glued to my back, and you do what I say." He'd gladly die to protect her, if he had to.

She hugged him harder, her fingertips digging into his biceps.

"Hey." He turned his head to look at her. A pinhole of light shone through a crack in the seam of the trunk. "I'll get you away from all this," he promised. If he had his way, she would never, ever go through anything like it again.

"I'm not worried about me, Ike." Her words surprised him. "It's true I don't want to go back to the FBI, not at all. But chances are I'd be safe with them, now. They'd take extra precautions after the bombing, don't you think? It's you I'm worried about."

No one had ever said words like that to him before.

"You can take care of yourself," she added. "I know that. But I don't want you going to jail because of me."

"Shhh." Her words made him want to kiss her, not just because she was so goddamn nice to him but also to stop her from fretting. "I've been in worse places."

Even in the dark, he could see her eyes glimmering. "I know you have," she said, thickly. "But you deserve better—"

"No." He didn't deserve shit. He sure as hell didn't deserve her, not that he ever had her in the first place.

At his fierce tone, she fell silent. The only sound was the rumbling of the tires and pebbles hitting the car's undercarriage. With a lurch, the car bounced onto asphalt, and the white noise faded leaving the trunk suddenly quiet.

"Ike." She moved even closer, pulling his arm between her breasts.

"What?" Would he ever get to caress those breasts again, suck those raspberry nipples into his mouth?

"You have to forgive yourself for what happened to your teammates," she urged in a desperate whisper that made him feel like the end was near for them.

The advice closed a fist around his heart and squeezed. He pretended not to hear her.

But his silence didn't deter her. "You need to find the survivors and to talk to them. They don't blame you, Ike. I know they don't."

He could only hope she was right. But, damn it, this wasn't the time to discuss his issues. He needed to concentrate on the route the Sheriff was taking, so he could be sure they were headed in the right direction.

With a troubled sigh, she pressed her cheek to his shoulder. Longing sluiced through him, dragging him into an undertow of pointless yearning. More than anything, he wanted to rise up and surpass her expectations. He wanted to be worthy of her respect, but the road to redemption was dark and treacherous. A cold sweat breached his skin at the mere prospect of traversing it. He lay there, his stomach roiling.

Suddenly, the sedan, which had been clipping along at forty or so miles per hour, slowed to a stop. Ike braced himself to keep from sliding into Eryn. Outside, he could hear raised voices, the tramping of feet. He tightened his grip on his rifle.

"You see anything, Sheriff?" asked a voice Ike didn't recognize.

"Neither hide nor hair," said Olsen, in his distinctive drawl. "We went way back in the woods, all around Green Mountain. Didn't see nothing. Good luck findin' him," he added.

"Thanks. You can go on through," said the stranger, thumping the trunk as the car eased forward.

Eryn jumped at the sound.

The sedan swung left and picked up speed. Recognizing the angle of the turn, Ike let himself relax. They'd barreled through the first barricade. Now they were now headed swiftly toward Naked Creek Vineyards. In just a few more minutes, Eryn could take a hot shower, sleep in a comfortable bed, and enjoy the amenities she'd been without for days. It only drove home how little he had to offer her.

"Out you go," said the Sheriff, opening the trunk.

Sunlight blinded Eryn. Ike rolled out ahead of her like a coiled spring. A moment later, he hauled her out after him. As he reached back inside for his pack, she turned full circle, noting that the cruiser had stopped in the middle of a vine-draped field, on a dirt track that divided trellises as far as the eye could see.

Bright green tendrils with leaves just beginning to unfurl coursed the length of strings that stretched the length of a pasture. A mansion, painted lemon yellow, lorded over the vineyard a hundred yards away. Lovely, she thought, feeling her fear and weariness slip away.

"Sheriff." Ike extended his hand. "Thank you."

"My pleasure," said the older man, pumping with enthusiasm. "But it was Dwayne's idea. Felt he owed it to you."

Ike headed for the lowered passenger window. He and Dwayne shared a long look. "Sorry 'bout the other day," Ike finally said. "No hard feelings?"

"None," Dwayne agreed, grinning at him. The Sheriff slipped behind the wheel, and in the next instant, the cruiser started backing away, leaving them standing on what had to be a tractor road.

"Come on." Ike shouldered his pack and grabbed her hand. Together they followed the tracks in the dark earth, past the rows of trellises, headed straight for the house.

"Who lives here again?" The sweet-smelling soil and the tidy lines combing the fields soothed her lingering concerns.

"Former trainee. Some punk kept vandalizing his vineyard, screwing with the machinery. Chris took my course to put a stop to it; caught the culprit and sent him to jail."

"So, Chris owes you a debt of gratitude." She shot him a look. "Is he expecting us?"

"He is now."

As they passed the last line of grape vines, the house came fully into view, and Eryn's eyes widened. "Now that's a house," she exclaimed, impressed by the French architecture.

In the same instant, a tall, raw-boned man slipped out of an adjacent building. Crossing the pebbled courtyard, he gestured for them to follow.

Entering the mansion via a rear entrance, Eryn found herself in a mud-room with tiled flooring, a sink, and state-of-the-art laundry appliances. She took a deep breath, savoring the scent of fabric softener.

"I thought you might come here," said the man, grasping Ike's hand. He slid Eryn an assessing look.

"This is Eryn McClellan," said Ike. "Eryn, Christopher Axtel."

"Chris," said the giant, engulfing her hand in his. Speculative blue eyes shone from a weathered face. "Your father is the ISAF Commander."

Startled, Eryn glanced at Ike.

"How do you know that?" Ike demanded. "And why'd you think I'd come here?"

"You were just on the news, my friend," Chris explained, making Eryn's stomach drop. "Rumor has it the FBI is searching for a former Navy SEAL who supposedly abducted the ISAF Commander's daughter. Sounds like hogwash to me."

"Shit," Ike breathed, rubbing his neck.

"Ike didn't kidnap me," Eryn protested.

"Of course not." Chris put a comforting hand on her shoulder. "The rumors are ridiculous. If he's doing anything, he's protecting you. Am I right?"

"That's exactly what he's doing."

"Look, the less you know, the better," Ike cut in, sounding tired. "You think you could spare us a bed for a few hours then loan me a car once the sun sets?"

"You already know the answer," their host assured him. "Take your muddy clothes off here. I'll have them washed." He ran a look over Eryn's figure. "I'll be right back with clothes for both of you."

Eryn murmured her appreciation. Shocked by the reports that Ike was wanted for kidnapping, she studied his inscrutable expression as he released the buttons on his filthy jacket. She could tell by the mask on his face that he was deeply discouraged. "I should turn myself in," she offered quietly.

His green gaze jumped up and skewered her. In the next instant, he stepped closer, caught her face lightly between his hands and said, "If you do that, then every risk I've taken—that *we've* taken," he amended, "—was for nothing."

Memories of their week together replayed in her mind's eye. She thought of Ike whisking her from the safe house. Warming water for her bath. Training Winston. Teaching her to shoot, to defend herself. "It hasn't been for nothing," she argued. "You've made me stronger, Ike. You've showed me how to fight back, not be a victim."

"You're *not* going to turn yourself in," he insisted, his lips firming. "We've come this far. We're almost in the clear."

"Okay," she soothed, sensing his distress. "I just hate the thought of you being vilified. You're not a kidnapper, Ike, you're a hero."

Her assertion made him step back abruptly, as if she'd slapped him. He bent over and wordlessly untied his muddy boots.

* * *

With one eye on the blue Buick parked across the street, Farshad slipped into the noisy auto shop to look for Shahbaz. If he could have things his way, he would never be meeting Vengeance face-to-face, but circumstances had changed suddenly and dramatically. Farshad desperately needed a car, one that didn't stand out like his cousin's black taxi, and a scapegoat. Shahbaz could provide him with both.

"Excuse me," he said, intercepting an employee in grease-stained coveralls. Farshad himself was as immaculately dressed as always, wearing a business suit and carrying a briefcase. "I am looking for Shahbaz Wahidi."

"Right there," said the mechanic, pointing to a youth who was leaning over the engine of a large, rust-colored American car.

Farshad sidled up next to him. "*As-salaam alaikum,*" he murmured, and the youth pulled his head out from under the hood. So, it's this boy, he thought, dismayed by the stumped look in the boy's eyes.

"It's you!" he exclaimed suddenly, his puzzlement clearing. "Allah's blessing be upon you," he added, demonstrating to Farshad that he didn't speak Arabic well enough to answer him properly.

Farshad frowned. Had all Muslim American youth cut ties with tradition? He stepped closer, only to be assaulted by odors of oil and gasoline rising off the boy's work clothes. "Allah has revealed the woman's whereabouts," he disclosed on a whisper. He was mollified to see Shahbaz's slow, gap-toothed smile. Perhaps what he lacked in culture, he made up for in enthusiasm.

"Where is she?" inquired the youth, wiping his hands hastily with a rag.

Farshad flicked a glance toward a television, just visible from where they stood, in the waiting area. "On the news," he said, withholding details for now. "We must leave right away."

"Now?" Shahbaz looked nonplussed.

"While the agents across the street are eating," Farshad explained. "Come, you have better things to do than to change the oil in this car."

"Alternator belt," the boy corrected him. "I already fixed it."

"Is the car reliable?"

"It runs."

"Then we'll take it," Farshad said, daring him with a look to defy his authority.

Shahbaz hesitated only briefly. "Very well, Teacher."

At least he seemed to understand that defending Islam took precedence over keeping his job. As Shahbaz shut the hood with a *clang*, Farshad rounded the vehicle to slip into the passenger seat, his briefcase on his lap. Shahbaz took the wheel. Backing them cautiously from the auto shop, he circled the parking lot before heading to the street. Farshad kept a wary eye on the Buick, but the agents did not remark their leaving. No one would report the car stolen for a while.

Within minutes, they were clipping along Connecticut in the direction of the Beltway. Farshad held his hand out. "Give me your cell phone," he demanded Shahbaz pulled it from his breast pocket and slowly surrendered it. Farshad lowered the window and tossed it onto the street, where it shattered into pieces. "Now you can't be followed," he explained, ignoring the boy's dismay.

"Where are we going?" Shahbaz asked.

"Patience," Farshad advised him, none too lightly, as he opened his briefcase. "This will explain everything." Inside his briefcase was his laptop. He opened it and powered it on. With the wireless card from Verizon, he could get Internet anywhere within a fifteen mile radius of a cell tower.

Accessing the website for MSNBC news, he clicked on the video for the day's top story and cranked up the volume so Shahbaz could hear.

"The manhunt continues in Rockingham County, Virginia for Eryn McClellan, daughter of General McClellan, leader of the International Security Assistance Force in Afghanistan. The twenty-six-year-old teacher from Washington, D.C. has twice been targeted by Muslim extremists protesting her father's actions in Afghanistan. Miss McClellan disappeared from a bombed FBI safe house a week ago and is believed to be in the company of former Navy SEAL Officer, Isaac Calhoun. It remains unclear whether Calhoun, who once served under her father, is protecting Miss McClellan or whether he has abducted her. The FBI and state officials refuse to comment. We will keep viewers advised as soon as we have an update."

Farshad shut the laptop, sending Shahbaz a satisfied smile. "*Alhumdulillah*," he murmured.

"So," Shahbaz said, clearly still processing what he'd overheard. "She is in Rockingham County. Where is that?"

"Not far," Farshad replied. "Go south on the Beltway up ahead."

* * *

Eryn exchanged her borrowed clothing for one of the fluffy white robes hanging on the back of the guest bathroom's door.

A couple of hours had elapsed since her and Ike's arrival. Showered and dressed in borrowed clothing, they had joined their hosts in the sunny, gourmet kitchen to enjoy a luncheon of club sandwiches and pickles. Over glasses of the vineyard's award-winning Fiore, they had touched on several interesting topics, while never once mentioning Eryn's circumstance. By late afternoon, the morning's harrowing events had faded from her mind.

Relaxed by the delicious wine and lulled by the luxurious accommodations, Eryn had ceased to fret about the FBI pursuing her and Ike. When Chris suggested they indulge in an afternoon nap, Eryn's first thought was would she get to make love to Ike again? She'd overheard Ike thank their host as he took a set of car keys from him. He'd mumbled that they would leave around midnight when, hopefully, the roadblocks would be gone.

Leaving at midnight meant she and Ike would have seven hours of interrupted time together. Wasting not another minute of it, Eryn eased from the guest bathroom while still tying the robe's belt around her waist.

At her entrance, Ike, who sat waiting in the bed, shut off the television abruptly, cutting short the news program he was watching. With the drapes already pulled across the tall, narrow windows, shadows filled the vast space, inviting restful sleep. But the word "manhunt" hung in the air, stealing a portion of Eryn's anticipation as she crossed to the far side of the bed.

"Are you sure we won't be found here?" she asked, apprehension nipping at her heels.

"Not here," he said with confidence. The massive headboard framed his torso as he sat watching her impassively. To her dismay, he wore an expression as withdrawn and aloof as the day he'd brought her to his cabin.

Oh, no you don't. With a surge of defiance, she unbelted her robe and let it fall from her shoulders, leaving her standing in the nude. His gaze slid helplessly over naked offering and his features tightened. But he said and did nothing to encourage her.

Slipping between the lavender-scented sheets, Eryn scooted across the wide mattress, groaning aloud at its comfort. "This feels like heaven," she professed, edging closer. "Every muscle in my body aches."

"Rest," he suggested, making her wonder if that was all he had in mind.

In desperation, she reached out to touch him and encountered nothing but naked, male flesh. If he wanted just to rest, he would have come to bed wearing Chris's clothing, she thought, encouraged. Snuggling against his stiffly held body, she refused to be deterred by his lack of affection. After all, he was bound to have a lot on his mind right now.

Laying her head on his chest, she discerned the swift, sure thud of his heart beneath her ear. He wasn't as aloof as he seemed. Moreover, as she gazed downward, there was no mistaking the tent in the sheet for anything but a full-blown erection. Obviously, Ike wasn't so overwrought that he didn't still desire her.

"I'm exhausted," she admitted, tipping her head back, "but I don't know if I can sleep right away. You?" she asked, softly kissing his jaw.

"Probably not," he admitted, gruffly.

It was all the prompting she needed to strain upward and touch her lips to his. He closed his eyes, passively letting her kiss him, until she slipped her tongue into his mouth, offering him a foreshadowing of what was to come. His restraint snapped so abruptly that she had to smile. At last, he was kissing her back with the focused passion she'd come to expect from him.

Throwing a knee over his leg, Eryn took charge. She straddled his hips, pulling away just long enough to coil her damp hair into a knot. Ike's gaze fell raptly to her swaying breasts. There was a tremor in his touch as he cupped her fullness.

Determined to repay the pleasure he'd given her at the cabin, she settled over him, kissing his lips, cheek, ear, and neck. Nibbling the length of sinew that ran into the muscles of his shoulder, she trailed her mouth lower, over the expanse of his chest where she encountered a number of scars that made her heart ache. She traced them one by one, with the tip of her tongue. Ike didn't think of himself as heroic, but the scars were evidence enough. He was *her* hero, and she would reward him for his commitment.

As she followed the line of fuzz that bisected his abdomen, she saw him clench the sheet with expectancy. *That's right. You know what's coming to you, don't you?*

He emitted a groan as she cradled his turgid sex. Caressing him with her cheek, her chin, her lips, she let him know by the look in her eyes that she would settle for nothing less than his complete capitulation.

Maybe then, he wouldn't leave her with Cougar. Maybe then he'd stick around.

Drawing him into the heat of her mouth, she pushed aside her insecurities and luxuriated in his maleness.

See what you'll lose if you give me up? She licked and swirled then took as much of him inside her mouth as she could, over and over again, until he gasped for breath, swearing incoherently.

Without warning, he lunged toward her. With a hook and a twist, he flipped her over, onto her back. Throwing himself on top of her, he wrested the reins of power. Pleased to have pushed him beyond his limits, Eryn welcomed his immediate and powerful possession, as he filled her in one thrust.

Ike caught Eryn's keening cry into his mouth in the nick of time. Her slippery heat reassured him her outcry was a sign of pleasure, not pain. She opened to him like a flower, her thighs encircling his hips, her pelvis undulating sinuously.

He should have known she would do this to him, pushing through the door he'd tried half-heartedly to close. From their first encounter, she had refused to let him retreat into isolation. What made him think she'd back off now? With every undulation, she pulled him closer, deeper.

This connection between them would only make it harder to part. They should have climbed into bed fully dressed and gone straight to sleep. His head knew that; only, the rest of him had had an agenda more like Eryn's. At least his reticence had wrought its own rewards, prompting her to make the first move.

The memory of her hot, hungry mouth on his cock would remain with him forever. She would soon be lost to him, but the gift of her passion would be his to cherish, always.

Oh, crap. Reality hit him like a hammer over the head. He'd forgotten about the condom he'd stowed beneath his pillow.

"Shhh," he warned, groping for it and, at the same time, withdrawing regretfully from her warmth. Palming a breast to console himself, suckled her flushed nipple as he tried ripping into the foil with just one hand. Once he'd covered himself, he shifted lower, burying his face in her steamy heat. There was no restraining himself, this time. He devoured her with all the yearning and desperation that roiled inside him, while still withholding what she begged for.

He wanted her looking him in the eye when she finally came.

Unable to wait any longer, he crawled over her. Bracing his weight on his elbows, he caught her face between his hands. He didn't have to ask her to open her eyes. She was looking up at him with eyes that shone with warmth and surrender. His heart expanded painfully. The way she looked at him, it was like she felt the way he did.

He sank into her snug, slickness, gritting his teeth as her muscles contracted, milking him.

You going to remember me, Eryn?

Buried to the hilt, he paused, fighting to shut off his awareness of how sweetly, how snugly she gripped him. Easing a hand between their straining bodies, he thumbed the swell that he had brought to sensitivity. *Going to think of me at all when we're apart?*

"Say something," he heard her gasp over the humming of his own blood. "What are you thinking, Ike?"

She must have sensed his desperation. Weighing the risk of sharing even a portion of what he felt, he ground out, "Don't forget me."

Tears filled her eyes, turning them to shimmering, violet pools. "How could I ever forget you?" she demanded. In the next instant, she threw her head back and bit her bottom lip. Her body tensed beneath him, and her beautiful face creased with rapture.

With his own release steamrolling over him, Ike fought to keep his eyes open, to memorize the way she looked climaxing with him inside her, a single tear sliding from the corner of one eye.

Shed for him.

CHAPTER FIFTEEN

Sleep eluded Eryn. She lay on a three thousand dollar mattress, surrounded by down pillows, her body flat-out exhausted and sleep-deprived. But her troubled heart kept her eyes from closing, and Ike's request rippled over her heartstrings in an endless melody. *Don't forget me. Don't forget me.*

How could he think, even for a moment, that she ever would? And why did he have to imply that they'd never see each other again? She wished now that she'd articulated her feelings more clearly, except that she'd been beyond speech at the time. She wanted to tell him how important he'd become to her in just five days.

When, exactly, had the jerk who'd accused her of self-medicating proven himself a sterling human being? Somewhere between heating water for her bath and rappelling down a cliff with her in his lap, she'd fallen head-over-heels in love with him.

Ike had more integrity than any man she'd ever known, yet he was humble to a fault. He was competent and capable beyond belief, while still patient when it came to teaching his skills to others. He might appear to be unfeeling, but beneath his tough veneer there dwelled a man utterly sensitive to her needs and wishes, especially when it came to fulfilling her in the bedroom.

What woman wouldn't want to hold onto him forever? But how could she ask more of him when protecting her had gotten him into trouble with the law already?

She rolled slowly away from him, careful to keep her troubled thoughts from disturbing him. For the first time since she'd met him, he slept soundly, neither moving nor snoring.

Why was the FBI doing this? she raged, quelling the urge to punch up her pillow. They'd had their chance to keep her safe, and they'd blown it by using her for bait.

Ike, in contrast, had removed her from the threat of terror. He'd taught her how to protect herself, how to shoot and fight and think through her fear.

And for that he would get punished, if caught?

The more she considered the injustice of it, the hotter she burned. She carefully peeled back the sheets to cool off. All Ike had ever done was to carry out her father's wishes: to liberate her from the FBI, who'd insisted she was a guest, staying in the safe house voluntarily. How, then, could they claim Ike had abducted her?

Surely Jackson saw the fallacy of such logic. If she could just talk to him, she might persuade him to convince his superiors to curtail their search.

Her gaze went thoughtfully to the chair by the window where she'd left her purse. Jackson's business card was still tucked into one of the little side pockets.

Her pulse quickened as she debated her odds of success. Using a house phone was out of the question. The FBI would trace her call and know exactly where to find her. But what about a cell phone? She recalled seeing one on the island in Chris's kitchen. Wouldn't that give her a little anonymity?

She had to do *something*. Ike had risked so much for her; she couldn't just lie here thinking about it.

With a held breath, she rolled slowly out of bed, praying she wouldn't disturb Ike. To her relief, he slept on.

Redressing in the jeans and T-shirt belonging to Chris's wife, Marie, Eryn collected her purse. She slipped into the quiet hall and closed the guestroom door behind her. The mansion stood still and silent. The vineyard's owners had retreated to the adjacent building to finish up the day's work.

Tiptoeing to the tidied-up kitchen, she spied the purple cell phone she had seen earlier.

With one eye on the window, she pulled Maddox's business card out of her purse. Picturing his compassionate gaze, she punched his number into the keypad with fingers that trembled and hit talk.

On the other end, the ringer shrilled over and over. Just as she deliberated whether to leave a message, he picked up.

"Special Agent Maddox. Hello?"

"Jackson?" She had difficulty finding her voice.

"Who's this?" She could hear men speaking in the background.

"It's Eryn McClellan." Her heart beat so heavily it rocked her on her bare feet.

"Hold on a sec." The voices faded and a door clicked shut. "I'm here," he said, confidentially. "Are you okay? Are you safe?"

"Of course I'm safe. Why wouldn't I be? We've been through this before, Jackson."

"Then why are you calling me?" he asked.

"I want to know why you're treating Ike like a criminal. You told me I was a guest at the safe house, free to leave any time. Just because Ike helped me leave that doesn't make him a kidnapper!" she railed.

"I understand why you're upset," he said calmly.

"Then stop chasing us!"

"I can't." His deep, melodic voice grew monotone. "It's not up to me."

She ground the heel of her palm against her throbbing temple.

"Is Calhoun there with you?"

"What difference does it make?"

"If you two turn yourselves in, I'm sure we'll drop the charges against him; they're too flimsy to hold up, anyway."

She remembered how strongly Ike was opposed to the idea. "That's not going to happen," she informed him.

Jackson was silent a while. "Then I need to tell you, Eryn, that I have the technology to pinpoint your location," he said regretfully. "We'll be showing up any minute to pick you up."

What? The blood drained from her head, making the room spin. "No!" She glanced wildly around.

"If you don't want us arresting Calhoun, you need to distance yourself from him, now. Keep this phone with you and start walking. I'll find you."

"Please," Eryn begged, regretting her decision to call him. "Don't do this, Jackson. Just pretend I never called. Please!"

"This is an agency phone, Eryn. People scrutinize my calls. I'd be neglecting my duties if I let you both go. I'll give you thirty minutes." He hung up abruptly.

For a full minute, Eryn stared in shock at the phone in her hands. *What do I do?* The cell phone wasn't even hers. How could she just take off with it? How could she just take off, *period?*

She had to wake up Ike, tell him what she'd done.

She cringed at the thought. He would assume she'd betrayed his trust, having gone and done the single thing he'd told her not to do. But that hadn't been her intention at all.

"Oh, God." There was just one course of action left: to do exactly as Jackson had suggested. It was the only way to keep Ike from getting arrested. Once she was back in FBI custody, she'd convince the agents that he hadn't broken any laws.

Scribbling a note promising to return the phone or to pay for the cost of replacing it, she left it on the counter.

Then she pivoted toward the mud room and found her Skechers drying with the laces untied and the tongues hanging out. Feeling guilty and ungrateful, Eryn slipped them on without socks. She tied them numbly. Her heart, sitting like a block of ice in her chest, scarcely seemed to beat.

How could she leave without saying goodbye to Ike, without explaining or thanking him for everything? Jackson had given her a thirty-minute lead, scarcely any time at all. She would need every second to get as far away from Naked Creek Vineyard as possible.

Please understand. She sent the message kinetically as she cracked the rear exit and eyed the distance from the house to the trellises—fifty yards, or so.

If Chris's security system was anything like Ike's, she might not pull this off at all. But she had to try. Her hero didn't belong in jail. Ironically, it was now her job to protect him.

Ike awoke to a brisk knock. He jerked to one elbow, noting with a sweep of his eyes that Eryn was not in bed with him; the clock by the bed read 4:53 **P.M.**, and her purse was missing. His heart skipped a beat. "Yes?"

"Isaac," Chris leaned into the room wearing an urgent expression, "do you know that Eryn left?"

Shock hit Ike squarely in the chest and radiated to his extremities. He leapt out of the bed, only to recall that he was completely naked.

"Do you want me to try and stop her?"

He tried to think through the memories crowding him. That single tear sliding from the corner of her eye... Had she known she was going to leave him?

"Isaac?"

"No, wait for me." He jammed his feet into the pants that were several sizes too big for him. Strands of thought caught one upon the other, leading him to a startling conclusion. "She's turning herself in," he guessed, threading a belt with fingers that started to shake.

"She took Marie's cell phone," Chris added. "I found a note in the kitchen saying that she'd compensate us."

The sequence of events came together in Ike's mind. Eryn had called the authorities to reason with them, probably, and had realized, too late, that she'd exposed their hiding place. She'd then bolted, no doubt hoping to protect Ike.

"God *damn* it!" He stuffed his head into a clean T-shirt. *Why, Eryn?* They'd come so close to making a clean escape.

Maybe it wasn't too late to stop her. He *had* to stop her. With the FBI fiasco all over the news, they'd managed to disclose her whereabouts yet again. No doubt the terrorists who wanted her dead were just waiting for the opportunity to finish her once and for all.

Sprinting past fertile furrows of grape vines, Eryn arrived, at last, at the dirt track where the Sheriff had dropped them off earlier. She followed it uphill, where it spit her out on a country road.

Looking both ways, she broke right, away from the vineyard, away from Ike. Ignoring a cramp pinching her midsection and the fact that her sockless heels were rubbing the backs of her shoes, she lengthened her stride, drawing on the strength of will that Ike had taught her.

All it took to gain top speed was to picture him behind bars.

Never! She pumped her arms, sucked more air into her lungs, and stretched the ligaments in her thighs, running as swiftly as she ever had.

Rays of late afternoon sunlight combed through the branches of trees that lined the adjacent field. Pastures of bright green grass and wildflowers stretched in all directions, broken up by fences like the one she paralleled.

Sweat cooled her upper lip and trickled down her spine. Her heels began to burn, but she did not slow down.

Just as she approached a crossroad, a helicopter, larger than the one that had chased them earlier, broke over the horizon ahead of her, shattering the bucolic quiet.

Startled, certain it belonged to the search party hunting her, Eryn broke left, onto a rural route where she hugged the shadows of the trees that lined it. Uncertainty had begun to weight her legs, limiting her stride. Tears stabbed at her eyes.

She had no way of knowing if she'd done the right thing. Without Ike, she felt suddenly vulnerable, suddenly exposed. God, she missed him already! The road beneath her feet blurred before her eyes as tears rolled onto her cheeks and dried in the air that sent her hair streaming.

Hearing an engine behind her, she craned her neck to look back. A truck had turned off the road behind her and was drawing nearer. The hope that Ike might be in it made her tremble with hope, but as it overtook her, the driver proved to be a bearded stranger, who gawked at her as he drove past.

The encounter sapped her energy. Loneliness and desolation overtook her abruptly, and she slowed to a brisk walk, peering about, feeling lost. There was no more traffic here, only trees and yards and an occasional clap-board home, nestled in flowering bushes. A steeple rose over the treetops up ahead, and the helicopter sounded farther away.

Ike might well have realized she was gone by now. He would be frantic when he found she'd left. Furious. He would search for her.

Please don't, she prayed, dreading the prospect of him and the FBI converging on her at the same time. There would be a confrontation. Ike would be arrested.

Picturing him cuffed and stuffed into a vehicle, she picked up her pace, hobbling now for the blister on her left heel. As she limped past the church and several dwellings, a dog chained to a tree, lunged at her and barked. The curtains in the window twitched.

Feeling eyes on her, she tried to run again. But her energy stores were all used up. Suddenly, the phone in her pocket vibrated. She slowed to a walk and pulled it out. "Yes," she gasped, expecting to hear Jackson's voice.

"Where are you?"

Ike's voice, gruff with urgency, brought her to a halt. She pressed a fist to the stitch in her side and swallowed the sob rising up her throat. "You shouldn't call me. They'll find you," she warned him.

"I told you not to do this." His voice cracked.

Was he furious or fearful? she wondered. "I didn't mean for it to happen," she cried, desperate to absolve herself in his eyes. "I just had to talk to Jackson, to persuade him to stop chasing us."

Movement in the corner of her eye drew her gaze toward the house with the dog. An old woman now stood in the shadows of her porch, watching her intently. Eryn's nape prickled. "He told me if I got away from you quickly, he would pick me up and leave you out of this. I'll talk to them, Ike. I'll make them see you were just trying to help me."

"What the *hell* am I supposed to tell your father?" he thundered quietly.

Was that all he was worried about, what her father thought? "I'm sorry." Regret choked her, making it hard for her to speak. "I didn't know what else to do! I love you, Ike," she added, throwing caution to the wind in telling him the truth. "I can't stand the thought of you getting in trouble because of me." Tears tracked her overheated cheeks.

The silence on the other end was so complete that Eryn glanced at the phone to check her reception. "Ike?"

"Just tell me where you are," he implored, and her heart gave a pang of disappointment. He hadn't even acknowledged her confession.

The sound of an approaching car had her whirling around to see a familiar, green sedan turning the corner and speeding toward her. "It's too late," she answered, torn by the possibility that she would never hold Ike again. "They're already here. Good-bye, Ike. I hope I see you soon." With profound regret, she ended the call.

Ike stared sightlessly out the mud-splattered windshield of Chris's off-road Jeep. The click against his ear as Eryn hung up tore into him like shrapnel. His fist closed over the cell phone until it bruised his palm. At the same time, he savored the words that pillowed his heart against blows of frustration.

I love you, Ike. How could four small words change everything? Yet, they did. He'd intended, after dropping Eryn off with Cougar, to head straight for Canada, where the FBI wouldn't find him, where his survival skills would serve him well. There on some cold, remote mountain, he would nurse his misbegotten infatuation for a woman he did not deserve.

But her words swept away those plans in an instant. They filled him with a sense of destiny and purpose. Knowing Eryn loved him made abandoning her unthinkable.

Chris's knock on the window, startled him back to the present. Ike rolled down the window.

"Did you reach her?" his friend asked. "Are you going?"

Ike handed him back his cell phone. "It's too late," he conveyed with numb acceptance. "They're picking her up right now."

Chris's blue gaze reflected sympathy as they searched Ike's expression. "So what will you do?" he asked. "Are you still taking off?"

"No." He realized he had every reason in the world to protect Eryn, still. And, given his special skill set, it seemed like fate, for he knew exactly what it would take to liberate her from terror, once and for all. "I have a job to finish," he added, glancing at the pack on the seat beside him. Everything he needed was there, including a bottle of Naked Creek Vineyard's 2008 Meritage. Thrusting his hand out the window, he wasted precious seconds thanking his host properly.

With a wave at Marie, who stood at the winery doors looking concerned, Ike cranked the Jeep's engine, worked the gears, and pulled away.

Grim but ennobling determination spurred his heart into a trot.

All he had to do was kill the terrorists before they struck again.

Eryn wilted with relief to see Jackson alone in the government issued Taurus. The sight of Winston in the back seat chased away a portion of her despondency.

"Hop in," said the agent, his light-colored eyes flicking toward the house with the dog. "We're being watched."

Eryn leapt into the front seat and turned to hug Winston. Her face was still buried in the fur at his neck when the car lurched forward.

"I'm surprised you came alone," she muttered, sitting back and latching her seatbelt. "I'd have thought the whole posse would come after me," she added bitterly.

With a sidelong glance of sympathy, Jackson executed a three-point turn and took off with a spray of loose gravel. "You hear that helicopter?" he asked, glancing toward the treetops.

"Yes."

"That's MSNBC news. If three agents went streaking off to pick you up, they'd be right on top of us."

Eryn stared at him aghast. "This is getting national coverage," she realized.

"Correct. That's what happens when you bring an army into a small town," he added, mocking the FBI's tactics. They sped down the country route toward the wider road.

"Then why'd you do it?" Eryn demanded. "I was perfectly safe with Ike."

His full lips quirked ruefully. "Believe me, I've tried convincing my boss of that, but he won't listen to reason. And, unfortunately, Calhoun's got a glitch in his military record—"

"I know all about that. It wasn't his fault." As they turned left toward town, she glanced in the direction of the vineyard, longing for Ike.

"He's got an arsenal in his basement," Jackson added, "and he fired his weapon at a federal agent."

"He is *not* a criminal! And that stuff in his basement is for the course he teaches." Heat surged into Eryn's face as she whipped her head around to glare at him. "Why the hell is the media saying he abducted me?"

Jackson shook his head. "Because my boss is an ass. The media made that assumption when he called in our Hostage Rescue Team. Why else would they be needed?"

Tears of frustration stabbed at her eyes, threatening her composure. She turned her face away to collect herself.

The soothing hand Jackson placed on her shoulder put a lump in her throat. "You have every right to be upset, Eryn. Believe me, I've been upset on your behalf. But don't worry. I'll keep a closer eye on you this time."

She could tell he meant it, too, but the promise failed to reassure her. She would rather have Ike watching her. Hugging her dog's neck, she stared blindly at the asphalt ribbon unraveling before them and wondered if the terrorists were watching the news, plotting their next course of action. A sense of unease pulled her scalp tight.

"So, where is Calhoun now?" Jackson's casual question drew her attention back.

"You know I'm not going to tell you that."

"I hope he has the sense to keep his distance."

Seeing him glance into the rearview mirror, she looked into her own side mirror at the mud-splattered Jeep pacing them. It was too far back and too stained with mud for her to make out the driver. Still, something told her Ike was in it. A thousand butterflies spread their wings inside of her and lifted off.

It would be just like Ike to ignore the threat of imprisonment to keep a watchful eye on her. She didn't know whether to cry for joy or weep in despair.

To her sharp dismay, the Jeep turned off at an intersection and disappeared. Jackson's grip on the steering wheel relaxed. Eryn sat more heavily in her seat and expelled a long breath.

As they turned up the ramp to take the highway to Elkton, she saw that the blockade was still in effect. Tapping his horn, Jackson swerved around the waiting cars and broke into the oncoming lane. The National Guardsman waved him down irately. Jackson displayed his badge, scarcely slowing, and the guardsman let them through.

At the same time, the media helicopter honed in on them. It hovered over them, moving at the same speed as the Taurus. As its thundering rotors sent the windows vibrating, Winston started to whine.

Maddox shot the helicopter a dark look. "I think the woman watching you earlier alerted the media," he said, having to raise his voice to be heard over the ruckus.

Eryn peered in consternation at the white helicopter with the MSNBC logo clearly displayed on one side. "They know I'm in this car?"

"I think so."

"Where are you taking me?"

"To the Sheriff's Office. Sorry," he added, "but it's the only safe place. The entire town is crammed with journalists and media. They're going to make a rush at us. Stick close to me when we get there," he added. "Keep your head down and don't talk to anyone."

Eryn considered his instructions. "Maybe I want to talk to the media," she considered out loud.

Jackson shot her a worried look.

"To clear Ike's name," she added. "So everyone knows he was protecting me."

"Not today, Eryn. I promised you, I'll try to get his charges dropped."

"But what if you can't?"

"Look, all my supervisor wants is you. Once he has you, he'll forget about Calhoun."

"He damn well better," she retorted with prim indignation.

Jackson quirked an eyebrow at her. "You've changed," he said, approvingly.

"You're right. This is my life, and no one's going to stop me from living it—not the terrorists and definitely not the FBI."

Her outburst made the agent grin. "Now you're talking."

Letting the Taurus out of his sight put a fist of anxiety in Ike's stomach. But he couldn't ignore the manhunt underway for him. Every main road in and out of the area was choked by National Guardsmen screening vehicles.

Tuning the radio to the local station, he listened for a moment and concluded that the agent would take Eryn into Elkton. Shifting into four-wheel drive, he eased off the road, lurched through a ditch, and forded a field that would be planted with corn shortly. Getting closer to Eryn without being caught would entail a little bit of trespassing and circumlocution, but for a former Navy SEAL, there was no such thing as impossible.

Whatever it took to keep her in his sight, he would do.

Eryn drew a sharp breath at the sight awaiting her. Block after block of
Elkton's downtown area was lined with news vans, cars, even motorcycles.
Pedestrians toting cameras or wearing sharp-looking suits that marked
them as journalists milled aimlessly in front of the two and three-story
buildings, a hodgepodge of quaint, historical structures and cinderblock
eyesores.

Maddox pressed the accelerator, intent on sweeping her through the
crowd unnoticed. But one by one, individuals caught sight of the green
sedan and gesticulated. Heads swiveled in their direction. Fingers pointed.
In one accord, the crowd began to surge toward the official-looking brick
building advertised as Elkton Town Hall.

Maddox swept into the parking lot, scattering the crowd by beeping
the horn. Individuals seemed determined to get run over. They surrounded
the sedan as Maddox drew alongside a huge RV and killed the engine. The
hum of voices and a sense of chaos enveloped Eryn as she met Jackson's
reassuring gaze.

"I'll come around and get you," he said. Pushing out of the car, he let
Winston out first. Cameras clicked as the media photographed Eryn's dog.
Elbowing his way to her door, he curtly ordered the crowd to back up. Then
he opened her door, curled a steady hand around her elbow, and pulled her
out.

Still, the journalists pressed in on them, thrusting cameras in her face,
bombarding her with a barrage of questions. She could see her pale reflection in several of the lenses. A sea of microphones danced before her eyes.

"Miss McClellan, do you have a comment for our viewers?"

"Move aside," Maddox snarled. The impeccably dressed journalist
thinned her lips and stepped back.

"Were you mistreated by the Navy SEAL who abducted you?" asked
another voice.

Eryn jerked to a stop, her temper ignited by the ridiculous and tactless
question.

"Not now," Jackson grated. Using his broad shoulders to clear a path,
he escorted her toward two men dressed like the soldiers she and Ike had
encountered in the forest. The armed men stepped aside, revealing a door
marked Sheriff's Office. Jackson pulled it open and propelled her inside.
They collided with two men on their way out, Jackson's colleagues, Ringo
and Caine.

Both men looked startled to see them.

"You found her!" Ringo exclaimed.

The fair-haired agent who was their supervisor divided an incredulous gaze between them, his nostrils flaring. "Where in hell have you been, Rookie?" he demanded. "How the fuck did you find her?"

"I've already told you, sir, that I won't tolerate being cursed at, especially not with a lady present," Jackson retorted, ignoring the man's question.

"Don't get smart with me, Rookie." The supervisor's pale eyes narrowed. "Now, what's going on behind my back?"

In what was clearly a gesture of solidarity, Jackson looped a casual arm over Eryn's shoulders. "Nothing, sir. Miss McClellan called my cell phone, and I went to pick her up."

"Is that right?" The man's complexion turned an unbecoming shade of red. "Then where the hell is Calhoun?" he grated.

"No idea, sir," Jackson said, easily.

It was all Eryn could do to conceal her gratitude. She hadn't realized Jackson had picked her up without the other agents' knowledge. She looked down at the floor to keep her satisfaction from showing.

Caine finally addressed her, forcing her to look up. "How are you feeling, Eryn?"

His concern sounded so forced in the wake of his disgust that she heard herself retort, "Do you honestly care?"

The agent wearing glasses sniggered, drawing Caine's wrathful attention. He looked back at Eryn, his cheek muscle twitching. "Well, of course, I care. What kind of question is that?" He shifted his focus back on Jackson and lips thinned with resolve. "Hand over your phone, Rookie," he demanded, thrusting out a hand.

Jackson surrendered it impassively. Eryn watched the exchange with concern.

"Take her down to the Sheriff's Office," Caine ordered, while accessing Jackson's call history. "We'll find Calhoun ourselves."

Concern weighted Eryn's footsteps as Jackson pulled her toward a set of stairs. As they started down them, Eryn overheard Caine add, "Ringo, find out where this call was made and send the airborne HRT unit to that location."

She would have turned back and pleaded for Ike's freedom, but Jackson hushed her, sending her a reassuring look.

"Don't worry," he murmured. "He's long gone, Eryn. Trust me on this. They won't get to him in time."

As they entered the musty-smelling basement, she mulled over Jackson's assertion. If anyone could disappear into thin air, it was Ike. But to think of him as "long gone" did nothing to bolster her spirits. At least, he would get to keep his honor and his freedom, she cheered herself. Plus, he had taught her to be courageous, to face the future on her own.

But who would teach him how to share his feelings and accept the love and admiration he obviously felt unworthy of?

CHAPTER SIXTEEN

Over the heads of the crowd in Elkton Town Hall's parking lot, Farshad caught sight of his target's burnished head. "Keep driving," he said to Shahbaz as the youth drove slowly past the building. Farshad's heart warmed with exaltation.

Praise to Allah! Not only had the National Guard departed just as he and Shahbaz arrived, but Allah had led him straight to the Enemy's treasure, sparing them the difficulty of locating her amidst this crush of people.

Shahbaz pressed onward, threading the large car through a street jammed with vans and cars and hundreds of milling pedestrians. "Teacher!" he exclaimed suddenly, and Farshad saw what troubled him. A deputy was directing traffic up ahead.

"Keep calm," Farshad urged. "If he asks, we are car salesmen."

As the deputy waved them through, they held their breaths against his careful scrutiny. In spite of his suspicious gaze, he let them pass. Shahbaz wiped his brow with a stained sleeve.

Farshad caught sight of a warehouse abutting the railroad tracks. "Park over there," he instructed. The brick structure stood deserted on this Saturday afternoon, its cargo doors firmly shut. As they eased between the empty loading docks, he powered down his laptop and pulled out his copy of the *Qu'ran* tucked inside his briefcase.

"What do we do now?" Shahbaz asked, turning off the engine.

"We reflect and we pray," said Farshad flipping through the worn pages to find the passage he had memorized. Having performed this brainwashing ritual numerous times with the newest generation of Taliban recruits, he did not necessarily need to read it.

"Hear the words of Allah: *Whosoever shall oppose Allah and His Prophet shall be severely punished. Therefore cut off their heads, and strike off all the ends of the fingers. This shall they suffer because they have opposed Allah and His Prophet.*"

"*We* shall punish them!" Shahbaz agreed, thumping the steering wheel with the palm of his hand.

Farshad reached inside his briefcase and retrieved the pistol he had stolen from Mustafa Masoud's bedside. Through their email exchanges, he had learned that, in addition to violent video games, Shahbaz was a paintball aficionado. As such, he was capable of firing a weapon with moderate competence.

Not too well, though. Farshad didn't want him killing the target—though he would not tell Shahbaz that. He needed the boy to be his scapegoat. Once the FBI believed they had stopped the man hunting her, the security around Miss McClellan would ease, giving Farshad more of an opportunity to capture her.

"For me?" The boy's eyes widened.

"The time has come to glorify Allah and to take back the Cradle of Islam," Farshad intoned.

Shahbaz turned the gun over in his grease-stained hands and said nothing.

Farshad flipped the pages and read again, "*Allah has purchased of the believers their persons and their goods; for theirs is the garden of Paradise: they fight in his cause, and slay and be slain.* You must be willing to give your life, Shahbaz."

The youth's expression darkened. He did not look up.

"When you shoot the target, you will be killed instantly by those protecting her," Farshad admitted. "You will not suffer," he promised. "You will ensure your salvation as a martyr for Allah. Trust me, if you were taken alive, you would be tortured and questioned by the FBI. You would be forced to betray your brothers in faith." *Namely me,* he added silently. "You would be cast into eternal damnation!"

"But I would never betray them," Shahbaz insisted.

Farshad made no comment. "Do you believe in the holy scripture?" he inquired.

"Yes, yes."

"You would not wish for Allah to punish you, would you, Shahbaz? You would not wish to die the way Itzak died."

The boy's frown froze into a look of fear. "It was you who killed Itzak," he realized, his eyes rising to regard Farshad in horror.

"He deserved it," Farshad answered simply.

Thoughts flickered in Shahbaz's eyes.

"Think of what you have to gain," Farshad continued. "You will be greeted in Paradise by seventy-two virgins. You will never have to suffer humiliation, pain or poverty again."

Memories flickered in the boy's eyes: memories of a tortured life, of disillusionment and discrimination. At last, his eyelids fluttering, he met Farshad's gaze. "Tell me what to do," he said with youthful determination, "and I will do it."

* * *

Caine's cell phone rang, jolting Eryn's heart. She held her breath as he answered, dreading the news that Ike had been apprehended by the HRT unit. But as his face fell with disappointment, her anxiety subsided. Ike had eluded the law, yet again.

Knowing he was safe gave her the courage to speak up. "I want to make a statement to the press," she said the minute Caine put his phone away.

An awkward silence filled the narrow room. Between the high windows and the poor ventilation, she'd begun to feel like she was sitting in a prison cell, only she hadn't been granted a phone call yet.

"No." It was Jackson who answered from his seat on the other side of the table. "Absolutely not."

"It's not a good idea," seconded Ringo.

"Wait a minute." Caine waved them into silence. A crafty look usurped his frown of disapproval. "Let's hear what Miss McClellan wants to say to the press."

She sat up straighter, lifted her chin in the air. "I want to clear Ike's name." Her gritty eyes burned from lack of sleep. Her head throbbed, but she refused to accept their offer of a motel bed as long as the man she loved was being maligned.

"Sir." Jackson all but growled the word. "Can I have a word with you in the hall?"

"I don't need your input, Rookie," Caine shot back.

"What about my input?" said the second agent on a strained note. "Sir, this story's been in the news all day. That's plenty of time for the terrorists to have seen her on TV."

Caine sent Ringo a reprimanding look. "Now, don't say that. You'll scare her." His gaze swung back toward Eryn. "At this given moment, we have over forty HRT soldiers patrolling the town. You're completely safe, Miss McClellan."

Neither Jackson nor Ringo seemed to agree, but Eryn wasn't as concerned about terrorists right now as she was about Ike's reputation. He was already burdened by guilt for what had happened in Afghanistan. He didn't deserve to have the media calling him a kidnapper.

"I just need to make a statement," she insisted.

"We can arrange that," Caine said, sounding as if he relished the limelight. Turning to Ringo, he instructed him to advise the press of her decision. As the man took reluctant leave, Caine looked back across the table at Eryn. "So, where do you think Ike, as you call him, is at this moment?"

"I have no idea," she answered with a heavy heart. He'd been planning to hand her off, anyway. Maybe he hadn't followed her as she'd first supposed. What made her think he'd want to stick around to watch events unfold, anyway?

* * *

The cellular tower on Highway 33 was by far the tallest structure within Elkton's city limits. Buffeted by a breeze that blew an evening thunderstorm closer, Ike climbed the tower's inner ladder to its pinnacle, two hundred feet off the ground. Throwing one leg over a rung, he grubbed in his pack for his field glasses.

He'd avoided all roadways by four-wheeling through pastureland. Nor did he wish to test his luck by trying to sneak past a glut of reporters in broad daylight. With his face all over the news, he'd be recognized eventually. For now, this was the closest he dared to get.

Peering through his field glasses, he quickly located the RV owned by the Feds, made glaringly apparent by its size and shiny appearance. Parked alongside it, in front of the Sheriff's Office, was the green Taurus he'd followed earlier.

The activity teeming around Town Hall made his gut coil. North Stuart Avenue was jammed with vehicles all parked fender to fender in a town that hadn't seen this much activity since Stonewall Jackson headquartered here during the Civil War.

Blue lights flashed at every street corner as police directed traffic. Spectators and media personnel thronged the nearby shops and restaurants, all awaiting a follow-up report on Eryn McClellan's so-called abduction and recovery.

The crowd infuriated Ike. Her story had been on the news all day. The odds were extremely high that, amidst all those reporters and thrill-seekers, there were gun-toting or bomb-carrying terrorists just waiting for Eryn to make an appearance.

God damn it!

The wind gusted suddenly, and he shot out a hand to keep his seat. This was exactly the kind of situation Stanley would have wanted to avoid.

The buzz of an incoming helicopter had Ike peering through his field glasses over the treetops.

The MH-6 Little Bird that had chased them earlier that day slowed over a field outside of town and nestled onto it. An armored vehicle drew up alongside it to collect the crew as they leapt off the exterior benches. Then the vehicle took off with the added personnel, lumbering down 340 toward Elkton, blaring its horn to clear traffic.

At first Ike was relieved to note the heightened security. But then he considered that it was probably in response to a corresponding increase in threat-level. He counted a total of twenty four soldiers as they jumped out of the vehicle. Half went to work clearing a perimeter around Town Hall. The other half disappeared into nearby buildings, popping out on rooftops, where they positioned themselves over the crowd.

Such precautions could only mean one thing: Eryn was due to make an appearance, possibly even speak to the press. Christ, could he trust any of those soldiers to pick out a terrorist in a crowd? He needed to get the *hell* over there before the worst possible scenario took place.

* * *

Shahbaz tugged down the brim of his baseball cap, concealing his dark eyes. The Teacher had sent him into a drugstore with a wad of cash to transform his appearance. He had bought a baseball cap, a T-shirt, shorts, and a sweat shirt with a large pocket in front, in which he stowed the gun. Figuring he looked like any other American youth, he had returned to the car, only to be banished to the drugstore once again for shaving cream and a razor. In the employee restroom, he had shaved the five o'clock shadow that darkened his already swarthy complexion. The Teacher had taken one more look at him and nodded his approval.

Now, blending seamlessly into the crowd, Shahbaz eyed the ominous clouds that billowed closer, turning the sky a charcoal gray. The rumor that Miss McClellan intended to make a statement rippled from the front of the crowd to the back. The impending storm reflected Shahbaz's agitation. All his life he had idolized martyrs for their courage and sacrifice. He had imagined what it must be like to go out in a blaze of glory while making such a clear statement of protest.

Death wasn't such a terrible thing, provided it came swiftly. It was life that was hard, a grueling struggle for income, a hopeless battle against prejudice. Death had to be easier, especially if the scriptures could be believed, and all those virgins would be there, fulfilling his every desire.

The crowd pushed closer to the building, shrinking the clearing that the soldiers fought to maintain. Shahbaz joined them, jostling for a better view.

His gaze flicked to the soldiers positioned on the rooftops. When he took his shot, the crowd would scatter, and bullets from those snipers would end his life, whether he managed to kill the girl or not. Hitting a target with a paintball wasn't the same as hitting one with a bullet. His hands had never trembled playing paintball.

Abruptly, the door on which every eye was fixed flew open. Thunder rumbled in the distance. With an electrical current dancing in the air, the Commander's daughter stepped out, escorted by men in dark suits. Shahbaz vied for a view of her. He was surprised to discover that, even with her tawny hair in disarray, wearing nothing but a white T-shirt and jeans, she appealed to him.

"Miss McClellan would like to make a public announcement," shouted an agent.

Microphones extended on poles swung into the clearing. An expectant hush fell over the crowd as the woman's face appeared between her body guards shoulders. They remained in front of her, like human shields, so that only her head was exposed.

Shahbaz slipped a moist hand inside his pocket. As his fingers curled around the cool pistol, his attention was drawn to the LCD panel on the camera in front of him, and he stared in wonder. Why, the target's eyes were the color of pottery glazed in Karachi, a lovely purple-blue!

When she opened her mouth to speak, he found himself straining to hear her words.

"Thank you all for your concern, but I was never in any kind of danger. I want to make it clear that the FBI's hunt for Isaac Calhoun was misguided. He was chosen by my father to protect me. He is a hero, a friend, and his privacy should be respected. Thank you."

Shouted questions followed immediately on the heels of her statement.

"No questions." The dark-skinned agent threw an arm around her, drawing her away from the crowd. Moving as a unit, the agents hustled her toward the immense silver motor coach parked strategically nearby.

Adrenaline fueled Shahbaz's heart to a gallop. The chance to kill the Commander's daughter was evaporating like the streams in the Rigistan Desert.

Now, Shahbaz, now! He willed himself to draw his pistol, to aim at the part of her that he could still see and squeeze the trigger. Only, the memory of her eyes kept him spellbound.

And then it was too late. She had disappeared into the motor coach, and the crowd was beginning to disperse.

Distress grappled with relief as Shahbaz stood in one place, jostled by the parting crowd.

The Teacher's furious face leapt before him. He grabbed Shahbaz's arm and tugged him in the direction of their car. "Hurry! We can't let them get away."

Dreading the Teacher's wrath, but giddy to be still alive, Shahbaz hastened after him.

* * *

Ike lowered his rifle just as raindrops started pelting the tiles of the rooftop on which he lay. Arriving at the edge of town, he'd climbed to the height of a towering Victorian. Just as he'd hoped, he was able to scrutinize the crowd at Town Hall through his scope while hiding from the soldiers patrolling the nearby rooftops.

Within minutes of crawling to the height of the steep roof, he'd seen Eryn exit the building. All he could make out was the top of her head. The crowd around her grew hushed, as if listening, but if she spoke at all, the sound of her voice was carried off by the breeze.

With his finger crooked over the trigger, Ike had scanned the crowd incessantly, ready to drop anyone who showed the least hint of aggression.

To his dizzying relief, no one had.

In the next instant, Eryn was being escorted toward the FBI's RV. Jackson stuffed her into the motor coach so quickly that Ike never caught a glimpse of her face. Jealousy vied with gratitude as he acknowledged Jackson's vigilance. At least someone in the FBI was doing his damn job. But as long as they considered her bait for terrorists, her future remained uncertain.

He couldn't let that motor coach out of his sight.

Looping his rifle strap over his shoulder, Ike let go and slid on his belly toward the gutter, where he caught himself on the sturdy lattice work below it. Rain soaked through his clothing as he swung down onto a second story balcony. The occupants of the home all appeared to be out. Braving the long leap onto the wet grass, he rolled to break his fall and came up running.

Chris's Jeep was parked a hundred yards away, hidden out of sight in a deep ditch. Sprinting through the downpour, Ike set his mind on finding and following the RV before it disappeared on him.

* * *

"You weak-minded fool."

The Teacher's lecture made Shahbaz burn with resentment as he drove them out of town. The windshield wipers slapped a frenzied tempo, doing little to clear the blurred view of dozens of taillights up ahead, including those of the FBI's motor coach, which they were following. "Why didn't you take the shot?" the man raged.

Shahbaz gripped the steering wheel. He could not explain his hesitation. He'd always believed that martyrdom was glorious. But it required more courage than he'd realized. He wanted nothing to do with it now. He was too weak. Until tonight, his target had been a faceless entity, a worthless woman. It had never occurred to him she would be so...pretty.

"Don't forget what happened to Itzak," the Teacher threatened him again.

A droplet of rainwater slid inside of Shahbaz's collar and down his neck. He darted his companion a look, wondering what would happen if he pulled out the pistol now, aimed it at the man's head, and blew his brains out. This martyring business would be over then, wouldn't it?

The sound of a switchblade ringing free brought his fantasy up short. The tip of it gouged the soft flesh beneath his jaw. In the next instant, the Teacher was reaching across him, taking the gun from the pocket of his sweat suit. Shahbaz's bravado went with it.

"I understand your cowardice, son," hissed the older man, even as he sliced through the first layer of skin. The steering wheel wobbled in Shahbaz's grip. "You have lived for years among the infidels. You've been tainted by their corruption. But for your mortal soul's sake you must be obedient to Allah, or you will face his chastisement, just as it is written."

Shahbaz concentrated on not crashing. Sweat bathed his pores.

At last, the blade was withdrawn. He heaved a sigh of relief, watching wistfully as the gun went back into the Teacher's briefcase.

"Do not let the motor coach out of your sight," the man cautioned, his voice gentle once more. "We will watch and wait. When the opportunity to kill her arises, you will then ensure your salvation."

* * *

The last thing Ike expected was for the FBI's RV to turn into the Elkton Motel. As it eased off Highway 33, he barreled past it, rainwater spraying off the Jeep's wide tires. He drove half a mile farther before executing a quick U-turn. But he didn't go back to the motel. Instead, he turned up the driveway of an adjacent property and extinguished his lights.

The house at the end of the driveway appeared abandoned. He veered off the pavement onto the unkempt lawn, rounded the unattached garage, and bumped his way across a wet field.

Back-dropped by trees that kept him camouflaged, he could see the rear of the motel clearly. Between the separated units, he spotted the FBI's RV, already parked. He stopped where he had the clearest view of it, killed the engine, and lowered his window.

Just then, Eryn dashed from the RV into a motel room, her purse over her head. The sight of her filled him with yearning, relief, and a steely determination. The door closed, putting her in the company of two agents, he guessed, as the third one, Jackson, took Winston for a walk in the rain.

Jealousy gnawed at Ike. Winston was *his* dog; he'd spent hours training him.

Once they'd paced the perimeter of the motel, the agent put Winston back into the RV. He then knocked on the motel room door. Two agents came out carrying duffel bags and went into the room next door, leaving Eryn alone with Jackson.

Ike scowled. Whose idea was this? Why hadn't they just continued on to Washington, instead of staying one more night in a town that had been put on the map today by the media?

Raindrops spattered the Jeep's canvas roof as he assessed Eryn's safety. The helicopter had departed a while ago. The armored truck was probably halfway back to Quantico by now. All she had were three armed agents to protect her. At least the rooms had no windows in the rear, and local law enforcement could be summoned in a heartbeat.

But Ike didn't like it. Staying in Elkton wasn't smart. Stanley wouldn't like it either. He considered calling the Commander to reassure him. He had to be frantic by now, having seen his daughter on the news, back in FBI custoody. But the NSA would be monitoring Ike's registered cell phone at the FBI's behest. They would pinpoint his location at once if he used it. Too bad he'd thrown away that prepaid phone in a fit of frustration. Could've used it now.

The motel's neon sign blinked on suddenly, finding colorful reflection in the RV's steel hull. Picturing Eryn alone with the agent whose business card she kept in her purse, Ike wrestled with envy.

He missed her. Her scent still clung to him from their lovemaking. Memories spooled in his mind, feeding the hunger to keep her. He'd known it would be this way.

Isolation crept over him. He couldn't believe he used to enjoy his solitude. Now he just felt cheated.

In an attempt to lighten his spirits, he turned on the radio. The tail end of a news summary had him turning up the volume.

In a brief statement to the press, Miss McClellan confirmed what locals have insisted all along: that the former Navy SEAL wanted for questioning by the FBI had been protecting her. Here is what Miss McClellan had to say about him:

Eryn's voice, coming out of the radio, made Ike hold his breath. "He is a hero, a friend, and his privacy should be respected." The words quenched him like a warm summer shower.

With the search called off, things are returning to normal here in the Shenandoah Valley. Up next, Mozart's Piano Concerto, Number 24 in C minor.

As mournful notes filled the Jeep's interior, Ike shut the radio off, stunned.

He's a hero, a friend. He held the words like a treasure, saving them for later comfort, along with her earlier confession. *I love you, Ike.*

In less than a week, Eryn had turned his world inside out. Before he'd met her, he could hardly face himself in the mirror; dreaded the endless, sleepless nights in which his dead teammates demanded to know why he had quit the fight and made their sacrifice meaningless. The weight of his guilt had kept him paralyzed, unable to move forward.

But now he was ready to walk that road to redemption. Eryn's essence would light the way.

Moisture stung Ike's eyes as he peered through the curtain of rain at the motel door, envisioning her inside. Maybe, if he survived the treacherous months to come, he would one day answer her words with a confession of his own.

CHAPTER SEVENTEEN

Brad Caine sat by the motel window, his bleary gaze fixed on the rain-drenched parking lot. Since it was easier to stay awake than to rouse from a deep sleep, he'd assigned himself first watch. The day's events coming on the heels of last night's failed rescue made his eyelids heavy. It didn't help any that the neon sign outside infused the billions of raindrops with hypnotizing color.

He couldn't afford to fall asleep. The report that Shahbaz Wahidi had eluded the agents trailing him meant a terrorist was on the loose, free to target the Commander's daughter. Brad had thought for certain he would strike during her media address, but the tight security must have deterred him—hence Brad's decision to release HRT to return to Quantico. He couldn't make this any easier for the fucker.

So far, however, there was no suspicious activity around the motel. Ringo had run all the tags in the parking lot, and they'd all come up clean. The hotel guests appeared to be in their rooms, lights out, sleeping.

Brad ordered himself to stay alert. Something *had* to happen. He would never get promoted if he didn't make an arrest soon.

* * *

Cruising past the motel every thirty minutes, Shahbaz waited, just as the Teacher had instructed, for all the lights in the rooms to go out.

The Teacher had been able to rent a room without arousing suspicion. But Shahbaz, who drove the stolen Pontiac, had been instructed to circle the area until the early hours of dawn. Hungry and cold, he drove aimlessly along dark, adjacent roadways. But he did not abandon the Teacher as he had considered doing earlier, for he rather liked the Teacher's new plan which eliminated the need to martyr himself.

When all was still and dark, Shahbaz would park the Pontiac near the motel, take the tools and the length of copper wire they had purchased at a hardware store, and crawl under the FBI's RV. Once there, he would run the wire from the ignition to the fuel tank, which he would puncture, inserting the wire inside it. When an agent turned over the engine in the morning, the RV would blow sky high. With any luck, their victim would be inside it.

Shahbaz let loose a punchy giggle. The prospect of blowing up the RV kept his weariness at bay. Any hour now he would avenge America for her false promise of the American Dream. And the best part was he didn't have to die to publicize his disillusionment.

* * *

The bark of a dog, familiar in pitch and quality, roused Ike from a light slumber as he allowed himself to rest while still remaining vigilant. *Winston?*

The Jeep's fogged windows obscured a light drizzle. He glanced at his watch. It was just after four in the morning, and the clouds would keep things dark for another hour.

Lowering the driver's side window, he breathed in the cold, wet air to sharpen his dulled senses. As he peered across the sweet-smelling field toward the motel, he wondered if he'd imagined Winston's bark. The scene looked much as it had in the hours preceding midnight, when he'd allowed himself to cat nap. But then the dog barked again.

Lifting the rifle propped beside him, Ike poked it out the window and peered through his scope. His blood froze at the sight of a man lying on the pavement, under the RV.

Who the hell?

Ike held him in his crosshairs. Was it one of the agents checking out a problem? Or could it be a terrorist, up to no good? There was only one way to find out. And the fastest way to do it was to drive across the field, counting on the rain to muffle the approach of his engine.

Easing away from the tree line, Ike kept the lights off as he forged across of field of what looked like seedling watermelons. He kept his gaze fixed on the shadow under the RV, hoping to identify him. To his disappointment, the man saw him coming, stilled, then abruptly squirmed out the far side of the RV.

Not a special agent, obviously, Ike deduced, gunning the engine.

With his lights off, he didn't see the low cement barrier edging the parking lot. The Jeep hurtled over it, bouncing him in his seat. When he landed on the other side, he caught sight of the suspect jumping into a car at the edge of the motel.

Ike swerved toward him. He could hear Winston barking. The doors to the FBI's units sprang open. Lights flared, casting a burgundy Pontiac into relief as it squealed out of sight. Ike pursued it. A glance in his rearview mirror showed two FBI agents racing for their Taurus.

And the chase is on, Ike thought, focusing on the car flying down the rain-slick highway ahead of him. The driver had turned east, where the road curved upward into the Shenandoah National Forest. Switching on his headlights, Ike snapped on his seatbelt in preparation for the steep, twisting inclines up ahead.

There appeared to be just one man in the getaway vehicle, a circumstance that disturbed him. There could be more back at the motel. With two agents in hot pursuit, that left just one man guarding Eryn.

Not good enough.

Groping in his pack, Ike located his trusty satellite phone, thumbed it open, and dialed 9-1-1, relaying a message to Sheriff Olsen through the operator that he was needed at Elkton Motel. So what if NSA picked up his phone call on their satellite. The FBI was right behind him anyway.

Tossing his phone back into his pack, he depressed the accelerator to the floor in an effort to overtake the car ahead of him. Only the old Jeep's four-cylinder engine lacked power to accelerate on such a steep incline. The Taurus behind him battled a similar problem. The six-cylinder Pontiac was outstripping them both.

God damn it, Ike thought, uncomfortable with the fact that he was moving farther and farther away from Eryn. He'd never wished so badly that he could be in two places at once.

* * *

Caught in a state halfway between sleeping and waking, Eryn was disturbed by her dog's disruptive barking. "Quiet, Winston," she mumbled, burying her head beneath the pillow.

Her subconscious tried to rouse her, but exhaustion kept her in a stupor. She heard the door open, felt a breath of cool air on the tops of her shoulders. Engines revved and roared. Tires squealed. A male voice barking out orders made her drag the pillow off her head. What the heck was going on? She cracked an eye to find a light on and Jackson's bed empty. Special Agent Caine stood by the window putting on a bullet-proof vest.

"Make sure you catch Calhoun this time," he snarled into his cell phone. "Better put him in handcuffs."

Eryn came wider awake at the mention of Ike's name. "What's happening?" she demanded. "Where's Jackson?"

Caine cranked his head around. "Arresting your boyfriend," he said with a nasty smile and putting his phone away. "Time to get up," he added. "We're moving to the RV."

"Why? What happened?"

"There's been an incident," he announced, his eyes bright with excitement.

The word *incident* pulled more of the wool from Eryn's mind. "What kind of incident?" she asked, snatching up the jeans folded on the foot of her bed and slipping them on beneath the covers.

"It's too soon to tell, but we're moving to the RV." Caine peeked under the curtains, looking out the window. "Hurry up," he said, sounding nervous.

"Can I use the rest room first?"

"There's no time for that. Use the one in the RV."

"Why are we moving to the RV?"

"Because it's armored," he retorted, making her think of bombs and bullets, causing her heart to palpitate. He wheeled from the window as she jammed on her shoes.

"I want to know what's going on," she insisted as he seized her arm in a bruising grip and hauled her toward the door.

"Not now. I'll explain later."

As he cracked the door open, peering outside with a wary eye, Eryn was surprised to see a pink sunrise burnishing the tin roofs of the other motel units. It felt like she had just fallen asleep. With his gun drawn, Caine drew her out after him.

Crisp, clean air brought her fully awake as he hustled her toward the RV. Inside, she could hear Winston issuing evenly spaced barks, like a car alarm.

As the agent turned a key and scanned his thumbprint on the biometric padlock, Eryn searched the quiet parking lot. The owners of the half-dozen cars appeared to be sleeping through the excitement.

"Go on in." He swung the door open. "I have to take a quick look around."

Climbing into the RV's dark interior, she ran into Winston, who greeted her enthusiastically. The door closed behind her and locked shut. Calming her excited dog, Eryn felt her way into the galley, which housed a kitchen on one side, a seating area on the other. Unable to find a light switch, she raised one of the blinds, admitting soft pink sunlight and catching sight of Caine, who was bending over, inspecting the underside of the RV.

Something must have caught his eye, for in the next instant, he was down on his hands and knees, crawling under the chassis. At the same time, a slender figure detached itself from the shadows between two units and approached him. As she watched him, sunlight glinted on a pair of spectacles. She determined it must be Ringo.

A clanking sound had her looking down at her feet. What was Caine up to, down there? With a puzzled shrug, she turned toward the tiny restroom beyond the galley to empty her bladder.

She was just pulling up her jeans when a scream unlike anything she'd heard curdled her blood. *Caine!*

An ominous growl rumbled in Winston's throat as the scream curtailed abruptly. Eryn rocketed out of the restroom only to pull up short, uncertain what to do. She strained to hear over her thudding heart.

There came a muffled thump and a sliding sound. Winston prowled toward the door, his hackles rising. The lock gave a click and the door swung open.

A glimpse of Caine's blond hair had her releasing her held breath, but then he slumped out of sight, and a stranger stepped over him. As he leapt nimbly into the RV, his face still in shadow, the air surged back into Eryn's lungs. Her blood froze as she recognized his silhouette.

The taxi driver.

Shock rooted her. He was older than she'd imagined, with salt-and-pepper hair, a hooked nose, and an oddly benign countenance. He closed the door behind him, holding up a blood-streaked knife. Caine's blood, Eryn realized, nearly fainting. In his free hand, he carried a briefcase.

Suddenly, with a loud snarl, Winston lunged at the man, just the way Ike had taught him.

"Winston, no!" Eryn flew into action, grabbing her dog around his midsection and pulling him away from the terrorist's flashing blade.

Winston's claws scrabbled on the fiberglass flooring as he fought her hold.

"Get him away!" ordered the stranger, sounding panicked. He glanced briefly at the blood appearing on his forearm then pointed with the knife at the bedroom behind her. "Both of you. In there, now," he said, in peculiar-sounding English.

She was quick to obey him. Menacing the dog's nose with his bloody knife, the terrorist pursued them. Eryn tried snatching up her purse as they passed the restroom, but with the knife so close to Winston's nose, she opted for retreat.

No sooner had they entered the dark recesses of the back room than the terrorist slammed the door in her face and locked it from the outside.

Get help. The words seemed to come from a part of her brain that remained untouched by the drama.

Eryn cast her gaze about. Beams of sunlight skimmed through the cracks at the edges of the blinds. In lieu of a bedroom, she found herself in a space crammed with consoles, computers, and monitors. Hence, the lock on the outside of the door, keeping out unauthorized persons.

Spying a phone on the far wall, she lunged for it, only to hang it up again in despair when she heard no dial tone. The cell she'd taken from the vineyard had been confiscated yesterday. Even if she had her purse with her, she'd have no way of getting help.

A throaty rumble and a sudden vibration under her feet robbed her of logical thought. In the distance, she heard the wail of an approaching siren, but her relief was short-lived, for the RV lurched suddenly into movement. She stumbled, falling into one of the seats bolted to the floor.

Numbness seeped into her bloodstream, desensitizing her to the situation at hand, but also silencing the reasonable voice inside her head. She felt detached, like this was happening to someone else, only she knew it wasn't.

Her mind looped away to the haunting dreams of her nightmares. Was this real or was she dreaming? She'd been abducted by the terrorist who'd killed Itzak. The man had plunged a knife into Caine without hesitation, just because he could. There wasn't a doubt that he would kill her just as heartlessly.

As the RV gained speed and swerved out of the motel parking lot, the sound of the siren grew more and more faint. Her hope diminished with it. The police had failed to intercept the RV. Nor would Ike be coming to her rescue, not if the FBI was arresting him. All she had was Winston, who leaned heavily against her legs, panting as if he'd gone for a long run. She was utterly alone.

Tears of terror clouded her vision. Her throat felt tight as she tried to swallow the lump that threatened to choke her. "God, help me," she croaked.

* * *

There was only one way to stop the Pontiac before it lured them farther from Eryn.

Ike tugged on the zipper that kept the Jeep's canopy secured. It flapped loudly in the chilly breeze. Then with a ripping sound, it pulled away from the zipper and sailed out of sight.

The frigid air stung Ike's eyes and numbed his ears. Drawing his Python from the holster under his arm, he negotiated another sharp turn with his left hand while releasing the safety with his right. All four tires squealed. When he finally hit a straightaway, he strained upward in his seat, aiming over the windshield at the Pontiac's right rear tire.

Crack! One discharge from his double-action revolver shattered the Pontiac's taillight. *Crack!* The second round punctured the rear tire.

With a shriek of rubber on slick asphalt, the Pontiac slid into an embankment at over fifty miles an hour. Ike saw what was coming next and winced. Sparks flew into the air as the vehicle careened into the guard rail. It bounced off it and wobbled wildly to the other side of the road where it plowed headlong into a wall of blasted granite. *Crash!*

Slowing to avoid the spray of metal and glass, Ike swerved onto the opposite shoulder and set the parking brake. With his gun still drawn, he leaped from the Jeep and sprinted toward the crumpled vehicle.

The driver's side of the car was stove in. Anyone in the front seat had to be dead. With his gun still drawn, he took a peek and saw a disfigured body covered in blood that gleamed wetly in the rosy light of dawn. The airbag had failed to deploy.

Ike dropped his gun and turned away. Christ, he hadn't meant for that to happen. He'd have preferred for the terrorist to rot in jail.

With a bitter taste in his mouth, he noted the Taurus pulling up behind his Jeep, catching the accident and his lone figure in the full glare of its high beams. "Freeze!" shouted a voice. "FBI. Drop the weapon and back away from the vehicle. Put your hands on your head!"

Fuck it. Ike let the Python clatter onto the roadway, where a river of oil had begun to ooze downhill. "Set some flares," he cautioned, "before we cause another accident." Backing away from his weapon, he laced his hands together on top of his head and struck a docile pose.

"I'll get them," said a second voice.

"You." The first agent approached him warily, gun pointed at Ike's chest. His hair looked tussled, and his glasses sat askew on his narrow nose. He warily snatched up Ike's weapon then peeked into the crushed car. "What the hell did you do? Jesus." He averted his gaze.

"He was tampering with your RV." Ike assessed the man automatically. "Call your leader. Warn him about the RV. Tell him not to start it."

The tussled agent just stared at him, then looked to his partner, who jogged up to him, handing him two lit flares.

"Isaac Calhoun?" It was the agent he'd shot at. The man stuck out a hand unexpectedly. "Jackson Maddox."

Noting that he'd omitted his title of special agent, Ike accepted the man's firm handshake.

"Maddox," said the first man. "Look who the driver is." He held up a flare so his partner could see inside.

Jackson winced and looked away. "Shahbaz Wahidi." He flicked Ike a grim look. "We could have used him alive."

"Didn't mean to kill him," said Ike, experiencing very little remorse. "He was pulling away from us. We need to get back to Eryn." In that exact moment, he detected the wail of sirens coming from both directions.

"You can stand at ease," Jackson said, betraying his military background. "Just don't try anything."

Ike lowered his arms. "Call your other man," he urged again. "Tell him not to start the RV. "

"I heard you," the agent said, reaching for his phone. "Don't worry. The LE was on their way when we left."

That's because I fucking called them, Ike thought with exasperation. Anxiety made his blood pressure rise. He hated feeling helpless.

Instead of reaching for his phone, Jackson pulled out a set of handcuffs. "Sorry, but I was told to bring you in," he said with a grimace.

"Just make the fucking call." Ike didn't care what happened to him. It was Eryn who was vulnerable right now.

CHAPTER EIGHTEEN

"Caine's still not answering," Ringo stated, as they flew down the winding highway back to Elkton Motel.

Jackson flicked a nervous glance in the rearview mirror. Isaac Calhoun sat in the middle of the seat behind him with his hands cuffed behind his back, his green stare fixed on Jackson through the mirror. They had called their supervisor two times already at Calhoun's urging. The tendons in the man's neck were standing out, his jaw muscles jumping.

"Maybe he can't get cell reception," Jackson suggested in an attempt to dispel the man's palpable concern.

Or maybe Wahidi wasn't alone in targeting Eryn.

The unspoken possibility was etched all over the former SEAL's taut face, making Jackson nervous as hell. It was all he could do to concentrate on getting them down into the valley without swerving off a cliff. His phone rang unexpectedly, making him heave a private sigh of relief. That had to be Caine.

But he didn't recognize the number. "Special Agent Maddox," he clipped, slowing on a particularly tight turn. All four tires squealed.

"Yes, this is Hugh, the paramedic?"

"What have you got?" Before they'd left the crash site, Jackson had tasked one of the paramedics to type Wahidi's blood in the hopes that it matched the blood on the holly bushes, left by Mustafa Masoud's killer, the same man who'd likely killed four others, including Pedro the Landscaper and Itzak Dharker.

"The victim's blood type is A-negative," the man announced.

Jackson swallowed against a suddenly parched throat. "Thank you." He dropped his phone into his lap. "A-negative," he croaked to Ringo.

"Oh, shit," Ringo exclaimed.

Shit was right. The killer's blood type was O-positive.

"Wahidi didn't kill our asset," Ringo stated aloud.

Jackson tightened his grip on the steering wheel and gunned the accelerator. "Call Caine," he pleaded, avoiding eye contact with the man glaring into his rearview mirror. "Put him on speaker phone. I'll tell him."

In the tense silence now in the car, Caine's phone rang and rang. A rumbling voice not belonging to Caine finally answered. "This is Sheriff Olsen."

"Sheriff?" Jackson flicked the phone in Ringo's hand a puzzled glance. "This is Special Agent Maddox," he said, speaking up in order to be heard. "I was calling for my supervisor."

"He can't take calls at the moment." The Sheriff sounded like he'd been chewing on gravel.

"Why? What happened?" Jackson asked.

"You'll have to see it to believe it."

Goosebumps sprouted all over his body. "Is Miss McClellan there?" He prayed for an affirmative.

"Negative," said the Sheriff.

A glance in the mirror showed Calhoun looking as wound up as a pissed-off rattlesnake.

Jackson wet his lips. "Where's the RV?" he asked.

"Don't see the RV anywhere. Just a body sittin' in a pool of blood next to copper wire and a puddle of gasoline."

"Fuck!" Jackson exclaimed.

"We'll be right there." Ringo said for him, severing the call.

Jackson left twin strips of rubber on the last tight turn. Holding down the horn, he overtook a slower car and swooped into the Shenandoah Valley on the final straightaway. One more mile and they'd be back at the motel.

"We fucked up, didn't we?" Calhoun's voice struck them like the tip of a whip.

At least, the man had included himself in the subject of the sentence. "Yes, we did," Jackson admitted.

* * *

Where is he taking me? Eryn struggled to raise the blinds at the back of the RV.

As her initial shock began to wane, it had occurred to her that she could signal for help through the large rear windows. Surely other drivers would see her and call the police. But once the blinds were raised, the expansive windows revealed nothing but an empty road behind them. It was too early in the morning for commuters to be going to work. Nor would they later because it was Sunday, she realized, stricken by a yawning sense of isolation.

Her gaze fell to the myriad monitors and computers jammed into the tight space. She sought every power button she could find, booting up instruments she couldn't name let alone operate. Who knew, maybe one of them would signal her location.

Abruptly, the RV slowed, turning onto a road that climbed to higher elevations. Forest hemmed it in on both sides. The engine roared to battle the grade. With a stab of poignancy, Eryn thought of Ike's mountain and wondered if she would step foot in his cabin again, ever sleep in his bed, in his arms.

How could I ever forget you? She never wanted to forget.

Shivering with fear and grief, she nonetheless noticed that the powerful engine had begun to sputter. Her breath came in ragged gasps as she watched out the back window, waiting to see what would happen next.

The motor coach was losing momentum. Minute by minute, its speed declined, until it rolled to a crawl, then stopped altogether in the middle of the road.

Eryn's heart seemed to stop, as well. As long as the terrorist had been driving, she'd been safe. But she could hear him now, engaging the parking brake, moving down the length of the RV. He paused in the galley, his stealthy movements terrifying. What the hell was he doing, fixing himself a sandwich?

It was Ike's voice inside her head that seemed to growl this question. She would have given anything, *anything* to have him there in person. Her respite was coming to an end. All too soon, the terrorist would unlock the door and...

She refused to picture what might follow. If she didn't think of something, she would have to fight for her life with her bare hands. Ike had tried to prepare her for this moment. But could anyone truly ever be prepared?

Closing her eyes, taking a deep breath, she tried to remember everything Ike had taught her. All that came back to her was: *Stop and feel, and you'll end up dead.*

* * *

Sitting handcuffed in the rear seat of the Taurus, Ike could see enough of the body being bagged to tell that the blond FBI agent's neck had been slit wide open.

As firefighters went to lay foam on the spilled gasoline, Jackson patted down his pockets, failed to find what he was looking for, and strode back to the car. His swarthy complexion had taken on a yellowish hue. Flicking Ike a wary glance, he reached through the driver's window, found his cell phone, and walked a few yards from the car to make a lengthy phone call.

Ike's temples throbbed. There wasn't any time for lollygagging. The terrorist had taken Eryn away in the RV. They had to fucking find her, *now!*

Finally, Jackson's call ended.

"Take these cuffs off me," Ike demanded, recapturing the agent's attention.

Jackson sent him a distracted look, reached into his pocket, and tossed a set of keys onto the rear seat. He then called Ringo over.

As Ike groped for the keys, awkwardly inserting them into the handcuffs, he could hear Maddox telling Ringo that their field office was trying to ping the phone aboard the RV, but with only one cell tower within a five-mile radius, the signal couldn't be triangulated.

"It'll be like looking for a needle in a haystack," Ringo muttered, jamming his hands into his pockets.

"Hostage Rescue's been alerted," Maddox added. "It'll take them thirty minutes to get a chopper out here."

"We're not waiting thirty minutes." Ike shoved out of the back seat. Fueled by a desperate, nerve-fraying need to take action, he studied the spot where the RV used to be parked. The rank smell of gasoline was in no-way relieved by the foam now billowing across the lot.

Remembering Wahidi under the chassis, Ike realized the leak had been made by him. And given the length of copper wire still lying on the ground, he must have been trying to rig the RV to explode upon ignition. His gaze went to the dark stain zipping out of the compound onto Highway 33.

The gasoline leak was dissolving the asphalt, creating tar. *Well, I'll be damned.* Heart thumping, he swiveled, stalking back to Jackson and Ringo. "We don't need to ping the phone," he said, pointing at the stain on the road. "The RV left a visible trail."

For a full second, Jackson didn't seem to grasp what he was saying, but then his gaze slid up the highway, and he bolted for the driver's seat. "Let's go!"

Ike slapped a hand on the lid of the trunk. "Open up first," he demanded, wanting the weapons and rucksack that had been taken from him.

Jackson hesitated.

"Just do it!" he raged. "Hostage Rescue isn't going to get here in time. I'm the next best thing you've got, Maddox."

Jackson glanced at Ringo, who sent him a short nod, then he released the trunk from inside the car. Ike grabbed up his gear and dove into the back seat. "Go," he growled.

The Taurus rocketed from the parking lot.

Cold, hard determination usurped Ike's earlier agitation. He refused to consider that Eryn could be dead right now, killed in the most horrifying manner possible. God forbid. He'd die inside if he were too late. He would absolutely die. The only acceptable outcome was locating the RV and apprehending the terrorist.

"Drive faster." The verdant pastures mocked him with their expansive apathy.

"Pedal's to the floor," Jackson answered, glancing in the rearview mirror. "They can't have gone more than ten miles, not with the tank leaking like that."

They zipped off Highway 33, following the stain in the asphalt as it arced onto a smaller, winding road, one that climbed toward the height of Green Mountain.

Ike's thoughts went back to the last time he'd hunted terrorists. He'd been forced to watch his fellow teammates fight for their lives and get picked off, one at a time. He'd thought there couldn't be anything more awful. But there was. His men were warriors, trained to fight. Every one of them had taken several combatants' lives before succumbing to his wounds. But Eryn was no warrior. And even with the training he'd given her, she was no match for a man.

"Who is this guy?" he demanded, wanting more information. "What kind of profile do you have on him?"

Jackson and Ringo shared a sheepish look.

"We don't know who he is," Ringo confessed. "If he's the one who bombed the safe house, then he's blown up one civilian and slit the throats of five men already, counting Caine." His voice had become as rough as sandpaper.

"I served in Iraq," Jackson added. "I knew this guy was a fanatic when I saw his handiwork. I don't think he's a national."

A desert-like breeze blew through Ike's mind. "Then you don't mind if I kill him," he said, his tone impassive, his heart devoid of any emotion but justice.

Ringo gave a nervous laugh. Jackson darted Ike a warning look. "*I* don't mind," he said with conviction, "but the FBI needs to question him to make certain there aren't any others."

Ike nodded and went to check his ammunition. He considered their best approach once they came upon the RV. Anything to keep from envisioning what Eryn had to be going through. Don't go there, he ordered himself. Don't fucking feel. But when it came to possibly losing the woman you loved, that was easier said than done.

* * *

With a click that made Eryn jump, the door to the rear room swung open. A rope sailed through the air, landing at her feet.

"Tie up the dog or I will kill him," the terrorist demand, slamming the door shut again.

Eryn eyed the rope as she would a snake. Then she looked at Winston, noting his bared fangs, his bristling coat. She could hear Ike's voice urging her to let the dog attack. Winston was her only weapon. Ike had trained him well, and the terrorist was clearly wary of him.

Only, she couldn't. She couldn't let her loyal Shepherd mix get stabbed because of her. Tears of frustration and fear gushed from her eyes as she bent over and picked up the rope.

Pulling her dog closer, she attached it to the sturdy ring on his collar, praying both the knot and the collar would hold. Then she looped the other end of the rope around the base of the second bolted chair, knotting it as securely as she knew how.

"Five seconds," warned the terrorist through the door, "or I'll shoot him dead."

"It's done," she called in a small voice.

The door opened an inch. As he peeked inside, Winston rushed at him, snarling. The rope pulled taut, catching him back. As the muzzle of a gun appeared, Eryn leapt in front of her dog, defending him. "Please don't do this." In a voice that quaked with fear, she tried negotiating. "I'm not your enemy. I've never meant you any harm."

The man's soft chuckle, brimming with bitterness, made her fall silent. "You are the daughter of my enemy," he replied. Seeing that the rope restrained the dog, he opened the door wider. "Your father killed my son. Did you know that?"

"No." She saw him differently, then, as a father tormented by grief. But then she remembered Itzak, whom this man had killed. Itzak had also had a father. And so had Caine. "I'm sorry about your son," she said, praying that if she kept him talking, she might convince him to abort his plans. "What was his name?"

"Osman. He was a Taliban chieftain, a warrior. Come." He crooked a finger at her. "Come out, or I'll shoot your dog first and then you."

She would rather be shot than to have her head cut off, wouldn't she? And yet, seeing him release the safety, she found herself obeying him, too much a coward to accept a bullet so willingly.

As she edged closer, he seized her, pulling her out the door swiftly. Winston flew into a rage, but the rope caught him back, and then the door shut between them, muffling his distress.

Feeling the gun prod her back, Eryn let herself be propelled toward the galley where she could see that the terrorist had set up a laptop and a webcam on the table. A chill seeped through her veins, turning her blood to ice.

"Sit." He forced her onto the bench in front of the equipment. She was startled to see her pale reflection jump onto the screen. "Look! More than thirty thousand Muslims have logged on to watch your execution," he said, with delight. "Yours shall be the first of many, as my students take back the cradle of Islam from our enemy invaders."

Depositing the gun inside the open briefcase on the opposite counter, he transferred his grip to her hair. The blade with which he'd killed Caine reappeared, flashing before her eyes as he pressed it to her throat.

Eryn struggled wildly, but terror in a dose she'd never experienced, sucked the strength from her, making her efforts as feeble as a child's. With just the grip on her hair, he was able to subdue her, forcing her to sit before the webcam.

He hit a key, and the program began filming. As stream of Arabic issued from his mouth, she realized he was reciting scripture. Sure enough, he switched abruptly into English, translating what he'd just said.

"The only reward of those who make war upon Allah and corrupt the nation of Islam is that they will be killed or crucified, or have their hands and feet on alternate sides *cut off*, or will be expelled out of the land. Such will be their degradation in the world, and in the Hereafter. Theirs will be an awful doom!"

Dear God, thought Eryn. I don't want to die this way. Not now. Not like this. Not when I have so much to live for.

* * *

"There it is!" Ringo cried, pointing up at the road that wound through the trees above them.

Jackson had already caught sight of it. There was no mistaking the Mobile Command Center's silver hull for anything else.

"Get as close as you can without exposing us," the former SEAL instructed.

"Roger that." Jackson slowed his approach.

There had been no overt discussion of who would be in charge. When the HRT had updated them minutes ago that they were still twenty minutes out, Jackson had glanced at Ringo, who grimaced and shook his head. They weren't going to sit around with their thumbs up their asses. They were going to put Calhoun's specialized skills to work. And that meant doing exactly what he told them to do.

"Right here," the former SEAL said, and Jackson pulled them alongside a holly bush to conceal their vehicle. "Maddox follows me. Ringo, you hang back fifty feet in case he's not alone and someone gets past us. Weapons check," Calhoun added.

There was something hugely inspiring about the man's focus. Eryn was up there in the clutches of a fanatic intending to behead her, and the former SEAL was making them count their rounds and back-up magazines. "Let's go. Keep quiet."

They leapt from the vehicle, crossed the road and moved swiftly and stealthily through the woods toward the MCC, startling a kestrel pulling entrails from a dead mouse. As it winged away, Calhoun signaled Ringo toward the street. He and Jackson proceeded further uphill, making their way to a boulder just a stone's throw from the RV.

Jackson felt like he was back in Iraq, sneaking up on an insurgent stronghold. His heart pounded somewhere in the region of his Adam's apple. He would have thought after all the military action in which he'd taken part he'd be inoculated to the stress. But nothing ever went down the same way twice.

"There's something you should know," he gasped, having pushed himself to keep up with the more fleet-footed Calhoun. "The MCC is supposedly bullet proof, though we've never tested it. All the windows are air tight. The only way in is through the front door, which requires both a key and a fingerprint scan."

Calhoun glanced at him sharply. "Do you have a key?"

"Caine had it last. The terrorist must have taken it. But we can shoot the electronic key pad which might slip the magnetic lock. Or it might lock it permanently." In which case, they'd be screwed.

The former SEAL shut his eyes briefly. "Describe the RV's layout," he said in a flat voice.

Jackson described the interior as quickly and concisely as possible.

"You shoot the lock," Calhoun said, glossing over the possibility of it jamming. "I'll go in first while you cover me. You clear right, I'll clear left."

"Keep in mind that any bullets fired inside might ricochet," Jackson added. "Don't kill the terrorist."

"You hear that?"

Jackson could hear Winston barking stridently inside the RV.

"*Now*," grated the SEAL, bolting from their hiding place.

Jackson scrambled after him, chasing his shadow around the back of the MCC. Calhoun waited by the door as Jackson blasted bullets in rapid succession into the biometric lock, sending the components flying, sparks spraying.

Inside, Eryn screamed, a sound that spiked Jackson's adrenaline. Dropping his empty magazine, he slammed a new one into his pistol as Calhoun tried to wrench the door open. To their mutual dismay, it didn't budge.

"Fuck!" Calhoun threw his shoulder into it, and the lock released with a *clunk*. He practically ripped the door off its hinges as he flung it open, ducked into a crouch, and stormed inside. The only way to cover him was to fire up at the sky.

Ike honed in on Eryn like a heat-seeking missile tracking its target. But training dictated that he clear his left corner first, while Maddox cleared the right. Only then did he let himself absorb the horrifying vision that awaited them.

His revulsion made him want to fly headlong at the enemy without any thought to the consequences. He reined himself in, shifting over to give Maddox room to join him in the living nightmare.

The terrorist held Eryn captive, one bloodied arm locked around her neck, a knife pressed to her chin. Ike assumed the blood was hers, but then he saw puncture wounds on the man's forearm and realized Winston must have bitten him. *Hooyah!*

On one side of the terrorist stood a laptop and webcam; on the other, an open briefcase containing a copy of the *Qu'ran* and a nine millimeter pistol. Looking back at Eryn, Ike was dismayed to see a thin line of blood sliding over the blade toward the terrorist's hand.

Her face was ashen, her pupils dilated. She appeared to be in shock, but—thank you, Jesus—she was still alive and that was exactly how Ike intended for her to stay.

"FBI!" Maddox announced. "Release the woman and back away."

With his left hand, Ike withdrew the Python holstered under his arm. He aimed it at the terrorist's forehead, while lowering his rifle. Firing at this range, even with the Python, would splatter gray matter all over the RV. What a shame he'd been told not to kill the fucker.

Maddox tried again. "Surrender now or be shot."

The terrorist pressed his cheek closer to Eryn's while shrinking behind her frame. "We will die together," he predicted with preternatural calm.

"Like hell," Ike growled. He thumbed off the safety.

"Don't," Jackson warned under his breath. "I'll take him down."

He did have a better angle, but if the terrorist moved at all, Eryn might take the bullet that was meant for him. "Wait," Ike pleaded. "Eryn." He addressed her directly, desperately. "Change the dynamics." If she ended up shot, he'd never forgive himself.

Recognition flickered in her eyes. Her fingers flexed on the terrorist's arms. "Remember?" he prompted.

"Yes," she whispered.

Hope hit Eryn's nervous system like a mainlined drug, beating back the fear that had kept her docile. She knew what Ike was asking her to do.

Ignoring the blade tip embedded in her chin, she ordered the sequence of motions in her head. *Now!*

Time seemed to slow as she executed each step with all the precision and power she could muster: tug, breathe, bend, sweep, twist, yank.

Yes!

She had no sooner wrenched free than a loud *pop!* left her ears ringing. The terrorist screamed in agony. A deep red stain blossomed on his thigh as he crumpled to his knees beside her. She stumbled against the kitchen cabinets, adrenaline storming her system.

The terrorist's gun gleamed in the open briefcase right beside her. Eryn snatched it up, whirled, and aimed it at him. Over the residual buzzing in her ears from the gunshot, she heard Ike's voice telling her distinctly to put the gun down.

"You!" she raged, her focus entirely on the terrorist. "You pathetic excuse for a man. You killed Itzak and Agent Caine. Don't you think their fathers loved them, too? Don't you?"

Clutching his wounded leg with one hand, his knife with the other, the terrorist gaped at her uncomprehendingly. "Shoot me," he pleaded, clearly terrified of being captured.

"Don't listen to him, Eryn." It was Jackson's voice this time, sounding like it came from a great distance.

She would never have to fear him escaping from jail if she shot him, would she? She wouldn't miss, either, not at this range.

"Do it," the terrorist pleaded, his eyes brimming with desperation.

The desire for vengeance burned in her, making her grip tighten. But then she realized killing him would make her just like him. "No." She shook her head in horror. "I'm not like you," she insisted, lowering the gun.

With a roar of frustration, the terrorist turned the blade in his hand and plunged it unexpectedly into his own chest.

Eryn's legs folded with shock. She fell to her knees at the same time that he keeled over, landing on the floor right next to her. A grunt tore from his throat as he pulled the knife out again. Blood spurted out like a fountain. With a cry of alarm, Eryn scuttled away, running into Ike's legs.

He hauled her up swiftly. Scooping her into his arms, he carried her past Jackson, who'd dropped down beside the convulsing terrorist to staunch the wound with a towel.

Without a backward glance, Ike transported Eryn out of the RV into the sunshine.

CHAPTER NINETEEN

Gripping Ike's neck in a hold that might have strangled a smaller man, Eryn took in her pristine surroundings in amazement. How could such a God-awful experience have happened here, in this untainted landscape?

The soaring trees formed a canopy of every shade of green; the sky beyond it was a deep, cerulean blue. Not even the stench of gasoline could overcome the fresh purity of mountain air or the familiar scent of the man she loved. He carried her wordlessly past Ringo, who charged into the RV, and crossed the road, lowering her on a bench-sized boulder on the other side.

"Let me see," he said, inspecting the slit that oozed blood down her neck. In the next instant he was ripping the material off the bottom of his T-shirt.

"I can't even feel it," she reassured him, surprised by the unfamiliar tremor in his fingers.

Ike was obviously shaken, his glazed eyes reflecting all the things that might have gone wrong.

"It's okay," she reassured him. "You saved me, Ike."

Her words had him blinking furiously. "You saved yourself," he insisted, smoothing her hair from her face. "I promise you'll never have to again," he added.

The words were uttered with such solemnity that she sensed some special significance to them, but, just then, Winston bounded toward them, giving her no time to decipher what he'd meant. The dog flung himself onto Eryn, licking her face and barking with unbridled joy.

"Oh, Winston." She hugged him fiercely, grateful that he'd come out unscathed.

Finally, Ike pulled the dog down. He briskly rubbed his ears. "You bit that bad guy, didn't you? Good boy."

The memory of Winston's loyalty thawed the last trace of shock that kept Eryn composed. As she burst into tears, Ike hauled her to his chest and held her tightly.

The clatter of an approaching helicopter forced her to collect herself.

"Hostage Rescue," Ike shouted, searching the sky.

Worry punctured Eryn's newfound contentment. "What happens now, Ike?" She kept her arms locked around him.

"Guess it's up to them," he said.

"They're not going to charge you, are they?"

He shrugged. "I'm not worried."

Just then, a familiar, black helicopter skimmed over the treetops, disturbing the fragile canopy.

It's over, Eryn realized. The nightmare that had begun with her failed abduction was finally over. And yet, everything felt so unsettled. What was to come of her and Ike now that she no longer needed his protection? As she met his inscrutable gaze, she begged him, "Stay with me."

The kiss he placed on the top of her head was her only reassurance. But she would take what she could get right now.

The sound of a car alarm startled Eryn awake. Snatching her head off Ike's chest, she found herself slumped against him, in the back seat of the Taurus while Jackson parked on a one-way street in downtown Washington, D.C. Winston, sitting shot gun, had steamed up the passenger window.

"We're here," Ike murmured, looking ruefully at the wet spot on his T-shirt.

"Sorry." But her chagrin was forgotten as she recognized where she was. The Washington Field Office lorded over the corner of 4th and G Streets. They weren't that far from her townhouse in Georgetown.

She wondered if, once the debriefing was over, she would get to return to her old life. Was there any guarantee that one of the so-called students viewing her execution wouldn't pick up where the terrorist had left off? Moreover, her old life seemed so far removed from the highs and lows of the past month, she wondered how she was supposed to go back, like nothing had happened.

Jackson cracked the windows for Winston. "We'll only be a short while," he promised.

Clinging to Ike with one hand, to her purse which Ringo had retrieved from the RV with the other, she crossed the busy street, hopeful of getting answers.

Forty five minutes later, Director Blooomberg's phone rang, interrupting the debriefing.

Eryn met Ike's protective gaze and managed a weak smile. Bloomberg had insisted she give a detailed recounting of the events, forcing her to relive every second of the worst day of her life. What she really wanted was to put the nightmare behind her and concentrate on the future—a future for her and Ike.

"Go ahead and send him up," Bloomberg said. "Your father's here," he announced, looking suddenly perturbed. She was reminded that Bloomberg had resisted her father's attempts to remove her from FBI protection early on.

"He is?" Eryn glanced at Ike, whose face was suddenly devoid of expression.

Bloomberg pushed away from his desk, seemingly eager to wrap things up. "Miss McClellan, on behalf of the Bureau, please accept our apologies." He rounded his desk to extend her a hand. "We'll soon know exactly how this happened, and we'll take every conceivable step to ensure it won't happen again," he said sincerely. With scant nod at Ike, he dropped her hand and headed for the door. Pulling it open, he startled back at the sight of General McClellan, his hand raised, about to knock.

"Daddy!" Eryn dashed across the room to throw herself at her father. His thick arms crushed her close, squeezing the air right out of her.

"Sweetheart."

Ike intercepted Stanley McClellan's wet gaze as it cleared the top of Eryn's head. The feelings reflected in the man's blue eyes were a mirror image of his own unwieldy emotions.

"Ike." Gratitude softened the Commander's blunt features as he extended a hand to him. "How the hell are you, son?"

Joining them, Ike found himself hauled into a big group hug. He was glad his teammates weren't around to witness this, but, damn, it felt good to know he'd earned Stanley's forgiveness.

Eryn drew back, her eyes watering, her nose bright pink. "You came home, Daddy!" she marveled.

"Course I came home. Would've been here weeks ago if the damn insurgents would take a vacation." His astute gaze swung between them. "So, how's my soldier been treating you, sugar?" he asked his daughter.

The blush that suffused her face made Ike want to melt into the carpet. She couldn't have made it any more obvious just how he'd been *treating* her.

"Fine," she said brightly. "He taught me to shoot and to defend myself."

Her father chuckled as he took in Ike's discomfiture. "I expected nothing less," he assured him.

Ike breathed a silent sigh of relief.

At last, the Commander took note of the two FBI men watching their happy reunion. His embrace eased. "Well, Alan," he said, sending Bloomberg a cool nod. "I hear you lost a good man over this case."

"We did," Bloomberg acknowledged, holding himself stiffly.

"I'm sorry to hear that," Stanley murmured. "Probably should have left it to my soldier," he added, clapping Ike on the back.

Bloomberg flicked Ike a disdainful look and said nothing.

"Well, enough red tape. My daughter needs to see a doctor." He started to draw Eryn with him as he made to leave, but then he swung back abruptly. "Oh, I believe you have her dog in your car," he said to Jackson.

Smiling, Jackson held up his car keys and jiggled them. Glancing at Bloomberg for permission, he followed them out the door.

"I have a driver waiting outside," Ike overheard Stanley divulge as he escorted Eryn toward the elevator.

"Where did you fly in? How'd you find me?"

"Quantico. Got there right as the Hostage Rescue Team landed with a dead terrorist aboard. Special Agent Ringo told me where to look for you. He filled me in on what happened." Pausing at the elevator, he pulled Eryn into another fervent embrace, hiding his face in her hair.

Watching them, Ike felt his confidence waver. There wasn't any question he was capable of loving Eryn the way her father did, completely and wholly. He might not have been shown much affection as a child, but he knew how to love. Once his commitment to the Teams was over, he knew he could give Eryn all the stability she deserved.

But it would take time for him to make peace with the past. He couldn't fulfill her needs when he was far across the ocean picking off terrorists so that she never had to look over her shoulder in fear again. Nor could he expect a woman so accustomed to love to go without for months on end. She'd already given more of herself to him than he deserved. Asking her to wait for him would be too much.

Hell, he'd served his purpose. It was over between them. His heart went leaden at the thought.

With red-rimmed eyes, Stanley looked up and intercepted Ike's pained regard. "You did good, Ike," he told him hoarsely. "You did real good."

"Thank you, sir."

"No need for the sir," Stanley needled. "You're a civilian now, right?"

Ike narrowed his eyes at him.

"Unless, of course, you've realized you want back in," Stanley tacked on, raising his eyebrows.

With a sharply drawn breath, Eryn withdrew from her father's embrace to witness his reply.

Ike couldn't bring himself to look at her. Stanley had put him directly on the spot, the sonofabitch.

And yet he'd made up his mind, already, so what was the point of concealing his decision? The sooner Eryn knew the truth, the sooner she could return to the life she used to lead. Abandoning Team Five last year had made him a deserter and a traitor to the memory of his fallen comrades. If he didn't go back, he would always be the selfish bastard Cougar thought him to be. There was only one way to redeem himself.

"I want back in, sir," he acknowledged quietly.

CHAPTER TWENTY

Eryn attempted to cheer herself. Here she was, eating Thai takeout in her townhouse in Georgetown with the two men she loved most in the world. The luxuries of home surrounded her. But Ike's shocking announcement that he wanted back into the military had stolen her contentment.

Pushing aside her cup of *tom yum*, she asked her father, "When do you have to go back?" The thought of both men leaving at once threatened to plunge her into despair.

"I'm not," he answered unexpectedly. "I've resigned my command, honey."

Eryn stared at him. "You what?"

"I'll be working at the Pentagon," he added, "advising the President and the Joint Chiefs of Staff. I hope you don't mind if I stay here while I look for my own place?"

She glanced at Ike and found him stirring his *pad thai*. "Of course not." At least she wasn't going to be utterly abandoned. "I hope you didn't do it just for me, Daddy."

"No, no." He twirled his own noodles. "I've given thirty years to the Marines; that's long enough. Time to enjoy my daughter and my grand-dog."

Her gaze shifted to Ike, who wouldn't look at her. If only he felt the way her father did.

"You realize there's going to be a period of readjustment," her father added, gently.

Thinking of the confidence it would take to walk alone again in public places, Eryn swallowed hard. She had hoped Ike would be the one to see her through the days and weeks following her ordeal. But with her father here to do it, there was nothing to keep him from rejoining the war effort right away.

She reached for the empty food cartons, using them as an excuse to leave the table. "I'll be right back," she said, fleeing to the kitchen to compose herself.

Once through the swinging door, she dropped the cartons into the trash and fanned her flushed face with her hands, hoping to dry the tears that threatened. She had promised she wouldn't cling to Ike when the time came to go their separate ways, but...

Her gaze came to rest on the brightly painted ceramics on the shelves that lined her galley-style kitchen. It was suddenly clear to her why her mother had chosen to live in Jordan when she could have gotten better medical treatment in the States. The thought of an ocean separating her from her husband had been too much for her, especially when she knew their time together was dwindling.

Eryn felt the same way about Ike, and they had their entire lives still ahead of them.

Hearing her father begin to excuse himself from the table, she snapped herself out of her anguish and hurried back into the dining room to offer him dessert. But in an obvious ploy to leave her and Ike alone together, he claimed he had a belly ache and headed for the stairs.

Ike started clearing the table wordlessly. Eryn joined him, trailing him into the kitchen where they rinsed the plates and put away leftovers with familiarity that was nonetheless charged with underlying tension.

"How's the chin?" he finally asked, reaching for a dishtowel.

"The Lidocaine's wearing off," she admitted. It had taken several stitches to close the cut made by the terrorist's knife.

He expelled such a deep sigh that she wondered if her chin was the cause of his regret or whether they were finally going to discuss the future.

"You should rest," he said, not bringing it up. "I'll crash on the sofa."

"Ike, we need to talk," she said.

"Come on, Eryn. You've had a hell of a day already."

His reply was anything but encouraging. "I'm fine," she insisted, determined to get this discussion behind them. "I want you to know that I understand why you're going back, Ike." She went straight to the point. "I do. You feel like you abandoned your teammates, like you turned your back on them." She swallowed hard, determined not to try and talk him out of his decision. "I get that. I just want you to know that I'm going to wait for you—"

"Don't," he said, cutting her off abruptly.

She blinked at the harsh word. Didn't he want to see her again? How could he walk away from what they'd shared? "Wh-what do you mean, don't?"

Fuck. Ike tossed the dishtowel aside. The hurt in Eryn's eyes was killing him because now *he* was the cause of it. Couldn't she see he was letting her go for her own good? Why put herself through the torment of separation, not knowing if he'd come back in one piece, depriving herself of the kind of love she deserved. "I don't want you to wait for me," he growled, forcing the lie through his lips.

She made a sound that was part-laugh, part-sob. "Why not?" she cried.

"Lots of reasons."

"Name them."

"First off, I might not make it back."

"You will!" She seized the edges of his open jacket and shook him. "You will, Ike! Don't you dare say that!" But her face was white with fear.

"Come on, Eryn." He refused to go down the list. "I'm not what you need." He went right to the main reason. "I'm just a sonofabitch with a crap-load of issues and really good aim. You know you can do better than me. Don't go wasting your life on me."

"Don't tell me what to do!" she snapped, showing her feisty side, which never failed to amuse him. "It's my life. And I don't consider you a waste!"

Her stubbornness, however misguided, filled him with gratification. Maybe he should ask for her to wait for him. Suddenly, he just had to kiss her, to hold her, to enjoy her passionate sweetness one more time.

He crushed his mouth to hers, and the room went into a slow spin. The friction between their dueling tongues sparked a desire fraught with desperation. He turned hard against her softness.

"Make love to me, Ike," she begged between his soul-sucking kisses.

An act like that would cancel out his words. Yet the memory of her passion might just get him through the blistering heat, the cold winds, and the nerve-fraying danger to come.

He backed her blindly against the counter, lifting her onto the edge to put her at a better height. There she coiled her legs around him, and the hem of the dress she'd put on rode the tops of her thighs. A glimpse of peach lace fueled his heart into turbo drive.

As always, his surroundings seemed to dwindle as he lost himself in her taste, her texture. With his heart jumping like a piston, he sought the steamy cleft between her thighs. Eryn bucked, pressing eagerly against his touch as he delved beneath her panties to plumb her wetness.

With a burning need to claim her one last time, he released the buttons of his fly and freed his erection. Pulling her hips to the edge of the counter, he edged aside her panties and drove blindly into her heat, muffling her cry of encouragement with a searing kiss.

He thrust deeper, pulling her roughly to him. Eryn's response was equally as fierce. Hands braced on the counter behind her, she clamped her legs around him and drove herself down his length. The only sounds in the kitchen were their ragged breaths, her muffled moans, and the moist friction between their straining bodies.

Under the hand that cupped her right breast, Ike could feel her heart hammering. Thumbing a stiff nipple, he spurred her toward her release, praying she'd get there before he did.

He was at the verge of incinerating in a flash of white heat, when he realized they were having unprotected sex.

Ah, shit! But he couldn't stop. Eryn's grip had tightened. He could feel her tensing with rapture. If he didn't cover her mouth right now, her father would certainly overhear.

She cried out into his mouth, her tight walls contracting around him so sweetly that he succumbed, his knees nearly buckling at the white hot pleasure that exploded through him. He expended himself deep inside her.

His first thought, when he could think again was, *You selfish dog.* How was she supposed to get on with her life if he left her pregnant?

Disengaging, he lunged for the paper towels beside the sink, yanking off a handful and thrusting it at her. "Sorry," he muttered, watching her slip off the counter and adjust her dress, her face bright pink.

Feeling like the lowest form of scum, Ike put himself back together. He'd just misled her into thinking there was hope for them. He had to do something to open Eryn's eyes to reality. But what?

Just then Eryn closed the space between them. Slipping her arms around him, she lay her cheek against his chest, filling him with bottomless yearning. "Do you love me, Ike?" she whispered, gazing up. Her eyes were exquisitely blue, her lips swollen from his kisses.

Shit. He couldn't look her in the eye and tell an outright lie. But neither would he condemn her to months, even years of waiting for a man who would put his life on the line every day for a year.

"I want to take you somewhere tomorrow," he said, inspired by a sudden idea.

"Where's that?" Her voice reflected hurt that he'd ignored her question.

"Walter Reed Hospital."

She frowned. "You know someone there?"

"Your father says my spotter, Spellman, is there."

"The one who hid with you in a hollow log," she recalled, proving how closely she'd listened.

"Yeah. He stepped on a mine after I left."

The freckles across her nose grew more pronounced.

"Will you come with me to visit him?" he persisted.

"Okay," she said. She released him, reluctantly, every line in her body reflecting the pain of his rejection.

It was all he could do not to pull her back and say, *We can try, baby. I'll give it my best.* But then he pictured her waiting for him, lying alone in bed at night, praying for his safety, watching the news in fear, and his resolve hardened. Hell, no. She'd suffered enough this past month. He didn't want her thinking about the War on Terror ever again. That was his job.

"I'll leave a blanket and pillow on the couch," she mumbled, turning toward the hall.

"Thanks." But between the agony of leaving Eryn and his fears for the future, he doubted he would sleep.

"See you in the morning," she added on a stubborn note.

She wasn't going to give up on him that easily, he realized both heartened and dismayed. But once she saw Spellman and realized what could happen to him, she would change her mind. He was counting on it.

* * *

Walter Reed Army Medical Center was a behemoth of a hospital, tastefully appointed with wide, sparkling hallways and modern artwork. But it still smelled like a hospital, reminding Eryn of a frightening time in her life. *I'm tougher now,* she reminded herself.

Still, when she and Ike knocked at Spellman's door, she couldn't quell her apprehension. Glancing at Ike, she saw no fear, only firmness of purpose on his face.

"Come in," called a robust voice.

Ike pushed into an apartment designed for patients needing long-term rehab. He'd warned her that Spellman had lost several limbs; still, Eryn wasn't prepared for what she saw: a young man so terribly maimed, it was just appalling. Reconstruction and plastic surgery had given him a face but it wasn't symmetrical.

"LT!" he exclaimed with a lisp indicating damage to his palate. "Holy shit, is that you?" He laid aside the controls to the game he was playing on the TV.

"Yeah, it's me." If Ike was as shocked as Eryn, he didn't show it. "What the hell happened to you?" he demanded.

To Eryn's relief, Spellman chuckled at Ike's candor. Better to address the elephant in the room than to ignore it, right?

"Had my head up my ass, that's what. Wasn't watching where I was going." Spellman waved them closer. "Get over here!"

Ike clasped the extended hand then bent to embrace his former team-mate. The emotion that contorted Spellman's features even further put a lump in Eryn's throat.

Ike finally straightened. "I want you to meet Eryn, General McClellan's daughter. Eryn, this is Anthony, the Eagle Eye."

"Not anymore, LT." Spellman held his only hand out to her. "Saw you in the news," he said, his grip that of a strong, healthy male. His good eye roamed over her appreciatively. "You're even prettier close up."

She flushed. "Thank you."

"Couldn't believe there was a manhunt for you, LT. I was tempted to call CNN and set their story straight. You guys want something to drink? I've got beverages in the 'fridge."

"I'm good." Ike looked at Eryn.

"No, thank you," she said, looking around. "This is really nice. Were you playing a Wii game?"

"Yeah, it's part of my therapy. I'm networking my brain so that the right side will take cues from my right hand."

"Really?" As an educator, Eryn was intrigued. Questions sprang to mind, but a glance at Ike found him studying Spellman covertly. They had things to discuss, she realized. "I think I will take a drink," she said, moving away.

Fetching a Diet Coke from the mini-fridge, she settled on the window seat and watched the traffic circling the U-shaped drive below. With one ear tuned to Ike and Anthony's conversation, she heard the former spotter describe how the Dear John letter he'd received from his girlfriend had put his thoughts into such a tailspin that he'd stepped right on a mine, real-izing too late what it was.

The top of Eryn's head turned cold.

"That's not what Cougar told me," Ike said.

"What'd he say?"

"Said you blamed yourself for what happened in Yaqubai."

"Hell no. We cast a vote, remember? We did what we thought was right."

Across the room, Ike shot Eryn a rueful glance. "Yeah, well, I took it pretty hard. But I'm ready to go back."

Spellman looked startled. "Really?"

"Planning to drop by Navy Recruitment this afternoon. General McClellan says he can get Team 18 to pick me up within six weeks. Once in, I'll hook up with a unit that's about to deploy. I should have boots on the ground in four months."

Spellman cut a quick glance at Eryn. "Six month tour?" he asked.

"Yep."

Tallying up the number of months Ike would be committed—nearly a year—Eryn's heart trembled. Could she wait a whole year? At least from what she understood about reservist duty, one year's mobilization guaranteed no more lengthy overseas tours.

"Man, do yourself a favor," Spellman murmured, pitching his voice in such a way that Eryn wasn't supposed to hear, only her hearing had been sharpened by years in the classroom. "Set her free. You gotta keep your mind clear out there."

"I hear you," Ike muttered.

With the feeling that she'd been trampled on, Eryn gazed unseeing at the life forms below. Suddenly she realized what Ike might have been trying to tell her last night: That he couldn't afford to have a girlfriend. He had to be in the moment, every second of every minute of every hour, if he wanted to stay alive.

Dear God. The last thing she wanted to be was a danger to him! Of course, he hadn't worded it like that. Instead, he'd insisted that he wasn't what *she* needed; that she deserved better. In reality, it was she who had the power to hurt him—she could see that now. Things happened.

She was sure she wouldn't change *her* mind the way Spellman's girlfriend had, but any kind of news from her could wreck Ike's concentration. She could get into a car accident, break a leg skiing, arouse his jealousy without meaning to. The slightest distraction could end his life.

Oh, Ike! He'd tried telling her this last night, only to end up comforting her, making love to her. It was up to her to set *him* free, or at least pretend to. She would have to convince him that seeing Anthony had made her change her mind.

Thirty minutes later, after Ike had attempted and failed Anthony's video game, he suggested it was time they leave.

Eryn kissed the former spotter's cheek, whispering in his ear that she'd come and visit. He would be her only link to Ike, aside from her father, who she knew would monitor Ike's career.

Neither one of them spoke as they traversed the hallway and took the elevator to the ground floor. She was aware of his every sidelong glance, but she kept her face averted, giving him no reason to suspect her heart was already suspended in time.

They took the bus and the subway back to her neighborhood in Georgetown. All the while, Ike remained her vigilant protector.

Too bad for her, she didn't need his protection anymore. What she needed was a good long cry in the shower, followed by a nap with Winston, her loyal Golden Shepherd.

A year would seem like a lifetime.

As they climbed the steps to her townhouse, Ike caught her by the wrist, tugging her to a halt. Turning reluctantly, she gazed down into his bloodshot eyes from one step higher than his.

"You see what could happen to me?" he said roughly.

This is it, Eryn thought. The scent of cherry blossoms, exhaust, and exotic restaurants mingled as a cool breeze stirred her hair. She wanted to say, *I still plan to wait for you.* But Anthony's warning echoed in her mind, leaving her no choice.

"Go ahead and leave, Ike, if that's what you want." Her voice came out remarkably steady as she memorized his dear face. "Just promise me you won't even think of me, not once." She swallowed hard, tacking on the words she didn't mean. "And don't expect me to be waiting for you, like I said. I've changed my mind."

All expression vanished from his face, making her heart break. After all the work she'd done to get him to open up to her, she couldn't believe she'd just pushed him away. But she'd only done it to protect him.

Ike lowered his eyes and nodded, accepting her decision without comment. But then he dropped his forehead onto her shoulder. He stood there, in that posture of surrender and despair for several minutes. Tears brimmed Eryn's eyes. Her hand came up to stroke the soft, silver bristles at his nape.

I'm sorry, she sought to communicate. *Of course, I'll wait. I'll wait for as long as it takes.*

Time ticked relentlessly away as they shared their final few moments together.

Before she knew it, Ike would be gone for months. But it had to be done. This was the only way he believed he could redeem himself and honor his fallen teammates. If only it didn't entail such tremendous risk, such painful separation. But she knew how it worked. After all, she'd grown up a military brat.

It wasn't like she really had a choice. Her heart belonged to Ike alone. And regardless of her words to the contrary, she would be the first one to welcome him home when he finally did come back.

CHAPTER TWENTY-ONE

"Jackson!" Eryn smiled in surprise at the special agent standing on her doorstep.

"How are you?" His dusky skin had darkened in the August sun, making his blue-green eyes all the more startling.

"I'm great. What are you doing here?"

"Well, I was going to drop this in your mail slot when I heard your music playing."

"Yeah, I was working out." She gestured at her snug-fitting yoga outfit. "You want to come in?"

"Only if I'm not interrupting," he said with a quick once-over.

"No, I'm pretty much done," she assured him, stepping back. "Now that it's summer, I have gobs of free time, anyway. Come on in out of that heat."

"Hey, Winston." Jackson paused in the entryway to greet the Shepherd mix who leaned against him, wagging his tail enthusiastically.

"Can I get you a drink? Iced tea?"

"Sure."

She left him in the living room to fetch him a tall glass from the kitchen.

"Nice place," he said when she returned.

"Thanks. I'll never take home for granted again. Have a seat."

He sat down on the couch with his drink. Turning off her exercise DVD, Eryn took a seat across from him. Her gaze slid to the envelope in his hands. "What is it?"

"It's the final report on the investigation." He extended it over the coffee table.

As Eryn hefted the thick packet, memories of last spring's horrors assaulted her. She was in no great hurry to read the report, yet there were questions she still wanted answers to. "Would you mind giving me the highlights?" she requested.

"No problem. The terrorist's laptop gave us most of the information we needed. He had multiple accounts registered under the name Franklin Smith. TSA paired that name with his photo and determined that he flew into Dulles in January, carrying an Australian passport and a student visa. But his dental records don't match those of the real Frank Smith, whose identity he acquired along the way."

"If he wasn't Frank Smith, who was he?"

"TSA gave us the address he'd reported on his I-94 Form. He'd been living with distant cousins who called him Farshad. Farshad of Helmand Province."

"Farshad," she repeated, shivering as she recalled his strangely gentle-looking face. "Are the cousins terrorists, too?"

"Doesn't appear so. All of them are U.S. citizens. Some are moderate members of the Brotherhood. They insisted they had no idea what he was up to."

"Are you sure you can believe them?"

"There's nothing to suggest they share his extremist bent. None of them lost any sons in Afghanistan either. Farshad's son was killed in 2008 in a Coalition-led airstrike."

"Ordered by my father," Eryn added somberly. "He told me his son's name was Osman." She clutched the arms of her chair, thinking of Ike who still dealt with terror on a day-to-day basis.

"The details are all in the report," Jackson added gently. "The reason we didn't catch the man earlier was because he never met face to face with the extremists we suspected, not until he had to. They shared an online email account, leaving messages for each other in the draft folder. There was nothing being transmitted, nothing for us to intercept."

"Clever," she acknowledged, recalling poor Itzak with a pang. He would have graduated in June.

"I probably shouldn't even tell you this, but…"

Jackson's words snatched her head up. "What?"

"We learned that Farshad was a teacher of religion back in Helmand. When he was still there, he taught radicals how to circumvent U.S. security measures. He went first, paving the way, providing inspiration. His aim was to put a new face on terrorism."

Eryn blanched, recalling the viewers who'd logged in to witness her execution.

"Not to worry," Jackson rushed to reassure her. "NSA is all over it. The CIA already has a year's worth of Intel, and Spec Ops has been given a list of all the suspects. They're going to hunt them all down."

Stunned, Eryn envisioned Ike's grim pleasure in participating in such a mission.

"Mind you, that's classified information. You'll need to keep it to yourself," Jackson added.

"Of course."

His gaze lingered on her. "How are you making out without him?" he asked unexpectedly.

Obviously, her thoughts of Ike were showing. "I'm okay," she lied. Back when school was still in session, the days hadn't been so bad. But with less to keep her occupied in the summer, the ache in her chest became a constant companion. She'd felt bereft when her period came two weeks late, toppling the impractical hope that she carried Ike's baby.

"I lost my wife to a car accident about two years ago," Jackson said unexpectedly.

"Oh, Jackson." She regarded him in stunned surprise. "I'm so sorry. I had no idea."

He looked down at the carpet a moment, cleared his throat. "I'm just saying, if you ever need a friend—" his dusky complexion pinkened "—just someone to hang out with...I'd be honored."

She searched his face for his intentions. "You should know that I'm waiting for Ike," she said steadily.

He inclined his head in acknowledgment. "Then he's a lucky man, but the offer still stands."

He had caught her off guard, but why not? Most of her girlfriends had husbands to keep them occupied. She needed to get out more, especially in the evenings when time slowed to a crawl. "Okay," she agreed. "That'd be great."

"Okay," he repeated, flashing strong, white teeth. "I'll give you a call soon."

With her step a fraction lighter, Eryn followed him to the door, called farewell, and watched him slip into the familiar Taurus, her gaze automatically scanning the street for danger.

Jackson could never be a substitute for Ike, but he might prove to be a friend. And she could really use a friend right now.

* * *

A frigid wind whipped along the dark, narrow streets of Naw Zad, sending trash fluttering, cans rolling. Doors and shutters that hadn't been blown off in the siege three years ago groaned on their hinges. Ike pressed his back against a crumbling wall and questioned the apprehension brewing inside of him.

The last time he'd seen Naw Zad it had been laid to waste in an Operation called Cobra's Anger. The massive Coalition effort had left hundreds of Taliban insurgents dead, including Osman of Helmand Province, the son of Eryn's terrorist. Survivors had fled the ravaged city. There had been nothing left but gutted buildings, blood-stained streets, and wild dogs feeding off the refuse.

Upon his return four months ago, he'd been amazed to see over sixty shops thriving in the downtown area, as well as a bustling market. Afghani forces patrolled the streets hoping to dissuade the re-infiltration of insurgents, but no one could tell militants from farmers when they kept their guns hidden under their tunics.

Signaling his squad to wait, Ike queried his senses like a vine sending out tendrils. The cold air smelled of hard-packed dirt and stale sewage. An empty can rolled past their feet. In the distance a dog howled.

The intelligence supplied by the FBI had proven flawless in the beginning. Ike's squad had surprised half a dozen Taliban—former students of the Teacher, Farshad—within weeks of their arrival. But as weeks turned to months, the remaining few got harder to find, leapfrogging from one village to another. The last man they'd cornered had shot himself in the head before they could lay hold of him. That meant only one thing: the insurgents were expecting them, and that was never good.

Sliding along the wall of a vacated building, Ike stole a peek at the next street over. The night-vision-enhanced visor on his helmet showed a wavering light shining in a second story window just across the street. The rest of the block appeared deserted. Their target had taken refuge in what had once been a hospital on the outskirts of Naw Zad.

Ike's thoughts flashed to an image of Eryn getting her chin stitched at the clinic in Georgetown. How bizarre that her world and this one had intersected the day that Farshad took her hostage in the RV.

Yanking his thoughts back to present time, he glanced at his watch. They had twenty minutes in which to reconnoiter the building and determine their points of entry. With the capture of the last of Farshad's students, the movement being dubbed The New Face of Terror would die out before it ever gained momentum, sparing the families of military leaders from the horror Eryn had endured.

He couldn't stop thinking of her, even though she'd ordered him not to. He risked his life every day for two reasons: to honor his fallen teammates and to make certain Eryn never lived in fear ever again. She might not be waiting for him. But this was all worthwhile, providing they got the job done right.

So focus, damn it.

Turning to his men, Ike conveyed his sighting with a series of hand signals, adding that he would take point. Typically, Rogue, who was small and light on his feet, went first. But the uneasiness that prickled Ike's nape urged him to assume the greatest risk. The others were younger, less experienced.

Under the watchful eye of Rogue, Ivy, and Jones, he darted in a crouch across the road, hurtling a pothole left by aerial cannon fire. Rats, startled by his approach, squealed and scattered. The fact that they were here at all meant the pile of garbage stacked against the building was fresh.

Ike spared the reeking pile a cursory glance. As he shouldered his weapon and raised a hand to signal Rogue over, a sudden foreboding yanked his scalp tight. He glanced back at the trash a second time, signaled for Rogue to halt.

Plastic and bottles and boxes of broken glass had been carefully piled one atop the other. Too carefully. It was as if someone had meant to cover up a...*Fuck!* With a warning cry, he started to run.

He felt the hot blast of the improvised explosive device before he heard it. At the same time, the air seemed to shatter around him. He felt his left eardrum rupture. *Wump!* The explosion sounded dull and hollow.

He became aware that he was hurtling through the air. *Oh, shit,* murmured a calm, emotionless voice just before a cinderblock wall, lit up by the explosion's flare, slammed into his face.

* * *

As Jackson pulled his sleek Nissan GT-R along the curb, Eryn noted the brightly lit windows on both levels of her townhouse and wondered why her father was still up.

Jackson set the handbrake but kept the engine running. Heat poured out of the vents to ward off the February chill. In the six months they'd been friends, he'd kept his word about just hanging out. The fact that her father still lived with her might have deterred him.

"Well, thank you," she said, sending him a strained smile. "That was fun." They'd taken his eleven-year-old daughter to the Pentagon Row Ice Skating Plaza. Naomi Maddox had clung to Eryn's hand all evening—when she wasn't pushing Eryn into her father in an obvious effort to spark romance.

Angling his head to see her better, Jackson searched her expression. "What's wrong, Eryn? Something's bothering you."

With a sigh, she eyed the naked elms that lined her street. When the trees sprouted leaves again, Ike would be back from Afghanistan. At least, that was what her father had told her. "We can't do this anymore, Jackson," she decided. "It isn't fair to Naomi. It isn't fair to you."

He sucked in a deep breath and let it out. "We're just friends, Eryn," he said tiredly.

"Naomi needs more than that. You saw her tonight. She needs a mother."

Bowing his shaved head, he kept quiet.

"I'm so sorry," she murmured, touching his coat sleeve.

He forced a smile. "Don't be. I guess I'm still hoping Colleen will come back, the way Calhoun will."

"Oh, Jackson." Twisting in her seat, she gave him a swift hug. "I wish I could make it better."

He kissed her forehead. "It's okay. I'm okay, Eryn. Don't worry about me."

She drew away, searching his stoic features for signs of suicidal thoughts. "We can still be friends," she offered. "Just keep an eye out for the right woman, okay?"

"I will."

"Good night, Jackson." Pushing out of his low-slung sports car, she gave one last wave and rushed through the frigid air toward her door.

As she mounted the stoop, the memory of Ike's forehead against her chest made her eyes sting. She wriggled her key into the lock, only to find the door unbolted.

Behind her, Jackson's engine roared and receded. As she stepped inside, her father emerged from the living room. One look at his haggard expression and she felt the blood drain from her face. "What happened?"

He approached her slowly, put his hands on her shoulders. "It's Ike," he said, somberly. "He was hurt."

Her house keys fell to the hardwood floor with a *chink*. "How hurt?"

"I don't know. I got the news an hour ago. He was caught by an IED."

"Oh, God." A vision of Ike looking like Anthony Spellman sprang into her head.

"They're transporting him to Lanstuhl, Germany."

Dark blotches obscured her vision. The hallway began to spin. Feeling herself fall, she groped for her father's shirt. Her last thought as she felt him catch her was that she'd end up empty and alone, just like Jackson.

* * *

"Excuse me," called a doctor, intercepting their march down the hospital corridor. "Only family members are admitted into ICU. Who are you?"

"I'm General McClellan." The Commander's tone conveyed the importance of his rank. "This is my daughter, Eryn. We're here to see Isaac Calhoun."

The doctor looked unimpressed. "Are you family?"

"No."

"Then you can't go in."

"Please," Eryn begged. "We just flew all the way from the States. Can't you make an exception?"

"No exceptions."

"Do you realize who I am?" Her father's thundering question caused the staff at the nurses' station to freeze and look at them.

The doctor's lips curled. "Rules are rules. Plus, I'm a civilian contractor," he added with a mocking lift of his eyebrows.

"How's Ike doing? Can you tell us that?" Eryn pleaded. "He's the Navy SEAL brought in from Afghanistan."

The doctor thought for a moment, glancing down the hallway toward ICU. "Oh, yes. Well, he's got a serious concussion, shrapnel wounds, and second degree burns. There may also be some spinal issues, but it's too soon to tell. The good news is that he *is* responsive."

"What...what does that mean?" A clammy sweat breached her skin. "What's his prognosis?"

"Our most immediate concern is that he'll slip into a coma and not come out. Right now his odds are fifty-fifty," said the doctor dispassionately. "If he remains responsive, those odds will improve."

She felt like she might faint again. *Fifty-fifty?*

Her father put an arm around her as she sagged against him. *Ike.* She had to see him. She had to.

"I'm sorry," said the doctor with scant sympathy. "If you'd like to pray with a chaplain, there's one around here somewhere."

Her father perked up. "Chaplain. Yes, we would," he declared. "Find him for us, would you?"

Rolling his eyes at the General's heavy-handedness, the doctor nonetheless turned to do his bidding. Eryn pulled back to send her father a questioning look. He squeezed her shoulder, enjoining her to keep quiet until the doctor disappeared.

"Daddy, what are you planning?" she whispered.

He looked down with a twinkle in his eyes. "I have an idea," he admitted, "and I don't want to hear any protests."

"What kind of idea?"

"Trust me, it's the best thing for both of you," he said. Pulling her closer, he whispered his idea into her ear.

Eryn gasped. "That's awful! We can't do that."

"Why not?" Her father didn't look the least bit apologetic. "The doctor said he was responsive. If he doesn't want to do it, he'll find a way to say no."

"And how humiliating will that be?" she cried.

Stanley's mouth split into a grin. "Not at all," he promised, "because I know that boy, Eryn. He'll marry you in a heartbeat."

It took twenty minutes to persuade the Marine Corps chaplain to do the honors, in secret without the doctor's knowledge. Stanley's threat to make or break his career had ultimately ensured the man's cooperation.

"Who'll sign the register?" asked the chaplain in a final bid to escape the plot.

Stanley waved a piece of paper under his nose. "Calhoun named me his agent when he rejoined the military. If he can't sign it, I will."

With a grimace of resignation, the balding chaplain escorted them down the hall toward ICU. Peeking around a corner, he waited for a doctor to disappear into surgery before darting across the hall and waving them furtively through a closed door.

"I'll be right back," he whispered, leaving them alone.

Eryn looked around. They stood in a gently lit room jammed with instruments and monitors that bleeped and whirred and pulsed. A blanketed figure lay strapped to a gurney surrounded by half a dozen instruments attached to him via wires and tubes. *Ike?* His neck was encased in a thick brace.

She willed her weak knees to carry her closer. Shock had her clutching the cold metal railing as she realized how much of him was swathed in white gauze. Looking past the bandages and the tubes conveying oxygen to his nostrils, she recognized the firm contours of his mouth and jaw, so dearly familiar that a sob escaped her throat. *Oh, Ike!*

She bent over him, assailed by a sweet, medicinal odor that smelled alien on him. The un-bandaged portion of his face was red and swollen, his eye blackened, but thankfully not disfigured. Lowering her mouth to his one good ear, she murmured to him. "Ike, honey, it's Eryn. I'm here. I came to be with you."

His lashes flickered, but his eyes remained shut.

That's responsive? Reaching for the hand that lay atop the blankets, she laced her fingers through his and was reassured by his warmth. "Can you hear me, Ike?"

There was no mistaking the slow curling of his fingers. Tears flooded Eryn's eyes. She looked up at her father, who now stood at the foot of the bed. "He heard me." Then she bent over Ike again. "You're going to be okay, love. You're going to make it." He *had* to. Fifty-fifty odds were nothing for a man like Ike, a man who'd defied the odds from the day he graduated SEAL training.

"Ask him," Stanley prompted, glancing at the door. "We don't have much time."

Eryn hesitated. She wasn't comfortable with forcing marriage down Ike's throat. What if he didn't want to marry her? After all, he'd chosen returning to the service over staying with her. What made her think he felt differently now?

On the other hand, she'd be sick if she were told to get away from him now and to stay away till he was out of ICU. "Ike, honey, I need to ask you a favor," she began, speaking slowly and clearly in his ear. "Dad and I aren't allowed to be here. Only family can come in. But Dad suggested...that if you and I got married, here and now, then we could stay and visit you till you're all better."

She searched his impassive face for any sign of panic or revulsion. "I never thought I'd be the one to do this, but...would you marry me, Ike? I understand if you don't want to, but things have changed with you being injured and all. So, tell me by squeezing my hand, okay? One squeeze means, yes; two means—"

He squeezed her hand, once, so quickly she had to wonder if he understood what she was asking.

"What'd he say?" her father demanded.

"He squeezed once. I think he said yes. Was that a yes, Ike?"

He squeezed her hand again, harder, slower. That was definitely a yes. Her heart tripled in size. She laughed out loud, half joyous, half scared.

The door squeaked open, curtailing her outburst. To her relief, it was just the chaplain, slipping into the room with two nurses, one of whom set a vase of daisies on Ike's beside table. "We're the witnesses," she explained with a conspiratorial smile.

"Let's get this over with," said the chaplain, who was visibly sweating. He cracked open a liturgical book and started reading. "Dearly beloved, we are gathered together in the presence of friends and family..."

Suddenly, Ike's eyes opened. Eryn gave a startled cry, and the chaplain paused before continuing the rite at double the cadence. His words seemed to fade into the distance as Eryn leaned over, trying to catch Ike's eye, only his gaze remained fixed and staring.

Suddenly, the chaplain was addressing her. "Will you, Eryn McClellan, take this man to be your husband, to have and to hold, for better or for worse, in sickness and in health, from this day forward, for as long as you both shall live?"

Never had that familiar, lengthy question seemed so loaded. Ike's chances for survival were grim. He was in danger of slipping into a coma. His injuries might well leave him cognitively impaired. And here she was linking her future with his. Was she crazy? Then again, was any bride ever guaranteed happily ever after? No. Not one.

But she could guarantee him unconditional love, something Ike had probably never experienced, not even as a boy. Whether his life lasted just hours or for decades, she would love him with all her heart.

"I will," she said with conviction. One of the nurses sniffled.

Just then, the door swung open and they all swiveled in alarm. There stood the doctor, bristling with indignation. "What the *hell* is going on in here?" he demanded.

The chaplain's face turned seven shades of red. Ignoring the interruption, he plowed forward with the service. "And will you, Isaac Calhoun, take this woman to be your wife, to have and to hold, for better or for worse, in sickness and in health, from this day forward, for as long as you both shall live?"

All eyes flew to Ike's hand while Ike stared fixedly at the ceiling.

"This is absurd. The patient can't speak!" shouted the doctor.

"Wait," implored one of the nurses.

The only sounds were that of the heart monitor racing at a strong, steady trot, the oxygen machine whirring, and the muted lights overhead buzzing quietly. With the breath locked in her lungs, Eryn waited for Ike's tanned, powerful hand to signal his decision.

Come on, Ike. Say yes. Let me be here for you.

At last, he enclosed her fingers in a sure, powerful grip that showed no sign of easing up, ever.

"That's a *yes!*" her father announced, shooting a triumphant grin at the speechless, outraged doctor.

"Then, in the name of the Father, the Son, and the Holy Spirit, I declare you both husband and wife!" the chaplain finished quickly, making a sign of the cross in the air.

The nurses turned and hugged each other. General McClellan went to sign the marriage register on Ike's behalf. The doctor threw up his hands and left without another word.

Eryn's misty gaze remained fixed on her new husband. She longed to seal their union with a kiss. Ignoring the tubes that snaked into his nose, she dropped a light kiss on his lips, encountering gauze and a hint of facial hair. Carrying their linked hands to her lips, she kissed his knuckles. Slowly, one finger at a time, his fist unfurled. He seemed to be reaching for something. She put his palm to her cheek and his hand grew still, wetted by her tears.

From the moment his possessive gaze first landed on her, she'd been his. She would remain his for as long as they lived.

"You have to live for me, Ike," she told him quietly. "Live for me."

A bead of moisture escaped the corner of his eye and ran into his bandage. She knew he'd heard her. She knew he'd fight to pull through.

EPILOGUE

Eryn sat up taller in the driver's seat. "I can't believe we're here," she breathed, nosing Ike's Durango between the brick pillars and onto the driveway leading straight up to their mountain getaway. Theirs, that was, if he didn't annul their marriage.

In the back of the Durango, delivered from Little Creek Amphibious Base by a teammate, Winston whined, echoing her excitement.

"Need to shift into four-wheel drive," Ike instructed, a small smile on his lips.

"Like this?" she asked, doing what she'd watched him do a couple of times last year.

"That's it."

Not only had Ike cheated death, coming out of ICU the day after their marriage, but four months of cognitive rehab in Bethesda had left him practically as good as new. He still got headaches sometimes; his back was scarred by burns; his limbs flecked with shrapnel scars. He hadn't been cleared to drive yet, but for a man whose odds had been fifty-fifty, he looked pretty darn good to her.

They had spent every evening of those four months getting to know each other better. From what Eryn could see, Ike had come a long way from the grim, silent man who'd played her protector last year. He seemed at peace with himself. But he still kept so much inside him that she had no idea if he was content to be married to her, or not.

The future of his career was equally uncertain. Ike's hearing loss, which was a result of the explosion, meant that he was being medically discharged from the Teams. But Homeland Security had approached him with an offer to head up a new counterterrorist taskforce. He seemed excited by the job offer, which would have him working out of D.C.

Still, he'd been so eager to escape to the mountains upon his release from the hospital that she had to wonder if he'd be content living in the city. After all, he had declined to recuperate in her townhouse, even though her father had finally moved out. Maybe he didn't want to consummate their marriage vows—unspoken vows, on his part.

The fact remained that nothing held Ike to her but a scrap of paper signed by her father, who'd served as Ike's agent.

She gunned the accelerator in private panic.

"Slow and easy," Ike soothed.

The driveway sported several new gullies where melting snows had washed away the gravel. The Durango jiggled through them.

"Got my work cut out for me," Ike muttered.

Cut out for me. Why hadn't he said *for us?*

Gripping the steering wheel harder, Eryn saw him lower the passenger window. A brisk, spring breeze gusted into the car's interior, smelling of young leaves and warm granite. It brought back memories of her and Ike running past soldiers and hiding from the helicopter.

That all seemed like a high adventure in retrospect, at least up until Farshad of Helmand had ruined all the fun he'd inadvertently caused.

Almost home, Eryn thought, speeding them around the final turn.

There stood the cabin, looking as quaint and bucolic as ever in the shade of the oak tree. The paint was still peeling; the porch now listed to one side. But the cherry tree and forsythia were in full bloom, adding lavish color to an otherwise simplistic setting.

"It looks just like I remember," she stated, parking by the rope that dangled from the oak tree, slightly yellower now.

"Only more run down," Ike agreed, glancing toward the sinking sun.

"Not after I—" Eryn cut herself off.

He slanted her a curious look. "You what?"

"Nothing." She had no right, at this point, to introduce her thoughts for renovating.

"Just leave our stuff in the truck," Ike said, "I want to show you something."

Intrigued, she spared a quick thought for her purse and their luggage while Ike released the dog from the back. Then trapping her hand in his, he drew her around the house toward the jogging trail. Memories of their morning runs assailed her. The scent of wild grass and the whisper of the wind welcomed them as they hiked into the sparsely-leafed forest, chasing the sun, which had started to sink behind the pinnacle of the mountain.

Eryn struggled to keep up. "Where are we going?"

"You'll see." For all his time in the hospital, Ike seemed no less fit than he'd been twelve months ago. He pulled her up the last part of the incline and over to the boulder from which he'd once surveyed the valley.

"Up there?" Eryn eyed the massive rock, thoroughly puzzled.

"C'mon. I'll boost you up."

A moment later, she was crawling on hands and knees across the sun-warmed stone. Ike joined her, urging her closer to the ledge that stuck out over a sheer drop. Settling next to her, he put an arm around her waist and drew a deep breath.

She could sense the stress leaving him. The feeling that they had come full-circle crept over her.

Below them, the Shenandoah Valley sprawled under an amber sunset. A hawk coursed the heavens, and somewhere down in the hollow, a cow lowed.

"I like it here," he admitted, glancing at her sidelong. "You?"

Suspended over nothing but air, she wasn't quite as relaxed as he was, but she'd never let him know that. "It's spectacular," she agreed.

He leaned suddenly away and delved a hand into the pocket of the jeans she'd bought him, along with a new wardrobe in repayment for the one he'd purchased at Dollar General the year before. Something glimmered between his fingertips.

Eryn's heart skipped a beat. "Ike!" He was holding out a diamond ring.

"Never got to ask you myself."

In stunned silence, she admired the sunset's reflection in the fiery stone.

"So. It's kind of late, but would you marry me?" He sent her a crooked smile.

Relief whipped through Eryn, turning her weak. Yet she still hadn't heard a confession of love from him. If he was having second thoughts, she owed him the chance to back out. "Are you sure it's what you want?" she whispered, even as she eyed the ring longingly.

His smile vanished. "Why? You having second thoughts?"

"No," she said at once. "But I thought maybe you might be. I mean, I practically forced you to marry me."

He exhaled with such a look of relief that her fears evaporated. Then he jammed the ring firmly onto her fourth finger. "Listen, I've told you this," he reminded her, hearkening back to their conversations in the hospital. "I only pushed you away because I thought you deserved better than to wait for me."

"And I pushed you away so you wouldn't think of me and get hurt." She shook her head at their mutual foolishness.

"Didn't work," he pointed out ruefully.

"I know." Needing to hear his true feelings for her, Eryn swung a leg over his thighs and sat on his lap so that he was forced to look at her.

"Easy, girl," he warned with a gleam in his eyes.

"Ike, I thought you were going to ask me for an annulment," she admitted.

Tipping his head back, he studied her incredulously. "Why the hell would I do that?"

"Um, well, you've never told me that you love me," she answered.

He looked stunned. "I haven't?"

She shook her head. "And you haven't made love to me in almost a year," she added, on a distinctly sulky note.

He gave her a slow grin. "Thought about it every day in rehab," he confessed, "but there wasn't a lock on the door."

"We don't need a lock out here," she hinted.

"My thoughts exactly." He caught her face in his rough hands. "Eryn," he said hoarsely, and then he kissed her.

She felt her heart float away. Maybe words weren't really necessary.

But then he spoke against her lips. "I wanted you the second I laid eyes on you," he admitted thickly.

"Go on," she gasped. She would never have guessed that.

His grip on her face was both fierce and gentle. "I am fucking crazy about you," he added with intensity.

Pleasure pulsed through her. Her fears seemed so ridiculous now. "So, you love me," she prompted, biting her lip against a smile.

"I totally love you," he agreed.

Desire had her clamping her thighs around him. "Let's go back to the cabin," she begged.

"What's wrong with here?" His hands slid purposefully up under her cashmere sweater.

Her eyes widened as he unlatched her bra. With a look, he challenged her to protest his actions. She was suddenly highly conscious of the hard ridge testing his zipper. "Up here?" she asked in disbelief. "Now?"

"What's the point of owning a mountain if you can't get naked on it?"

She had to concede he had a point, but, "Someone might see us up here."

"How do you think Naked Creek got its name?" he shot back, studying her through narrowed eyes.

It took her a second to realize he was teasing. "Oh, what the heck." Thrilled by her own audacity, Eryn whipped off her sweater and tossed up higher onto the rock.

In the next instant, she was topless. The cool breeze contrasted exquisitely with the heat of Ike's skilled mouth. "Oh, Ike, I've missed you," she cried, cradling his head.

He rolled over, lowering her gently onto a carpet of lichen. "Missed you, more," he murmured, settling between her legs. And then he peeled off the remainder of her clothing, raining kisses on every inch of skin that he exposed. Lost to pleasant sensations, Eryn watched the sky blush a pretty shade of pink.

By the time Ike's own pale backside was facing the heavens, the sun had slipped behind the highest crag on Overlook Mountain, casting a shadow of modesty onto what was known from that day on as Naked Rock.

ACKNOWLEDGMENTS

When I finished this book, I felt like I'd given birth to a baby elephant. Seriously, the labor was intensive; the gestation period endless. My poor readers have waited forever, for this prequel to my Counterterrorist Taskforce Series. I trust they will not be disappointed.

My new baby elephant is the result of an awesome team effort shared by a group of amazing individuals, all of whom volunteered their time and talent without a lick of monetary reward. Words fail me in expressing my gratitude, but I wish to acknowledge each of you individually.

Timeshare salesman Stephen Winegard, you overlooked the need to sell me a timeshare at Massanutten Resort. Instead, you took me on all the back roads around your hometown of Elkton, providing me with the perfect setting for my book. Thank you!

FBI Retired Supervisory Special Agent Steven Brown, you worked tirelessly with me in making my FBI investigation sound authentic. Best wishes for your health and for the publication of your own books including your fabulous mystery: *Redeeming the Dead*.

Rachel Fontana, friend and reader, you suffered through every manifestation of this story as it morphed into a tale worth telling. And you made me jump off a rope swing fifteen feet above the water, an experience I never would have enjoyed if you hadn't gone first. I hope you know how much I value your friendship.

Don Klein, a true gem of a human being, you drove all the way from Minnesota to Virginia to meet me; became the first and only dues-paying member of my fan club; and edited every blessed word of my working manuscript, multiple times. Love hath no greater gift than this.

CPSIA information can be obtained at www.ICGtesting.com
Printed in the USA
BVOW032244201211

278871BV00001B/129/P